"Amateur sleuth Tucker Sinclair is smart,
unflappable and wickedly funny,
and so is her creator, Patricia Smiley."*

Praise for Patricia Smiley

"Full of colorful characters . . . a real treat."
—Janet Evanovich, author of *Lean Mean Thirteen*

"Smiley keeps the complications coming and moves
the story along at a speedy clip thanks to a breezy,
good-humored voice that's tremendously enjoyable."
—*The Baltimore Sun*

"Smiley's feisty heroine boosts the bottom line."
—*Entertainment Weekly*

"Deft plotting and an appealing heroine who calls to
mind Sue Grafton."
—*Denise Hamilton, Edgar® Award finalist and
bestselling author of *Prisoner of Memory*

"Fast, funny, and sure to find many fans. Smiley and
Sinclair are off to a wonderful start."
—Robert Crais, author of *The Watchmen*

"An engaging, down-to-earth heroine."
—*Publishers Weekly*

"Fans of Janet Evanovich's Stephanie Plum will appreciate the gutsy and klutzy Tucker."
—*Booklist* (starred review)

"Patricia Smiley and her heroine, Tucker Sinclair, are
two of the brightest stars to light up detective fiction in
a long time."
—Elizabeth George, author of
What Came Before He Shot Her

Also by Patricia Smiley

False Profits
Cover Your Assets
Short Change

Cool Cache

A Tucker Sinclair Mystery

Patricia Smiley

AN OBSIDIAN MYSTERY

OBSIDIAN
Published by New American Library, a division of
Penguin Group (USA) Inc., 375 Hudson Street,
New York, New York 10014, USA
Penguin Group (Canada), 90 Eglinton Avenue East, Suite 700, Toronto,
Ontario M4P 2Y3, Canada (a division of Pearson Penguin Canada Inc.)
Penguin Books Ltd., 80 Strand, London WC2R 0RL, England
Penguin Ireland, 25 St. Stephen's Green, Dublin 2,
Ireland (a division of Penguin Books Ltd.)
Penguin Group (Australia), 250 Camberwell Road, Camberwell, Victoria 3124,
Australia (a division of Pearson Australia Group Pty. Ltd.)
Penguin Books India Pvt. Ltd., 11 Community Centre, Panchsheel Park,
New Delhi - 110 017, India
Penguin Group (NZ), 67 Apollo Drive, Rosedale, North Shore 0632,
New Zealand (a division of Pearson New Zealand Ltd.)
Penguin Books (South Africa) (Pty.) Ltd., 24 Sturdee Avenue,
Rosebank, Johannesburg 2196, South Africa

Penguin Books Ltd., Registered Offices:
80 Strand, London WC2R 0RL, England

Published by Obsidian, an imprint of New American Library, a division of
Penguin Group (USA) Inc. Previously published in an Obsidian hardcover
edition.

First Obsidian Mass Market Printing, June 2009
10 9 8 7 6 5 4 3 2 1

Copyright © Patricia Smiley, 2008
All rights reserved

Dedicated to George and Lillian Smiley

Acknowledgments

I wish to express my gratitude to the following people:

First readers William Solberg and Patricia Fogarty.

Los Angeles Police detective Rich Householder for answering endless questions with infinite patience. Captain Andy Svatek for coaching me on how to fly an airplane to Santa Catalina Island and for coming up with the title for this novel. John Bibb, MD, for enlightening me about chest wounds and ER/ICU procedures. If I got anything wrong, it was no fault of theirs.

My editor, Kristen Weber, and my agent, Scott Miller. How fortunate I am to have you both in my corner.

Finally, my heartfelt appreciation to the readers who have followed Tucker through her many adventures. You make it all worthwhile.

Chapter 1

It was the light in the display case that made me stop. Helen never left it on. It was past eight p.m., and Nectar had been closed for hours. That wouldn't matter to most people, but I have an overly developed sense of duty. When I take on a business client, it's like adopting a puppy. Fluffy may leave teeth marks on my favorite shoes or whine to get up on the bed when I'm trying to sleep, but I've made a commitment to her and I'm going to see it through to the end. Helen Taggart engaged my firm to save her chocolate shop, and since Tucker Sinclair and Associates had only one associate—me—it was my job to make everything right.

Rain from an early-November storm swept across the Boxster's windshield in unrelenting sheets as I drove around the block past the palm trees on Brighton Way and the arched doorway of Christie's auction house. The street was still lined with cars. I nosed into the alley in back of the building and found a Hummer as large as the Rose Bowl in one of the shop's two reserved parking spaces. It had a BABY ON BOARD sign hanging in the back window. TOT IN TANK seemed more appropriate. A Mercedes was parked in the other spot. The Mercedes was new. It still had the GARVEY MOTORS—ALHAMBRA advertisement where the license plate should have been.

Neither car belonged to Helen Taggart. Both drivers had ignored the threatening NECTAR PARKING ONLY sign painted on the stucco wall. Helen would be upset if the valets from the restaurant next door were using her spaces for overflow traffic. She'd warned the owner on numerous occasions that she often stopped by the shop at night to drop off supplies or do paperwork, and even if it was chichi Beverly Hills, she didn't want to walk alone in the dark from the public garage a block away. Her polite requests had been ignored time and again. Friendly reminders eventually escalated into skirmishes, then to battles, and finally to all-out verbal warfare.

The windows of the Mercedes were tinted, so I couldn't see through the glass, but steam billowed from the exhaust pipe. The engine was running. I activated the turn signal and honked the horn, hoping whoever was in there would get the message.

A moment later, the driver's-side window glided halfway down. A man's hand appeared, holding a burning cigarette. He flicked the butt into the air. It flashed red as it arced upward and then fell into a puddle of rainwater. The window closed. The car eased forward and headed down the alley. If the driver was a valet from the restaurant, his lazy pace seemed abnormal. Usually it was all about screeching tires and burning rubber. At least he'd vacated the spot.

The alley was dark. The streetlights cast eerie shadows on the distant boulevard. Rain drummed the soft top of my convertible as I pulled in and cut the engine. I didn't have an umbrella, so I stepped out of the car and took off my cotton jacket, spreading it over my head like a pair of wings. In no time, I'd be soaked.

I ran toward Nectar, drawing in the odor of rotting food from the nearby Dumpster. That's when I noticed the back door was ajar. There was no sign of forced entry, so Helen was probably in the store. It just seemed odd she'd leave the door unlocked this late at night. I thought about calling the police, but I didn't want to overreact. So I decided to investigate before doing anything rash.

Curiosity had gotten me in trouble before, so I dug out a canister of pepper spray from my purse. I poised my finger on the release button and nudged open the door with my shoulder, listening to the groan of hinges in need of lubrication.

It was dark inside. Tiny needles of tension prickled the flesh along my neck. I fought to keep my voice from faltering as I called out Helen's name. There was no response. I leaned toward the blackness, listening for sounds like breathing or shoes slapping against the tile floor. All I heard was the muted hum of a compressor motor from the walk-in refrigerator.

I ran my hand along the wall, searching for the light switch. I flipped it on. Nothing. The fluorescent bulbs must have burned out. Helen would need to replace them in the morning. One more expense for her challenged budget.

My fingers groped inside my purse for the flashlight. My thumb pressed against the switch. I aimed the beam of light toward the gloom, half expecting to see a dark figure crouching in a corner, waiting to pounce. But the workroom was empty. I stepped over the threshold. The smell of wet cotton from my jacket mingled with the aroma of bitter cocoa and something else, something foreign—the faint odor of garlic.

There was a round aluminum foil container on one of the marble tabletops where Helen worked her magic. The lid was off but the food looked untouched—shrimp sautéed in garlic. If she was experimenting with some kind of seafood truffle, I didn't think it had much of a future.

The shop consisted of four rooms: the front retail store, the back workroom, a small bathroom, and a cubbyhole Helen used as an office. There was no sign of life in the workroom or in her office, so I inched along past metal shelves lined with baking pans, dipping forks, chocolate molds, graters, and copper pots until I reached the retail store. I turned on the overhead light and stepped into a room filled with the heady aromas of chocolate and coffee beans. A wave of relief swept over me when I saw I was alone.

The room held tiered glass cases and small round tables where Nectar's customers lingered over cappuccinos and artisanal chocolates Helen made from recipes passed down from her Belgian great-grandfather. Hanging on the wall behind the counter was an article I'd pitched to the *Los Angeles Times*. The paper had featured the store in the food section two weeks earlier, along with a photograph of Helen in the retail store. Since then, Nectar had seen a bump in sales.

Something about the retail store looked different. I just couldn't put my finger on why. I glanced at the photograph again. In it, Helen was holding a tray of chocolates. On the wall behind her were three shelves, each displaying various chocolate-related objects—vintage cocoa tins, a Spanish *molinillo*, an antique Cadbury heart-shaped candy box, and a replica of a Mayan spouted chocolate pot. That's when I realized what was wrong. The shelves weren't there anymore.

I raised the pepper spray to eye level and listened for sounds. Silence. I switched off the light in the display case and the one overhead and was making my way back to the workroom when I felt pressure under my foot. The beam from the flashlight revealed one of Helen's molded chocolates, called L.A. Noir, crushed beneath my shoe. I scraped off what was left of the shell and the soft ganache and tossed it in a nearby wastebasket.

There was another chocolate under the table and another by the door of the walk-in refrigerator. Helen was meticulous in her kitchen. She wouldn't have been that careless. I followed the trail to the refrigerator and pulled on the cold metal handle of the door.

Inside, a single lightbulb illuminated shelves lined with packages of unsalted butter, heavy whipping cream, sugar, and bars of solid chocolate. On the floor were several more candies. My clothes were damp from the rain, which made the air seem unbearably cold. My body began to tremble. I stepped out of the refrigerator, closing the door behind me.

The darkness was making me edgy. I wanted to go home to the light, but first I had to call Helen to let her know about the unlocked door and the missing shelves.

The chocolate had left my fingers feeling sticky. I needed to wash my hands. I headed toward the bathroom, pausing just outside the closed door. It was the only room in the store I hadn't checked yet. Prickles of tension snaked up my spine. I told myself I was being a wuss. No one was in there. I took a deep breath to calm my nerves and slowly opened the door.

A metallic stench hit me like a wrecking ball. I covered my nose to ward off the smell. Gagged. I scanned the room and saw that the paper towel dispenser had been ripped from the wall. Brown towels were strewn across the floor like autumn leaves. On top of them lay the body of a woman. She appeared to be a Latina in her forties. Her eyes were open and red, her pupils dilated. Bruises marred her neck. Her right leg was twisted at an odd angle to her torso. One outstretched arm had turned a purplish color. A feather lay in a pool of blood next to the body. It was long, eighteen inches or so, and brilliant green edged in white. The light made it seem iridescent.

I stumbled out of the bathroom. Out of Nectar. Out to my car. I fumbled for the cell phone in my purse. Clenched my hands to control the trembling. Dialed 911. Then I called Helen.

Chapter 2

Helen Taggart was just leaving the Century City shopping mall when I reached her cell phone. She made it to Nectar minutes after the arrival of a patrol car from the Beverly Hills Police Department and shortly before the homicide detectives and a few members of the paparazzi who must have been cruising Rodeo Drive, looking for celebrities going commando. Before long there were more flashbulbs than at a Hollywood movie premier. After years of hosting movie stars, Eurotrash, and tourist looky-loos in its trendy shops and restaurants, Beverly Hills was used to the attention.

While his partner interviewed Helen, a male homicide detective named O'Brien questioned me in the backseat of a patrol car that smelled like vomit and urine. My clothes would have to be torched before the night was over. He probably couldn't conduct the interview inside Nectar because it was a crime scene, but the setting he chose seemed calculated to make me feel uncomfortable.

O'Brien was a tall redhead in his midthirties with a boyish face and an attitude that was all business. He sat behind the wheel of the patrol car, staring at me under the dim overhead light. His arm was draped over the bench seat as his fingers drummed against the faux leather. The movement and the red hair on the back of his digits reminded me of a quartet of Irish step dancers.

"It stinks in here," I said. "Can you open the door?"

O'Brien paused for a moment as if considering my request. Then he lowered the window an inch or so. The annoyed expression on his face made it clear I'd just used up all my goodwill chits. I suppose homicide detectives were trained to suspect everybody, even me, but this guy needed a Miss Manners makeover. Uncooperative witnesses sometimes ended up as dead witnesses, and since I wasn't into police-assisted suicide, I kept my irritation in check.

O'Brien tilted his head to the side and cracked his neck, an act that must make his chiropractor rub his hands with glee. Then he pulled a small notebook and a pen from his jacket pocket and prepared to take notes.

"So what brought you to Beverly Hills tonight?" he said.

"I had dinner with a friend. I was on my way home when I saw the light in the display case. I knew something was wrong because Helen never leaves it on."

"Why's that?"

"Because heat melts chocolate."

He glared at me. "What's that supposed to mean?"

"I'm just explaining the basic principles of physics."

A quarter-sized flush appeared on each of his cheeks. "Did you see anybody going in or out of the store?"

I shook my head. "A Mercedes was parked in the back when I got here. Somebody was inside. I assumed it was a valet from the restaurant next door."

"What can you tell me about the driver?"

Our breath had fogged the window glass. I fought claustrophobia by wiping away the condensation with my hand, forgetting for a moment about all the drug-resistant microbes I may have just acquired.

"The car windows were dark. I saw only his arm. No tattoos, but he was a smoker. He flipped a cigarette out of the car window just before he drove away. It's probably still by the Dumpster, if you want to check for DNA."

O'Brien seemed dismissive, as if he thought I'd been watching too many episodes of *CSI.*

"Did you recognize the victim?"

I shook my head. "Helen might know."

"Does Helen Taggart have any enemies who might want her dead?"

I was taken aback by his question. In the short time I'd known Helen, I'd pegged her as a chronic nurturer. She was president of her condo association. She made chocolate centerpieces for the garden club's annual fund-raiser. She showered people with attention and gifts. I'd found ample examples when I'd gone through

Nectar's financial records—a new Baume & Mercier watch for her assistant manager's birthday, and gift certificates at Neiman Marcus for all her employees. She'd once given me a twenty-minute course on how to roast and skin hazelnuts when all I'd asked was "Why are they so shriveled?" Sometimes Helen got touchy, especially when she didn't feel appreciated, but that didn't put her at the top of anybody's hit list. At least I didn't think so.

"I don't know," I said. "You'll have to ask Helen that question."

"I'm asking you."

O'Brien must have missed the training that taught detectives to establish rapport with a witness, because he stared at me with smoky-blue eyes that were cold with suspicion. A moment later, I heard knuckles tapping on glass.

O'Brien's partner, wearing a yellow hooded raincoat, stood outside the cruiser. Detective Gatan was slim and exotic-looking. She seemed more like a woman who sprayed perfume on a paper strip at the Nordstrom half-yearly sale than a homicide detective investigating a murder in a rain-soaked alley in Beverly Hills.

O'Brien leaned over and opened the door. Gatan slid into the passenger seat with the fluid grace of a woman who knew she turned heads. As she pushed the hood off her sleek black hair, a drop of rain slid down her broad nose and disappeared into the folds of her suit jacket.

"The owner IDed the victim," she said. "Lupe Ortiz. Forty-six. Married. Four kids. She cleans the store five nights a week."

"Just what we need," O'Brien said. "Another domestic violence case. I wish these people would settle their beefs on their own turf instead of spoiling a perfectly good night on mine. Does Taggart know where we can find the husband?"

Gatan looked as if she was anticipating trouble. "I didn't ask her."

O'Brien narrowed his eyes. "Strike one. Go get her."

Detective Gatan waited for what seemed like a long time before shoving open the car door with a tad more force than necessary. I felt like shoving something, too. O'Brien was out of line for a lot of reasons, least of which was his assumption that Lupe's husband was the only suspect. It was too early in the investigation to close every door but one.

A few minutes later, Gatan returned with Helen in tow. The two detectives sat in the front of the patrol car. Helen climbed into the back with me.

Helen was somewhere in her fifties, with soft brown hair, which she kept styled and sprayed to perfection between once-a-week appointments at a Beverly Hills salon. Her figure was expanding with middle age but she made the best of it with well-cut clothes that camouflaged any flaws. The double strand of pearls she wore was a remnant of a past life she could no longer afford to maintain. At least the necklace disguised the loose flesh below her chin. I didn't want to look at it, because it reminded me of the ghost of sagging necks yet to come.

Helen was what my grandma Felder called high-strung, and at the moment, she looked like Mount Vesuvius ready to blow. Her lipstick was smeared and her nose was red from crying. Identifying Lupe Ortiz's body must have triggered a range of emotions, from sorrow to apprehension. No surprise. Nectar wasn't a lark for her. It was her life. She must know death and chocolate were a hard combo to spin even for an experienced marketing expert like me.

"What time did Mrs. Ortiz get to work?" O'Brien said.

Helen dabbed at her nose with a shredded tissue. "Around six. She has a key, but I usually stay at the store until she gets here just to make sure she's okay. Lupe was always telling me how much she appreciated that. Today I had to leave at five thirty for my hair appointment. Then I drove directly to the mall. I was supposed to get together for dinner and a movie with my boyfriend, but he called at the last minute to say he had to work and couldn't make it. I skipped dinner and went to the seven o'clock showing of that new Nicole Kidman movie. I had some popcorn and called it a night."

"Did Mrs. Ortiz usually leave the door open while she worked?" he said.

"I don't know," Helen said. "Maybe."

O'Brien began tapping his fingers again, but it was hard to separate that sound from rain that was pelting the roof of the cruiser. "Other than you and the victim, who else has a key?"

"Just my assistant manager, Kathy."

Detective O'Brien's long legs weren't made for sitting sideways behind the wheel of a car. His torso was twisted. His face was in profile. A red scratch blemished his right cheek. I wondered if he'd had a shaving mishap or had run into an angry fingernail.

O'Brien made a note in his book. "Did Mrs. Ortiz have any problems with her husband?"

"There were a couple of minor issues, but I helped her work through them. After that, her marriage seemed solid. I'm sure she would have told me otherwise."

"Any of her kids gang members?"

Helen hesitated for what seemed like a long time. I wondered why. It was almost as if she was filtering her response through some sort of politically correct colander.

"They're just normal kids," she said.

O'Brien stared at Helen with a deadpan expression. "Is there anybody who might have killed Lupe Ortiz to get back at you?"

Helen's lips parted slightly, but no words came out. It was as if something had cut off the air that gave power to her voice. I held my breath, hoping she could hold it together until the interview was over.

When she finally spoke, her voice was a whisper. "Nobody hates me that much."

"When you were inside the store, did you notice if anything was missing?"

"My recipes are the most valuable thing I have, but the books are still on the shelf. I checked the cash register, too. No money is missing."

"The display shelves in the retail store are gone," I said. "Maybe Lupe interrupted a burglar."

O'Brien's frown made it clear he didn't welcome my

interruption or my theory. Either something or someone had put him in a foul mood or else he just didn't
like women.

"The shelves aren't missing," Helen said. "I took
them down yesterday to make room for another table.
All that stuff is in the trunk of my car until I can find a
place to store it. Anyway, none of it's valuable. It's just
collectibles."

That was bad news all around. If a burglar had killed
Lupe Ortiz, he'd left without taking anything except
her life.

"Look," Helen continued, "I have to take my recipes
home tonight. If something happens to them, I'm in
big trouble."

"Once we're done processing the scene," O'Brien
said, "you can take anything you want."

"How long will that be?" Helen's voice was becoming shrill.

"We're done when we're done."

"That doesn't tell me anything. I have to know."

Detective Gatan's lips were pursed, as if her partner's hard-line tactics were annoying her. She turned
toward Helen. "Check back with us in a couple of
hours. Maybe we can release the books then. Meanwhile, I'll make sure nobody disturbs them."

"Helen, the police are here," I said. "I think the books
are safe for now."

Gatan measured me with her dark eyes before returning her gaze to Helen. "I tried to call the Ortiz
house. The line was busy. Does the husband have a cell
phone?"

Helen shifted her gaze from me to the detective. "I don't know. Probably. Lupe has one. It's a gaudy purple thing with rhinestones on it. But it doesn't matter if he has a cell phone or not. You can't reach him. He's in Guatemala. Visiting a sick relative, I think."

O'Brien shifted in the seat. "The kids are home alone?"

Helen moaned. "Those poor babies. I can't believe this is happening."

O'Brien glanced at his partner. "Call children's services and have them check into it. They'll probably have to take the kids into custody."

Helen leaned forward and grabbed the back of the seat. "They just lost their mother. You can't leave them with strangers. I know the three little ones. Lupe brought them to the store several times. Let me take them to my place."

Detective O'Brien shook his head. "You're not a relative. We have to go through channels. That's children's services. End of story."

Helen fingered the pearls around her neck as if they were worry beads. "Lupe has a cousin in the area. I'll get her to stay at the house until we locate Mr. Ortiz."

A thick silence settled in the car, displacing the stench and the tension. Gatan stared at her partner as if she was searching for operating instructions on his forehead.

"Let her try," she said to him. "What can it hurt? The kids are better off with family."

O'Brien's jaw muscles twitched as he pointed his index finger in Gatan's face. "If this goes south on us, Detective, it's on your head."

Something about their relationship reminded me of a dysfunctional couple on a TV drama. I wondered if O'Brien's Irish digits had ever danced over the soft brown skin of his partner's butt.

Gatan handed Helen her card. "Call me when you locate the cousin. I'll handle the rest."

As we got out of the patrol car, dozens of camera flashes lit up the alley. A crowd was gathered outside the yellow tape, people drawn by curiosity, boredom, or maybe just a sense of the macabre.

The rain had stopped but the street was still wet, so I offered Helen a ride to her car. As soon as she slid into the passenger seat of my Boxster, she pulled out her cell phone and dialed a number. I could hear the blare of the busy signal from where I sat. I backed out of the parking space and waited while a patrol officer lifted the crime-scene tape and motioned the crowd to step away from the alley.

By the time we got to Helen's car, which was parked on the street a couple of blocks away, her breathing had become shallow. I asked if she was okay.

"I will be as soon as I know Lupe's kids are safe."

"Is that her cousin you're trying to call?"

She closed her phone with an audible snap. "I'm trying to reach Roberto, but the line is still busy. I can't leave him alone with those children."

A feeling of dread settled in my chest. "Helen, what's going on?"

"Lupe was having problems with Roberto. He was running with a bad crowd, experimenting with drugs. His dad tried to straighten him out, but he wouldn't listen. Other people tried to help, too—school counselors, her parish priest. I told her I'd pay for a psychologist, but her husband was against it. He didn't want people to know he couldn't control his own son."

"Why didn't you tell O'Brien?"

"Because I didn't want to cause more problems for the family."

Helen got out of the car and slammed the door.

I lowered the passenger-side window. "What are you going to do?"

"Drive to East L.A. and talk to Roberto."

"Helen, that's insane. You have no idea what kind of mess you're walking into."

She glared at me. "And Lupe's children? What about them? Their lives are a little messy right now, too."

"They don't even know their mom is dead. Are you going to tell them?"

"I'll have to."

"Why are you doing this? Lupe's not even your employee."

"I don't want to do it. I have to because there's no one else."

I hoped Helen's compulsion to meddle in other people's lives wouldn't become a problem, but if rescuing Lupe Ortiz's children was her latest cause, trying to talk her out of it was futile. There was only one thing I could do to save her from herself.

"Get in the car," I said. "I'm going with you."

Chapter 3

There were many reasons why a trip to see Roberto Ortiz could turn into disaster. It was late at night. The streets were slick with rain. The freeway would be a mess. And East L.A. could be a dangerous place. At the moment, telling a troubled teen that his mother had just been murdered seemed like the least of my problems.

Locals call East Los Angeles East Los or ELA. Once home to Russians, Jews, and Japanese immigrants, the area is now ninety percent Latino and the largest Mexican-American community in the United States. It's larger than Manhattan. Larger than Washington, D.C. One million people. Hundreds of colorful outdoor murals. Graffiti. *Discotecas. Farmacias.* Pastry shops. Hardworking people. ELA also has young mothers in short skirts carrying babies that already know how to hold a gun, and young men with no work and few alternatives, selling weapons from the trunk of a car. There are good neighborhoods in East L.A. Lupe Ortiz and her family didn't live in one of them.

The house was a downtrodden bungalow that looked like a child's crude drawing—a square box with a slanted roof and a front door flanked by two small windows. A few blocks away, a police helicopter swept a spotlight over the neighborhood, searching for something or someone I didn't want to know about.

Cars and pickups lined the street, so I parked in the driveway behind an older-model Toyota. Gang graffiti marred the surface of a three-foot cinder-block wall that barricaded the neighbor's yard from the outside world. A man stood on the porch, struggling to restrain a pit bull that was lunging at us with bared teeth. The barking triggered a response from canines up and down the block until it sounded like the doggie version of Tchaikovsky's *1812 Overture*.

"I hope that collar doesn't break," Helen said.

I wanted to allay her fears, but it was all I could do to keep my own in check. "We're here now. We might as well go to the door."

No fence barred us from entering Lupe Ortiz's yard. We made our way up the sidewalk through a lawn that was dead except for tufts of grass that reminded me of hair plugs on the pate of a desperate man. Paint was peeling from the wood siding of the house. The doorframe was hollowed out in places, probably from termites. The windows were covered in blue floral bedsheets that would make Martha Stewart proud.

I knocked on the front door and waited. A faint rustling sound could be heard from inside the house. A moment later, the bedsheet on the window to my left parted, revealing the face of a girl of around eight. I waved to her. She waved back.

"Angelica," Helen said through the glass. "I'm looking for Roberto. Is he home?"

The girl stared at us for a moment and then stepped away from the window. The curtain drifted shut. We waited, but nobody came to the door.

"Try calling the number again," I said to Helen.

She dialed and listened. "Still busy."

I knocked, louder this time. A short time later, the door jerked open and an unpleasant chemical odor drifted onto the porch. A young man of about sixteen stood in front of us. I assumed he was Lupe's son Roberto. Small bumps covered his face. They looked like a crop of mini Botz dots that had gone on a rampage. Heavy, arching eyebrows accented his broad face. A metal stud pierced the skin just below his lower lip. He had on an oversized white T-shirt and a pair of jeans that were so large they would have fallen off if he hadn't been holding on to his crotch.

Behind him were three young children—the girl I'd seen in the window and two younger boys, age three and four, I guessed. They were all huddled in front of a television set.

"Roberto?" she said. "I'm Helen Taggart. Your mother cleans my chocolate store. I'm sure she's talked about me."

Roberto raked his nails over the blemishes on his

face. His gaze flitted from me to Helen and back again, as if our presence had made him hyperalert. His lips were dry and cracked. He moistened them before speaking.

"I know who you are," he said. "What do you want?"

Helen reached out as if she was going to embrace him. "Oh, honey. I'm so sorry. Your mother's dead. The police asked me to identify the body. It was awful. I drove all the way over here to see if I could help."

I grabbed her arm before she blurted out any of the gory details.

Roberto seemed repelled by Helen as much as by the news of his mother's death, but the two younger boys didn't even look away from the TV. Angelica did. Her dark eyes burned with anger as she stared at Helen and me.

Pain etched Helen's face. "I'm sorry. I didn't mean to—"

"Listen, Roberto," I said. "It's important for you to contact your father right away and tell him to come home. In the meantime, you need to find an adult relative who can stay at the house."

He lifted his chin and looked down his nose at us in a gesture of defiance. "I don't need a babysitter."

Helen broke free of my grasp. "The police said—"

I interrupted her. "Of course you don't. But you might have to leave the house, and your brothers and sister will need someone to watch out for them. What about your cousin? Would you like me to call her?"

He didn't answer for some time. Perhaps it was

shock or just machismo that allowed him to stand in the doorway without shedding a tear.

"I don't need your help."

I felt the music before I heard it, that loud, thrumming base that reverberates in your chest like thunder. I turned toward the street and saw an older-model American sedan with tinted windows, maybe an Oldsmobile, cruising down the street. It slowed to a roll as it neared us. The neighbor pulled his pit bull into the house, and the barking grew muffled. The rear window of the sedan rolled down. Rap music pounded into the night.

Roberto's eyes narrowed. The last image I saw was the glow of the television screen and three wide-eyed children scurrying for cover as the door slammed shut. A moment later, the lights in the Ortiz house went out.

In my mind's eye I saw tomorrow morning's newspaper headline: NOSY BUSINESSWOMAN MOWED DOWN IN DRIVE-BY SHOOTING. Next to the article would be that old high school picture of me with the perm that looked like a mushroom cloud over the Nevada desert. People would come to my funeral. People I didn't know. Just to see if my hair really looked that bad. I couldn't let that happen.

"Get in the car," I whispered.

"We can't leave without the children," Helen said.

"Get in the car," I said, louder this time.

Helen seemed to sense the urgent tone in my voice, because she followed me down the sidewalk toward the Boxster. Once we were both inside the car, I locked the doors—for all the good that would do. You didn't need a PhD to know that bullets penetrated glass.

Every house on the street seemed to be dark now. I watched the taillights of the sedan grow smaller as it continued down the block. When the car was out of sight, I turned the key in the ignition and backed out of the driveway.

Helen pressed her forehead to the window, staring into the darkness. "I failed Lupe. They'll take the children away now."

I didn't answer right away because I was focused on navigating us out of the neighborhood and back to the freeway.

"You did what you could," I said. "The police will take care of the rest."

That was easy enough to say, but I couldn't shake the feeling that Lupe Ortiz's death was only the beginning of Helen's problems—and mine. The next challenge was convincing Detective O'Brien to release Helen's recipe books, but I had a feeling he wasn't going to let them go without a fight.

Chapter 4

By the time we got back to Nectar, Lupe's body had been taken to the morgue. Detective Gatan promised to arrange for the Ortizes' cousin to stay with the family until the father could be located. I'd been right about O'Brien. He wasn't going to let the recipes go without a fight, but it wasn't with Helen or me. It was with his partner. After a heated discussion between the two, Detective Gatan escorted Helen into the store to get her recipe books, plus several boxes of business records she'd need while Nectar remained closed.

There wasn't room for everything in Helen's car because the trunk was filled with the collectibles display from the retail store, so she asked me to take the cocoa tins, the heart box, and the spouted chocolate pot home for a day or two until she could free up some space at her condo. Of course I agreed.

It was past two a.m. by the time I pulled the Boxster into the driveway of my beach cottage just north of Malibu. There were no lights on at my neighbor's house. Mr. and Mrs. Domanski had likely been lulled into slumber hours ago by multiple martinis and years of marital ennui.

Cold November sea air seeped into my lungs as I got out of the car. In the distance I heard the surf slam the shore, sizzle, and withdraw to renew the cycle. I pulled my coat tight around my neck and walked toward the house, watching the moon spotlight the water with a milky yellow glow. The only other light I saw was from a house in the middle of a wide arc of beach that sloped gently into the Pacific Ocean.

I made my way through the sand toward my deck, pausing for a moment to admire my house. It wasn't much to look at, just a small brown rectangle I'd inherited from a grandmother I'd never known, but I loved the place more than anywhere I'd ever lived.

Unlike Lupe Ortiz's neighborhood, mine felt quiet and safe. I trudged up the wooden steps leading to the side door and tried to imagine what it would be like for her children in the days ahead. My father had died before I was born, which had left a void in my life, but I'd never had to mourn a parent who'd been loved and lost the way Lupe's kids would have to do now.

I heard barking from inside the house—my West Highland terrier. Muldoon had a good voice, but he'd never make it to Carnegie Hall. He was too handsome to be talented, too. That just wouldn't be fair. The pup had leading-man good looks—broad shoulders, bedroom eyes, and a melancholy expression that melted hearts.

The door swung open and Muldoon charged out to greet me. I threw him a couple of air kisses and stepped over the threshold, nearly tripping over his yellow cashmere sweater. It was just one of many gifts from Mrs. Domanski, whom Muldoon had come to view as a generous but eccentric aunt.

I paused near the small alcove that functioned as my home office and flipped on the lights in the living room and on the deck. By the time I'd laid my coat on my grandmother's steamer trunk, Muldoon was staring at his empty food dish. The expression on his face read *Uh . . . excuse me. Empty!*

I negotiated my way around my apartment-sized kitchen to the refrigerator, where I kept Muldoon's food. I moved his dish to the round rooster rug on the kitchen floor and filled it to the top from a sack of low-fat kibble, waiting for him to dig in. He studied the cuisine for a moment, flicking his tongue at the pellets. Several shot out of the bowl like skeet off the back of a cruise ship. He plopped his butt on the floor and began to whimper. I hated to see the little guy unhappy, so I caved in and nuked a frozen panini that was big enough for two.

While Muldoon was eating, I changed into a sweat-suit and checked for messages on the answering machine located on the kitchen counter. No one had called. I went to my office and booted up the computer to check my e-mail. Nothing. I was beginning to feel like the Maytag repairman.

I didn't feel like going to bed, so I slipped an Aretha Franklin CD into the player and molded myself into the cushions of my rose and celery floral couch with my half of the panini, waiting for a little R-E-S-P-E-C-T.

Muldoon finished his sandwich and jumped on the couch to gape at mine as if his X-ray vision might magically transport it from my hand to his mouth. It didn't work. After I'd finished eating, he settled next to me on the couch while I rested my hand on his bristly coat.

A photo album lay on the coffee table. It was filled with pictures of a recent cycling trip I'd taken in France with my friend Venus Corday and her boyfriend, Max Huffman. I picked up the book and flipped through the pages of familiar photographs. In every one I saw a thirty-year-old woman who was almost thirty-one. She was tall and thin with brown shoulder-length hair and eyes the color of Old Grand-Dad Kentucky bourbon. All were shots of me. Me, in Paris leaning on a bridge over the river Seine. Me, posing for a portrait in Monmartre. Me, straddling my bicycle in front of the Romanée-Conti vineyard. Me, sipping espresso in an outdoor café in Bonne. If the Tour de France had a wallflower jersey, I would have been wearing it.

Venus had billed the trip as salve for my broken heart. It was something less than that, but at least for two weeks, the exercise and the French food distracted me from thinking about the end of my relationship with an LAPD homicide detective named Joe Deegan.

There was nothing profound or poetic to say about our breakup. The relationship had been challenging from the start. He was accustomed to calling the shots.

So was I. There had never been any man in my life telling me what to do—not a father, not even my ex. Maybe I was just meant to be alone.

A moment later, a rumble of thunder jolted me out of my reverie. Lightning flashed through the sky, which sent Muldoon bolting from the room like a reluctant bridegroom. He hated loud noises. It would take a T-bone steak to lure him out from under my bed. I sat up and braced myself for another thunderbolt. None came. I knew thunder. It would wait until I felt safe before shattering my nerves a second time.

I gazed through the glass of the French doors at the gritty film of sand on the deck and my fake wicker deck furniture, which was covered for the season because even plastic degrades in L.A.'s winter storms, and I thought about Lupe Ortiz. By nature I was a curious person. I wanted to know what had happened to her. Maybe she'd gone out to buy garlic shrimp and had forgotten to lock the door when she came back. Maybe a thief entered the shop, looking for a quick score. Except nothing was missing. Why would a burglar kill Lupe Ortiz and not even take the money in the cash register, which seemed easy enough to find? The other possibility was that somebody came to Nectar with the sole purpose of killing her. Helen said Lupe's son was troubled. I wondered if he'd been involved in her death. It was a chilling thought because just hours before I'd been standing on a front porch in East L.A., talking to a murderer.

The rain was launching its full attack now. I could hear the branches of the Domanskis' trees being whipped by the wind. The deck light illuminated the metal railing that led down the steps to the sand. Drops of water had accumulated on the underside of the pipe. They looked transparent in the light. One grew plump and fell to the ground with a Humpty-Dumpty splat. All the king's men in the nursery rhyme had failed Humpty. I doubted they could put the Ortiz family back together again, either.

That night I lay awake wondering if Lupe's children were with their cousin or in a foster home, surrounded by strangers. I wanted to believe the dawn would bring good news, but I knew in my heart that life, like nursery rhymes, didn't always have a happy ending.

Charley Tate was a private investigator and a former cop. He might have some ideas about who killed Lupe Ortiz and how long Nectar would be closed for business. I decided to ask him.

Chapter 5

The next morning, I overslept. There was no time for breakfast, so I made a cup of coffee for the road and loaded my purse and laptop computer into the car. Then I dropped Muldoon off at Mrs. Domanski's house for a play date and headed for the office.

It was still raining. Not the deluge from the night before, but a gentle spray that darkened the sky and covered the highways with a thin coat of water mixed with oil that made for dicey driving conditions. Los Angeles had been experiencing unusually cold weather, thanks to a storm blustering south from the Gulf of Alaska. My response to the chill was a heavy coat and a wool hat with earflaps that made me look like a llama herder in the mountains of Peru.

Forty minutes later, I arrived at the pie-shaped slice of land between Washington Boulevard and Washington Place in Culver City, where I shared a second-floor office suite with an ex-cop–turned–private investigator named Charley Tate.

Charley was a combination of father, brother, uncle, and friend. He was sometimes cranky and obstinate and we often disagreed, but we'd been through trouble together and had come out on the other side with a healthy measure of mutual respect. I could count on him 100 percent to cover my back in a crisis.

He'd taught me a lot in the short time I'd known him, including how to pick locks, not that he'd set out to do that. We'd been chatting in the car one day about copy for a new brochure I was writing for him, and one thing led to another. I guess he felt if I was going to learn to defeat locks I should have the proper tools, so a few months back he'd given me a lock-picking set of my own.

Charley had learned some things from me, too, like how to change the color of Tate Investigations' bottom line ink from red to black. Our businesses were separate, but we shared rent, a lobby, and an administrative assistant named Eugene Barstok.

There was no elevator in our building, so I walked up the stairs to the second floor and found Eugene at his desk, staring trancelike at his computer screen. He was in his midtwenties with a slight physique, round blue eyes that always looked surprised, and a cowlick on the crown of his head that reminded me of an antenna on a spaceship.

A small plastic object hung from a chain around his

neck, humming in a low monotone. It was an air purifier he used to relieve allergy symptoms, which were
especially bad in November when the Santa Ana winds
blew in pollen from the desert. He also used the purifier
when it rained, because he worried about killer mold.
Truth be told, he wore the thing in the off-season, too,
because he was a bit of a germophobe. The downside
to this was that Charley and I were forced to read peri-
odic bulletins from the Center for Disease Control. The
upside? The office was always immaculate.

I wanted to tell Charley about Lupe Ortiz's murder, but that meant telling Eugene, as well. His psyche
was on the fragile side of the spectrum, so I had to be
careful how and when I laid out the story. Charley's
door was closed, so I assumed he was busy working or
with a client. I decided to wait until he was available
so I could break the news to both of them at the same
time.

"How's the chocolate research coming?" I said. "Find
anything I can use in Nectar's advertising campaign?"

Eugene craned his neck and squinted at the screen.
"How about this? Belgium produces one hundred
seventy-two tons of chocolate a year. They have two
thousand chocolate shops. The Swiss each eat twenty-
one pounds of chocolate per person per year. Belgians
and Brits eat sixteen pounds. Americans eat only
eleven and a half pounds, but I think those numbers are
skewed. Venus accounts for most of that herself. Too
bad all that sugar hasn't sweetened her disposition."

I ignored his comment. He and Venus had a quirky

kind of friendship that sometimes included trading barbs. None of them were meant to hurt. It was just the way they interacted.

"What's happening with the mailing list for the chocolate symposium?" I said.

He pointed to a stack of labels on an in-basket supported by elaborate Corinthian columns and decorated with laurel wreaths. Eugene had recently become fascinated with the Greek Revival period. I was surprised his computer wasn't wearing a toga.

"I have the labels all made up," he said. "As soon as the invitations are printed, I'll mail them out."

"Good work."

I'd arranged for Nectar to partner with a UCLA professor who'd recently published some interesting journal articles exploring the effects of chocolate consumption on depression. He'd organized a panel of experts and planned to present his findings to the public. Helen was providing a chocolate buffet. The university was paying for publicity, so it was a way for her to reach a new audience without breaking her budget, a sweet deal for her. I just hoped Lupe's death didn't upend all those plans.

"This is going to be *the* event of the season," Eugene said.

I picked up a stack of mail on his desk and began sorting through it. "Well, maybe not *the* event—"

"Give yourself credit, Tucker. Organizing this affair was a real coup. It's high-profile and it came just at the right time. Helen's seemed so uptight lately. I've been calling her every day to cheer her up, but this symposium should make her feel more confident about Nectar's future."

"You call her every day? What do you talk about?"

"Everything. I practically know her whole life story. Did you know she was raised on a farm in Vermont? She's the only friend I have who knows how to milk a cow. If you discount the *eeuu* factor, it's quite an accomplishment. Plus, she had a father who never said 'I love you.' Not once in her life. I can *so* identify. I admire her for rising above her childhood. After everything she's been through, it takes gumption to start all over again at her age. Remember how hard it was for me to leave corporate America for the private-eye business? And I was young."

Helen had never confided in me about her barnyard history, but I knew a little about Eugene's past. He'd been my assistant at Aames & Associates, the corporate consulting firm where I'd worked before I left to start my own company. After I left, he wasn't happy there anymore, so a few months back he quit and came to work for Charley and me. I didn't want to downplay the stress involved in changing jobs, but at least milking cows wasn't part of his job description.

"Um, Eugene—"

"I know, I know. I'm not a pro, but I could be and so could you. Even Charley thinks so."

I doubted Charley would agree with him, but I didn't say so. Instead, I took the mail and headed toward my office. Eugene followed, carrying what looked like a telephone message in his hand.

My room was understated but professional-looking.

I hadn't been sure if sharing space with Charley would work in the long term, so I hedged my bets and found a furniture rental outlet with an in-house interior designer. She'd put together some pieces, including a pair of metal file cabinets, that were boring, but at least they didn't look as if they'd been pilfered from a Quonset hut on Iwo Jima. On the wall next to a couple of beach-scene watercolors was a framed blue Frisbee sporting the caption, *Don't Forget to Play*. Deegan had given it to Muldoon a few months back, but the pup never used it much. He wasn't interested in flying through the air to catch anything short of a turkey wiener.

Eugene laid the message on my desk. "You have an appointment with a new client this afternoon at three."

I set my purse and the computer on my desk, disrupting a stack of papers in the process. "That's good. What kind of business?"

Eugene eyed the mess and frowned. He moved both bags to a guest chair and straightened the papers. "She was a little vague. She wouldn't tell me the name of the company, just that it's a dating service and she wants to expand."

I pulled off my coat and hat and threw them across the chair. "She wants *me* to give her advice on dating?"

"I know. It's not exactly your forte, but I know you'll rise to the occasion."

"What's her name?"

He folded my hat into a neat triangle and tucked it into the pocket of the coat. "Elizabeth Bennet."

The name sounded familiar but I wasn't sure why.

I nodded. "Sounds great. Is Charley in yet?"

Eugene slipped my coat on a hanger from the rack near the door. He buttoned the top button so it would hang just right, and brushed a piece of lint from the sleeve.

Over his shoulder he said, "He's in his office, hibernating. He hasn't been himself for the past few days. He's not even insulting me anymore. You need to talk to him, Tucker. I'm worried Lorna has finally succeeded in making him average."

"What's the problem now?"

Eugene looked toward the door to make sure Charley was out of earshot.

"You didn't hear this from me," he said, speaking in a hushed tone, "but she's pressuring him to have a baby."

I narrowed my eyes. "How do you know that?"

"I sort of overheard him talking to Lorna on the telephone."

"You were eavesdropping again."

Eugene threw his arms up in frustration. "You're missing the point. The whole thing is freaking him out. He did the fatherhood thing with his first wife. Now his son is an adult, at least technically speaking. Charley feels he dodged the bullet once, and he doesn't want to tempt fate by trying it again. And he's fifty-eight. I'm worried Lorna will wear him down and he'll do something stupid. You have to talk to him."

"Lorna's ticking biological clock is not my problem."

"What's all the noise?"

I turned toward the voice and saw Charley Tate standing by the doorway, ramrod straight, running a freckled hand over his crew cut. His normally mischievous smile had been replaced by a scowl. I hoped he hadn't overheard us gossiping about him.

"Eugene and I were just discussing my new client," I said.

He turned to leave. "Well, keep it down. I'm trying to get some work done."

"Charley," I said. "I have something to tell you."

He swung around slowly, looking at me as if he was reading tea leaves in the bottom of a china cup. "What now?"

"You should probably sit down for this."

Eugene's eyes lit up like they always did when he smelled a good story. "Come on, Tucker. The suspense is killing me."

Eugene didn't know how prophetic his words were until I told them both about Lupe Ortiz's murder and described the exotic green feather I'd found next to her body. Eugene looked pale and subdued. I could tell by Charley's expression that he was calculating what might have happened.

"Have either of you seen a feather like that before?" I said.

Charley crossed his arms over his chest. "That's none of your business."

Eugene rolled his eyes. "Tucker's not asking what kind of sex toys you and Lorna use when the lights go out."

"Yeah?" he mumbled. "Well, there's not much of that going on these days."

"A feather seems like an odd thing to find at a murder scene," I said. "I'd like to know where it came from."

"Robin Hood's hat?" Eugene said.

Charley looked at the ceiling as if he was praying for patience. "It probably fell out of her duster."

"Maybe," I said, "but most dusters I've seen have brown feathers."

Eugene leaned forward in the chair. "Why speculate? Let's look it up on the Internet."

"What's Tucker supposed to look for? Long, green iridescent feather?"

Eugene flapped his hand toward the computer. "Don't be a pessimist. Give it a try, Tucker."

To humor him, I opened my search engine and typed in *long green iridescent feather*. A list of links appeared on the screen, including the word *quetzal*. I clicked on the link and found a photograph of a male bird with a spiky hairdo that made him look hip. There was only one way to describe the guy—magnificent. His brilliant crimson chest feathers stood in stark contrast to the snowy white ones below his breast. The two long green plumes of his tail looked exactly like the one I'd found near Lupe Ortiz's body. A short article accompanied the picture.

Charley's curiosity got the better of him. He walked around the desk and started reading over my shoulder. The article claimed the quetzal—pronounced ket-

ZAHL—was a rare bird found in the isolated jungles of Central America. The Maya and the Aztecs revered the bird for its strength of spirit, and used its feathers in ceremonial costumes. It was also the national bird of Guatemala. I scanned a few more pages but saw nothing that told me if the species was living or extinct.

Helen had named her store Nectar because the Maya, who had used chocolate thousands of years before the Europeans, called cacao the Nectar of the Gods. Now a feather from a bird revered by the same ancient culture had been found at her store next to a murder victim. It was a creepy coincidence.

"Check the L.A. Zoo Web site," Eugene said.

I did, but found no quetzals listed in its inventory.

Charley apparently grew tired of reading about zoos and feathers because he returned to the chair, staring into midspace as if he was deep in thought. "Do the police have a suspect?"

I shrugged. "They asked if Lupe had problems with her husband or her kids. The husband has an alibi. He's out of town. Her teenage son is a possibility. He looks like trouble."

Charley frowned. "How do you know?"

I told him about going to East L.A. and my encounter with Roberto. Charley seemed uneasy, especially when I described the bumps on the teenager's face and his chemical odor.

"Sounds like a tweeker," he said.

I raised my eyebrows. "A what?"

"Somebody who's addicted to methamphetamines. The drug plays havoc with both your mind and your body. The kid has all the classic symptoms. Was there anything in the paper this morning?"

"I was running late and didn't have time to look."

Charley turned and walked out of my office.

"See?" Eugene whispered. "I warned you. He's really cranky."

A short time later, Charley came back to my office, carrying the California section of the *Los Angeles Times*. He handed it to me, folded open to page six. I scanned the columns, stopping at a small article near the bottom of the page.

Woman found strangled to death

A 16-year-old boy was taken into custody early Friday morning on suspicion of strangling his mother to death following an argument, according to a Beverly Hills Police Department spokesperson. Authorities said the boy was arrested without incident at the family's residence after the body of his mother, Guadalupe Ortiz, 43, was found at Nectar, the Beverly Hills candy store where she worked. She was pronounced dead at the scene.

Once again, Nectar's name had appeared in the newspaper, this time in connection with a homicide investigation. I just hoped that old saying was true that there was no bad publicity.

"I have to tell Helen," I said.

Charley and Eugene watched as I pressed numbers on the telephone keypad. As I listened to Helen talk, I felt my forehead muscles constrict into a deep frown. When I ended the call, my legs felt rubbery.

"What's going on?" Charley said.

"The police just left Helen's house."

"That was fast."

"It wasn't about Lupe Ortiz. Somebody broke into her condo last night and tore the place apart."

"Looking for what?" Charley said.

"She doesn't know. She asked me to drive over. I'd like you to come with me."

"What for?"

"I need your opinion. To me, it seems odd that both Helen's condo and her store were broken into on the same night. I think the two events are connected."

"The authorities will sort it out."

"Maybe, but that means cooperation from two police departments and a lead detective who's willing to push the envelope. What's the likelihood that'll happen any-time soon? Look, maybe I'm just being paranoid, but Helen has a lot riding on Nectar's success. If it fails, she loses everything. All I want you to do is evaluate the situation. If you think the break-ins are random, then fine. If you don't, I'm going to suggest Helen hire you to find out who's targeting her and why."

Charley hesitated. "I have a lot of cases on my desk right now."

"Then one more isn't going to make any differ-ence."

Eugene's hand was clutching his throat as if he

needed help swallowing. He looked ashen. "Charley, can't you see how important this is to Tucker? You can't say no."

Charley crossed his arms over his chest and stared out the window as if he was rearranging appointments in his head.

"Okay," he said. "Let's roll."

Chapter 6

Charley suggested we take separate cars to Helen's place. He claimed he didn't like riding in my Porsche, which was true, but that wasn't the whole story. A hit-and-run driver had totaled his van the previous June. He'd used part of the money he earned from solving a missing-heiress case to buy a Subaru Forester. I warned him the Forester had a reputation as the vehicle of choice for the nerdy but intellectual Birkenstock crowd, but he pooh-poohed the theory because he loved driving the thing. Twenty minutes later, we were standing in the foyer of Helen Taggart's Brentwood condo.

Helen hadn't slept all night and it showed. Her makeup needed refreshing, and a few hairs had defied the hairspray and were poking out of her coiffure like swizzle sticks. Her boyfriend was there, holding her hand in a show of support.

Dale Ewing worked as a part-time political science instructor at Santa Monica College, where he'd met Helen while she was teaching an evening candy-making class. He was tall and portly with white hair and a bushy mustache and goatee that concealed a weak chin. His crumpled tweed jacket had leather patches on the elbows and may have been designed to look professorial, but succeeded only in making him seem like a cliché. I'd seen Ewing only once. He'd come into Nectar on the pretense of buying chocolates, but I sensed he was there to check on Helen. He was taciturn, probably a decent guy, but as stimulating as a long, boring novel.

The window in the kitchen door had been broken and glass still covered the floor. The crime scene investigators were finished collecting evidence, but they'd left the place in a state of disarray. Black fingerprint powder was everywhere in the kitchen and in Helen's bedroom, as well.

Somehow in the chaos, Helen had managed to brew a pot of coffee. Several dirty cups sat on the kitchen counter. It wouldn't have surprised me if she'd served the criminalists a light buffet as they dusted for prints.

The living room was small but tastefully decorated with traditional furniture. The only material trappings that may have been a target for thieves were a Persian rug that was too big for the room and a modern painting hanging on the living room wall. The artist had probably meant it as an expression of something profound, but to me it looked more like an aerial shot of New Guinea.

Charley and I sat on the overstuffed chairs. Helen sat

on the couch across from us. Several sympathy cards were laid out on the coffee table. One was already addressed to the Ortiz family. Knowing Helen, she probably kept an assortment of disaster-appropriate greeting cards tucked away in a file somewhere.

Ewing retired to a corner of the room, away from the circle of conversation, and began paging through a *National Geographic* magazine. His apparent lack of interest seemed unusual under the circumstances, but maybe he just didn't want to interfere.

"So what happened?" I said.

"After I left Nectar last night, it finally sank in. My store was a crime scene. I was a wreck. I didn't want to go home, so I drove out to Simi Valley to see Dale. We talked. I told him I'd done all I could to help Detective O'Brien, but instead of being grateful, he'd been quite rude. Poor Dale. He was so upset, he called O'Brien's supervisor to complain. He told her I needed to reopen the store as soon as possible and wanted to know when they'd be finished collecting evidence. He said he'd stay on the phone until he found out, all night if necessary."

Complaining to O'Brien's supervisor took cojones. Maybe I'd misjudged Ewing. Maybe he wasn't so boring after all.

"After that, Dale told me to go home and get some rest," she went on. "So for his sake, I did. I got to the condo at around three a.m. and found the window broken. Food was pulled out of the cabinets. The closets in the bedroom had been ransacked. Drawers were open. Clothes were thrown all over the floor. I called the police."

Helen hadn't seen the newspaper. She was shaken when I told her Roberto Ortiz had been arrested for killing his mother.

"He was at home last night," she said. "We saw him there. How could he have murdered her?"

"I'm sure the police are working on a timeline," Charley said.

Helen shook her head in disbelief. "How could he kill his own mother and then go home and watch television?"

I turned toward Charley. "Lupe had a key to the store. Do you suppose Roberto duplicated it and was using Nectar after hours to sell drugs? Maybe she found out and confronted him about it."

Charley shook his head. "Too risky. It's easier to work out of his backyard or from the nearest street corner." He turned toward Helen. "It's an odd coincidence your place was broken into on the same night Ortiz was killed. Is anything missing?"

"Some cash I had laying on the dresser. It wasn't much. A hundred dollars, I think."

"How long have you known Lupe Ortiz?" Charley said.

"About three months. She started cleaning the shop the week it opened. Back then I worked late every night, so I saw a lot of her. She was sweet and easy to talk to. We chatted about our kids, our lives. . . . A lot of things. She brought the three youngest children into the store several times. I even taught her daughter how to make brownies."

"Did Lupe ever come to your condo?"

"She cleaned for me a couple of times when my regular girl was sick. She didn't normally do that sort of work, so I appreciated the favor."

"Did you talk to her about any valuables you had? Things she might have mentioned to her son?"

"You think Roberto Ortiz broke into my condo?"

Charley shrugged. "Anything is possible. From what Tucker said, it sounds to me like the kid is hooked on methamphetamines. Drugs cost money. Most tweekers steal to support their habit. I suggest you call the detective in charge of the Ortiz investigation. Tell him everything you know."

It was clear from Helen's careworn expression that Charley's advice was not welcome. "If Nectar gets associated with another crime, it could ruin my business. The store can't fail, Mr. Tate. If I lose it, I lose everything."

"You'll lose more than your business if you withhold possible evidence in a homicide investigation."

Dale Ewing looked up from the magazine he was reading and cleared his throat. "I don't want Helen to have any more contact with O'Brien unless it's absolutely necessary."

"You want me to call him?" I said.

Charley shot me a warning glance. It was clear he didn't think that was a good move, but it was too late for a retraction.

"Before you do anything," Ewing said, "I think Helen should tell you the rest of the story."

She swallowed hard and met Charley's gaze. "I think somebody tried to get into the condo before last night. A couple of days ago I noticed the lock plate on the back door looked bent, like somebody had jimmied it with a tool. I didn't report it because I wasn't sure."

"Do you think these break-ins are related to Lupe's death?" Charley said.

"I don't see how that's possible. I'm just thankful my recipe books were in the trunk of my car last night or they'd be gone, too."

"Who'd want to steal your recipes?" I said.

She hesitated. "I'm not sure. At first I thought it might be Bob Rossi."

"The guy who owns the restaurant next door?" I said. "He would ruin you over a parking dispute?"

Helen glanced at Ewing and then at me. "Our problems started long before that. I didn't tell you this, Tucker, but right after I opened the shop, Bob approached me with an offer. He wanted to serve my chocolates as a dessert option at the restaurant. What he offered to pay didn't cover the supplies, much less my time, but his customers were all raving about my chocolates, so I told him I'd think about it. He was so sure I'd say yes he went ahead and printed new dessert menus. Dale convinced me I couldn't afford to do it. When I told Bob, he was furious. He wanted me to reimburse his printing and design costs. I refused."

"Did he threaten you?"

"Not directly."

"Tell them the rest, Helen," Ewing said.

She took a deep breath. "For the past couple of weeks, I've been getting strange calls in the middle of the night. The person never speaks. All I hear is heavy breathing and then he hangs up."

"You sure it's a he?" Charley said.

"No, but I sense that it is. And chocolates have been disappearing. At first I thought we were just busy because of that newspaper article you pitched to the *Times*, but the cash receipts don't account for the missing inventory."

"Helen," I said, "why didn't you tell me?"

"Because I knew you'd worry."

"What about your employees?" Charley said. "Maybe somebody's developed a sweet tooth."

"I don't think so. My assistant Kathy brought the problem to my attention. She's the only one I leave alone in the shop."

"Except for Lupe Ortiz," he said.

Helen closed her eyes as if she wanted to shut out the world. "It may seem odd to you, but Lupe and I were friends. I did whatever I could to help her. If one of her kids was sick, I always encouraged her to leave early. When she sold her car, I told her how to transfer the title. She always seemed so appreciative of everything I did for her. I can't believe she would steal from me."

"Has anybody been hanging around the shop lately?" Charley said. "Somebody that looked suspicious?"

She shook her head. "We have a lot of regular customers now, but nobody I'd consider strange."

At least not by Beverly Hills standards, I thought. I told Charley about the Mercedes I'd seen parked at Nectar the night Lupe was killed.

He frowned. "Did you get a license number?"

"There wasn't one. Just a dealer advertisement behind the license frame."

"Do you remember what it said?"

"Garvey Motors. Alhambra."

Neither Helen nor Ewing had seen the car before.

"You said Rossi might want to ruin your business," Charley said. "Was there anybody else?"

Helen looked at Ewing before answering. "My ex-husband."

Charley and I exchanged glances but kept quiet as Helen told us about living the good life in Greenwich, Connecticut, with her CEO husband of twenty-six years. On her fiftieth birthday, Brad Taggart had sent her an e-mail, canceling the dinner they had planned for eighteen of their closest friends and telling her he was leaving her for the company's twenty-nine-year-old corporate attorney.

The divorce had split the family in two. Helen's grown daughter had sided with her ex. The son supported his mother. Helen couldn't face running into Taggart or his new wife at the local market, so she took the money from the divorce settlement and moved to California. She drifted for a while, too emotionally damaged to worry about what the future held. Eventually, she took most of her savings and opened Nectar.

I remembered Eugene's comments earlier in the day about Helen and all she'd gone through. He must have been referring to her messy divorce. I was surprised he'd grown so close to her in such a short amount of time. Chocolate and bad family relationships must be strong bonding agents.

"Brad was involved with this woman a year before he left me," Helen said. "All during that time he was hiding our assets in secret accounts. After he filed for divorce, I hired a forensic accountant to track down the money. He was livid. He said all sorts of horrible things to me. Told me he'd make me pay."

"The Ortiz woman's murder changes everything," Dale Ewing said. "Her death may have been collateral damage. Helen could have been the real target."

Collateral damage was an interesting choice of words. I wondered if Ewing had been in the military. If so, it must have been a long time ago. He looked doughy and benign now, but I'd learned over the years that looks could be deceiving.

"Do you have any evidence Helen was the target?" Charley said.

Ewing shifted in his chair. "I'm only speculating. The police have made an arrest. As for the break-in, we'll probably never know who it was. The detective told us these burglaries are rarely solved. You're probably right about the Ortiz kid. He killed his mother and then broke into Helen's condo looking for something valuable he could fence on the street."

"Helen," I said, "Charley is a private investigator. Maybe you should hire him to look into the problems you've been having."

Helen stared at a black footprint that had been tracked onto her beige living room carpet. Her facial muscles were slack from too much trauma and too little sleep.

"I can't afford that, Tucker. I could barely come up with the money to hire you."

"Maybe Charley and I could combine our efforts, sort of a marketing-slash-investigating service. You know, two for the price of one."

Ewing closed the magazine he'd been reading. "I think that's a good idea, Helen."

She picked up the Ortizes' sympathy card from the table and ran her thumb over the stamp to make sure it was secure. "All right. If that's what you all want."

Charley pulled a small black notebook from the breast pocket of his jacket. "I'll need some info on your ex, like addresses and telephone numbers."

She gestured toward the black fingerprint powder. "Can it wait until later this afternoon? My address book is in the bedroom. I want to vacuum before this powder ruins the carpet."

"Is there anything I can do to help?" I said.

"Kathy is alone at Nectar. Can you stop by the store and make sure everything is okay? Tell her I'll be there as soon as I can."

I stared at Helen in disbelief. "Nectar is open for business?"

Ewing cleared his throat. "The watch commander called after Helen went home last night. She said they were done collecting evidence and promised to have the place cleaned up in time to open this morning."

Past experience told me police departments didn't clean up crime scenes. That was the responsibility of the family or the business owner. I wondered what strings Ewing had pulled to get that kind of service.

"That's Beverly Hills PD for you," Charley said. "I'm surprised she didn't ask her publicist to hold a press conference."

A Cheshire cat smile stretched across Ewing's lips. It

was obvious he enjoyed Charley's snide comment, but he wasn't about to say so.

"Helen, maybe you should have waited a day or two before opening the store," I said. "Just to catch your breath."

She flashed a wan smile. "I couldn't do that. My customers are counting on me. Plus, I have to make chocolates for the symposium. Don't worry. I'll be fine."

My watch read eleven a.m. I had enough time to stop by Nectar and still make my three o'clock appointment with Elizabeth Bennet, but being a business doctor and now a hand holder was becoming a bona fide juggling act.

"Don't worry," I said. "I'll make sure everything is okay."

Before we left, Helen gave me a package for Eugene, six of his favorite Mango-Tango chocolate squares. She said a study just published in the *Archives of Internal Medicine* had found that chocolate lowered blood pressure. She thought Eugene could use a little stress reducer. Maybe I'd down a few of those babies myself.

Charley and I walked to my car, dodging puddles filled with earthworms stranded aboveground after the rain. None of them looked as if they were strong swimmers. I guess learning the backstroke wasn't a high priority in worm world.

"Thanks for taking this job, Charley. I appreciate it."

"Like I told you this morning, I'm pretty busy at the moment, so I may need some help from you and the kid. Computer searches. That sort of thing."

"You can count on us, Charley. Do you really think Roberto Ortiz broke into Helen's condo?"

He shrugged. "It's just one theory. We might get lucky if they find fingerprints and match them to a suspect, but Ewing is right: these types of burglaries are rarely solved."

"How come?"

"For one thing, this wasn't done by a pro. They don't ransack a place. That's usually done by somebody acting on impulse, like a hype looking for his next fix. He cruises by a residence, checks the door to see if it's open or if the lock can be easily defeated. He's in a hurry because he doesn't know who lives there or when they'll be home. He breaks in and tears the place apart, looking for anything he can fence on the street. Then he moves to another neighborhood."

"Do you think Lupe's murder and Helen's burglary are one crime or two?"

"I don't want to speculate. I just don't have enough information."

When we reached the car, I opened the door and slid into the driver's seat. "So what do you want me to do?"

Charley watched as I buckled my seat belt. "Nothing at the moment. I'll check out the ex and that Rossi character later this afternoon. For now, I'm going to hang around here and talk to the neighbors. See if anybody saw anything unusual last night. I can also contact a buddy of mine who used to work for the Beverly Hills PD. He might be able to call in a few favors and find out what evidence they have against Roberto Ortiz."

"I'll ask Eugene to do an Internet search to see if he can find out any more about that quetzal feather."

"What for?"

"It might be a clue. I mean, how did a feather of a rare bird found only in the jungles of Central America end up in a chocolate store in Beverly Hills?"

Charley was silent for a moment. "Okay. He can look up stuff on the computer, but that's it. I don't want him pulling a Philip Marlowe on me, thinking he can solve the case himself."

His concerns were justified. A few months back, Eugene had invented an alter ego and set off on his own to interview suspects in one of Charley's cases. The information he collected had been helpful, but he could have ended up in a body bag. Charley didn't want any more close calls. Neither did I.

"Don't worry," I said. "I'll make sure he understands."

Charley ambled back toward Helen's condo to interview her neighbors, and I headed to Nectar.

Chapter 7

"I can't believe Helen's being victimized again," Eugene said. "How is she holding up?"

"I'm on my way to Nectar right now. I'll tell you more when I get back to the office. In the meantime, Helen hired Charley to look into a few problems she's having. We're going to help him with some research. Can you look up more information on the quetzal?"

"It's a clue, isn't it? I knew it. Have no fear. Bix Waverly is on the job."

Bix Waverly was the pretext name Eugene had used in that unauthorized investigation he undertook for Charley. In private investigator parlance, a pretext is a lie you tell people in order to get information you probably wouldn't get under normal circumstances. It's a tricky and sometimes dangerous game to play. I remembered Charley's admonition.

"All I want you to do is download anything you find on the bird. No phone calls. No interviews. No nothing. Got it?"

He huffed out some air. "Honestly, Tucker, was that little lecture really necessary? I've worked for Charley for almost six months now. I know what I'm doing."

I could only hope that was true.

When I got to Nectar, I parked in the alley and went inside. The retail store was packed with customers, more so than usual. Maybe I'd been wrong. Maybe murder and chocolate did mix.

The decor in the shop was done in the rich autumnal colors of gold, cinnabar, carnelian, and bronze. On the wall was a framed drawing of chocolate molds reproduced from the pages of a 1907 Parisian catalog for professional chocolate makers. There was also an oil painting of a cacao plant growing in the jungles of Central America and a reprint of an 1885 poster Helen had purchased at the chocolate museum in Brule. It was a copy of an original advertisement from her great-grandfather's chocolate shop, which had once been located in the Grand Place in Brussels. Helen had done a masterful job of combining elements of European and Central American cultures to create a place that made you want to kick off your shoes and stay awhile.

Kathy seemed overwhelmed by the crowd of customers, so I grabbed an apron and got behind the counter. Before Nectar, I hadn't been much of a chocolate eater, but Helen was educating me. I now knew that the cacao tree rarely survived outside an area twenty degrees north and twenty degrees south of the equator, and its large pods sprouted from the trunk of the tree as well as from its branches. I'd learned that white chocolate wasn't chocolate at all. Real chocolate had both cocoa butter and cacao solids. White chocolate contained no cacao particles, which was why it didn't taste or look like the real thing. Helen used only the finest chocolate in her recipes, claiming it required less sugar. She also used a higher percent of cacao, at least 65 or more. You didn't have to be an expert to taste the difference between grocery store chocolate and Helen's rich, dense, somewhat bitter, and decidedly orgasmic creations. I hadn't become a chocoholic yet, but I was moving in that direction.

Just as we were gaining control over the crowd of customers, a woman in a blond wig and a pink Chanel suit stormed through the front door. She looked to be in her seventies, but it was hard to tell because of all the work she'd had done by some plastic surgeon who didn't know when to say no. She used her Fendi handbag as a battering ram and shoved her way to the front of the line. Her rudeness prompted a chorus of angry outcries from her fellow customers.

"I'm late for a doctor's appointment," she said with a haughty edge to her voice. "Give me six apricot truffles and six bourbon balls. I want them in the gold box with a red ribbon. And give me a gift card."

In her rush to be served, the woman pushed aside a stocky man wearing a navy blue suit. His white shirt was starched to perfection and stood in stark contrast to his dark skin. He was probably in his sixties but he seemed older, almost prehistoric, like a pre-Columbian stone god in the jungles of Belize. The man seemed unfazed by the brouhaha. His expression was placid, almost meditative. He held up his hand to address the crowd, exposing fingers stained brown by nicotine.

"Pardon," he said, trilling the "r" like a Latin lover. "A woman in a hurry is a dangerous thing. Wouldn't you agree? To save us all, I will allow this lady to take my place in line."

As Kathy hurried to put the woman's chocolates in a box, the man strolled to the back of the store. Out of the corner of my eye, I saw him studying the pictures on the wall and waiting patiently.

A moment later, a black SUV pulled up to the curb in front of the store. A mountain of a man, dressed head to toe in black, exited the driver's seat and walked around to open the rear door. Everything about him screamed *bodyguard*.

A young woman stumbled out of the car wearing a skimpy getup that made her look like a contestant in a new reality show called *America's Top Tart*. Cradled in her arms was a white rat with a pink nose that matched his pink-jeweled collar and leash. As she walked through the front door, she tripped on her four-inch platform shoes. The bodyguard caught her just before she did a triple-header into the glass display case.

When the young woman was upright again, she pushed her way through the crowd to the counter and threw her scrawny arms across the top, knocking over a basket of chocolate bark. The rat must have sensed trouble, because he jumped over her shoulder and scurried down her back as far as the leash would allow.

"I hear somebody got creamed in your back room last night." Her words were slurred by booze, drugs, both, neither. "You should call this place Death by Chocolate." She giggled at her joke.

She didn't look like a member of the newspaper-reading public, so she must have heard the scoop about Lupe Ortiz's death someplace else, maybe by word of mouth. I imagined the store becoming a stop on some macabre tour of famous crime scenes. It was troubling that Nectar's profile had been raised by a murder in the bathroom, but there was nothing I could do about it at the moment.

Kathy seemed flustered by the appearance of the morning's second unruly patron. She picked up the spilled bark and set it on the back counter. "I'm with a customer right now. I'll be with you in a minute."

"A minute?" The young woman's voice squawked as if she had just been startled awake from a bad dream. "Don't you know who I am?"

Maybe Kathy didn't recognize her, but I did. She was Alexis Raines, a pop princess for the bubblegum crowd, who'd ruined her career by growing into adulthood, physically if not emotionally. In the past year, she'd had a succession of DUI arrests and unflattering mug shots plastered across the front page of every tabloid newspaper and celebrity magazine in the country.

The woman with the Fendi bag whipped around. "Excuse me, young lady. Can't you see I was here first?"

That's when she saw the rat. She screamed and raised the Fendi above her head, as if she was a trendy cavewoman about to bag dinner. I knew if I didn't do something fast, the rat was going to end his life as a pancake. I rushed from behind the counter in time to catch the blow from the purse just as the bodyguard pulled Alexis to safety.

The Fendi woman gaped at me, stretching the surgery scars near her ears to a pearly white. Her gaze cut to the bodyguard looming over Alexis. Without so much as an apology, she grabbed the box of chocolates Kathy had packed for her and left the store.

"Christ on a cracker," Alexis said, cuddling the rat in her arms. "You saved Aldo's life. I owe you."

"No big deal—"

"I mean it. You deserve a reward."

"How about buying chocolates for a hundred of your closest friends, and we'll call it even."

"That's all you want?"

"That's all."

"It's not enough. I'm going to send you tickets to my next concert. Front-row seats."

I didn't have the heart to tell Alexis if she didn't get her act together, there would be no next concert. There may not even be a tomorrow. While Kathy and I filled her order, Alexis lurched up to the newspaper article mounted on the wall. She turned and scanned the room.

"Hey, what happened to all the stuff in the picture?"

It took me a moment to realize what she was talking about. The display shelves.

"The owner took them down to make room for more tables."

"Why don't you put it over there?"

As Alexis swung her arm toward one of the glass cases to illustrate her point, she nearly upset a jar of cacao nibs. I grabbed the jar before it went flying across the room. The crowd of customers stood frozen, as if they were watching a train wreck.

"Thanks," I said to her. "I'll mention your decorating ideas to the owner."

Alexis liked the look of the *molinillo* in the picture and wanted to know what it was. I told her it was used for frothing chocolate. She wanted to buy it. I told her it wasn't for sale. She expressed interest in the heart box and the chocolate pot, too, but I demurred. Her negotiating skills were lucid and surprisingly sophisticated, which made me wonder if all that stumbling and slurring was just an act.

Two hundred dollars' worth of chocolates later, the bodyguard carried the bags and Alexis out to the SUV and drove away. Raines was a disaster waiting to happen, but if she came back and brought all of her celebrity friends, she could guarantee Nectar's success.

When Kathy and I were finished waiting on all the customers, the man in the back of the room stepped up to the counter.

"Thanks for waiting," I said to him. "You're a real gentleman."

He smiled like a contented lizard sunning himself on a desert stone. "I did not know that buying chocolates today would earn me the praise of a beautiful woman."

"I'm sorry for what happened. It's usually not this crazy. I hope you'll come back."

"It is a long drive for me, but worth the trip. I tell my wife that cacao is good for my health, but she says my guilty pleasures will kill me one day. Too bad that young woman has no one to warn her of her fate."

"Money and immaturity are always a bad combination."

The man selected six chocolates. It wasn't many for the length of time it took him to pick them out. The last he chose was my all-time favorite. Helen called them Forget-Me-Nots, because once you sampled one, you weren't ever likely to forget. A delicate flower was stenciled on a thin crust of dark chocolate that covered a chocolate ganache so rich and sensual it made you want to say, "It was good for me, baby. Was it good for you?"

"If you work here," the man said, "you must share my passion for cacao."

I handed him the box. "I love Helen's chocolates, but I don't work in the store. I'm just filling in today. I'm a consultant, sort of a business doctor."

He nodded. "This Helen is a wise woman to seek help. I myself own a small business. I am always looking for new ways to make money so I can continue to indulge those guilty pleasures of mine."

I reached under the counter and handed him a card from my purse. "I've worked with a lot of small businesses. If you ever want to discuss your options, call me at any of these numbers."

"Perhaps I will." He gave me a placid salute and made his way toward the door.

It was getting late. I didn't want to miss my appointment with Elizabeth Bennet, so I hung up my apron and headed for the door. I was just backing out of the alley when I was startled by a knock on the passenger-side window. I turned and saw Detective O'Brien staring at me through the glass. He didn't look happy.

Chapter 8

I got out of the car and stood facing O'Brien over the roof of the Boxster. The sun at his back made his red hair look like a burning bush. I hoped I wasn't about to meet my destiny.

"What are you doing here?" I said.

"Looking for Lupe Ortiz's cell phone. It's missing. Too bad the crime scene was closed without consulting me. Otherwise, it wouldn't be a problem."

The scratch on O'Brien's face seemed to be healing, but his disposition was still raw. He was probably pissed that Dale Ewing had complained to his supervisor.

"I thought you solved the Ortiz case."

"We made an arrest, but the investigation isn't over. You never know what else might turn up if you dig deep enough."

His words sounded ominous, sort of like a threat.

The last thing Helen needed was a Beverly Hills cop with a little power and a lot of attitude.

"You think somebody else was involved?" I said.

"That feather we found at the scene is from a bird called a quetzal. It's a symbol used by a street gang called the MayaBoyz. Roberto Ortiz is a member. We think he killed his mother because she was interfering with his gang activities. Now we want to know if any of his homeboys helped him out."

As I'd promised, I told O'Brien about the break-in at Helen's condo and asked if he thought Roberto might have been involved. He didn't express an opinion; just said he'd check it out with the LAPD.

It was around one thirty before I got back to the office. Eugene was working at his computer. The air purifier was still hanging around his neck, whirring. I handed him the chocolates Helen had sent. He clutched the bag to his chest in ecstasy.

"Isn't she just too wonderful?"

"Yeah," I said. "She's a peach. Did you find out any more about the quetzal?"

He set the bag on his desk and handed me a stack of notes. "Yes, but it's going to make you sad. I still don't know if they're extinct or not, but it doesn't look good. The birds were considered a symbol of freedom to the Maya because they couldn't be held in captivity. If you put them in cages, they'll kill themselves in a sort of live-free-or-die suicide pact."

For a moment, I imaged a cult of colorful birds wearing black tennis shoes and toasting the arrival of the Hale-Bopp Comet with poisoned punch.

"I found a book in the library's online database," he went on. "It's about an East L.A. street gang called the MayaBoyz. And—get this—there's a picture of some gang graffiti on the book cover. There's a feather that looks a lot like it came from a quetzal. At least, it was long and green. There must be something about it in the book, or the link wouldn't have come up in my search."

"O'Brien told me Roberto Ortiz is a member of that gang, but I'd like to find out more."

"I'll stop by the library this weekend."

The library. That didn't sound dangerous.

"Great," I said.

I was heading toward my office when Charley strolled into the lobby.

"Any luck with Helen's neighbors?" I said.

"Nah. Only one person was home—the guy who lives next door. He said he was home sick all day Thursday, but didn't see anything unusual. Claims he took enough cough syrup with codeine to sleep through an earthquake. He didn't want to talk to me, wouldn't even open the door. Said he was afraid I might catch whatever he had. The guy was weird, like one of those quiet types who turn out to be a serial killer. He gave me the willies."

"Somebody must have seen *something*," Eugene said.

Charley shrugged. "The place is secluded, lots of trees, and all the units have separate entrances."

Eugene's face was flushed. "Doesn't Helen's condo have a security gate or a concierge?"

"Sorry, kid," Charley said. "The place doesn't have anything like that."

"So Helen loses again, and nobody can do anything about it." Eugene's voice was laced with futility and indignation. "We're private investigators. We should be able to solve a simple burglary."

Charley put his hands on his hips. I could tell he was about to scold Eugene about the use of the word *we*. I didn't want Eugene pressured before he downed a couple of Mango-Tango squares, so I caught Charley's eye and shook my head.

"What about that police contact of yours?" I said. "Did he know anything?"

"Not much. One of the neighbors heard Ortiz arguing with his mother at around four thirty. The kid wanted money to buy drugs, and she wouldn't give it to him. The neighbor saw her leave for work at around five o'clock. Roberto left a few minutes later."

"So the police think Roberto followed Lupe to Beverly Hills to kill her?" I said.

"Yup."

"That doesn't make sense, Charley. If he needed money for drugs, why didn't he steal the cash from Nectar's register?"

"Beats me."

Charley walked into his office. Eugene and I followed. Several file folders were stacked on his desk chair. He dropped them on the floor and sat.

"Where did they find Lupe's car?" I said.

"She was driving a van from the janitorial service she worked for. Beverly Hills PD found it in a parking garage about a block away. Funny thing, though: her cleaning bucket and some supplies are missing."

I cocked my head. "That's odd."

"Who knows? Maybe her kid took them."

"Why would he take cleaning supplies? Roberto's a druggie who needed a fix. It's not like a can of Old Dutch Cleanser is worth big bucks on the street. I just talked to Detective O'Brien. He says her cell phone is missing, too."

Eugene picked up the files and set them on top of the cabinet. "Roberto didn't do it. The police arrested the wrong guy."

Charley and I exchanged skeptical glances.

"Believe me," Eugene continued, "I understand the lure of matricide, but Roberto Ortiz had too much on his plate last night to pull it off. He had to drive all the way from East L.A. to Beverly Hills, kill his mother, and then drive home to open the door when Helen and Tucker got to his house. From what Tucker said, the guy was high on drugs. I don't know how he could drive, much less accomplish all that."

Charley crossed his arms over his chest in a defensive posture. "Like I said before, we don't know if it's possible until we know the timeline of the murder."

True, but Eugene's point was well taken. If Roberto's motive for killing his mother had been revenge for meddling in his gang life, why had he driven to Beverly Hills to kill her? That seemed risky. Even if he'd been angry and desperate for a fix, it seemed more likely that he'd kill her at home at the moment she'd refused to give him money.

Eugene stood. "Roberto is innocent. I just know it. I think Lupe's murder is a carefully planned conspiracy to destroy Helen Taggart."

Charley rolled his eyes. "How so?"

"First came the harassing telephone calls, then the theft of her chocolates, then the break-in at her condo, and now murder. Somebody wants to drive her out of Beverly Hills."

Charley picked up one of his number 2 pencils and shoved it into the electric sharpener. Over the noise of wood grinding to a fine point, he said, "And who would that be?"

Eugene began to pace. His words were punctuated with sweeping arm gestures. His breath grew shallower with each hypothetical. "Maybe the European chocolate industry is threatened by her success, or a band of antisugar terrorists wants to kill the candy industry one chocolate store at a time, or maybe it's her ex-husband or that Rossi guy. He's been vile to Helen. I bet one of them is behind all these problems."

Charley blew the lead dust off the tip of the pencil. "Calm down. I have to go to the courthouse for another client. I'll see if I can find a criminal record on either of those guys. If I learn anything, I'll let you know."

"Let me do something," Eugene said.

"If I need help, I'll ask for it."

Eugene turned and stomped out of the room. Over his shoulder he said, "I just wish you two had more faith in me."

Charley loaded his sharpened pencil and a notebook into a battered leather briefcase and left for the courthouse. I returned to my desk. Soon after, I heard the outer door open. I glanced up and saw Lorna Tate strutting into the office like a cartoon runway model. I was surprised her hip joints could withstand the gyrations. I walked to the lobby to see what she wanted.

Charley's wife was in her late thirties, with violet eyes, chestnut hair, and a butt as flat as a tortilla grill. She had on her porn-queen outfit—high-heeled leather boots and a fake leopard coat. She looked like an escapee from a stuffed toy factory. She set a large Bloomingdale's shopping bag on Eugene's in-basket, collapsing the plastic Corinthian columns. He caught my gaze and stuck his finger down his throat, pretending to gag. Eugene and I tolerated Lorna, but you'd never see the three of us sitting around a campfire singing "Kumbaya."

Lorna glanced into Charley's office and saw it was empty. A pout began forming on her mouth. "Where is he?"

"At the courthouse," I said.

She gestured toward the bag. "I have something to show him. When is he coming back?"

"I don't know. Did you call his cell?"

"He doesn't answer."

I walked back toward my office. "Then I guess you'll just have to wait until tonight."

Lorna grabbed the shopping bag from Eugene's desk with enough force to rip off one of the handles. "Thanks for nothing, Tucker."

"My pleasure," I mumbled under my breath.

A few moments later, the door to the outside hallway slammed shut. Eugene came into my office, his finger making a circular motion next to his ear.

"When I think of Lorna procreating," he said, "I get *Village of the Damned* flashbacks."

"Half the kid's genes would be Charley's."

"And *that's* supposed to make me feel better?"

I smiled. "Yeah . . . you have a point."

Elizabeth Bennet's appointment was at three. I didn't want to seem clueless about the matchmaking industry, so in preparation for our meeting, I searched the Internet for information on modern-day dating practices. I found several research papers on the public library Web site and discovered that a person has only a 17 percent chance of hitting it off with a blind date arranged by a friend. I didn't need a research study to tell me what I'd already verified in the field.

I also read that people spent over forty billion dollars a year on weddings, and that in the past four years, annual revenues from matchmaking businesses had increased 300 percent. The researchers estimated that 75 percent of adults in the U.S. were looking for true love. I wondered what the other 25 percent were looking for. Lorna Tate?

Elizabeth Bennet was in a competitive field, but the potential was promising. She just needed to weed out the serial daters and the serial killers from her client list, price her services to beat the competition, and she'd soon be bringing in some cool cash.

I'd collected enough matchmaking facts to impress even the most jaded client, so I decided to search the Internet for Elizabeth Bennet to see if she had a presence on the Web. I got a number of hits, mostly for Jane Austen's heroine in *Pride and Prejudice*. No wonder the name sounded familiar. I just hoped *this* Elizabeth Bennet was as sensible and smart as the literary figure, because I wasn't in the mood to assume command of the bimbo brigade. A few minutes before three, Eugene called on the intercom. Elizabeth Bennet was waiting for me in the lobby.

Chapter 9

I straightened the papers on my desk into tidy piles. I wanted the place to look neat, but I didn't want Elizabeth Bennet to think I wasn't busy. I walked into the reception area and found a fair-haired, athletic woman in her midtwenties standing near Eugene's desk. She wore no makeup, but that didn't matter. It might have made her more glamorous, but it wouldn't have made her more beautiful.

"Ms. Bennet? I'm Tucker Sinclair."

She stared at me until her unwavering gaze made me uncomfortable. "I've heard a lot about you."

"Good things, I hope. Do you mind telling me who referred you?"

She hesitated. "Nobody, really. I've just heard your name mentioned a bunch of times."

That sounded suspiciously vague, but there was no

point in being confrontational. I'd press her for more information during our interview. I led her into my office and we both settled in chairs across the desk from each other. As she set her handbag on the floor, a bottle of water rolled out and clunked against her shoe.

"I understand you run a dating service," I said. "Sounds challenging and entrepreneurial."

"I'm just getting started. You know, still trying to get clients, make good matches, that sort of thing. My goal is to get a few of my couples married. Don't you think that would be good advertising?"

"I'm sure it would be."

"Are you with anybody right now?" she said. "If not, maybe you could be my test case."

Her smile was mischievous and appealing. I smiled, too, just so she knew I got the joke.

"I'm afraid I'd be more of a challenge than you need right now. So, tell me about your company. What's it called?"

She hesitated, unsure of herself. "Luv Bugs."

I felt myself do a mental cringe. My negative reaction must have played out on my face, because she looked crestfallen.

She took off the jacket she was wearing, exposing toned arms. "You don't like it, do you? Me neither. In fact, I think it sucks. I considered Happily Ever After, Mixed-and-Matched, Strangers to Soul Mates. All of them were terrible."

"Naming a company isn't easy."

She planted her elbows on the desk and held her face in her hands. "It's harder than falling in love."

"How long have you been in business?"

"Not long."

"How long is that?"

"About three months."

"How much working capital do you have?"

She stared out the window behind me, avoiding my gaze. "It's sort of depressing to talk about that."

I leaned back in my chair, frustrated by her cryptic answers. "Just so you know, Elizabeth, I charge for my work."

Her expression seemed pained. "I know that. Don't worry. I have enough money to pay you."

"Do you have a business plan?"

"Not a good one. That's why I need your help."

"What are your goals for Luv Bugs?"

Her eyes sparkled with youthful exuberance. "I want to make love happen. So many people make bad relationship decisions. I see it everywhere. People who should be together but aren't. People who shouldn't be together but are. I want to fix all that, give people a chance to find real love."

If Elizabeth Bennet had been any sweeter, I'd be suffering from insulin shock. While she talked about her plans to save the romantically challenged, her long, graceful fingers were in perpetual motion, punctuating each sentence with swoops and loop-de-loops. Her voice danced up and down the scales, stopping with a sudden squeak that doubled as an exclamation point. She was serious one moment, laughing the next, sometimes all in the same sentence. Even her nose was expressive, wrinkling to make some point or another.

She was mesmerizing. I didn't want to take my eyes off her for fear of missing something delightful. Her naïveté would probably doom Luv Bugs, but by the time she'd finished talking, I was ready to bail water from the deck of her sinking ship.

"It's an interesting coincidence," I said. "Your name, I mean. Elizabeth Bennet is the woman who tamed Mr. Darcy."

Her cheeks flushed.

"I'm sorry," I said. "You've probably heard that a million times before. What I meant was, it's a lovely name."

She fidgeted with the neat stacks of papers on my desk, making them neater. "I have a confession to make. My name isn't Elizabeth Bennet. I told you that because I didn't think you'd help me if you knew my real name."

The possibilities flashed through my head, but I couldn't think of anybody I disliked enough to turn down business because of an association with this young woman.

"My name is Riley." She studied my reaction with her earnest blue eyes. "Riley Deegan. You used to date my brother, Joe."

I felt my muscles grow tense. Joe Deegan was the man who had driven me to seek solace on that bicycle trip in France. There had been some trouble for him a few months back, for which I was partly to blame. A disgruntled ex-lover had filed a complaint against him, accusing him of selling confidential government information to a private investigator—Charley Tate. It was a lie. It was also a felony. Not only could Deegan have lost his job; he could have gone to prison. I offered to help clear his name, but instead he chose to end our relationship.

I stared at Riley Deegan, wondering what kind of game she was running on me. "Does he know you're here?"

"No. I need business advice, and I don't know who else to ask."

"This isn't a good idea."

Her shoulders slumped in defeat. A moment later she rose from the chair. "I'm sorry I bothered you."

I felt as if I had just melted a snowflake with a blow-dryer. There was no reason to punish Riley Deegan for my failed relationship with her brother, and there was no excuse for turning down business, either. I needed clients to pay my rent and my half of Eugene's salary. Besides, we were all adults. Relationships fail. Love dies. Blah, blah, blah.

"Sit down, Riley."

She returned to the chair, but waited for me to speak first.

"How's he doing, anyway?" I said.

She bowed her head as if the gesture would make the words come out easier. "The Board of Review finally cleared him of all charges, but it was hard on him."

I tried to make the next comment seem offhand, but my cheery tone sounded false even to my ears. "I hope he's happy."

She shrugged. "I guess so. He's engaged."

I felt as if someone had just punched me in the

stomach. It had only been five months since Joe Deegan and I stopped seeing each other. I didn't expect him to be pining away for me, but it was painful to think he'd gone from zero to sixty with some other woman in such a short amount of time. In a way, it wasn't surprising. He was a charming and funny guy who also happened to be eye candy. He'd had other women before me, lots of them. Now he had only one, and it wasn't me.

"I wish him well," I said.

Riley's shoulders relaxed. "So you'll work with me?"

I handed her a packet that included my schedule of fees, a resume, and several client recommendations. "Why don't you look this over? If you want to proceed after that, we'll have a strategy meeting, at which time I'll ask you to provide any financial statements you have."

Riley glanced at the cover of the packet but didn't open it.

"I'm giving a party for some clients tomorrow night," she said. "There'll be a lot of people there. Why don't you come? I can give you all of the paperwork then."

"That's very kind of you," I said. "I'll check my calendar and let you know."

"I think it's important for you to see how I work the crowd. You know, how I break the ice, match people up. That sort of thing."

"Why don't you look at the material I gave you first? Make sure you can afford my services. If you want to proceed, we'll sign a contract and you'll give me a retainer."

"I've decided. You're hired."

"Okay." I stretched out the word until it became one long, skeptical sentence.

"Look," she said. "I don't know when you'll have another chance like this. These events are a lot of work. It could be months before I set up another one. Then it might be too late."

"Too late for what?"

She seemed to be struggling with the answer to my question. "Too late for Luv Bugs."

She had a point. If it was a business-related function, it might be a good idea to check out her clientele and her matchmaking skills. I'd stay just long enough to size up the operation. I made a pretense of checking my calendar, but of course, I knew the following Saturday night and all of the subsequent Saturday nights in the foreseeable future were wide open.

"You're in luck," I said. "Looks like I'm free."

"The party's at my sister's house." She handed me a piece of paper. "Here's the address. Come by at around seven."

"Your brother won't be at this party. Right?"

She frowned. "Why should he be? He's not single anymore."

Nothing like rubbing salt into the wound.

As soon as Riley left, Eugene bustled into my office with a wide-eyed look on his face. "She's Joe Deegan's sister?"

I shot him a wary glance. "You were eavesdropping again."

"No, I just happened to be standing by the door when she told you. Do you think it's some kind of setup?"

"It's hard to say, but I don't think so."

"Are you really going to work for her?"

I slid all of the dating research I'd printed from the computer into a file folder. "Yup, as long as her check clears at the bank."

He shook his head in dismay. "I hope you know what you're doing."

"I'm going to one of her singles' parties on Saturday." I paused for a moment, remembering that he already knew since he'd been listening to our conversation. "How about coming with me?"

"Your offer is oh-so-tempting," he said dryly, "but Saturday's my day to volunteer at the old folks' home."

Eugene went back to his desk, and I started making a list of possible market niches for Luv Bugs. There were probably tons of busy executives who couldn't find love, especially since some companies had rules against coworker relationships, and others even encouraged workers to sign "love contracts" to protect them against legal fallout when in-house romances turned bad.

It was hard to come up with any good dating ideas. I hadn't had a successful relationship since my day-care days, when I'd shared my Binkie pacifier with a kid named Marvin Sidwell. My mother told me he and I had a groovy kind of love, until Marvin's mother got laid off from work and became a stay-at-home mom.

After a few more frustrating attempts to download dating statistics, I asked myself why I was sitting at the computer when I had access to a woman whose serial-dating exploits belonged in *Guinness World Records*: my friend and former coworker Venus Corday. I telephoned her at work and asked if we could meet.

"I'm booked all through the weekend," she said. "What about next Monday?"

"This can't wait. I need to brainstorm dating strategies."

"Are you back in the game?" Her tone sounded hopeful.

"Nope. It's for a client."

I heard what sounded like a pen tapping impatiently on a hard surface. "It's been months, Tucker. What are you waiting for?"

"I've been busy with work."

"That's a crock and you know it. You're stalling."

"Look, I just haven't met anybody that interests me. Okay? So when can we get together?"

I heard paper rustling. She was probably checking her appointment book. Venus was one of the few people on the planet who still organized her life with pen and paper.

"I'm having lunch with a client tomorrow at the Getty Center," she said, "but I can meet you for coffee. How about ten thirty?"

"I don't have a ticket."

"You don't need one anymore. Just park in the garage and take the tram to the plaza. I'll meet you at the café."

At around six, I packed up and got ready to leave. Eugene was still at his desk.

"Aren't you going home?" I said.

He looked up from his computer screen. "Nerine is flying into LAX at nine. It's too far to drive back to my apartment. I'm going to stay here and work until her broomstick is safely parked on the tarmac."

"Your mother is coming for a visit and you didn't tell me?"

"I knew you'd worry. I'm fine with it, Tucker. Really. I can handle her on my own."

I'd never met Eugene's mother before, but from what he'd told me over the years, she was controlling and hypercritical. I studied his face, searching for signs of panic. He seemed calm, at least on the surface, but I didn't want to tempt fate. He'd had his share of anxiety problems in the past. Therapy had helped. I just worried Nerine's visit would trigger a relapse, especially with everything that had happened at Nectar in the past two days.

"I'm surprised your dad is letting her out of his sight."

Eugene took a plastic bag from his desk drawer. Inside was a dusting glove he'd knitted after his therapist suggested it might relieve his anxiety.

"The colonel doesn't know it yet, but she's leaving him. I think she's saving it as a surprise."

I sat down because I had to be sure he was okay. "How long is she staying?"

He lifted his penholder and swept the glove over the surface of the desk. I noticed the popcorn stitch was starting to look flat from too many washings.

"I don't know," he said. "Not long, I hope."

"If she's leaving the colonel, it seems like she'd want to stay with your sister. You know, for a little female bonding time."

"Marilyn is living in an undisclosed safe house in Seattle. She's been there ever since my parents sent her away to college and then left her to rust. Last time I heard, she was working in the dusty stacks of some library."

"Sounds like it's been a while since you've heard from her."

Eugene brushed over the laurel wreaths and Corinthian columns of his in-basket. "I get a Christmas letter from her every year, sent from a post office box. It starts with *Dear Friends and Family. Hope this letter finds you well.* I salute her ingenuity for getting out of the house, but I wish she'd have left a note, warning me of what to expect."

"Your childhood sounds pretty awful."

He wiped off his computer screen and put the glove back inside the plastic bag. "Did I tell you I was a mistake? My father called me Oops until I was fourteen, when he finally stopped talking to me altogether. Just because I didn't make the football team. He didn't seem to notice I was small enough to be the ball."

"Why didn't you tell your mom not to come?"

His lips pressed together in a hard line as he returned the bag to the desk drawer. "I'd never hear the end of it. She'd accuse me of being a bad son, which wouldn't exactly surprise me. Nothing I ever do is right. I'll try my best to impress her while she's here, but if I don't do something spectacular in the next couple days, things could turn ugly."

"Do you want me to stop by your place and feed Fergie and Liza?"

"Thanks, but my neighbor offered to cat-sit until I get home."

I studied his expression, still looking for signs of panic. "In case of emergency, you know my number."

"In case of emergency, Eugene Barstok will step into the nearest telephone booth and come out as Bix Waverly, investigative reporter for the *New York Times*."

I imagined him as the caped office crusader. Faster than a speeding modem. More powerful than a million gigabytes. Able to leap tall stacks of case files in a single bound. At least we could joke about the situation.

Eugene's psyche would probably survive the weekend with his mother, so I turned my thoughts to my meeting with Venus. I knew she'd give me a new direction for Luv Bugs, but I also hoped she'd have some thoughts about the relationship between Helen's problems and a long, iridescent green feather.

Chapter 10

Saturday morning, I drove to the Getty to meet Venus. The J. Paul Getty trust is the wealthiest private art institute in the world, with an endowment of more than four billion dollars. The buildings and gardens that comprise the Getty Center sprawl across 110 acres of land on the crest of a hill in the Santa Monica Mountains, just as the 405 Freeway dips into what we Angelenos think of as the strange and alien land called the San Fernando Valley.

The museum had recently been forced to return several looted antiquities to the Italians. There was no evidence the Italians planned to return the items to the Greeks, from whom they'd been looted back in yon years of yore. My mother always says, "What goes around comes around," but sometimes justice takes a while to go full circle.

The parking-garage elevator took me to the tram station. There was no line, so I boarded one of the cars and rode to the travertine marble plaza at the top of the hill, stopping for a moment to take in the view. On a clear day you could see from the Pacific Ocean to the San Gabriel Mountains, but not today. The sun had broken through the clouds on the Westside, but a gray marine layer still blanketed the inner city.

Venus was waiting for me by the front door of the café. She was dressed for business in an imposing burnt gold suit accented with a chunky necklace made of carved wooden zebras, lions, and a giraffe or two. The outfit was a perfect complement to her caramel skin, coffee-colored eyes, and raven hair, which cascaded around her neck in loopy curls that looked as if they had spent the night rolled around orange juice cans. We did the girlfriend hug and strolled inside to a table near the window.

Venus was a consultant who worked mostly with large manufacturing companies, but she knew plenty about other industries, and even more about dating than anybody. For the next few minutes, we sipped coffee and brainstormed niche markets that might distinguish Luv Bugs from the competition.

It didn't take long to come up with a list that included serious daters, casual daters, straight men and women, gays and lesbians, the well-heeled, the over-fifty crowd, and the executives. We broke down the college educated into smaller groups, like Ivy League schools versus state universities and community colleges. Then there were people with similar religions, hobbies, interests, or professions.

"What about Catholic school survivors?" I said.

Venus poured two packs of sugar into her cup. "How about people who are afraid of clowns?"

"Video vigilantes."

"Celebrity impersonators."

"The possibilities are endless," I said. "Riley will have to do background checks to make sure her clients are legit, but Charley can help with that."

Venus added cream and stirred the coffee. "In case a match doesn't work out, she'll have to offer some kind of guarantee. She also needs to come up with a list of safe-dating tips."

"That won't be a problem. Her brother is a cop."

Venus's cup was midway to her mouth when she set it on the saucer with a loud clunk. Her eyes were full of suspicion.

"Who did you say this client was?"

I bit my lip, anticipating her disapproval. "Riley Deegan."

Venus inhaled deeply and squared her shoulders. "You're working with a Deegan?"

I nodded. "Joe's sister."

Venus shook her head. "Huh-uh, Tucker. Don't do it."

"It's just business."

"You're still vulnerable. You don't need a Deegan in your life right now, not even a sister."

"I've moved on."

"Why am I not convinced?"

"You worry too much. Look, Riley invited me to a singles' party she's throwing for some clients tonight. I think it makes more sense to introduce couples online and let them arrange their own dates, but I'll see how she works it. How about coming with me?"

"I'd rather be locked in a monastery cell, listening to Gregorian chants."

"That's it? Just no?"

"Okay, hell no. I hate singles' parties. It's like being in a room full of desperate shoppers looking for a fresh turkey the day before Thanksgiving. Everybody's sniffing around, checking the size and expiration date. Besides, I'm taking a break from men."

That was news to me. Venus had survived her share of failed relationships, including one with Max Huffman, the third rider on our French cycling trip. He seemed like a nice guy. Kind of a jock, but he adored her. They split shortly after we returned. She'd never told me why.

"I thought Max was the one," I said. "What happened?"

She wagged her index finger in my face. "Never get serious about a man until you've traveled with him. After three days cooped up in a hotel room, you start to see his dark side."

"We were on our bikes all day. The only time you were in a hotel room was at night. That couldn't have been all bad. I've seen Max in a pair of Spandex shorts."

Venus checked her watch and pulled a leopard cosmetic bag from her purse. "Sex wasn't the problem. The man was a virtuoso."

"Then what happened?"

Venus looked around to make sure nobody was within earshot. "He stole shower caps . . . from the hotel rooms."

"How do you know?"

She unzipped the bag and took out several items, including a mirror, lipstick, and liner. "I was sort of looking through his backpack the day before we flew home. It was full of them."

"Okay, stealing things from hotel rooms is bad, but it's not uncommon. Maybe he didn't like to get his hair wet when he showered."

"That's another problem."

"He didn't shower?"

"Oh, he showered all right. Every morning and every night and he stayed in there with a scrub brush until all the hot water was gone along with the top layer of his skin. No wonder he was so white."

"Seems like a shame to dump a nice guy like Max just because he likes to exfoliate under running water."

Venus was applying lipstick and talking at the same time, so her words seemed distorted. "Listen, Tucker. For once take my advice. Don't go to that party tonight. You'll just open a big can of worms."

"Deegan won't be there."

"Doesn't matter. His sister will be, and that's bad news for you."

"He's engaged, Venus."

She looked at me over the top of the mirror. "Excuse me?"

"Deegan's engaged. So you don't have anything to worry about."

She put away the cosmetics bag and studied my expression. "You okay with that, girl?"

"Perfectly okay."

The depth of my bond with Venus was mostly unspoken, but I knew she'd go the distance for me and she knew I'd do the same for her. She squeezed my arm in a gesture of support, and changed the subject.

I told her about Lupe's death and Helen's problems. I braced for a lecture about not getting involved. To my surprise, she seemed more worried than annoyed. Maybe the swearing-off-men thing had mellowed her.

"If you ask me, it was Helen's ex who killed Lupe. Sounds like the guy has issues."

"I found a quetzal feather near the body," I said. "It's a rare bird from Central America. You ever heard of it?"

"The only birds I know about come on dinner plates. What's the big deal with this feather, anyway?"

"It's a gang symbol. The police think Lupe's son left it there as some sort of statement. I'm not so sure. From what Eugene found out, quetzals don't live outside Central America. The L.A. zoo doesn't even have any. Where would gangbangers get feathers?"

"You need to ask one of those bird experts."

"I probably will. Or maybe somebody who knows about Central America."

Venus paused. "I have a client you could talk to.

He's a doctor on the board of a nonprofit called Air Health. His name is Jordan Rich. He flies to Guatemala all the time to work at a free clinic there. He knows a lot about the culture, and he's a nice guy. I'm sure he'll help if he can."

"Thanks, but I can find out about Guatemala on the Internet."

"That's not the same as talking to somebody who's been there."

Dr. Rich was probably a dead end, but it couldn't hurt to talk to him.

"Okay, maybe I'll call him."

Venus checked her address book and jotted down Rich's telephone number on one of her business cards. I put the card in my purse and headed for my car.

The wind was pushing the clouds east, creating a swath of blue sky over the desert. Riley Deegan's party wasn't for several hours, so I called Charley on my cell to see if he'd learned anything at the courthouse. All I got was his voice mail.

When I arrived home, I took Muldoon for a long walk on the beach. At around four o'clock, I felt restless, so I dialed Jordan Rich's number. As it turned out, Venus had already alerted him that I might be in touch. He said he would be happy to talk to me about Guatemala. In fact, he had tickets for a musical at the Ahmanson Theatre on Tuesday evening. A fund-raiser. Would I join him? He suggested we meet at the Pinot Grill before curtain time to have dinner and talk.

The invitation seemed calculated, almost like he was asking me out on a date. I hoped Venus hadn't said anything to lead him on, because I wasn't interested in jumping into another relationship just yet. On the flip side, what could it hurt? Dr. Rich might know something about quetzal feathers that might help me understand why one had been left at a murder scene. I agreed to meet him at the restaurant at six on Tuesday evening.

I fed Muldoon more kibble and headed for Riley Deegan's singles' party.

Chapter 11

The Luv Bugs party was being held at the home of Riley Deegan's sister, a large Spanish-style house on the cliffs overlooking the Pacific Ocean in Palos Verdes Estates. The roof was made of terra-cotta tiles, and the courtyard driveway was lined with lush vegetation. I wondered how Claudia and her husband, Matt, could afford to live in such fancy digs. I'd only seen Claudia once. She was my age, thirty or so, and attractive. I assumed her husband was the same. On the other hand, she could have married a troll with a trust fund.

I arrived twenty minutes late, to find light spilling out of every window in the house. I adjusted the spaghetti straps on my little black cocktail dress and pulled my Nanook of the North parka around my neck to ward off the cold. As soon as I got out of the car, I heard music blaring. The party was obviously in full swing.

The door was ajar, so I stepped inside. A moment later, Riley Deegan vaulted across the room like a member of the Olympic cheerleading squad. Her smile was welcoming, but there was tension in the creases around her eyes.

"How's it going?" I said.

She took a deep breath. "I should have opened a pet store."

I glanced at the half-dozen people standing in the foyer. A couple of them looked as if they belonged in a cage. "It's early. Give it time."

Riley grabbed my hand. "Come with me. I'll get you a glass of wine."

The decor in the living room was spare. There was a couch, a couple of chairs, and a few well-placed works of art, but the look was minimalist, which allowed visitors to see the centerpiece of the house—a 180-degree view of the ocean.

Claudia was nowhere in sight, but about forty singles were crowded into the living room, drinking wine and chatting. They all looked young, thin, attractive, and impossibly cool in their high-priced designer jeans and tight leather jackets. I felt like a dork in my little black dress. Along with my abysmal dating skills, choosing the proper attire for any event other than a day at the office had never been my forte.

Riley showed me where to stash my coat and then guided me through the living room and out to a patio overlooking the water. A boyish-looking man with an unruly head of reddish-brown hair was holding a pilsner glass filled with amber liquid and gazing at the ocean.

"Josh, I want you to meet Tucker Sinclair. Could you entertain her for a few minutes while I get her some wine? I have to change the music. Nobody's dancing. I need to play something . . . else."

Riley bolted toward the living room.

Josh smiled. "So, what's your sign?"

If this was an example of Luv Bugs's clientele, the company was in deep doo-doo. Josh must have noticed the look of incredulity on my face, because he laughed.

"I was just joking. My grandpa told me that line got him lots of action back in his day. I guess it's not ready for a comeback."

"I'm afraid that line went out with tube tops and wide lapels. So, you're a Luv Bug?"

He hesitated. "Not really. I'm sort of Riley's boyfriend."

"Sort of?"

"Yeah, as in she's sort of mad at me right now."

"What did you do?"

He threw his arms up, clearly exasperated. "See? Why do you women always think whatever happens is our fault?"

Before I had a chance to say, "Because it usually is," Riley came rushing out to the patio. A moment later, the doorbell rang. She looked as if she was being pulled in every direction and couldn't decide which way to turn first.

She grabbed the pilsner glass out of Josh's hand and slammed it on a nearby table. "I need your help. I ran out of white wine. There's a case downstairs in the cellar. In a box on the floor. Grab as many bottles as you can carry and bring them to the bar. Use the door in the kitchen."

Josh gave me a look that said *I told you she was mad at me.*

The doorbell rang again.

"You want me to get that?" Josh said. "Or the wine?"

"The wine. No, the door, then the wine. I have to go. Noah's freaking out. Emma has him pinned to the couch, talking about the mandible of the trap-jaw ant."

Just as Riley turned to leave, a young woman approached.

"Just thought you should know," she said. "There's no toilet paper in the bathroom."

Riley groaned and rushed from the room like a whirling dervish. Josh ambled toward the living room to answer the door.

Poor Riley. The party was full of bugs, but not the Luv kind. Since I was just standing around doing nothing, I decided to help her out by getting the wine from the cellar. My one-stop consulting service had now expanded. In addition to business doctor and hand holder, I could add wine wrangler to my list of services.

A door off the kitchen led to a flight of stairs to the lower floor. At the bottom was an arched wooden door. I opened it and entered a room filled floor to ceiling with racks containing hundreds of dusty bottles of wine. Either Claudia and Matt had invested major bucks in this cellar, or they'd been Dumpster-diving for empty bottles.

The light was dim. It was too cold down there for my little black spaghetti-strap dress. It took me a few moments to locate the box. I was stooping over to grab a few bottles when I was startled by a man's voice.

"Riley? You down here?"

I looked up and saw Joe Deegan standing in the doorway. Riley had lied to me. I'd been set up.

My gaze traveled over the familiar lines of his six-foot-two frame, from his spiky hair to his sensual lips to his oatmeal fleece jacket and stonewashed denim jeans. Under all that clothing, his body was hard and chiseled. I knew because at one time or another I had run my fingers over every inch of it.

"What are you doing here?" I said, not even trying to keep the irritation from my voice.

He seemed surprised to see me, too. "Maybe I should ask you the same question."

"I'm here because your sister hired me to do a business plan for . . ." I couldn't bring myself to say *Luv Bugs* in his presence. ". . . Her dating service."

Deegan shifted his weight to his left leg and leaned his shoulder against the doorjamb. His thumbs were hooked onto the front pockets of his jeans. He looked relaxed and confident.

"You're wrong if you think Riley set this up," he said. "Claudia called me this morning. Said there was a party at her house and invited me to stop by."

"Whatever."

He crossed his arms over his chest. "I just ran into Josh at the front door. He sent me down to pick up some wine. I didn't know you'd be here. Since you are, I guess we should talk."

I weighed wounded pride against curiosity. Curiosity won.

"Talk about what?"

He assessed me with his gaze. "You look good. Your hair is longer. I like it that way."

Cold air had crept into my bones. I started to shiver. I crossed my arms over my chest to keep warm. "Is that what you needed to say to me? You like my hair longer? Or is that just your version of foreplay?"

He cocked his head and smiled. "Some things never change. Do they?"

"Wrong. Some things do change. They change a lot."

He must have noticed I was shivering. "Cold?"

"A little."

He took a step toward me, unbuttoning the top button of his jacket. "I guess you want to know why I haven't called you."

"Not anymore."

That was a lie. Of course I wanted to know. I just didn't want him to know I wanted to know. Life was so complicated.

"Mind if I tell you, anyway?" he said.

"If it helps ease your conscience, go ahead."

"I almost lost my job."

"I hear you found a shoulder to cry on."

He kept moving toward me. "Who told you that?"

"A little bird."

"A Riley bird?"

He was so close I could smell the faint aroma of white T-shirts drying under a warm sun. All of the buttons were now undone. I wasn't sure if he was going to take the jacket off and put it around my shoulders, or if he planned to enclose both of us in one warm cocoon. It troubled me that I cared either way.

Before he had a chance to do anything, I heard the sound of footsteps on the stairway. A moment later, Riley burst through the door. Deegan and I stepped away from each other, but not before she saw how close we'd been standing.

"Omigosh," she said. "Tucker, I didn't know he was coming here tonight. I swear. You've got to believe me. I would never trick you like that."

"Cool your jets, Riley," Deegan said. "I already told her."

I heard another set of footsteps. I glanced toward the door and saw a woman standing on the threshold. In the real world, you rarely encounter anyone so beautiful they take your breath away. She was one of the rare few, the kind of person men love and women envy. Everything about her was perfect. Her blond hair had no split ends. Her luminous skin had no freckles. Her toned thighs had no cellulite. Even her breasts looked real.

The woman glanced around the room, from Riley to me to Deegan. "Did you find the wine, honey?"

The *honey* was unnecessary. She was just leg lifting,

marking her territory. Deegan's eyes narrowed. I could tell he was embarrassed, because he wouldn't meet my gaze. The woman seemed to sense the tension in the room. She smiled, but the gesture was forced.

"What's going on, Joe?" she said. "Am I missing something?"

"Jeez, Carly," Riley mumbled under her breath. "Where should I start?"

Deegan shot his sister a warning glance.

Carly frowned. "You don't like me, Riley. Believe me, I get that. But your brother does, and that's what counts. And just so you know, I love him."

Deegan was staring into the stacks of wine bottles. There was no flicker of emotion on his face.

"You love him?" Riley said. "You mean like last time? When you were engaged to my brother and screwing your boss?"

Carly looked at Deegan as if she was waiting for him to defend her. An uncomfortable silence followed before she turned and ran up the stairs. A moment later, I heard the door to the kitchen slam shut.

"What the hell was that all about?" Deegan's tone was low but intense.

A flush appeared on Riley's neck and began creeping toward her cheeks. "I have a right to my opinion. Carly McKendrick broke your heart once and she'll do it again. You're my brother and I love you, but somebody needs to save you from yourself."

Deegan gave his sister a look that could only be called intimidating. "I'll deal with you later." He sprinted up the stairs, and for a second time that night I heard the door slam shut.

Deegan had told me he was engaged once. He didn't give me details. Just said the woman cheated on him and he found out. I couldn't understand why he'd hooked up with Carly McKendrick again. If it had been another man, I might have said it was because she was so beautiful, but Deegan wasn't that shallow.

The relationship between Carly and her boss had obviously ended. The guy was probably married. As soon as it was over, she must have set her sights on Deegan again. Whatever she'd done to get him back, she'd used powerful mojo, because forgiveness seemed alien to his nature. At least he hadn't been willing to forgive me.

My chest felt crushed beneath all that heavy thinking. Maybe Venus was right. Maybe I *was* still vulnerable. I had to work on that before it became a problem.

Riley's shoulders were hunched inward as she stood staring into nowhere. I grabbed a couple of bottles of wine from the box on the floor.

"Hey, Riley. What do you say? Let's party."

Chapter 12

By the time Riley Deegan and I returned to the Luv Bugs party, a crowd had gathered in the hallway outside the guest bathroom, listening to a conversation through the closed door. Unless *oh, baby* and *lower* were entomology terms, Emma and Noah were no longer talking about ant mandibles.

The Noah and Emma show was about as good as the party got. Even so, I stayed until the bitter end. After the last person had left, Riley gave me some financial data on Luv Bugs and retired to her sister's spare bedroom for a good cry. I let myself out. On Sunday, I looked over the paperwork she'd given me, but the information was too sketchy to be of help. I'd have to start from scratch.

Aloneness has its merits, but by Monday morning, I was happy to be back at the office. The lobby was empty when I arrived, but I heard papers rustling in Charley's office. I went to investigate and found him sorting through stacks of files on his desk.

"What's up?" I said. "Where's Eugene?"

"I don't know," he mumbled. "I thought he was with you."

"No. Did he call to say he'd be late?"

"He's probably tied up in traffic. How about you stop worrying about Eugene and help me find the Seabrook interview notes."

Charley resumed pawing through the files on his desk. I walked to the drawer in the cabinet marked R-S-T, where I found the file. I pulled it out and handed it to him.

"Is this what you're looking for?"

He grabbed it out of my hand and studied the label. "Yeah, where did you find it?"

I started to tell him, but figured it was wasted breath.

"Find anything interesting on Friday?" I asked.

He sat at his desk and opened a Manila file folder marked HELEN TAGGART. "My buddy told me a road crew found Lupe's cleaning bucket in some brush near the Ten Freeway. The police think Ortiz threw it out of the window of his car after he fled the scene, but it's just speculation, because the rain destroyed any chance of lifting prints."

"What did you find at the courthouse?"

"Lupe Ortiz's criminal history came up clean. Nothing on Brad Taggart, which didn't surprise me. He lives on the East Coast. I didn't expect to find a record in California. I got a hit on Bob Rossi, though. He pleaded no contest to a domestic violence rap last January. He got probation and a one-way ticket to anger-management classes. I drove to the restaurant on Saturday to talk to him, but he wasn't there. One of his employees told me the guy is volatile and he doesn't like Helen Taggart. Guess what else I learned? His restaurant is serving Nectar's chocolates."

I sat in a chair and stared at Charley from across his desk. "I thought Helen said that deal fell through."

"She did."

"Then how did he get the chocolates?"

Charley leaned back and put his freckled hands behind his head. "Who knows? Maybe Rossi sent one of his employees to buy them."

"He wouldn't pay retail prices. That would cost too much."

He picked up a yellow number 2 pencil on his desk and made a note in the file. "The employee told me Rossi was friendly with Lupe Ortiz. He brought her dinner most nights she was cleaning at Nectar."

I remembered the container of garlic shrimp. It must have come from Rossi's restaurant, which meant he'd been at Nectar the night Lupe was murdered. I was beginning to think Eugene might be right. Roberto wasn't the only person who had the opportunity to kill Lupe Ortiz. Maybe he wasn't the only one who had a motive, either.

"What if Lupe was exchanging chocolates for garlic shrimp?" I said. "Rossi has a history of violence toward women. Maybe he killed her because the exchange rate wasn't working for him anymore."

"It's an interesting theory, especially since the employee claimed Rossi left the restaurant Thursday night at six thirty and didn't get back until eight thirty. What time did you get to Nectar?"

"About eight fifteen. Your snitch didn't mention what kind of car Rossi drives, did he?"

"No, but I can find out."

"You think Rossi is behind those crank calls Helen keeps getting?"

"That's going to be hard to prove unless we tap her telephone line. I mentioned it to her, but she didn't warm to the idea."

"We have to do something. I can't save Nectar if somebody keeps sabotaging my efforts."

By ten o'clock, Eugene still hadn't arrived at work. I called his cell phone number, but he didn't respond. He didn't pick up at home, either, and his answering machine wasn't on. I walked into Charley's office and sat in his guest chair.

"It's not like Eugene to be late," I said. "He always calls."

Charley looked up from the papers he was reading. "His mom probably grounded him."

"I know you're joking, Charley, but I'm worried."

"Look, Sinclair, I like Eugene, but the kid is high-strung. Give him some space and let him work out his issues with his mom. If you ask me, he needs to have a down-and-dirty talk with Nerine and make peace."

"You mean like all those down-and-dirty talks you've had with your son?"

"Leave Dickhead out of this."

Charley's skepticism aside, I knew Eugene. Something was wrong.

"I'm driving to his apartment to check on him," I said.

"It's a waste of time, but suit yourself."

Chapter 13

Eugene had recently moved to an apartment in Silver Lake, a quaint residential neighborhood just northeast of downtown Los Angeles. The lake isn't a lake. It's a reservoir that was built in 1907. It's not silver, either. More like blue, at least on a sunny day. The name came from Herman Silver, a member of Los Angeles' first Board of Water Commissioners. Renowned Los Angeles Modernist architects, like Neutra and Ain, from the 1920s and '30s had designed many of the homes and apartment buildings in the area. Eugene lived in an apartment featuring connected stucco cubes that had been inspired by the early work by R. M. Schindler.

A woman in her mid-to-late sixties answered the door. Nerine Barstok was around five-three or so and thin like Eugene. She had a prominent nose, and lips that had once been full but were now diminished by the crevices of time. On her wedding-ring finger was a boulder-sized opal. Her close-cropped gray hair and the navy gabardine pantsuit and white turtleneck sweater ensemble made her look militaristic. The plastic grocery bags strapped to her feet made her look as if she was about to perform surgery in the produce aisle of Ralph's supermarket.

Near the door to the kitchen was a carpet shampooer, the kind you rent at the grocery store. Paper towels had been rolled out on the floor, forming crisscrossed paths leading from the door to the living room to the kitchen and beyond.

I introduced myself and she invited me in.

"Please take off your shoes," she said in a pleasant tone. "One never knows what kind of nasty things you've been stepping in."

As instructed, I kicked off my shoes and left them by the door.

"Walk on the towels. The carpet may still be wet."

I put one foot in front of the other along the narrow strip of towels. By the time I reached the couch, I felt as if I'd passed some kind of quicker-picker-upper field sobriety test.

Eugene had filled his cozy apartment with furniture bought at garage sales and flea markets. He'd chosen pieces with a retro feel, adding paint and repairs where needed. A beat-up wooden hutch had been converted into a bookcase. It had been painted blue at one time, but the paint had chipped off. He'd chosen to leave it that way, and somehow it looked just right. An afghan in shades of rust, blue, and gold was draped artistically over the back of the couch. Beneath each foot of the bamboo couch, the matching chairs, and the end table was a square of waxed paper forming a barrier between the wood and the wet carpet.

A comforter and pillows were piled on a chair in the corner of the room, along with a stack of papers. The apartment had only one bedroom. I assumed Eugene had been relegated to sleeping on the couch. Framed photographs of his two cats sat on a nearby table, but I saw no sign of Liza and Fergie.

I sat on the couch next to a pair of sensible navy pumps that were parked on a paper towel on the floor. The toes were perfectly aligned, as if they were sister battleships docked in port after months at sea.

"I wish I could offer you a drink," Nerine said. "I can't believe my son doesn't have a properly stocked liquor cabinet. Not even a decent bottle of bourbon. I thought I taught him better than that."

I couldn't believe she was thinking about alcohol so early in the day. She must have had one of those clocks with every number marked five.

"That's okay," I said. "I'm not into booze in the morning."

Nerine stared at me as if I was something growing in a Petri dish. "I'm not talking about booze, dear. I'm talking about Booker's, the best bourbon money can buy."

I decided against pushing her toward any kind of showdown. For all I knew, Nerine could be housing nuclear warheads in that opal ring of hers.

"Is Eugene here?" I said.

She stood abruptly. "How about a macaroon? I brought them with me on the plane from Tallahassee. In a sealed container, of course."

She didn't wait for my response. She marched into the tiny kitchen, past a clock on the wall that Eugene called Big Ben. I heard the water running and the clatter of crockery. She returned shortly, carrying a paper doily and a plate filled with cookies shriveled from the interaction of coconut, cookie dough, and hermetically sealed plastic.

I craned my neck and looked down the hallway toward the bedroom. "Where did you say Eugene was?"

She set the doily on the coffee table and spent a few seconds centering the plate so it was equidistant from all edges.

"Running errands."

"When do you expect him back?"

"Soon."

"How long has he been gone?"

"A while."

Her answers seemed deliberately evasive. She was hiding something from me. Maybe she and Eugene had argued and she locked him in the cat carrier.

"Where are Liza and Fergie?"

"Hiding. I think they know I don't like cats. Neither does the colonel. In fact, we never allowed the children to have pets of any kind. We moved so often, it wasn't worth the fuss."

I leaned back into the cushions of the couch and crossed my legs, racking my brain for a way to circumvent the chitchat without appearing rude. I wasn't there to foment war. I just wanted to find Eugene. Nerine stared at my legs and frowned. I followed her gaze to make sure my feet weren't shedding germs on the cookies, but the distance seemed okay to me.

"You shouldn't cross your legs like that," she said. "You could get a deep vein thrombosis. It happens to people sitting on airplanes or cramped in a car all day. The blood clots up and you're dead, just like that. Besides, ladies should cross at the ankles. Modesty before comfort, they say."

"Mrs. Barstok—"

"How long have you known Eugene?"

I drummed my fingers on my thigh and counted to ten. "We've worked together for about five years. I'm surprised he didn't tell you."

She brushed at a wad of cat hair on her navy wool pants. "Perhaps he did, but it's such a chore to remember all the details. So where are your people from?"

"Los Angeles. Look, I need to find—"

She flashed a smug smile. "My goodness, don't you feel claustrophobic staying in one spot all of your life?" She didn't wait for my reply. "The colonel and I have traveled extensively. It's a broadening experience. Maybe one day you'll have a chance to try it."

"I went to France last summer," I mumbled.

She paused to center the opal on her finger. "As the colonel always says, France would be wonderful if it weren't for the French."

No wonder Eugene suffered from low self-esteem. It must have been toxic growing up with this woman.

Pookie had her faults, but she was merely unstructured and ill prepared. Nerine was a horse of a different color, as my grandma Felder always said. We all had to make the best of the cards we were dealt, but somehow Eugene's hand seemed even unluckier than mine.

I made another attempt to ask about him, but Nerine spoke over my words, as if she hadn't even heard them. "My son tells me you're a successful businesswoman. I wanted to be a schoolteacher, myself." She averted her gaze in a move that seemed pensive, almost melancholy. "Not very imaginative, is it? Anyway, then the children came along, and the rest is history."

"I'm sure you would have had a brilliant career," I said, "but Eugene must have been worth the sacrifice."

"Touché," she said, acknowledging the implied criticism. "Yes. I suppose it worked out for all of us. He was a challenge, though. I'm just grateful he's been able to keep a job. Personally, I never thought he was cut out for the sort of work he's doing now. He never had that killer instinct."

I wasn't sure what she was talking about. Being an administrative assistant for a business consultant didn't exactly require hazardous-duty pay. Even his work for Charley was mainly secretarial.

"Eugene has excellent skills," I said. "He can be anything he wants to be."

"That's very sweet of you, dear, but you know what they say. All bourbon is whiskey, but not all whiskey is bourbon."

My irritation bubbled over. "Mrs. Barstok, Eugene didn't show up for work today. That's not like him. I need to know where he is."

She seemed taken aback by my sharp tone. "Why don't you ask that private detective he works for?"

"Charley doesn't know where he is, either."

Nerine frowned. "I don't understand. I thought Mr. Tate was the one who sent him out of town."

My stomach was churning. "What are you talking about? Neither of us sent Eugene anywhere."

"I'm sure you're mistaken." Her voice had become brittle. "My son told me he was working on an important assignment. He asked me not to tell anybody. It sounded ridiculously clandestine, but I agreed."

"Did he say what kind of an assignment?"

"I didn't ask. He worked at the office all day Saturday. When he came home that night, he was rather quiet. I thought he was just tired. The next morning, he got up and packed a bag. He said he was going to work for a while and then he had to go away on business. He called that afternoon at about four thirty. Said he was just leaving and wanted to say good-bye."

I stood and walked into the kitchen, ignoring the paper towels.

"Excuse me," Nerine said. "The carpet—"

I checked the notepad near the telephone in case Eugene had left a message. The top sheet was blank. I held it up to the light to see if I could make out indentations from a previous message, but found none.

Eugene had an appointment book somewhere. If he hadn't taken it with him, it might still be in the apartment. I returned to the living room and opened each drawer of the bookcase. The address book wasn't there.

"Did Eugene say when he'd be back?" I said.

"Today."

I whipped around to face her. "Perhaps you haven't noticed, Mrs. Barstok, but it's today and he's not back. Aren't you worried about him? Even a little?"

She pursed her lips and glared at me. "Don't take that tone with me, young lady."

I walked down the hall toward the bedroom. The plastic bags on Nerine's feet made swishing sounds as she marched over the carpet behind me.

"Has he called since he left?" I said.

"I haven't been answering the phone. I thought it might be the colonel. We're having some difficulties right now, and I didn't want to talk to him."

Nerine's cosmetics were lined up on Eugene's dresser like soldiers in formation. His clothes had been shoved to one end of the closet to make room for hers. In the dark interior I saw two sets of eyes peering at me. The cats. There was no point in trying to lure them out now.

"What are you looking for?" she said.

"I don't know."

The bedroom held no clues to Eugene's whereabouts. Discouraged, I retraced my steps down the hallway, stopping at the bathroom. The medicine cabinet was stocked with over-the-counter items like aspirin and antibiotic cream but no appointment book.

A wastebasket sat in one corner. Several pieces of

balled-up papers lay in the bottom, including a receipt for gas from earlier in the week, and a piece of paper with a cryptic notation: *Six p.m. Sunday SB/MI.* It was Eugene's handwriting, but I had no idea what it meant.

I took the discarded paper and went back to the living room. On top of the bookcase was a framed photo of Eugene. He was holding Liza and smiling into the camera. I grabbed it and slipped it into my purse.

Nerine grabbed my arm. "Put that back. You have no right to take my son's things."

I shook her off. "Look, Eugene is missing. That's all the right I need. Call me the minute you hear from him. And if you leave the apartment, turn on the message machine."

Nerine clicked her tongue against her palate. "My God, what's that boy done now?"

My head was throbbing as I headed back to Culver City. It was one thing for Eugene not to tell his mother where he was going. It was quite another not to tell Charley or me. That set off all sorts of alarms. Not only were we his employers, we were also his friends.

Eugene was supposed to search the Internet for information on the quetzal. Nothing more. I'd made it clear to him. I was worried he'd taken the assignment a step further and gone off to investigate on his own. I had to find out where he was before he got himself into trouble.

I dialed Charley's number and waited for all hell to break loose.

Chapter 14

When I reached Charley, he was in his car on the way to the Century City shopping mall to return a six-pack of MY POPS IS TOPS onesies that Lorna no longer needed because the home pregnancy test she'd just taken had turned out negative. We agreed to meet outside Bloomingdale's to discuss Eugene.

The mall was crowded with people in business suits who had come from nearby high-rises for an hour of eating and shopping. I bought a latte at a coffee kiosk, but Charley demurred on caffeine. I was glad. He seemed hyped up enough already.

"She didn't even tell me she'd gone off the pill," he said. "I told her she better start taking them again or I'd be sleeping in the spare bedroom from now on."

"That must have gone over big."

"I can't take much more of this, Sinclair."

"Okay, but I think it's dangerous to press the snooze button on Lorna's biological clock. Taking away her onesies is a little radical."

"Look, I don't want that baby crap in my house. It's like Lorna is deciding something and forcing me to like it."

The talk about babies seemed to spike his blood pressure, so we shifted the discussion to Nerine Barstok and what she'd told me about Eugene.

"Where do you think he is?" I said.

"From the way you describe his mother, I'd say he's hiding until she leaves town."

"If Eugene was hiding from his mother, he'd tell us. Look, there was a lot going on in his life. He was upset about Helen's problems. He thought Roberto Ortiz was innocent. And he felt pressure to impress his mother. I'm afraid he went off looking for antisugar terrorists just to prove something to Nerine."

"He wouldn't do that."

"He would, Charley. You know he would. He's been fighting all of his life to show his parents he's more than just a mistake. He's more confident now, but Nerine could destroy all his progress with one little *oops*. I've seen her in action. The constant criticism could push anybody over the edge."

Charley pinched the bridge of his nose as if he was trying to cut off a monster headache. "I need to retire."

"If you retire, you'll be home with Lorna twenty-four/seven. Sounds like a life sentence to me."

He raised one eyebrow. "After all the time we've

known each other, you still can't tell when I'm joking."

"What are we going to do about Eugene? Can we file a missing person's report?"

"We can try, but he's only been out of touch twenty-four hours. He's an adult. The cops might tell you to wait a few days."

"I can't wait. I have to find him."

Charley brushed his hand over his crew cut, a sure sign he was thinking. "You can canvass our building. Find out if anybody else was working on Sunday. See if you can pinpoint when Eugene left work, what direction he was heading, and if he was with anybody. Then call all of his friends, and don't forget that old folks' home where he volunteers. See if anybody's heard from him."

After that, Charley went to Bloomingdale's to return the onesies and I headed back to the office. On the way, I called Venus. She and Eugene had a contentious sort of friendship, but there was a chance he may have contacted her. He hadn't.

"You know how he gets," she said. "He's probably locked up in a room at the Holiday Inn with a ball of yarn and a year's supply of lorazepam."

"Yeah, maybe." But I knew Venus was wrong. That may have described Eugene in the old days, but not anymore.

"I hear you called Dr. Rich." Her tone sounded teasing and just a bit coy. "You two are going to dinner and the theater."

"Yes, on Tuesday. It's some kind of fund-raiser for

Air Health. The invitation seemed odd, almost like he was asking me out on a date. You wouldn't know anything about that, would you?"

"The only thing I know," Venus said, "is that this is the first time in months you've been alone with a man."

I felt my jaw clench. "You didn't tell him that, did you?"

"I might have let something slip."

"I hope you didn't talk him into some kind of pity date."

"Don't be so sensitive. All Jordan's offering you is dinner and some adult conversation."

It was futile to argue with her. The damage had already been done. I'd just have to set Dr. Rich straight when we met on Tuesday. I ended the call with Venus and dialed the number for the assisted-living facility where Eugene volunteered every week. The administrator told me he'd called to cancel his regular visit on Saturday. She said there was an elderly resident with whom he spent a good deal of time. She didn't know if Mr. Winn would be able to provide any further information, but I was welcome to speak with him. The facility wasn't too far out of my way, so I told her I would stop by in a few minutes.

"I'll tell him to expect you," she said.

When I arrived at the home, an elderly man was leaning on a cane by the front door, smoking a cigar. His eyes were watery blue but intelligent. Age had expanded his ears and compacted his body into a tidy mass that measured less than five feet tall. He had on a white guayabera over gray slacks and a tasseled beret that was one of many Eugene had knitted for residents of the home. Only a flare-up of carpal tunnel syndrome had stopped him from making more.

"I bet you're here to see me," Winn said.

"How did you know?"

Even with the stogy in his mouth, there was room for a smile. "Eugene said you were a beanpole. He also said you had dark hair and a few freckles and a cowlick just like his. He didn't say you were pretty, but you are. I know why you're here, too. They called my room and told me."

He tottered over to a planter that rimmed the front facade and sat down. He tapped his cane on the brick, indicating he wanted me to sit beside him. I did. Traffic was heavy on Olympic Boulevard. The air was thick with dust and the sounds of car horns and screeching brakes—L.A. Symphony No. 3 in D Minor with horns.

"Nobody has heard from Eugene since Sunday," I said.

Mr. Winn glanced at me. "I haven't seen him since last week. I look forward to his visits."

"What did you two talk about?"

He winked at me. "You want me to start with my gall bladder operation or the cataract surgery?"

"Why don't you start with anything he may have told you about his life and what he was doing."

"We talked about his friends. You and the goddess of love."

I smiled. "Did you talk about anybody other than Venus and me?"

"Let's see." He puffed on the cigar and sent a cloud of smoke swirling around my head. "He mentioned the private eye and that wife of his. We don't like her." He paused to flip ashes from the cigar into the planter.

"Anything else?"

"We played a game sometimes. I think Eugene made it up to test my memory, but I don't care about that. It's fun."

"What kind of game?"

"Name the capitals."

"You mean the state capitals?"

"What else? He always starts with the easy ones like the capital of California. Then he tries to stump me with places like Rhode Island and Delaware. We got into an argument about Arizona one Saturday. He claimed the capital was Phoenix and he wouldn't back down."

"Mr. Winn, the capital of Arizona *is* Phoenix."

He studied the tip of the cigar to make sure it was still lit. "I know that, but what's the fun if everybody agrees all the time?"

"I'm worried about him," I said. "Is there anything else you can remember?"

His expression changed. It was as if a dark cloud had moved across the sun. "No, but when he comes back, I'll let him have Phoenix, no questions asked."

I gave him my business card and told him to call me if he thought of anything else. When I got back to Culver City, I stopped at the ground-floor office of our landlord, Manny Reygozo, Esq.

Manny advertised his specialty as products liability and medical malpractice, but his real talent was settling with insurance companies. He was a glad-handing, wiry guy who always looked dapper in his impeccably cut pin-striped suits. He had more than a few bad habits, like grinning with his mouth open. I'd seen his oral cavity so many times I knew how many gold crowns he had. Three. Charley swore he was humping Carmen, his bodacious paralegal, every Sunday while his wife was at mass with their three kids. I had no reason to doubt him. Charley was a private investigator and a former cop. I assumed he knew about such things.

I walked through Reygozo's front door and saw sheets of legal-length paper shooting out of the printer under Carmen's watchful eye.

"Hey, Tucker. You paying your rent early for a change?"

I had to be careful how I broached the subject of Sundays at the office. I didn't want her to think I was questioning her right to have a nooner with her boss.

"Carmen, I know you work a lot of overtime. Were you by chance at the office yesterday?"

"I went hiking in the mountains with my boyfriend on Sunday."

Her smile seemed frozen, her alibi canned. Carmen might have reached new heights on Sunday, but I doubted it was on any mountain trail. More likely it was on the leather couch in Manny's office.

"The reason I'm asking," I said, "is Eugene forgot to write down his hours. I want to pay him, but I need his time. He's out of town, so I'm trying to find out if anybody noticed when he left."

She flipped her long black hair over her back. "I didn't see anything."

There were only two other tenants on the second floor besides Charley and me. An accountant and a business called Aardvark Entertainment. Tax season was over, so the accountant hadn't worked on Sunday and nobody answered the door at Aardvark. In fact, none of us had ever seen a live body come or go from that suite. Charley joked that Dracula had rented the space to be closer to his bloodsucking lawyer.

I returned to the office, where I camped out at Eugene's desk, looking through drawers, hoping to find a note that might indicate where he'd gone. His dusting glove was there, along with a box of alcohol swabs, a list of telephone numbers in a sheet protector, and a receipt for a cell phone charger from Radio Shack dated the day before. Maybe he'd lost his and needed a replacement. I put it aside to show Charley and began calling the names on Eugene's telephone list. Of the people who answered, no one knew where he was.

My head felt heavy, so I rested it in my hands. If I concentrated, maybe I could channel Eugene's energy and get a feel for where he was. Nothing happened. As I looked up, my elbow brushed against the mouse next to his computer. The screen sprang to life. I wondered how long it had been on. He always shut down the operating system before he left for the day.

He was still logged on to the Internet. I clicked on

the page that listed his search history and found an odd mix of words and phrases, including *quetzal, L.A. street gangs, chocolate, the University of California–Davis, Osteen,* and the *Central Intelligence Agency.* I was surprised to learn that a secret spy organization like the CIA had a Web site, but when I opened its home page, I found a wealth of information, including a page for children. The government obviously thought one could never be too young to start spying.

Getting into the CIA site was easy, but there was no way to track information Eugene had viewed within the site. I skipped around from link to link until I found a page called the World Fact Book. An option allowed me to view information by country. Eugene had searched for the word *quetzal,* which I already knew was the national bird of Guatemala, so I started there. A map of the country popped up. I scanned it quickly and noticed a city named Puerto Quetzal. That was a good omen, so I continued scrolling down the page.

According to the text, Guatemala was a constitutional democratic republic with a population of 12.3 million. Forty-one percent were below the age of fourteen. Eight percent were Mayan. A section called "Environmental Issues" outlined the country's problems with soil erosion, water pollution, and deforestation.

I skipped to another site and found a journal article cautioning that global warming was forcing many birds to migrate away from their natural habitat in the Petén Forest, especially birds like the quetzal. I had no way of knowing if Eugene had been searching for articles on global warming, but it seemed clear that the quetzal's habitat and maybe the birds themselves were endangered by man's insatiable push to develop and pollute. I remembered Eugene's theory about antisugar terrorists. That seemed far-fetched, but ecoterrorists were real. There was a possibility the feather I'd found near Lupe's body represented some broader warning about the destruction of the environment.

Osteen produced thousands of links. I waded through about ten pages of them before I stumbled on a professor named Herbert Osteen, who had written an article for an anthropology journal about the feather work of the ancient Maya. A footnote at the bottom of page one revealed that Osteen was a professor of cultural anthropology at the University of California at Davis.

Eugene had located a quetzal expert and may have tried to contact him despite my warnings. I had to find out more, so I called the university's main number, and after being transferred from office to office, I spoke to somebody who knew Osteen. At least she knew of him. The professor was on sabbatical and wouldn't be back for six months. The woman wouldn't tell me where he'd gone.

I wasn't willing to give up that easily, so I called telephone information in Davis and was surprised to find Osteen's home number listed with directory assistance. His wife answered my call.

"Eugene called on Saturday," she said. "We had a lovely chat. Such a nice boy. He has cats, you know. I have three myself. All pound kitties."

"Did he say why he called?"

"He wanted to know about the quetzal. I told him

he'd come to the right place. Herbert is an expert on the subject."

"Did he speak to your husband?"

"He wasn't here. He's in Santa Barbara trying to finish his book. I called to let him know Eugene wanted to talk to him, but I'm not sure if they ever connected."

"Where's he staying?"

"The Montecito Inn."

The note I'd found in Eugene's bathroom wastebasket made sense now—SB/MI. Santa Barbara, Montecito Inn.

"I wonder if you'd call your husband one more time," I said. "Ask if he'd have time to talk to me."

"I'll try, dear, but he gets stressed just before deadline. I'm not sure he'll cooperate."

After I hung up, I waited for half an hour before calling the hotel, but there was no answer in Osteen's room. Sunday morning, Eugene had packed a bag and told Nerine he was going out of town. If he'd failed to reach Osteen by phone, he may have driven to Montecito to see the professor in person. I was still considering the likelihood of that when I heard a knock on the office door.

Chapter 15

The hallway door opened and a moment later Joe Deegan stepped into my room. I was once again taken with how handsome he was. Unlike other beautiful people I'd met, Deegan had never displayed an iota of narcissism. It was almost as if he wasn't aware of his good looks. That modesty was just one of the things I liked about him.

Neither of us spoke. Out of the corner of my eye I saw him glance at the framed Frisbee hanging on the wall, the one he'd given Muldoon the previous June. A faint smile lifted the corners of his mouth as he read the caption, *Don't Forget to Play*.

"I was on my way back to the station," he said. "I saw your car in the parking lot. I wanted to talk to you about the other day. The thing with Riley. I'm sorry that happened."

"No harm, no foul."

"And thanks for not giving me shit about Carly."

"It's okay, Deegan. Really. I'm seeing somebody, too."

He gave me the cop stare—narrowed eyes, wrinkled brow. "Oh yeah? Who is he?"

"A doctor. A thoracic surgeon. He's also a pilot . . . with his own plane. He's involved in humanitarian work with an organization called Air Health. They do free medical work in third-world countries. You know, they fly places and save lives."

Deegan broke eye contact and stared at the floor while I babbled on about my make-believe boyfriend the doctor. I don't know why I felt the need to make up a phony relationship to save face in front of him. It was so high school. I hadn't even met Jordan Rich and I was already talking as if we were planning our honeymoon. When I paused to catch my breath, Deegan looked up.

He hesitated as if he didn't want to leave. "So I guess that's it."

Maybe I didn't want him to leave, either, because I blurted out words guaranteed to make him stay. "I can't find Eugene."

He frowned. "What do you mean?"

"He didn't show up for work. He told his mother some bogus story about going away on a business trip. He was supposed to be back today, but he isn't. He didn't even call. He wouldn't do that unless something was wrong."

Deegan pulled one of the guest chairs up to my desk.

We sat knee to knee, facing each other, so close I could smell the Flitz he used to polish his badge.

"Tell me what's going on."

In the past I would have told Deegan everything, because he and I were in a relationship. This time I told him because he was a cop. I told him about Lupe Ortiz's death, the quetzal feather, her son's arrest, the break-in at Helen's condo, and the words Eugene had looked up on the Internet. Maybe I hoped he would offer some information that put my mind at ease.

"Eugene was upset about Lupe's death," I said. "He thinks her son is innocent. He came up with a couple of loopy theories about antisugar terrorists and chocolate conspiracies. I'm afraid he went off to find the real killer."

Deegan's gaze was probing and full of concern. "What makes you think that?"

"He tried to contact an anthropology professor he found on the Internet. Somebody named Herbert Osteen. He's a quetzal expert. Eugene was also researching street gangs. Ever heard of the MayaBoyz?"

Deegan leaned back in the chair and nodded. His detective's instinct for spotting trouble was in high gear. I hoped he didn't give me one of his macho lectures about meddling in police work, because he'd lost that right when he walked out on me.

"They operate out of a neighborhood in East L.A. near the county morgue. Most of the members are from Central America, new immigrants. When they came here, they didn't fit into any established Latino gang, so they formed one of their own. Right now they're killing each other over drug profits. Just yesterday a seventeen-year-old kid was killed in a drive-by while he was at a service station pumping gas. As usual, nobody saw anything, but we're pretty sure it was one of his own homeboys."

"What can you tell me about quetzal feathers?"

He leaned toward me. "How do you know about that?"

"Lupe's son is a member of the MayaBoyz. Like I told you, I found his mother dead in my client's store, lying next to a feather. I'd like to find out if the gang is behind any of the other problems Helen is having."

"There's a law enforcement database called CAL/GANG. It lists admitted gang members or anyone who has been identified as a gang member by a reliable informant." Deegan paused. "I hope you're not asking me to look him up for you."

"No," I said. "I'll find out on my own."

Deegan narrowed his eyes as if he wasn't pleased by my response. I ignored his disapproval.

"What about the other words he looked up?" I said. "Do any of them mean anything to you? I mean, would the CIA have any connection to L.A. street gangs?"

"About eight hundred tons of cocaine a year are shipped from Colombia to the U.S. straight though Central America. A lot of it ends up on the streets of L.A. The CIA might be interested in that."

Deegan leaned forward, resting his forearms on his thighs. He gazed at the floor between his feet for a moment. Then he looked up at me with a tender expression in his eyes. "If you're concerned about Eugene, you should report him missing."

"Charley says the police may not want to take the report."

"They'll take it."

"But will they do anything?"

"There's only so much they can do." His tone was soft. "They'll check the NCIC database, the morgue, local hospitals, psych wards. If that doesn't turn up anything, they'll probably wait a few days."

"Can they trace his cell phone calls?"

"They can, but they probably won't. Not without a warrant. And they won't get one unless the case turns into a homicide investigation. It's a privacy issue. Here's the deal. Eugene's an adult. Disappearing isn't a crime. People do it all the time. Most of them come back on their own."

"You don't make it sound very hopeful."

He reached out as if he was going to comfort me with his touch, but pulled his hand back at the last second. "I didn't mean it like that. Look, I can get you a telephone number and a person to call if you want."

"Thanks. I can do that myself."

"Yeah. I remember that about you." He stood but didn't leave right away. "It doesn't matter where Eugene was when he disappeared. You have to report him missing in the jurisdiction where he lives. And just so you know, there are four hundred sixty-three known gangs in Los Angeles, with over thirty-eight thousand members. If you think you can cruise over to the barrio and start asking questions about your friend, you're wrong. Report him missing, and let the department handle it from there."

"You should know by now I'm a better friend than that. I've already been to the barrio once, and I'd go back a hundred times more if it means finding Eugene."

"You can't save the world by yourself."

That's when I remembered why things hadn't worked out between Deegan and me. He didn't understand how I was wired. He would probably never understand. I stood to give greater emphasis to what I was about to say.

"Haven't you ever been scared shitless, worrying about somebody you loved?"

Deegan's gaze traveled over my body from the top of my head to the curve of my shoulders and downward, stopping only when forced to by the desk.

"Let me know if you need help finding that number."

He turned and walked out of the room, taking all of the energy with him. The office felt cold and empty. I sat down, resting my head on the back of the chair. I stared at the ceiling for what seemed like a long time, until I finally forced myself to the computer to look up the Web site for the Los Angeles Police Department. Silver Lake was listed under the Northeast Division. I jotted down the number for the front desk. If I hadn't heard from Eugene by the next morning, I was going to tell Nerine to report him missing. The information would carry more weight coming from his mother.

By the time I left work, it was after seven p.m. As

I opened the door leading to the parking lot, I saw a blur of movement near my car. My hands trembled as I reached into my purse for my flashlight and fumbled with the switch. As I turned the beam toward the car, I saw a man standing near the rear trunk. The light wasn't strong enough to see his features, but it was strong enough to startle him. A moment later, he loped over a low shrub at the edge of the lot and ran down the street.

It seemed too coincidental to find somebody prowling around my car so close after Lupe's murder and the break-in at Helen's condo. The office had never had any problems with break-ins in the parking lot. Why had someone been snooping around my car? Why now? It was almost as if the guy suspected there was something valuable inside. Like Helen's recipes? It sounded crazy, but if true, it meant only one thing. He had been watching Helen and me the night Lupe Ortiz was murdered. It also meant he had followed me to the office.

All the way home, I kept checking my rearview mirror, but saw no evidence I was being followed. I picked up Muldoon from Mrs. D's place and took Helen's collectibles out of the trunk of my car. She claimed the items weren't valuable, but I didn't want to be held responsible if anything was stolen.

Once the pup and I were inside the house, I spread the collectibles on the bed in the spare room to have a look. Muldoon jumped up and began sniffing like crazy at the heart box. No wonder. It smelled of chocolate, as if somebody had used it in recent days.

I looked him square in the eye. "Chocolate is bad for dogs. You're a dog. Enough said."

Muldoon is a terrier, so it took at least three more admonitions before he resigned himself to watching from the floor as I inspected the chocolate tins. There were five in all. All were old. Most were battered. None of the brand names were familiar to me. The companies must have gone out of business long ago. They were all empty, except for one. As I turned it over, a piece of paper fell out. It was brown and flaky with age. As I reached to pick it up, it disintegrated in my fingers. I put the fragments together. It looked like some sort of price tag.

The spouted chocolate pot was shaped like an hourglass: wide at the mouth, narrow in the middle, and seven or eight inches at the bottom. It had a half-moon handle, a long thin spout, and was about ten inches high from the bottom to the top. It reminded me of an old-fashioned spittoon. It appeared to be made of metal that had corroded, obscuring the graphics. It wasn't until I tapped my knuckles on the rough surface that I realized the material was ceramic. The pot might have been a replica, but the artist had done an impressive job of making it look old.

I thought about the man I saw standing in the shadows near my car when I left work. Whatever he was looking for, he didn't find it, which meant he was still out there, watching and waiting. I shook off a chill and shoved the collectibles under the bed. It wasn't the most creative hiding spot, but it would have to do until I found someplace better.

Before I went to bed, I checked my answering machine for messages. Pookie had called from the woo-woo retreat in Big Sur where she'd gone for a little R&R with her husband, Bruce. Pookie Kravitz isn't my mother's real name. She changed it early in her acting career because she thought it had more pizzazz than Mary Jo Felder Sinclair. She's never felt comfortable with Mom, either, so that's why I've always called her Pookie.

A few months back, she'd given up her acting career to help Bruce realize a lifelong dream to open a yoga studio they'd named Kismet. Her call was to let me know they were coming back from the retreat early because of some developing problems at the studio. That worried me. It wasn't good for her or the marriage if his dream turned into a nightmare.

There was a second message that had come in around noon. I pressed the Play button and waited. At first I thought it was a hang-up because nobody spoke. Then I heard a whispered voice.

"Tucker, it's me. I can't talk. I'm deep undercover. Don't worry. I'm okay. I'm making progress, but there's still work to do. And I have to do it alone."

It was Eugene's voice. I felt cold and hyperalert, the way I always feel when my imagination runs wild. I couldn't be sure what had driven him "deep undercover," but there were four possibilities: he was investigating the missing chocolates from Nectar, the threatening telephone calls to Helen, the break-in at her condo, or the last and worst alternative, the murder of Lupe Ortiz.

All of those events might be related, but I couldn't be sure. For the moment, I'd have to consider them as separate crimes and follow the available leads, starting with Professor Osteen. I still hadn't been able to reach him by telephone, so in the morning I planned to drive to Montecito and talk to him in person. I had to find Eugene before he got himself into serious trouble.

Chapter 16

The following morning, Professor Osteen still wasn't answering the telephone in his hotel room. I dropped Muldoon off at what was fast becoming the Domanskis' Pet Spa and Day Care Center and headed to Montecito.

The inn was on a two-lane street separated by a narrow greenbelt dotted with fragrant eucalyptus and lush vegetation. The street was congested with joggers and cyclists, mostly men who looked as if they had retired at fifty.

I pulled into an angle-in parking spot a block away. As I got out of the car, a strong Santa Ana wind stirred up the scent of rosemary from the greenbelt and carnations from a nearby vendor's cart. I made my way past a real estate office advertising a Tuscan Village, a Fine Southern Plantation, an Elegant Cape Cod, and an estate described only as Equestrian Elegance. In Montecito, anything was possible.

The inn was a three-story mission-style building with arched windows. Flowers and vines spilled from green window boxes. A fire burned in the lobby fireplace. I glanced down the narrow hallway, hoping to find somebody who looked professorial, but all I saw were the red marble treads and wrought-iron handrails on the staircase leading to the second floor. The ambiance reminded me of a bygone era, where grandiose was still spelled with a small "g."

Near the antique elevator was a statue of Charlie Chaplin, one of the hotel's early investors. He was sporting heavy eye makeup and leaning on a cane, wearing his famous Tramp costume—oversized clown shoes, baggy pants, and a bowler hat too small for his head.

I made my way over the brown and beige floral carpet to the desk clerk, a clean-cut young man who had the look of a student working his way through college. I asked him to ring Professor Osteen's room.

"He's expecting me," I said.

The desk clerk dialed a number and waited. "No answer."

"Any idea where he might be?"

He shrugged. "There's a swimming pool out back. He might be there. If not, check the bar on the other side of the driveway."

Osteen wasn't at the pool. I was walking toward the bar when I noticed a man in his seventies standing by the window, holding a coffee mug. Age had bowed

his back and jutted his hips forward, making his body
S-shaped. He was thin, almost gaunt. Wisps of long
white hair fluttered over his brow as he leaned over a
tall stack of paper on the table next to him. I walked inside and glanced at the top page. It was scrawled with
red markings. It looked like a book manuscript to me.

"Professor Osteen?"

The man squinted as if that might help jog his memory. "Do I know you?"

"My name is Tucker Sinclair. Your wife may have
called about me."

He paused as if thinking. "Yes. Something about
your assistant. All I can tell you is we talked on the
telephone."

I felt a rush of hope. "When did he call?"

Osteen ambled over to a coffee thermos sitting on the
bar and picked up a cup. "Sunday evening, I believe.
It's so hard to keep track of time when I'm writing."

"Did he say what he wanted?"

Over his shoulder he said, "Why don't you ask
him?"

"He didn't show up for work today."

Osteen pumped the plunger on the thermos. Coffee
gushed into the cup in spurts. "That's none of my concern. I don't want to get involved in your personnel
issues."

"I need your help. I'm afraid Eugene is in some
kind of trouble. You may have been the last person
he spoke to."

Osteen didn't respond right away. He took his coffee
to the table and sat in the chair next to the manuscript.

I followed him. He studied my expression, as if looking for some sign of worthiness. A moment later he gestured for me to join him. As I pulled up a chair and sat down, he shoved his manuscript aside like a man needing a reprieve from all that paper and red ink. I guess isolation sounds better in theory than it does in practice.

"He asked about two topics that are of interest to me, chocolate and quetzals. He was mistaken in his thinking about the Maya. I had to correct him. They were not the first to process the pod of the *Theobroma cacao* tree. That discovery is credited to the Olmec civilization, around fifteen hundred years before Christ. I explained to him that chocolate back then was nothing like what you find today in heart-shaped boxes on Valentine's Day. It was liquid poured from a pitcher held from a height of three or four feet, so it entered the cup thick and frothy. It was often spiked with unusual flavorings like hot chili peppers."

"I've seen a replica of one of those pots," I said, "but I didn't know how they were used. What got you so interested in the Maya?"

He cupped his hands as if they contained secrets from the ages. "I lived in Belize as a child. My father was a diplomat. He immersed my brother and me in the culture. We attended local schools. We didn't learn Quiché, which is the language spoken by many of the Maya, but we did learn Spanish. The Mayan ruins captivated me. I went there every chance I got. Their civilization was highly advanced. They were the first to come up with the concept of zero. Imagine that! They had the only developed language in the pre-Columbian Americas. At their pinnacle, the Maya were one of the most culturally advanced peoples of the ancient world."

I described the feather I'd found near Lupe Ortiz's body and asked him what he could tell me about it.

"Your assistant asked about that, too. I told him it sounded like the tail feather from a *Pharomachrus mocinno*, also known as the Resplendent Quetzal."

"Does the bird still exist or is it extinct?" I said.

"The official term is *near threatened*. That means the bird may be threatened with extinction in the near future."

"From what?"

"Myriad causes," he said, "all man-made, I'm sorry to say. Development. Pollution. Global warming. They're destroying habitat and forcing many species of birds to move north into new territories. Some can adapt, but the quetzal is already at risk. They are not good fliers, which makes them vulnerable to predators. In some areas, quetzal chicks are being attacked by species moving to the cloud forests to escape the heat. If the earth continues to grow warmer as predicted, we will see mass extinctions in the next hundred years. Entire ecosystems will disappear."

"What were the quetzal feathers used for?"

He used the table to push himself upright and then strolled to the counter to top off his coffee. "In the Mayan culture, the bird was considered sacred and its feathers highly prized. They were used in royal headdresses, capes, and fans. Unfortunately, no artifacts survived, and feather work is now a lost art. We only know about the quetzal's place in Mayan society from drawings left behind on glyphs and monuments."

"Do you have any idea how a person could gain access to these feathers? I understand the birds can't live in captivity."

He walked back to the table, dribbling a trail of brown liquid on the floor. "That's what the Maya believed. To them, the quetzal was a symbol of freedom. Alas, the myth isn't true. There's a zoo in Mexico that has kept birds in captivity since the early nineties. Several years ago, they started an active breeding program, which has shown some promise."

"Where is this zoo located?" I said.

He set the cup on his manuscript, oblivious to the ring of brown coffee seeping into the paper. "In Chiapas. It's called the Miguel Alvarez del Toro Regional Zoo."

If the zoo had a quetzal-breeding program, it meant there were birds that got old and died or maybe just molted their feathers. Someone who worked in that program or visited the zoo might have access to one, perhaps even the one I found near Lupe Ortiz's body.

"Have you ever heard of the MayaBoyz?" I said.

"Sounds like a rock band." He chuckled at his joke.

"It's a street gang. Most of its members are from Central America. Their symbol is a quetzal feather. You said the bird was sacred to the ancient Maya. Do you have any idea what it might mean to an East L.A. gangbanger?"

Osteen drummed his fingers on the manuscript as

if that might help him think. His hands were dotted with age spots and his knuckles seemed swollen. "The quetzal is still important in the Guatemalan culture. Its image is on the national flag, and the country's currency is named after it. As far as what the bird might mean to a street gang, I suppose you could say its mythology has a kinship with violence. There's an ancient fable that claims the Resplendent Quetzal was a *nahual*, a spirit guide or guardian angel to the warrior-prince Tecún Umán. It is said that the bird got his red breast from Tecún's wounds in a battle against the conquistador Pedro de Alvarado."

"So a modern-day gangbanger might think the feather was his *nahual* against rival street gangs or even against his own homeboys?"

"It has a certain poetry to it, wouldn't you say? An ancient and sacred symbol of your people, watching over you, protecting you from violent death?"

Osteen was right. The story was poetic. Too bad there had been no *nahual* protecting Lupe Ortiz.

"Did Eugene mention where he might be going next?"

As Osteen lifted his cup once more, he noticed the stain on his manuscript. He tried to wipe it off, but it was too late. The coffee had already spoiled the page.

"He didn't say. He seemed quite interested in the history of the Mayan spouted chocolate pot, so I told him about an exhibit called 'Chocolate: The History.' It's showing at the Natural History Museum in Los Angeles. They had such success with the Field Museum chocolate exhibition a few years back they brought in this smaller show. I told your friend to ask for Marianne Rogers if he wanted to know more about chocolate pots. She's an expert."

I didn't know why Eugene had been so interested in Mayan spouted chocolate pots, but it was more than a coincidence that I had a replica of one hidden in my spare bedroom. I thanked Osteen for his help and hurried back to my car. I planned to make a brief stop at my house to pick up the pot before dropping in on Marianne Rogers.

Chapter 17

I t was three o'clock by the time I arrived at the Natural History Museum of Los Angeles County in Exposition Park and walked across the grassy commons it shared with the University of Southern California's coliseum. The guidebook I'd consulted listed the architectural style as Spanish Renaissance, but the blocky stucco building seemed more Socialist-Realist to me.

I walked up the steps and entered the lobby through the heavy bronze doors. Inside, the floor was covered with travertine marble, accented with intricate multi-colored inlaid tiles. Doric columns stood guard over the bones of a prehistoric critter. The columns were less elaborate than the ones on Eugene's Greek revival inbasket, but they still served as a painful reminder that he was missing.

A security guard sat on a stool at the information

desk, scrutinizing a line of people waiting to buy tickets. I asked to speak to Marianne Rogers. A few minutes later, she walked into the lobby. As soon as I mentioned Eugene's name and told her he was missing, she led me past dark wood display cases that looked as old as the exhibits they held.

Rogers looked like a skeleton in somebody's biology lab. I could almost hear her bones clacking as she guided me to a small office on the third floor where the curators worked. Even though her body fat was low, her enthusiasm was high, especially for all things chocolate.

"Eugene stopped by the museum yesterday morning," she said. "He was interested in Mayan spouted chocolate pots. As Professor Osteen probably told you, I have a passion for the subject. Eugene wanted to know if we had one in our exhibit. I told him we didn't."

"Did Eugene say why he was interested in chocolate pots?"

"He was researching information about chocolate for a client and he ran across a doctoral dissertation on the Internet about the pots. He couldn't open the link, but it piqued his interest."

I pulled Helen's replica from my tote bag.

"How interesting." Marianne Rogers reached for the pot, holding it up to the light streaming through the window. She seemed almost reverent as she studied it from every angle.

"Where did you get this?" she said.

"It belongs to that client Eugene mentioned. I'm not sure where she got it."

Rogers shifted her gaze to meet mine. "It belongs in a museum."

I was taken aback by her comment. "You think it's real?"

"If it isn't, it's a magnificent reproduction. We'd have to run some tests to know for sure. Authentic Mayan chocolate pots are rare. Several were uncovered at Colha in Northern Belize in 1981, but those are now housed at the University of Texas at Austin. At least one was stolen from a museum in Guatemala City during the civil war. It's never been recovered."

"Did you mention that to Eugene?"

She nodded. "He seemed interested in knowing everything I could tell him about the theft. All I remembered was an article from several years ago. The Guatemalan police suspected it was an inside job, but they couldn't prove it. The case is still open, but I don't suppose anybody's looking very hard. The country has too many other problems to solve."

I gestured toward Helen's pot. "Do you think this could be the missing chocolate pot?"

"I doubt that, but may I keep it for a couple of days? There are a few people I'd like to show it to."

"As I said, it's not mine. I'm sure my client has no idea it may be valuable. In any event, I'd have to ask her permission before I let you have it."

Rogers looked stricken by my response. She pointed to my tote bag. "If the pot is real, it's also priceless. You can't carry it around in a tote bag. I'll get some packing material and a box from the back room."

If the spouted chocolate pot was real, that changed everything. It created a motive for murder. Anybody who was knowledgeable about Mayan antiquities could have seen the pot in Nectar's retail store and realized its value. For that matter, the chocolate pot had been clearly displayed in the newspaper photograph of Helen at the shop. Anybody who saw that picture knew she had it, including pop princess Alexis Raines. I remembered her looking at the newspaper photograph of Helen's chocolate display. She'd seemed overly interested in buying several of the collectibles. I was beginning to wonder why.

It was plausible that somebody broke into Nectar to steal the pot. Lupe got in the way and paid for it with her life. It was also possible she was tied to the pot in some other way. Eugene had come up with a couple of wild conspiracy theories before he disappeared. I could almost see his take on this latest development— the chocolate pot had been stolen during the Guatemalan civil war. Lupe Ortiz was Guatemalan; at least I assumed so. Her husband was in the country, visiting a sick relative. Maybe she witnessed the theft and now, years later, somebody had hunted her down and silenced her forever. In fact, it didn't sound all that far-fetched. If I kept spinning tales, I was sure to come up with a theory about Mayan tomb raiders and ancient curses. If the pot was real, uncovering its chain of ownership was vital. Eugene must have followed the same logic. I had to find out where Helen had gotten the pot.

When I arrived at Nectar, Helen was at the stove in the workroom, stirring up a batch of Buster Brownies to take to Detective O'Brien as a peace offering. Her white chef's jacket seemed to have sucked all the color from her face. She looked as if she'd aged ten years in the past few days.

"A messenger dropped off a letter for you today," she said. "It's in my office."

I hurried to her cubbyhole, thinking it might be another message from Eugene. Instead I found a note from Alexis Raines, thanking me again for saving her rat, Aldo. Attached to the note were four tickets to her concert scheduled for the following month. At least she'd been lucid enough to follow up on her promise.

The lobby of the retail store was full of customers. Murder in the workroom hadn't kept people away. On the contrary, it seemed to have added cachet to the store.

"Business looks good," I said.

Helen grabbed a thermometer to test the temperature of a bowl of chocolate melting above a pot of simmering water. "One of my customers told Kathy that Nectar is now considered the best chocolate shop in Southern California."

"That's great, Helen," I said. "By the way, I thought you might want to know I stored your collectibles in my spare bedroom. It's quite a collection. Where did you find all that stuff?"

"Various places. I bought the Cadbury heart box on-line. The chocolate tins came from yard sales and antique shops. I don't remember where exactly."

"What about the spouted chocolate pot?"

Helen transferred the bowl of melted chocolate to a trivet on the marble tabletop. Then she dumped some eggs and flour into the bowl and began blending the mixture. "Lupe gave it to me."

I was stunned by the news. "Where did she get it?"

"From one of her customers, I think."

"Why did she give it to you?"

Helen pestered the batter in silence. "I told you before. She liked me. She was probably just showing her appreciation for all I'd done for her. Why are you so curious about the chocolate pot?"

"I just showed it to an expert at the Natural History Museum. She thinks it may be a priceless antiquity."

Helen turned toward me. "That's absurd. How would Lupe get something valuable like that?"

"Maybe the person who gave it to her didn't realize how much it was worth. Or maybe Lupe took it without permission."

"Are you saying she stole it?"

"It's possible. If it's true, somebody might have killed her to get it back."

Helen folded a cup of walnuts into the chocolate. "So why didn't this person tell me or the police that the pot was stolen? He'd get it back eventually."

I thought about the Mayan pot that had been pilfered from the Guatemalan museum. I wondered if it had found a home with a collector in Los Angeles. Maybe that collector was also Lupe's customer. If Lupe had stolen the pot, the victim may not have reported the crime to the police, especially if he knew or suspected it had been looted from a museum. Dealing in stolen antiquities was illegal. The collector would not only lose his investment, but he might go to jail.

"Let's say he couldn't report the crime," I said, "because he had some reason to keep his identity hidden. He found out the chocolate pot was at Nectar and came to the store last Thursday night to get it back. Either he planned to kill Lupe all along or he panicked when he realized the pot wasn't in the store anymore. Maybe that's why he went looking for it at your condo."

"So Lupe interrupts a burglary," Helen said, "but before the guy kills her, she gives him directions to my home."

"Addresses aren't that hard to find."

Helen dropped the spatula she was holding, splattering chocolate on the tabletop. "Your theory is implausible. In fact, it's ridiculous. I don't understand what you're doing, Tucker. Lupe's death has nothing to do with a spouted chocolate pot. Her son killed her. He's a drug user and a gang member. He caused the family all sorts of problems. The police know all this. That's why he's in jail."

"At least you should find out if the chocolate pot is real. I'd like your permission to leave it with Marianne Rogers at the museum."

Helen looked pale and distracted. She picked up a towel near the sink and began wiping the spilled chocolate from the table.

"All right," she said. "Go ahead."

I couldn't argue with the facts. Roberto was the police department's only suspect at the moment, but if the chocolate pot factored into Lupe's death, I doubted her son was guilty of the crime. The theory just didn't add up.

On my way out of Nectar, I noticed one of the small signs Helen used in the glass cases to identify her chocolates. This one read DEATH BY CHOCOLATE. It looked as if she'd taken Alexis Raines' advice. She hadn't renamed the store, but I wondered if she was thinking about it. The thought left me feeling slightly unsettled.

As soon as I left Nectar, I called the museum. Marianne Rogers had been called away on a family emergency and couldn't be reached. I didn't want to leave the pot with anyone else, so I left a message for her to call me as soon as she returned. Then I hotfooted it home to change for my meeting with Dr. Jordan Rich.

Chapter 18

Once at home, I took the chocolate pot out of my car. As I carried it up the stairs to my side door, I heard the sound of someone playing single notes on a piano, followed by a woman's voice warbling *whoo-eee*.

It was my neighbor Mrs. Domanski. She'd recently started taking singing lessons again, hoping to revive her career. She claimed she'd once had a decent set of pipes, but the vagaries of her husband's career as a movie producer had forced her to give up any dreams of performing at Carnegie Hall. I didn't think all those gin martinis she inhaled every day helped her voice much, either.

I imagined Mrs. D's seventy-year-old body draped across the top of her Steinway, a baby spot illuminating her ruby pageboy, her boggy butt camouflaged under a sequined gown. At least she was following her dream, unlike Nerine Barstok, who seemed like a gray lizard hiding in the shadows, lashing her tongue at unsuspecting bugs.

Then reality intruded.

"Whoo-eee."

My grandma Felder would say, if Mrs. D was aiming at superstardom, she had a long row to hoe. I imagined Muldoon under her bed with his paws over his ears. Too bad. He'd have to tolerate the noise until I got back from my meeting with Jordan Rich.

The spouted chocolate pot was still swathed in padding inside the box Marianne Rogers had provided. It just fit inside the clothes dryer, so I decided to leave it there until I could make arrangements to drop it off at the museum.

At four thirty I left for Bunker Hill, wearing a conservative black dress that made me look like a mother-in-law at a Sicilian wedding. In case Venus had told Dr. Rich I was single and looking for love, the dress should keep his libido in check long enough for me to set him straight.

Traffic was a mess. I was on the road an hour and a half before I pulled into the Music Center's underground garage and took a series of escalators to the plaza level, where the Dorothy Chandler Pavilion, the Mark Taper Forum, and the Ahmanson Theatre were spread out over several acres of prime downtown Los Angeles real estate.

The night air was chilly. I pulled the collar of my coat around my neck and walked toward Pinot Grill, the outdoor restaurant on the plaza. To the east was the

Jacques Lipchitz sculpture, which arose amid the dancing waters of a circular fountain. I scanned the tables of people huddled beneath freestanding gas heaters, looking for a man alone. Everybody was with somebody. I was beginning to think I'd been stood up when I heard a man's voice call my name.

I turned to see a well-dressed male in his early forties, wearing a charcoal gray overcoat. You seldom see one of those on a man in Los Angeles. That was East Coast apparel, maybe Chicago, certainly not here. He was probably two inches shorter than I, five-seven I guessed. In lieu of traditional good looks, he had brilliant blue eyes and dimples that graced his cheeks when he smiled. He handed me a single red rose with a bow tied around the stem.

"Venus told me you were brilliant, but she didn't say you were beautiful, too. Just as well. It's more exhilarating to discover it for myself."

Beautiful. Brilliant. Exhilarating. I hoped Jordan Rich wasn't going to be a problem.

"I see you've been watching too many Cary Grant movies," I said.

His smile was warm and embracing. I was glad. There was no reason to offend him before the hors d'oervres arrived. The hostess set down a couple of menus for us at a table under one of those blazing gas heaters, so I was spared having to comment further. For many, it was invigorating to be at an outdoor café in Los Angeles in November, surrounded by genteel people enjoying the company of friends before a night at the theater. But for me, this night was all about business.

"Would you like a cocktail?" Jordan said. "Or should I order a bottle of wine?"

"Wine. I don't drink the hard stuff."

He caught the attention of the waiter and ordered Bordeaux, the most expensive bottle on the list.

"Venus tells me you're one of medicine's superstars," I said.

Jordan looked down at his hands and smiled. "I prefer to think I'm a good physician who cares passionately about his patients."

"What do thoracic surgeons do, anyway?"

He reached for a breadstick in the blue plastic cup on the table. "I'll give you the short version. We fix everything between the neck and the diaphragm."

"Venus says you travel all over Central America for Air Health."

"I've been involved for several years now. It's a wonderful organization."

A breeze fluttered the paper tablecloth. I anchored the corners with the salt and pepper shakers and the blue plastic cup filled with breadsticks. I held down the fourth corner with my hand. Traffic from the nearby freeway and tumbling water from the fountain created an urban symphony.

"So, tell me about Guatemala," I said.

He unwrapped the breadstick and broke it in half. "It's a beautiful country with many problems."

"Like what?"

"Poverty. Drugs. Pollution. The aftermath of a civil war that only ended in 1996."

He was the second person that day who had mentioned the war. I vaguely remembered reading about it in a college history class, but I couldn't recall any of the details except for one.

"Wasn't the CIA involved?" I said.

Jordan laid the breadstick down untouched. He leaned toward me. His expression was somber, his gaze intense. In the background, strings of small white lights glimmered like fireflies in trees shaped like monster broccoli.

"The conflict started in the 1950s during the peak of the McCarthy hysteria. A few wealthy Guatemalan landowners objected to President Jacobo Arbenz Guzman's land reforms, which they felt favored the poor. They sent representatives to Washington and whispered *communists* in the right ears. The U.S. government panicked and sent the CIA to Guatemala with a hit list."

The details were coming back to me now. "Wasn't there a coup?"

He nodded slowly, as if the movement took some effort. "Our CIA armed, trained, and funded a group of military dissidents that overthrew the legitimate president and installed a dictator in his place. What followed was a thirty-six-year political genocide carried out by the Guatemalan National Police. Hundreds of Mayan villages were destroyed and two hundred thousand people were murdered, or 'disappeared,' mostly poor, indigenous farmers."

The waiter arrived with our wine and went through the ceremony of showing the label, opening the bottle, and pouring a splash into the bottom of Jordan's glass for his approval. He ignored the ritual and told the waiter to pour the wine.

"Once our government realized what was happening," I said, "didn't they try to stop it?"

"Unfortunately not. The U.S. continued providing military aid and intelligence to death squads. The massacre is often called the Silent Holocaust."

I glanced at the table next to ours, where a well-dressed couple was seated. The woman had pushed the plump croutons from her Caesar salad to the edge of the plate, too many calories perhaps. She leaned over and spoke to her companion, who checked his Rolex watch, maybe to monitor how long before curtain time.

"What happened to the National Police when the war was over?" I said.

"Its legacy was so tainted it had to be disbanded and replaced with a new police force."

"Was anybody prosecuted?"

"Both sides agreed to an amnesty. Most of the officers melted into the population. Some came to the U.S., including Los Angeles."

Jordan seemed to sense how troubling this news was to me, but he couldn't have fully understood why. It was because of Eugene and the trouble he may have found looking beyond a long, iridescent green feather.

Jordan sat back in his chair. "I'm sorry. I didn't mean to turn the evening into a political rant."

"There's no need to apologize. I'm interested in anything you can tell me."

"Why this fascination with Guatemala?" he said.

I gave him a brief account of Eugene's disappearance and my search for anything that might help me find him.

"I'm not sure how history will help you find your friend," he said, "but I'm happy to help in any way I can."

"Have you ever heard of the MayaBoyz?"

"I've not only heard of them, I've operated on their victims in the ER. More gunshot wounds than I care to remember."

A pall settled over the table, caused by too much talk about war and death. The simple ritual of upper-middle-class Angelenos sipping wine at a trendy outdoor café seemed sacrilegious in light of the events Dr. Rich had just described. I averted my gaze toward the Lipchitz sculpture with its tangle of figures reaching up toward what looked like a dove perched on a gigantic tear. At the base was a caption I hadn't noticed before. It read PEACE ON EARTH.

The musical was lighthearted, but watching it didn't lift my spirits. I kept thinking about all those murdered Guatemalans, Lupe Ortiz, and the families destroyed by drugs and gang violence. And I thought about Eugene and where he might be. Even though he'd grown emotionally stronger, I still couldn't shake my urge to protect him. Not knowing where he was made me feel as if I was fleeing a tormentor without the benefit of legs.

When the show was over, Jordan and I walked toward the escalator that led to the parking garage. A man was sitting on a blanket, torturing the reed of his saxophone, playing a melody meaningful only to him. Jordan stopped to listen. He pulled a twenty-dollar bill from his wallet and placed it in the velvet lining of the instrument's case. The musician tipped his horn in appreciation.

Jordan walked with me to my car, steering our conversation toward lighter subjects. We chatted about the Lakers and Jordan's first run in the L.A. Marathon the previous March. When we reached the Boxster, he watched as I slid into the front seat.

"I'd like to see you again, Tucker. What about this weekend? A patient of mine has a vineyard in Santa Ynez. He's always trying to entice me to come for a tour. We could leave Saturday morning, spend the day."

Most people would have said Jordan Rich was a catch. He seemed to be an intelligent, compassionate person, a humanitarian. I considered both his offer and Venus' warning about traveling with a man. She claimed it destroyed a relationship. Jordan Rich and I didn't have a relationship to destroy, maybe we never would, but it was too soon to leave town with him.

"I can't go," I said.

He lowered his gaze as if searching for guidance from the parking-garage floor. "And why not?"

"I'm busy on Saturday."

He looked up, studying my expression. "I must have misunderstood. Venus told me you weren't involved at the moment."

"I'm not. I have to work, that's all."

He slid his hands into the pockets of his overcoat.

"Look, Tucker, I'm not going to pretend I don't find you attractive. The truth is you're a delightful woman, and I'd like to get to know you better."

His directness was both refreshing and intimidating. The easy way out would have been to say yes, and then send him an e-mail in a day or so telling him how truly sorry I was that my schedule didn't permit a wine-tasting trip to Santa Ynez. Except, I couldn't do that. It was dishonest. I just wasn't ready to plunge into another relationship. It was too much effort.

"It was a fun evening," I said. "I hope we can do it again sometime. But just so you know, I'm not looking for anything beyond friendship."

He nodded. "Fair enough. I'm willing to work with that."

I was leaving the parking garage when Charley called. He was just going to bed—on the couch, he wanted me to know. He'd been listening to the news when he heard Roberto Ortiz had been released from county jail.

My breathing became shallow. "I didn't think murder suspects were eligible for bail."

"He didn't make bail. They cut him loose by mistake. Confused him with another prisoner with a similar name. I don't think he's a threat to you, but just in case, watch yourself. Okay?"

I told Charley about the chocolate pot and the receipt for the cell phone charger from Radio Shack I'd found in Eugene's desk. He said he'd check it out.

After we ended the call, I couldn't stop wondering what Roberto Ortiz would do next. He was a sixteen-year-old kid. His family lived in East L.A. He couldn't leave town without money and a place to stay. I wasn't sure if he posed any threat to Helen, but I had to warn her he was in the wind.

There was no answer at her condo. Either she had unplugged the telephone because of all those late-night calls, or she'd gone to Dale Ewing's place in Simi Valley to spend the night. The information operator informed me that Ewing's number was unlisted. If Helen was in Simi Valley, she was probably safe. There was nothing else I could do at the moment. Besides, it was late. I wanted to go home to see if Eugene had left me another message.

Chapter 19

There was no call from Eugene that night or the next morning, so I called Nerine Barstok to see if she'd heard from him. She hadn't. I told her not to worry. Charley and I were on the case. I kept my voice breezy so she wouldn't detect my concern, but her only focus seemed to be on Eugene's lack of foresight, which had left her stranded in L.A. without a car.

When I arrived at the office, I found Riley Deegan sitting at the top of the staircase, looking listless and forlorn.

"What's up?" I said.

"I have a problem."

"What sort of problem?"

"Can we talk inside?"

I unlocked the door and walked across the lobby to my office. Riley followed. On my desk was a vase filled with a dozen red roses. The card in the plastic pitch-fork read *I had a wonderful time last night. Hope you did, too.* It was signed Jordan Rich.

Riley took a seat on a guest chair. "Wow. Somebody did something right."

I ignored her comment and moved the flowers to the top of the file cabinet. "So tell me what happened."

"I'm giving up Luv Bugs," she said. "My family thinks I should get a real job."

"Even your brother?"

"Joe and I aren't speaking. He told me to get a life and stop interfering in his. He thinks I'm wasting my time trying to run a dating service. He's probably right. I'm a failure. My party was a dud. Nobody connected on any sort of emotional level."

"Sex on a bathroom floor sounds emotional to me."

"You know what I mean, Tucker. Nobody made a soul connection. People drank my booze and ate my food and somebody went home with a spare roll of toilet paper from Claudia's bathroom. I mean, what kind of person would steal toilet paper at a singles' party?"

"Probably not somebody looking for love."

"Exactly my point."

"Look, Riley, you can't give up. Businesses take time to grow."

Tears had formed in the corners of her eyes. She reached up with her index finger to stop one from dropping onto her cheek. I handed her a tissue from a box in my desk drawer.

"I'm just no good at this," she said. "I can't even save

my own brother from a bad relationship. He doesn't love Carly. He just feels he has to defend her."

Nerine Barstok had given up her dream of becoming a teacher to have kids, and Mrs. Domanski had axed a budding singing career for marriage and martinis. Even my mother left her acting career to help Bruce open his yoga studio. True, she hadn't exactly been an A-lister, but she'd had a decent career playing ingénues, then young moms, and finally the ditzy neighbor next door, until her forties, when the acting jobs started to dry up. It had been a life of struggle, but she seemed to enjoy it until she met Bruce. Riley Deegan was too young to give up so early just because a man told her to do so. There was plenty of time to consider sacrifice when she was older and wiser.

"Look, Riley. You hired me to create a business strategy for Luv Bugs. At least give me time to do my job. These parties are okay, but they're not the best bang for your buck. I think you need to focus on Internet dating. You can reach more people and reduce your overhead. Plow all of the profits back into the business for a while. It'll work. You'll see."

She dabbed at another tear. "I don't know."

"Trust me. You can't give up before you even begin."

"The problem is my mom loaned me money to get started. If Joe tells her Luv Bugs is a loser, she'll cut me off."

"Let me talk to your brother. I'll make him understand how important this is to you."

She looked up. "You'd do that? Really?"

I smiled. "For you? Yes, I would."

I wanted to grab Joe Deegan by the lapels and shake him until he understood that loving somebody meant standing by her even when times got tough, even when you disagreed. It didn't take much insight to understand that I wasn't angry with Deegan because of Riley. I was angry with him because of me, the way he'd dumped me with no explanation. If I was ever to move on, I had to tell him how I felt, and this time he was going to listen even if I had to chain him to a chair with his own handcuffs. I just had to find the right moment.

Shortly after Riley left, Charley walked through the front door. "How about taking a ride?"

"Where are we going?" I said.

"To meet with Helen's ex-husband."

"We're driving to Connecticut?"

"To Orange County. Brad Taggart's company just opened a branch office in Irvine, and he's been flying into John Wayne Airport every couple of weeks to supervise the operation."

I felt a tingling sensation on the back of my neck. "I don't suppose he was in town the night Lupe Ortiz was killed?"

"How did you guess?"

"I'm surprised he agreed to talk to you."

"He not only agreed, he was gung-ho. Said he wanted to tell his side of the story. I need you to distract the guy with some business bullshit while I watch how he reacts."

"Do you think he's involved in Lupe's death?"

"Anything's possible."

"Is it likely?"

Charley walked toward the door and beckoned for me to follow. "Ask me again in a couple of hours."

Chapter 20

Brad Taggart had agreed to meet Charley at a coffee shop in Seal Beach, a town in Orange County just south of Long Beach. It's a small, middle-class, white-bread community where surfers, fishermen, rocket scientists, and Lions Club members enjoy the laid-back beach vibe under the watchful eye of the U.S. Naval Weapons Station. The town also has a national wildlife refuge, which is good because about a third of the population lives in a retirement village called Leisure World, and that's about the only wild life they see anymore.

The Espresso Express was located on a narrow main drag lined with low-slung buildings. Charley and I bought a couple of lattes and took them outside to a table under a tree in the adjacent courtyard. In the chill of the air, I welcomed the heat of sun and coffee.

A few minutes later, we saw a man in a dark blue

power suit, rushing down the sidewalk toward us, carrying a paper coffee cup in his hand. His ebony hair was turning gray. His jaw was clenched. The cords in his neck were taut, leaving the impression he was all nerves and hard edges. When he got closer, I could see his eyes were an intense hazel.

Brad Taggart exchanged a curt greeting with Charley and shook his hand without even looking at me. He centered the knot of his muted tie as he scanned the courtyard.

"I don't like this table," he said.

Taggart found another one toward the back of the courtyard and set his cup down to cement ownership. There was no reason for us to move. Nobody who might overhear our conversation was sitting nearby. The table wasn't in the sun. The way I saw it, Taggart just wanted to control the meeting from the get-go.

I glanced at Charley to see if the ploy registered on his bullshit meter. Apparently it didn't, because he got up and joined Taggart at the new table. As I sat down, I noticed the markings on Taggart's coffee cup, cappuccino with a triple shot of espresso. No wonder the guy was juiced up with nervous energy.

"I don't know what Helen told you about me," Taggart said, "but it's all a lie. She's the one who's out of control. I wouldn't be surprised if she killed that cleaning woman herself, whatever her name was."

I felt my chest welling with anger. "Her name was Lupe Ortiz. Mom, to her four kids."

"Why would Helen kill her?" Charley said.

"Helen thought the woman was stealing from her.

She told my daughter she was going to confront her. Maybe she did, and the argument got physical."

"Just for kicks," Charley said, "where were you last Thursday night?"

A flush appeared on Taggart's neck and began creeping upward. "I was at the gym in a spinning class."

Charley nodded. "I guess lots of people saw you there."

"I wouldn't know. The lights were low. People concentrate on their workouts. They don't care about the guy on the bike next to them."

"Helen thinks somebody is out to destroy her business," I said. "You know anybody who'd want to do that?"

Taggart glanced at me with narrowed eyes. "Helen isn't the victim she'd like everybody to believe she is. And she's no Goody Two-shoes, either. She has a mean streak—just ask my kids."

"Since they're not here," Charley said, "how about you tell us instead?"

Taggart took a drink of his triple cap and stared into the void as if he was dredging up a bad memory. "With Helen it's all about me, me, me. She's a perfectionist. She always rode those kids too hard. She turned our marriage into a civil war and made them take sides. My daughter, Pammy, barely speaks to her mother. Helen has brainwashed my son and filled his head with all kinds of lies about me. I can't even get close enough to knock sense into his head."

I glanced at Charley to gauge his reaction to Taggart's comment about his son, but he had on that mask of neutrality he frequently wore. I couldn't tell how the words had affected him, but I suspected the undercurrent of violence had not escaped his notice.

Charley ripped open two packets of sugar and poured them into his latte. "I understand your marriage broke up because of an affair."

Taggart looked less sure of himself now. "Helen drove me to it, all the time on my case for every little thing. A man can take only so much."

"Before he snaps?" I said.

Taggart's jaw clenched with tension. "Helen wants you to think I was angry because she got too much in the divorce settlement. That's another lie. I would have given any amount of money to get out of that marriage."

"Do you still call your ex-wife?" Charley said.

Taggart took a drink of his coffee. "No. Why should I?"

"If the police checked your phone records, would they find outgoing calls made to Helen from your home or office?"

Even though it was chilly outside, beads of moisture were forming on Taggart's forehead. "I can't guarantee they wouldn't be there. Pammy works for me, so she uses my telephone at home and at the office. She may have called her mother."

"I thought you said Pammy barely speaks to her mother," Charley said. "Now you say she calls Helen from both your home and your office. So which is it? Does she call her mother or doesn't she?"

Taggart clenched his jaw. "It's just my impression. I don't watch her every minute of the day."

If Pammy called Helen at all, the mother-daughter relationship couldn't be as bad as Taggart made it out to be. I had a feeling he was lying to make his ex-wife look bad. If so, one day those lies were going to catch up with him.

"What exactly does your company do?" I said.

Taggart paused as if he was assessing whether my question deserved his attention. "We're a multinational manufacturer of industrial ceramics and food-processing products. We have forty-two plants in eleven countries. We employ almost twelve thousand people."

Charley and I exchanged a glance. Then he sat back and let me take the lead.

"Do you have a plant in Orange County?" I said.

"Land is too expensive here. Our Irvine office is strictly administrative."

"You must travel a lot."

He adjusted his tie again, making it perfect. "A fair amount."

"I'm doing a strategic plan for a small pharmaceutical company. They're considering moving some manufacturing to Central America. Do you have plants there?"

"Yes, two. One near San José and one in Chiapas."

"How's it working out for you?" I said.

"We have the usual problems—unskilled labor and government regulations. I've had to spend a lot of time tweaking things, but the operations are finally starting to come together." Taggart checked his watch and downed the dregs of his triple cap. "I have to go. I have a meeting in thirty minutes."

"Just one more question," Charley said. "You ever hear of a guy named Eugene Barstok?"

"No. Should I have?"

"Nope."

"Then don't waste time asking the question," he said. "Let me leave you with a final word of warning. My ex-wife is a liar. Don't trust her."

Charley and I watched Taggart bolt from the table and disappear around the corner.

"Nice guy," he said.

"Yeah, a real jewel."

"What's your take on his theory that Helen Taggart has a dark side?"

"I've never seen any evidence of that," I said. "She can get intense because she worries all the time about failing and it scares her, but that hardly makes her evil. He's right about the me, me, me part, though. It can get annoying. On the other hand, Taggart is a piece of work. My guess is he's done something bad and he wants to deflect attention from himself by trashing Helen."

"What are the odds that Helen Taggart killed Lupe Ortiz?" Charley said.

"Slim. Helen may be overestimating the role she played in Lupe's life, but I think they had a good relationship. I suppose if she caught Lupe stealing chocolates from the store the friendship would have soured, but Helen insists Lupe's no thief. She got upset when

I suggested Ortiz stole the chocolate pot from her customer."

"I guess we should contact her employer," Charley said. "See if there've been any complaints against her."

"Let me do that."

Charley took the lid off his latte, looking at the foam at the bottom of the cup. "So, what about Taggart? You think he killed Ortiz?"

"If he did, Lupe wasn't his target. It was Helen. I don't know if he's guilty, but I do think it's interesting that one of Brad Taggart's plants is located in Chiapas."

"So what?"

"It's within spitting distance of a zoo that breeds quetzals."

Charley's eyebrows lifted in surprise. "You think Taggart left that feather?"

"It's possible. Taggart oversees two plants in Central America. He's traveled there a lot. He could have easily heard about the Mayan belief that quetzals symbolize freedom."

"What's your point?"

"Taggart claims he would have paid any price to be free of Helen, but what if he's lying? What if he went to Nectar that night to kill her and left the feather to make a statement? As hard as she tried, she'd never be free of him."

"But Lupe Ortiz got in the way?"

"You have a better idea?"

"It's an interesting theory, Sinclair, but way too deep for a guy like Taggart."

On the drive home, Charley gripped the steering wheel so tight his knuckles turned white. I asked him what he was thinking about.

"Nothing you'd want to know."

"Lorna?"

"She isn't talking to me since I took that baby crap back to the store. I keep telling her I'm too old to screw up another human life."

"Dickhead didn't turn out so bad. At least he doesn't have any felony convictions."

"Yeah, but he isn't doing anything with his life."

"You mean anything you want him to do."

"Listen, I worked my butt off to put that kid through college, and what happens? He goes out and gets himself a job as a bartender."

"He's just a late bloomer."

Charley stared straight ahead at the road. "I should have stayed single."

"You don't mean that."

He didn't answer for a moment, as if he had to think about how he felt. "You're right. So what should I do about Lorna?"

"You're asking me for relationship advice? I made up a fake boyfriend so I wouldn't look like a total loser."

He glanced at me and frowned. "You make fun of yourself, Sinclair, but you're a smart, good-looking woman. You could have ten boyfriends or a husband and ten kids if you wanted."

"Or I could be like Nerine Barstok, resentful because her children ruined her chance for a career."

"You wouldn't be like that."

"How do you know?" The words came out sharper than I'd intended.

An uncomfortable silence settled in the car.

"What are you thinking?" Charley said.

"Nothing you'd want to hear."

"Try me."

I adjusted my seat belt and moved the lever of the air vent so it wasn't blowing on my face. I was stalling for time to consider if I should confess what was really on my mind.

"Do you think there's somebody for everyone?" I said. "If a person keeps looking for true love, will they eventually find it?"

"You're talking to the wrong guy, kid. Ask me something I know about, like basketball scores or fly fishing."

"Or how to find Eugene?"

His hands tightened on the steering wheel. "Don't worry. We'll find him."

What Charley didn't say was if we'd find him alive.

It took us more than an hour to drive from Seal Beach to Culver City. Charley dropped me off at the office at about one, and left immediately for Garvey Motors in Alhambra to see if he could get a lead on the black Mercedes I'd seen parked outside Nectar the night Lupe died.

Someone needed to contact Lupe's family to follow the chocolate pot's trail of ownership. Charley was busy with other things, and despite Deegan's warning, I decided to go back to the barrio.

Chapter 21

When I called the Ortiz house, Lupe's cousin answered the telephone. Detective Gatan had arranged for her to care for Lupe's children, and that's what she'd been doing since the night of the murder. She didn't know anything about a chocolate pot, but she invited me to speak with Lupe's daughter, Angelica, who was due home from school in an hour. The cousin claimed she hadn't seen Roberto since he'd been released from jail and had no idea where he was. That made sense. He wouldn't risk returning to his mother's house. It was the first place the police would look.

Eugene hadn't been in contact with me since Monday. No one knew where he was. All I had to go on were the words he'd searched for on the Internet and a spouted chocolate pot. I called Nerine and told her to be on the lookout for any credit card statements that came to the apartment. No recent charges would likely be listed there, but it was worth checking.

"Tampering with somebody else's mail is illegal," she said. "If I see something that looks like a bill, I'll call. You can open it."

"Whatever," I said. "How are the cats?"

"I'm sure they're fine. I put them in a kennel."

I counted to ten to prevent myself from screaming at her, but in truth, Liza and Fergie were probably better off without Nerine. Her heart was a sack of ice.

I ended the call and sat for a moment, thinking. I hated not knowing things, but not knowing what had happened to Eugene was torture. I couldn't discount the possibility that I was missing the point with chocolate pots and civil wars. Just because I didn't know of any enemies Eugene might have didn't mean they didn't exist. He'd recently uncovered evidence against Tracy Fields, the deputy DA who could have sent Joe Deegan to prison. She lost her job because Eugene exposed her lies, so she had a motive for revenge. It just seemed unlikely that Tracy was behind his disappearance.

At two, I headed for East L.A. The neighborhood looked less intimidating in the daylight. The man and his pit bull were nowhere in sight. I parked in the driveway behind the Toyota. It looked dusty, as if it hadn't been moved since the last time I'd been there.

Lupe Ortiz's cousin was a barrel-chested woman named Connie. She had pencil legs and straight black hair that lay blunt and boxy on her shoulders. Though her telephone manner had been open and friendly, in person she seemed guarded. Behind her, Lupe's two preschool boys sat on the floor in the living room, watching cartoons on the television set.

To my right was a kitchen barely large enough for a small square table and four chairs. The counters were covered with cereal boxes, a cookie jar, and a variety of small appliances, but no evidence of Nectar's signature gold boxes. If Lupe had been stealing chocolates from the store, it seemed as though I'd see some evidence of the theft in her house.

Angelica was hunched over a book at the kitchen table. She had heavy black braids that dangled in front of her as she swung her legs back and forth, slowing the pace periodically to write something on a tablet with a yellow pencil.

Connie invited me inside the house and gestured for me to sit on the couch. She told me Lupe had worked for ten years for a company called Jay-Cee Janitorial Services. I asked her about Roberto's drug use and the argument he'd had with his mother the night she was killed. She answered in a hushed tone, as if she didn't want the children to hear negative talk about their brother, athough I didn't know how they could hear anything over the noise of the television.

"Roberto has many problems, but he didn't kill Lupe."

"How can you be so sure?"

She stood. "Wait here. I'll show you."

She disappeared down the hallway, returning a moment later with a leather purse, hand-tooled in an intricate pattern.

"Roberto made this for her. It took him months. A

boy who would do this for his mother would never kill her."

I studied the purse. Connie was right. It was beautiful and obviously made with loving care, but Roberto was a tweeker and drugs changed everything. I doubted he'd ever sit around hand-tooling leather purses again, except in an occupational therapy class in state prison.

"A quetzal feather was found near Lupe's body," I said. "The police think it belongs to Roberto."

Her eyes darted away from me, down the hallway. "Why would he have something like that?"

"Because he's a member of the MayaBoyz."

She shrugged. "Quetzals are everywhere in this neighborhood. It's no big deal. Even Lupe has a necklace with a bird on it."

"Where did she get it?"

"Her husband bought it to remind her of home."

"And where's home?"

"Xecoxol. It's a village near Guatemala City. She was fifteen when she came here with her mother. Back in the seventies. The family had a bad time during the war. Two of our cousins were killed. Lupe's brother, too. And her father. All disappeared."

"After Lupe's death," I said, "were you contacted by any newspaper reporters?"

"Sure, lots of them. From TV, too."

"Did somebody by the name of Bix Waverly ever call? He may have told you he was from the *New York Times*."

"He called yesterday. I remember him because of the funny name."

I was relieved to learn Eugene was okay, but annoyed with him for keeping me in the dark about his whereabouts. He had to realize how worried I'd be and what a dangerous game he was playing.

"What kind of questions did he ask you?"

"All sorts. He wanted to know about that pot, just like you. I told him I didn't know where it came from."

"Did you tell him about Lupe's family being killed in the war?"

Connie stood as if she'd grown weary of my questions. "Maybe I did. It's no secret." She moved toward the kitchen table. The two young boys glanced at her as she passed by, and then went back to watching TV.

"Angelica," she said, "this lady wants to ask you some questions about a chocolate pot."

The girl didn't look at me. She just kept swinging those legs, reading the book, and crushing the pencil in her pudgy hand.

"Angel, be good. She wants to know where Lupe got it. Tell her."

Angelica held the pencil like a dagger over the tablet. In large angry letters that tore through the paper she wrote *NO*. Connie reached toward the pencil as if she was going to take it away. I stopped her with my hand.

"It's okay," I said. "Let me try."

The cousin looked puzzled, as if she couldn't understand why I wanted her to give up so easily. I didn't know if I could pull Angelica out of the safe haven where she'd gone to nurse her pain. Maybe it wasn't even fair to try.

I knelt on the floor next to her. The book on the table was *The Secret Garden* by Frances Hodgson Burnett, a classic children's story about a young girl dealing with the death of her parents. It seemed particularly revealing that Angelica was reading it now.

"I'm sorry about your mother," I said. "If there was anything I could do to bring her back, I would."

My attempt at empathy was met with silence.

"My best friend is missing, and I'm worried. I need to know who gave your mother the spouted chocolate pot. Will you help me?"

She hesitated for what seemed like a long time. "I don't know her name. You have to ask Roberto."

I tilted my head back and stared at the ceiling. This was getting me nowhere. "Unfortunately, Roberto's not here—"

The smaller of the two boys jumped up from the floor. He clapped his hands, seemed proud of himself for what he was about to say. "He's in the bathroom."

Connie shouted at him in Spanish. His chin began to quiver. Tears formed in her eyes. A door slammed. I heard footsteps running down the hall. The two boys scattered. A moment later, Roberto Ortiz appeared in front of me, holding a baseball bat above his head. He looked poised to hit a home run.

For a moment, time seemed to stop. My heart was pounding. My breathing felt labored. Every possible action seemed wrong and dangerous. I held up my hands in surrender.

"I'm not here to cause problems," I said. "I just want to find my friend."

The muscles in his arms were taut. "I didn't kill my mother."

"I believe you."

He sneered and poised the bat as if he was going to swing it at my head. "You lie."

I wasn't sure if he was high on drugs or going through withdrawal. Whatever the case, it wasn't good news for me.

"Okay, so I don't believe you," I said. "Not yet. But I want to. That's why I need your help. Your mother gave Helen Taggart a Mayan spouted chocolate pot. I have to find out where she got it."

"Why should I tell you?"

"Because I think the pot is connected to your mother's death. If I can prove it, I might be able to prove you didn't kill her."

"How do I know I can trust you?"

"You don't. All I can give you is my word."

Roberto gave me the mad-dog evil eye, as if he was testing my resolve. I held his gaze until he lowered the bat to the floor. A moment later, he walked to the edge of the kitchen window and aimed a furtive look toward the street. I wasn't sure who he was looking for. The police? Fellow gang members? Angelica hadn't moved from the table, but she looked up periodically from her book, as though assessing her brother's mood.

"My mom found the pot in the trash at work one Saturday. She said the lady who owned the business found it when she was cleaning out her storage shed. She thought it was junk and threw it away."

"So your mom kept the pot."

Roberto pointed the bat at me. "The lady said it was okay."

"When did your mom give it to Helen?"

"The next Monday. My mom never kept anything for herself."

"Did the customer ever ask her to return the pot?"

Roberto glanced out the window again. "Not her. Her old man called a week ago. Said his wife gave away the pot by mistake. My mom told him she didn't have it anymore and couldn't ask for it back. That wouldn't be right. He kept calling and calling until she wouldn't answer her cell phone anymore."

"You think this guy killed your mom to get the chocolate pot back?"

Roberto looked as if somebody was running a scalpel over a raw nerve. "If he did, I'll take care of him myself."

"Look, you're in enough trouble. Tell me the guy's name. I'll report him to the police."

From out on the street I heard the sound of loud music. Roberto heard it, too. He dropped the bat and sprinted toward the back door. A second later, I heard an explosion. For a moment, I thought it was sound from the television set. Then glass shattered. I heard screams. I turned toward the kitchen window, where Roberto had just been standing, and saw a hole in the glass surrounded by a spiderweb of cracks.

I sank to the floor, so scared I could hardly breathe. Lupe's cousin cowered in the living room with the two young boys in her arms. Angelica lay trembling on the kitchen floor among shards of glass from the broken cookie jar. I crawled over, reached out to touch her, afraid of the blood I might see, afraid of the help I might not be able to give. I rolled her into my arms as if she was fragile parchment. She was bleeding, but only from cuts made by the broken glass. I held her to my chest, rocking her and speaking in soft, low tones.

I heard three more shots. I carried Angelica to her cousin, staying low, not wanting to become a target. Then I crawled to the living room window and parted the bedsheet curtain, unable to process the scene unfolding before my eyes. At the edge of the lawn was the body of Roberto Ortiz. He was lying on his side, facing the house. His white T-shirt and baggy jeans were black with blood. Out of the corner of my eye, I saw the back of an Oldsmobile racing down the street.

It was dark by the time the police allowed me to leave East L.A. I willed myself to perform the routine things I had to do to get home. Find the freeway on-ramp. Turn into my driveway. Find my house keys. What I couldn't do was come to terms with the shattered lives of Lupe Ortiz's children and the violent and capricious world we lived in. I stayed awake most of the night, hoping tragedy would take a holiday at least until daybreak.

Regardless of my fractured emotional state in the aftermath of Roberto's death, I couldn't stop searching for Eugene. In the morning, I planned to visit Jay-Cee Janitorial Services to get a list of the customers Lupe serviced on Saturdays. I hoped it would lead me one step closer to finding the owner of the spouted chocolate pot.

Chapter 22

On Thursday morning, I set out to visit Jay-Cee Janitorial Services, with two goals: to get a list of Lupe's Saturday clients, and to find out if any customers had accused her of theft. Helen didn't think Lupe was responsible for the missing chocolates, but I had to be sure. If she wasn't the culprit, somebody else was, and they had to be found. Helen couldn't afford any more losses.

Jay-Cee Janitorial Services was located just south of downtown L.A. in a gritty, light-industrial area on Soto Street, underneath the massive concrete pilings of the 10 Freeway. The neighborhood was between Boyle Heights and Vernon and featured stubby buildings, small factories, and a crisscross maze of parked cars. There weren't many people on the street, just freeway noise and dust.

The only vehicle access to the store was through a narrow alley behind the building. I parked in a small lot next to a fleet of Jay-Cee vans and made my way through the back entrance to the front of the store. On the left side of the lobby was a tiered metal shelf, lined with waxes, polishes, abrasives, and various cleaning utensils, including mops, sponges, and squeegees. On the right side were three vending machines loaded with soft drinks, coffee, and junk food.

A young Latina was hunched over a ledger at her desk. One finger was sliding down a line of figures. The other was working the keys of a calculator. A narrow hallway led away from the lobby to a cavern of offices where, I presumed, the big guns worked.

"Be right with you," the woman said without looking up. "I just gotta finish adding this up."

While I waited for her to calculate, I glanced at the counter, looking for a promotional brochure. All I found was a scratch pad with Jay-Cee's logo on it and a slightly chewed pencil.

A moment later, the woman threw her hands up. She ripped a long section of paper tape from the spool and tossed it in the wastebasket.

"Stupid machine comes up with a different answer every time." She stood and walked toward me. "Sorry you had to wait. Can I help you?"

I wasn't sure if the woman would release client information to me, so I made up a pretext.

"I'm looking for a service to clean my office," I said. "Your company came highly recommended."

Her wide smile exposed even white teeth. "Thank

you. How did you find us? People usually don't come here. We send our reps out to you."

"I was in the neighborhood. Thought I'd stop by."

"Okay. No problem. We're glad you came." She reached under the counter and handed me a brochure. "This tells you all about us. I'd have you talk to Mr. Rocha, but he's not here right now."

I scanned the brochure, and was disappointed it didn't include a list of clients.

"Actually, I'd prefer talking to you."

She blushed. "I'll try to help the best I can."

"I'm interested in a Saturday cleaning. Do you have a list of customers you service on that day so I can call for references?"

She looked puzzled by my question. "I don't know. Our reps usually handle that. I guess it depends on what kind of place you have. I mean, does it get real dirty?" She blushed again. "Sorry. That didn't come out so good. What I meant was, do you work with chemicals or grease or anything like that?"

"You mean like a restaurant?"

"Yeah, like that."

"No. I'm a business consultant. My office is small, just three rooms. But I don't necessarily want to talk to businesses like mine. Any of your clients will do. I'm just interested in things like honesty and reliability."

"We're both of those things."

"I'm sure you are," I said, "but I'd like some independent confirmation."

The door behind me opened. I smelled French fries.

I turned to see a man standing on the threshold, wearing an olive uniform with JAY-CEE JANITORIAL SERVICES embroidered on the pocket. He was struggling with a large box filled with paper bags that all sported the golden arch emblem of McDonald's. He and the clerk exchanged a few words in Spanish before he disappeared down the hall with the box. Whatever he said to her had made her frown.

"Is something wrong?" I said.

"No. Hector just wants me to help him carry stuff in from the truck."

"Go ahead. I don't mind waiting."

"No. Our customers come first. He can do it alone."

"Are you having a party?"

"Not really. There's no place to eat around here. Whoever isn't busy goes out for food. Hector gets mad when it's his turn."

"Then maybe you'd better help him."

She hesitated. "You sure it's okay?"

"I'm sure."

Hector returned from the back offices. She said something to him and the two disappeared into the dust and noise. They wouldn't be gone long. Hector's truck was probably parked in the lot off the alley. I hurried to the ledger on the desk and saw columns of names, invoice numbers, and dollar amounts. I grabbed the scratch pad and the chewed pencil from the counter and began flipping pages and jotting down names, but I soon realized names alone wouldn't help connect Lupe Ortiz with her clients.

There were several file cabinets lined up by the wall. I opened drawers until I came to one that was full of personnel files. Lupe Ortiz's name was written on one of the tabs. Inside was an evaluation sheet listing the clients she serviced, including Nectar. The list gave no indication of which days she cleaned any of the businesses. Under various columns that read *punctuality*, *neatness*, and *honesty* were letter grades. Lupe had earned all As and Bs in every category. There were no incident reports, no complaints. Nothing that indicated Lupe was a thief. If she had been, somebody would have caught her at it in the ten years she'd worked for the company. Somebody else was responsible for Helen's missing chocolates.

There was no copy machine in the lobby, so I jotted down as many companies and contact names as I could until I heard voices outside the door. My heart pounded as I stuffed Lupe's report card back in the file and closed the drawer. I ran to the other side of the counter, arriving just as the young woman appeared with a tray of sodas. I opened the door for her, breathing deeply to calm my nerves.

She thanked me and took the tray to the back room. When she returned to the lobby, I grabbed the brochure from the counter.

"Look," I said, "you've been very helpful, but I don't want to interrupt your lunch. Tell Mr. Rocha I'll call him tomorrow."

She looked stricken, as if she'd made a bad decision. "Okay. You're sure you'll call back?"

"Of course."

I felt guilty lying to her, but I didn't want to waste any more time. I had to get the list of Jay-Cee clients to Charley so he could call on them one by one until he found the person who had given Lupe Ortiz the chocolate pot.

Chapter 23

Beverly Hills was on my way back to the office, so I decided to stop at Nectar to tell Helen that Roberto Ortiz had been killed in a drive-by shooting. When I arrived, she was scooping up chocolate from her marble tabletop and molding it into egg shapes. Her reaction to the news was muted. Cumulative stress was beginning to make her look wasted. One of her fingernails was broken and jagged, and the circles beneath her eyes looked like the dark side of a crescent moon.

"I got another of those two a.m. calls last night," she said. "I unplugged the telephone, but I can't take this much longer, Tucker. I'm so tired."

"Charley's still looking into your missing inventory, and I'm trying to find out who gave Lupe that chocolate pot. I finally got a list of clients from her employer and—"

Helen smashed the chocolate egg onto the marble in one angry splat. "Please don't tell me you have another stupid theory about Lupe Ortiz's death. I'm getting sick of listening to you rag on and on about it. So far I don't see much progress in Charley's investigation. As for you, you're supposed to be marketing my business, not wasting time solving crimes that have already been solved."

I knew she was under stress, but I was taken aback by her anger. I remembered her ex-husband's warning that Helen had a dark side. I wondered if I was seeing it now.

"Helen, I'm not your employee. You're just one of my clients, and in case you're worried, I charge you only for the time I spend on Nectar's marketing plan. Here's the deal. Eugene is missing. I think his disappearance is related to your shop and maybe even to Lupe Ortiz's murder, so I have to investigate all theories, stupid or not."

Helen bit her lip as if that might prevent the tears from cascading down her cheeks. It didn't work. Exhaustion was making her hysterical.

"Missing? Why didn't you tell me? I just thought he was busy with his mother and didn't have time to call. I have to do something. Maybe I should organize a candlelight vigil or make up some fliers."

I did a mental eye roll. "That's not necessary. Charley and I have it covered. Look, why don't you stay with Dale tonight? Maybe you'll get some sleep there."

"He's having his house painted. He doesn't want me to come over. Says the fumes will give me a headache."

That was unfortunate. If Dale Ewing wasn't around to soothe Helen's anxiety, she might fall apart. If she did, all of the feature articles in the newspaper and all of the chocolate symposiums I could organize weren't going to save Nectar.

I didn't know who was behind those late-night telephone calls, but Helen's ex-husband was a prime suspect. I left the list of Lupe's customers and a note of explanation on Charley's desk at the office, and headed to Irvine to confront Brad Taggart.

Chapter 24

An hour later, I was cruising toward the entrance to Taggart's office building when a new Mercedes passed by. Taggart was driving. I did a U-turn and followed him, noting the license plate on the car. It wasn't a dealer advertisement, which meant it wasn't the Mercedes I'd seen at Nectar the night Lupe Ortiz was murdered—unless the plate was new.

Taggart drove to the Montage, an upscale resort located along the Laguna Beach coastline. I waited on the street as he rolled into the circular driveway. A young man in uniform opened the car door. The valet took Taggart's black leather duffle bag from the trunk and escorted him inside. If Helen's ex was staying at the Montage, his company was springing for top-of-the-line accommodations. Being a CEO was good work if you could get it. As soon as Taggart disappeared into the lobby, I pulled into the driveway, too.

The valet opened my car door. "Are you staying with us tonight?"

"No. I'm meeting a client at the bar."

"Perfect. Allow me to escort you."

He led me through a low gallery that opened to a lounge with a panoramic view of the Pacific Ocean. Out of the corner of my eye, I saw Taggart standing at the reception desk as if he was checking in. I didn't want him to see me, so I walked out to a balcony overlooking a swimming pool with a bottom mosaic depicting a rising sun. Rows of lounge chairs were lined up around the perimeter. Beyond the pool was a patch of lawn bordering a walking path. A few feet farther was a cliff that fell to the sea where waves broke over an outcropping of rocks just beyond the small beach.

Taggart left the reception desk and headed with his bag down a long hallway. I followed a short distance behind. He stopped at a door and slipped the key card into the slot, and went inside. I didn't know how long he planned to stay in the room. It was possible he was in for the night. At the end of the hall I found a door leading to the grounds and made my way to the ocean side of his room, where I discovered a private patio with a couple of lounge chairs.

Through the glass of a sliding door I saw a king-sized bed looming three feet above the floor. Climbing aboard required long legs, a ladder, or maybe just two consenting adults. A bottle of champagne lolled in an ice bucket on a stand near the door. I wondered if that was standard with the room or if Taggart was expecting company. The leather duffle was sitting on the bed. A moment later, Taggart came out of the bathroom and headed for the door. I ran inside to follow him, but by the time I got to the lobby, he was gone.

I couldn't stay all night waiting for him to come back, so I decided to have one last look around the hotel. I searched the spa area, the gift shop, the restaurant, and the lower-level meeting rooms. He wasn't anywhere. I was about to leave when I noticed him standing near the valet station. If he drove away, I'd never be able to get to my car in time to follow him.

Moments later, an Audi convertible drove up. The top was down. The driver was a young woman with blond hair. She got out of the car and handed the valet her keys. Taggart walked over to him and began gesturing toward an area near the front door. An animated discussion ensued that put a frown on the valet's lips. A short time later, he parked the Audi in the area where Taggart had been pointing. I remembered the day he made Charley and me change tables at the espresso shop. Taggart was used to getting his way.

The woman watched from a distance until the car was parked. She strolled over to Taggart as if she was walking the runway at a Paris fashion show. She was one of the few women I'd seen who actually looked good in a red leather jacket and matching pants. Taggart kissed her on the lips. She responded with a confident smile. She may have been Taggart's wife, but I didn't think so. The kiss seemed unpracticed.

He slipped his arm around her waist and guided her

to the lobby bar. Before long, they were toasting each other with martinis the size of birdbaths. I found a seat in a corner that wasn't in Taggart's direct line of vision and ordered a Shirley Temple, because I didn't want alcohol to dull my reactions.

It took only fifteen minutes for Taggart and his companion to finish their drinks. They must have been on a schedule, because they got up and headed down the hall toward his room. There was little doubt in my mind what they planned to do there. I gave them enough time to open the bottle of champagne and undress before ignoring the DO NOT DISTURB sign with a knock on the door.

From inside the room, I heard a man's voice shouting, "Can't you read? We don't want to be bothered."

I didn't want to cause a scene, so I kept my voice as low as I could and still be heard. "I'm sorry, Mr. Taggart, but I have an urgent message from your wife."

"Slide it under the door," he said.

Bingo.

"I can't. The envelope is too big to fit."

A moment later, Brad Taggart appeared in the doorway wearing a thick terry cloth bathrobe, which he held closed around his body. I'd have felt more at ease if the belt had been tied, because what was under that robe was more than I wanted to know about old Brad. Over his shoulder, I could see a pair of red leather pants draped across a chair.

In a flash, Taggart's expression transitioned from angry to confused, to angry again. "You."

"Yeah. Me."

"What the hell are you doing here?"

"Reconnaissance. Can I come in?"

"No, you cannot come in, and if you don't leave immediately, I'll call security."

He tried to close the door, but I blocked it with my foot.

"Here's what I think," I said. "You won't call security, because it might get loud. That's bad for you, because, if I'm not mistaken, you're in a hotel room with a woman who isn't your wife. Call me crazy, but I doubt the current Mrs. Taggart would be thrilled by the news."

Behind him, I saw a woman's arm reach out and grab the leather pants and pull them out of view.

"What do you want?" Taggart said.

"My assistant has disappeared. I want the truth this time. Has Eugene Barstok contacted you?"

"You seem to have an unhealthy curiosity about my appointment calendar. Too bad it's none of your business."

"My business, police business, whatever."

He smirked. "The police aren't interested in me."

"Not now, but you never know what might pique their curiosity."

"What are you after? Money?"

"Nope. Just information. I want to know where Eugene is."

"Why should I tell you anything? What's in it for me?"

"Here's what's in it for you, Brad. You tell me what you know about Eugene, and I won't tell your wife where you were tonight."

A flicker of uncertainty ghosted across his face. "My wife already knows where I am."

I chuckled. "Seriously, do I look like the sort of person who would believe that crap?"

The sliding glass door rolled open and a woman in red leather slipped through the opening onto the hotel grounds, bumping into one of the patio chairs in her haste to leave.

Taggart glanced over his shoulder, noted the situation, and turned back to me. "I told you. I've never heard of this Eugene character. As for my private life, you can't prove anything."

"The burden of proof is on you, Brad. Tell me where you were last Thursday night."

He glared at me. "I was here."

"With Leather Pants?"

"Her name is Lisa."

"Do you and Lisa come here every Thursday?"

His smile was smug. "Sunday. Tuesday. Thursday. I come with Lisa as often as I can and wherever I can."

"Jeez, Taggart. You're still a newlywed and you're already cheating on your wife. Why bother to marry if you want to play the field?"

He shrugged off the criticism. "What can I say? I'm easily bored."

"Will Lisa corroborate your alibi?"

"See, there's your problem. I don't need an alibi."

"Actually, Brad, you need a couple of them. One for

Thursday, the night Lupe Ortiz was murdered, and one for last night, when your ex-wife got another one of those late-night hang-up calls."

"I didn't kill anybody. And as far as those calls are concerned, we've discussed that already. Why would I waste my time calling Helen?"

"Because you're a control freak. You had your life all planned out. When the time was right, you were going to leave Helen and start a new life with wife number two. But she screwed up the plan by hiring a forensic accountant to find all the money you'd squirreled away. I think that stuck in your craw."

His eyes narrowed into slits. He put his hand on the door as if he planned to slam it in my face. "This conversation is over. Get out."

"I'll leave, but I suggest you stop harassing Helen, or I'll make a few calls of my own—to the police."

"I'll take your suggestion under advisement."

"Don't mess with me, Taggart. Phone companies keep records and don't say it was your daughter who made those calls. She isn't going to commit perjury to save your sorry ass. Keep playing this game and things could get ugly. It could even make the newspapers. I suspect your company won't be impressed by the negative publicity. Your wife won't be, either. Or Lisa Leather Pants."

He stared at the door for a long time before responding. "Okay, so I might have called Helen a few times. I probably forgot about the time difference. I didn't want to disturb her sleep, so I hung up."

"But you won't call her again. Right?"

Taggart's jaw was clenched so tight I thought I heard one of his molars crack. "Right."

Then he slammed the door. As predicted, it was loud. I decided to leave before somebody came to investigate. I picked up my car from the valet and made it back to Culver City by three.

Charley was in his office, studying the list of Lupe's clients I'd gotten from Jay-Cee. Eugene hadn't been in for four days, and Charley's office looked as if it had suffered a direct hit from a category-five hurricane. Files were stacked on the floor, and wood chips from his pencil sharpener were scattered around the desktop like mulch in a fall garden. I pulled Eugene's dusting glove from his desk drawer and started to tidy up.

Charley whistled. "I never thought I'd see you doing housework, Sinclair."

"Treasure the moment, because you won't see it again."

"I stopped by Radio Shack to see what I could find out about the cell phone charger Eugene bought. The clerk remembered him coming into the store, but nothing more."

I herded the wood shavings into a wastebasket. "Guess where Brad Taggart was last Thursday night."

"I assume he wasn't in a spinning class."

"Nope. He was screwing somebody who's not his wife."

"No shit? How did you find out?"

I put the dusting glove back in the plastic bag. "I followed him to a room at the Montage. He was with some blonde, and they weren't wearing clothes. He admitted to making those calls to Helen. He made up some flimsy excuse. Said he forgot about the time change."

"Did he say anything about the kid?"

"He said Eugene never called him. I tend to believe him. He was sort of low on bargaining chips at the time."

"There's still Bob Rossi," Charley said. "The guy has a criminal record for spousal abuse. Eugene knew about his parking feud with Helen. He might have gone to see him."

"When can you talk to him?" I said.

"As soon as I contact these Jay-Cee customers."

"Look, I have some free time this afternoon," I said. "I can talk to him."

"I don't know, Sinclair."

I returned the glove to Eugene's desk drawer. "Don't worry, Charley. I'll be careful."

Bob Rossi's restaurant wouldn't be open until dinner. That left me just enough time to take care of another urgent matter. Joe Deegan.

Chapter 25

I'd made a promise to Riley to discuss the rift in her relationship with her brother, and I intended to honor it. When I told Deegan I wanted to talk, he told me he'd taken the day off and invited me to stop by his house. I hesitated at first, wondering how I'd feel about being at his place again with its Carly McKendrick–inspired French cow plates and the baby grand piano he owned but didn't play, but I finally agreed.

Deegan grew up in San Pedro, which he and everybody else in the 'hood pronounced San PEEdro. The medium-sized town is home to one of the busiest deepwater ports on the West Coast and a diverse, close-knit community comprising longshoremen, entrepreneurs, doctors, and lawyers from multiple ethnic and cultural backgrounds.

Deegan had overcome the pedestrian architecture of

his small 1960s-style ranch house by using taupe paint on the wood siding and accenting the sash and trim with charcoal and white, a color scheme that enhanced the curb appeal and gave the place a solid, no-nonsense feel, sort of like that of its owner.

He answered the door wearing a pair of jeans and a white T-shirt. Braced against his hip like a football was a blond-haired baby who looked to be around a year old. He had round blue eyes and pillow lips and wore a long-sleeved shirt and a diaper that looked as if it might blow off in a strong breeze. I was taken aback by the sight. I'd never considered Deegan father material, but watching the tenderness with which he held that baby made me realize there was a side of him I'd never seen before. A side I would never see.

"Excuse me," I said in mock surprise. "I must have the wrong house. I was looking for a homicide detective by the name of Joe Deegan."

Deegan glanced at the baby and smiled. "My nephew Andrew. It's Claudia and Matt's anniversary, so I'm babysitting for the day. Come in. We were just eating. Weren't we, Rookie?" He threw the kid in the air, which produced waves of giggles and a string of drool.

All of my senses were on alert as I stepped inside the house. I scanned the living room, searching for the scent of unfamiliar perfume, a fashion magazine that didn't belong, or a pair of black lacy panties forgotten between the cushions of the couch. Instead I saw the familiar bleached oak floors, black leather sectional, two sleek accent chairs, and the white sheepskin area rug beneath the glass-and-chrome coffee table. Off in the corner was Deegan's baby grand piano.

I followed him into the kitchen and watched as he put Andrew in a low scooter on the floor next to his retro aluminum-trimmed kitchen table.

"Did Eugene come back?" he said.

"Not yet."

"Did you report him missing?"

"It's complicated."

Deegan seemed puzzled by my comment. "So, then, what can I do for you, Tucker?"

It was jarring to hear him call me that. Before things went bad between us, he had always called me Stretch because I was long and lean like a stretch limousine. It had been his nickname for me from the first day we met.

"I want to talk to you about Riley," I said. "She says you're not speaking to her."

Andrew didn't like being confined in the scooter. He began to fuss. Deegan tried to quiet him with a few empty promises, but that didn't work, so he took a set of keys from his pocket and dangled them in front of the baby's face. Andrew grabbed the keys and began to pound them on the tray. He seemed to find this amusing. I found it loud and irritating.

"Riley was out of line," he said.

"She doesn't like your fiancée. She's entitled to her opinion."

"I don't care who she likes or doesn't like. That's not the way to handle things."

"She's trying to protect you. She doesn't want to see you hurt."

Deegan reached for a jar of baby food on the counter. "Do I look like I need protecting?"

I didn't answer right away because I didn't want to state the obvious, that everybody needed looking after now and then. Even Deegan. Maybe even me.

He twisted the lid of the glass jar. The vacuum unsealed with a whoosh. The food inside was an unappetizing pumpkin-colored puree interspersed with green chunks. He put the jar in the microwave and set the timer for twenty seconds.

"Riley is a great kid," I said.

"Yup, she is."

"She thinks you want her to give up Luv Bugs."

He took a spoon from the drawer. "What Riley does with her life is up to Riley."

"Starting a new business is hard. I'm trying to help her, but she needs your support, too."

The timer on the microwave went off. "I'll tell you what I told her. She needs to get a life and stop interfering in mine."

He took the baby food jar from the microwave and squatted in front of Andrew's scooter. He loaded food onto the spoon and aimed it for the baby's mouth.

"Aren't you going to test that to make sure it's not too hot?" I said.

Deegan cocked his head. "Excuse me? You're telling me how to feed a curtain climber? Have you even seen one of these little guys before?"

"Okay, so I'm not an expert on babies, but I read in a magazine once that you're supposed to test the temperature so you don't burn his mouth."

Deegan stuck his finger in the jar. "It's fine."

"You're supposed to test it on your lips. Lips are more sensitive than fingers."

"I'm not going anywhere near that line."

"Okay, at least blow on it."

He tried but failed to suppress a smile. "Your offer is tempting, but no."

Deegan aimed the spoon for Andrew's mouth. At the last minute, the baby turned his head. The spoon hit his cheek. Pumpkin puree spilled down his face and onto his shirt. Deegan grabbed a nearby towel and wiped the food from the baby's face.

"Would you please talk to Riley?" I said.

"I will, but first she owes Carly an apology."

I wanted to defend Riley, but Deegan was right. His sister hadn't handled the situation with much grace. In Deegan's defense, I knew what it was like when a family member hated the person you loved. I'd been engaged back in college to a man named Evan Brice. My mother thought he was bad news. It was painful to know she didn't trust my judgment, but as it turned out, she was right. Evan was bad news. I couldn't help believing that Riley was right about Carly McKendrick, too. She *would* break Deegan's heart again.

"When you love somebody," I said, "sometimes you just have to forgive them. No strings attached."

Deegan parted his lips as if he was going to say something, but he remained silent. His expression held no clue to his emotions. He set the jar of baby food on the tray and fixed his gaze on me. We studied each other for what seemed like a long time, searching for cues to what might happen next.

The silence was broken by a loud clatter. We both turned toward the scooter. Andrew had crashed the keys against the jar of baby food and toppled it over, spilling the pumpkin puree. He slapped his hand in the food, splattering it all over the tray and all over his uncle. Deegan stood and picked up the towel again, wiping the front of his shirt.

"Were there any tips in that magazine article about how to get vegetable-chicken dinner out of a clean shirt?" he said.

I put my hand over my mouth to hide my smile. "I guess I should have read the whole thing."

There was a glob of food in his hair. Without thinking, I took the towel from his hand and wiped it off. He didn't say anything. He just stood there watching me with those smoky bedroom eyes of his and an expression I couldn't quite read. We were standing so close I could smell the aroma of fabric softener on his shirt.

I don't know what came over me, but the next moment my arms were around his neck. It was as if a memory chip had malfunctioned, the one that said Deegan and I weren't together anymore, that he was engaged to somebody else. My lips brushed against his. I felt his hesitation and then release as he pulled me closer. We stayed like that for a moment, rocking together in some sort of penance dance. I knew it could be more than that if I wanted it that way, but he wouldn't make the first move. That would be up to me.

My credo had always been once a cheater, always a cheater. Now I was on the verge of initiating Deegan into that select club. I thought about the consequences of making love to him. It would feel good until Carly found out. She'd be shattered. I knew because I'd been on the receiving end of an unfaithful boyfriend. I couldn't inflict that pain on another woman, not even Carly McKendrick, who knew a thing or two about cheating.

I backed away from Deegan's embrace. "I'm sorry. I shouldn't have done that."

He took a deep breath and lowered his gaze to the floor. Andrew squealed. Deegan turned toward his nephew to see what was wrong. I used the diversion to make my way to the front door.

I sat in my car for a few minutes, wondering if Deegan would come after me. If the closed door was any indication, I might be waiting forever, so I headed to Beverly Hills to interview Bob Rossi.

Chapter 26

My car was stopped at a red light at the corner of Santa Monica and Wilshire boulevards when my cell phone rang. It was Jordan Rich, asking if I got the flowers. I'd almost forgotten about them.

"Yes. They were beautiful. Thank you."

"You sound upset. Is something wrong?"

"I have a lot on my plate right now, that's all."

"Did you find your friend?"

"Not yet."

There was a long pause. "I'm sorry. How can I help?"

The light turned green and I headed into the intersection. "You can't, but thanks, anyway."

"I have an airplane," he said. "I can fly you anywhere you need to go, or I can just sit with you. I wouldn't even talk if you didn't feel like it. I'd just be there if you needed me."

"I'll let you know."

Jordan was quiet for a moment.

"Will you come to dinner with me Friday night?" he said. "I don't know about you, but I need some intelligent conversation." When I didn't answer right away, he added, "No pressure. Just dinner. You have to eat."

"Okay," I said. "Dinner sounds good."

After I hung up, I had a flash of clarity. I'd almost pulled a Deegan, turning down a perfectly sincere offer of help. I wondered what had happened in our collective experiences that made us always choose to go it alone. I suspected it had something to do with fear.

It was around five thirty by the time I got to Beverly Hills. The restaurant wasn't open yet, but the door to the service entrance was unlocked. The narrow hallway led me past a kitchen filled with the sounds of clattering pots and pans, and into a back room of the restaurant where I found Bob Rossi sitting at a table, folding napkins.

He looked up, startled. "We're not open yet."

"I need to speak with you about Lupe Ortiz."

"Are you a cop?"

"No."

"Then I have nothing to say to you."

"You're serving chocolates from Nectar in your restaurant. I know all of Helen's clients, and you're not one of them. So my question is, How are you getting them?"

His jaw muscles twitched, but he didn't respond. He just kept folding.

"Did you have some kind of deal with Lupe Ortiz?" I went on. "Maybe the chocolates were an even exchange for dinner, or maybe you just used the food to distract her while you raided Helen's store."

He pushed his chair back so hard it toppled over. "Get out of my restaurant."

"Either you talk to me or you talk to the police. Frankly, I'd choose me, because you already have a criminal record. Do you really need another arrest added to your rap sheet?"

Rossi's hands were balled into fists. He seemed to be fighting to control his rage. "What do you want?"

"Where were you Thursday night between six thirty and eight thirty?"

He paused before answering. "I had an appointment with my shrink."

"For anger-management classes?"

He smirked. "No. I finished those, but I'm still angry. Can't you tell? I didn't like the doc I was seeing, so I found somebody else, a lady this time."

"And she'll verify you were with her?"

He picked up the chair and set it upright. "You think I'm stupid enough to lie about that? Of course she'll tell you I was there."

"You brought Lupe dinner every night. Why?"

Rossi sat down and started folding again. "Because I'm a nice guy."

"How did you get into the store?"

"She always left the door unlocked."

"So you had an open invitation?"

"Yeah. So what? I felt sorry for her, having a no-good son like she did."

"How did you even know she had a son?"

"I broke up a fight between those two one night out in the alley. The kid was screwed up on drugs. I recognized the symptoms."

"So she owed you big time, and you decided to take it out in chocolates."

"You have it all figured out, don't you?"

"Not all of it," I said. "Why don't you fill in the blanks?"

"Why should I?"

"Better to tell me than the police."

He stared at the napkin in his hand as if he was weighing his options. "A bigwig studio executive came in for dinner one night with a party of eight. They all got drunk. Mr. Bigwig wanted chocolates, and not just any kind. He wanted Nectar chocolates. He started to get loud. If he'd been anybody else, I would have thrown him out, but you don't alienate politicians or Hollywood suits if you want to be in business next week."

"So you went next door and asked Lupe if you could raid the refrigerator."

His neck turned red. "She didn't know. I took a few when I brought her dinner. I figured nobody would ever miss them."

"One bigwig doesn't account for all of Helen's missing inventory."

"Okay, so maybe I did it a few more times. I lost a lot of money because of Helen Taggart. She owed me."

"Did you get chocolates on Thursday, too?"

He held his hands palms up in a gesture of mock surrender. "My shrink is a chocoholic. So sue me."

"My assistant is missing. I think he was looking into the murder of Lupe Ortiz. His name is Eugene Barstok. I'm wondering if he stopped by the restaurant to see you."

"Never heard of the guy."

I took the photograph of Eugene from my purse and showed it to him. "He may have been using another name."

Rossi studied the picture and frowned. "He looks like a guy I saw arguing with one of my valets last Saturday night, except he wasn't your assistant. He was a reporter."

"From the *New York Times*?"

"No. *National Geographic*."

Eugene was branching out.

"Is the valet working tonight?"

"Not tonight or any night. I fired him. He dented the fender of a customer's Bentley later that night. I gave him his final paycheck and told him to hit the road."

"How can I reach him?"

Rossi picked up the stack of napkins he'd folded, and I followed him to a busing station, where he offloaded the napkins into a storage cabinet.

"I don't know. I think he moved back to Avalon."

"On Catalina Island?"

"Yeah. He used to work at a golf cart–rental place on Casino Way. He might try to get his old job back."

Rossi told me the kid's name was Aidan Malloy. I had to talk to him. He spoke with Eugene on Saturday night, and he might have some idea where he was headed next.

Jordan Rich and I were having dinner the following evening. I hoped he'd be willing to have lunch instead—in Avalon. We could get there on the ferry, but it would be so much faster to fly.

Chapter 27

When I got home that night, I found a troubling message from my mother. Pookie was in Santa Barbara, but said she planned to be home sometime the following day. The tension in her voice worried me, but I almost didn't want to know what was bothering her. I had too many problems of my own to worry about.

All that deep contemplation was giving me a headache. I had to prove to myself I wasn't a total loner, so I called Venus and told her about Jordan Rich's offer to fly me to Avalon to question Aidan Malloy.

"He seems so strong and supportive," I said.

"Jockstraps are strong and supportive. Don't commit until you see his four-oh-one K. Any word on Eugene?"

"No. I'm worried, Venus."

"He's tougher than you think. He'll be okay."

At about nine p.m., I dialed Charley Tate's number. I was surprised when he suggested we meet at an Irish pub in Santa Monica for a Guinness and some conversation. The truth was, I didn't want to be alone, so I told him I could be there in half an hour.

O'Reilly's Pub was dark and brimming with attitude when I walked through the door. The room resonated with music and the chatter of men sharing a pint and a few war stories with anybody who'd listen. It took a moment to spot Charley sitting at a table in a corner, hunched over a glass filled with dark liquid. He looked glum. I strolled over and slid into a chair across from him.

"I'm surprised Lorna let you out of the house this late."

"Lorna doesn't care where I go these days. She told me if I wasn't going to give her a kid, there was no reason for us to be together."

I studied his expression but saw no sign he was teasing me.

"So what happens next?" I said.

He just shook his head. "Nothing. She'll get over it. By the way, I found out what kind of car Rossi drives. A Toyota Maxima."

"No Mercedes?"

"Nope."

"Interesting, but it doesn't matter anymore. Rossi didn't kill Lupe Ortiz. He was with his shrink on Thursday evening. What did you find at Garvey Motors?"

"Nothing. They wouldn't give me squat, except to say they sold twenty black Benzes last month."

"I'm getting desperate, Charley. The longer Eugene is out there on his own, the greater likelihood he'll run into trouble. He's looking for the person who gave Lupe that chocolate pot. We have to find him before Eugene does."

"I still think Ortiz could have killed his mother. The timeline is tight, but if the traffic gods were with him that night—"

"Roberto told me he didn't do it."

Charley tilted his head back to take a drink of his beer but his gaze didn't leave mine. "Dopers lie."

"And sometimes they die and can't clear their names."

"The truth will come out one way or the other."

I let his words settle in the air. "You always taught me to keep an open mind, Charley. Blaming Roberto for his mother's death seems too easy. We need to look beyond the obvious. How are you coming with the list of Lupe's customers?"

He stared into his beer. "Nothing to report yet. I'm still working through the names."

"Hurry, Charley. Okay?"

He nodded. "I hope to have some answers by tomorrow. Call me as soon as you get back from Avalon."

Chapter 28

The following morning before leaving for the airport to meet Jordan Rich, I called Nerine to see if she'd heard from Eugene.

"Who?" Her voice sounded way too mellow. Either she was having an early morning Booker's or she was in insulin shock from all those cookies.

"Your son . . . Eugene. Have you heard from him yet?"

"No, dear, I haven't, and I'm running out of sugar. Can you drop by the store and bring me some next time you're in the neighborhood?"

"Yeah, sure. Whatever."

I hung up and started packing a bag for Muldoon, who was spending the day with Mrs. D. We were just heading out the door when the telephone rang. It was Mr. Winn from the retirement home.

"I found a message from Eugene," he said. "I never

check my answering machine. I don't see very well, and I'm always in my room to answer the telephone. His call came in this morning at seven. I must have been at breakfast."

My heart was pounding. "What did he say?"

"He was sorry he didn't come last Saturday, but he'd be back for our usual get-together tomorrow."

"Anything else?"

"He said the capital of Arizona was still Phoenix, but there was a new capital of California. North Hollywood. I think he just made that up to tease me."

North Hollywood was a town in the San Fernando Valley and certainly not the capital of California. I wondered what Eugene meant by it. Maybe he'd found some evidence linking the city to the chocolate pot. If so, he was closing in on a killer, which meant he was in more danger than ever.

Armed with the photo of Eugene, I drove to the Long Beach airport to meet Jordan Rich for our flight to Catalina. I hadn't been to the island in years. I remembered it as rustic and quaint, an unspoiled treasure twenty-six miles across the sea from a string of crowded cities linked by ribbons of freeway. At one time or another, Catalina had been home to Native Americans, Spanish explorers, Yankee smugglers, and Union soldiers. In 1919, William Wrigley Jr., the chewing gum mogul, bought controlling interest of the island and turned it into a playground for sport fishermen, yachtsmen, and Hollywood celebrities. The island was now under the control of the Catalina Island Conservancy, whose mission was to preserve the land for posterity.

Once at the airport, I turned into the hangar parking area under the SIGNATURE AVIATION sign and left the Boxster in the visitor's area. I found Jordan inside the hangar, looking through a metal binder.

A young man stood behind the counter, speaking to him. "The seven-twenty X is right outside. Oil is checked, windshield cleaned, and preflight complete."

Jordan nodded but kept reading, as if he appreciated the information but preferred to verify it himself. I didn't want to disturb him, so I paused by the door to watch. He was dressed casually. His hair was ruffled by the wind, which made him seem boyish, but it was the compassion in his eyes that made him handsome. I waited until he set the binder down before walking toward him.

He flashed a warm smile when he saw me. "Are you ready to go?"

"I think so. What's that book you were just reading? I hope it wasn't *Flying for Dummies*."

He laughed. I was glad, because I hadn't meant to offend him.

"It's an aircraft logbook," he said. "I always check the maintenance history myself. Good pilots don't take anything for granted."

"That's comforting news."

I followed him through the hangar. Just outside the door, I spotted a miniature airplane perched on three toylike tires. I was hoping it was some kind of horrible mistake. The thing looked too frail to play with, much less to fly.

"This is your airplane?" I said.

"Actually, no. I have a Cessna Citation at John Wayne in Orange County. It's perfect for long-distance trips, like to Central America, but the Catalina runway is too short for the jet, so I borrowed this Piper Warrior from a buddy of mine. He's too busy with work to fly much, so he's always trying to get me to take it out more."

Contrary to its menacing name, the Piper Warrior didn't look as if it would fare well in a fight. Jordan and I climbed onto the wing and into the airplane. Then he settled into the pilot's seat and focused on his preflight ritual.

"Here. Put this on," Jordan said, laying a pair of large earmuffs in my lap. "The headset has a voice-activated hot microphone intercom. Talk in a normal voice and I'll hear you just fine. You can also hear me talk on the radio to Air Traffic Control, so that might be a good time to just listen."

Jordan Rich was telling me to keep my mouth shut. He didn't know me well enough to realize it was a risky move and not for the faint of heart. He saved himself by flashing a teasing smile to show he meant no offense. He fastened my seat belt and then his. A moment later, a twin-engine aircraft swung around in front of us, blasting the Piper with a gust of air so strong it made the airplane shudder.

"Maybe I should just interview Aidan Malloy on the telephone," I said.

Jordan smiled. "Don't worry. It's just prop wash."

Prop wash or not, the mini Piper wasn't winning any points with me.

Jordan shouted out the window. "Clear!" He put on

his headset and glanced around the airplane. A moment later, he engaged the starter. The Piper shook. Instrument dials spun into position. Panel lights flickered on.

"Are you sure this thing can fly?" I shouted over the noise.

Jordan raised a finger and tapped one ear of his headset. I slipped mine on and glanced around the cockpit, looking for parachutes.

Jordan's voice echoed through the headset. "We have a beautiful day for flying. You're going to like this."

Yeah, sure. Easy for him to say.

"Long Beach tower," he said. "Piper seven-twenty X at Signature, with information Kilo, ready for taxi. VFR to Catalina."

I heard an unfamiliar voice. "Piper seven-twenty X cleared to taxi to runway three-zero via Alpha, Foxtrot, Bravo, altimeter twenty-nine-point-ninety-seven inches."

Jordan responded. "Long Beach tower, Piper seven-twenty X is ready for takeoff, runway three-zero."

"Roger—cleared for takeoff. Wind three-ten at twelve knots."

I was so concerned about ceding control to a man I barely knew that I didn't notice the Piper lifting off the runway. Below us, the airport, the freeways, and soon the entire Southern California coastline slipped away as the airplane climbed in a gentle banking turn across the beach and headed out toward the Pacific Ocean.

We were in the air less than thirty minutes when Jordan said, "Okay, here's something you should know.

The runway at Catalina is safe, but depending on the weather, the approach and landing can be either a nonevent or very challenging. In a minute, you'll see a fifteen-hundred-foot cliff in the distance. Gusty winds come up that slope. They can make for a bumpy ride. I'll put us down in the first five hundred feet, but it may be a little rough."

My breathing felt shallow. "Sounds tricky."

Jordan scanned the skies, looking for air traffic. "Not really, but you have to pay attention."

All I could think was *What happens if you don't?*

As we approached the airport, I saw a barren hill dotted with sagebrush and a narrow strip of pavement that dropped off into nowhere. Beyond the cliff was nothing but the endless blue of the Pacific Ocean. It felt as if we were about to land on an aircraft carrier in the middle of nowhere. I hoped Jordan would tell me if we got into trouble. If my life was going to flash before my eyes, I wanted time to watch the show.

Despite my image of flaming wreckage, Jordan kept the Piper steady, countering the destabilizing gusts of wind with practiced ease. The airplane lightly touched down with an audible tire chirp and rolled smoothly to the runway exit. There was no control tower in Avalon, but nevertheless Jordan announced our arrival to no one in particular.

"Catalina Traffic. Piper seven-twenty X clear of runway twenty-five."

Jordan switched off the engine and removed his headset. I studied him for a long, pensive moment, admiring his capable handling of the flight and his jittery passenger. Surgeon. Pilot. Humanitarian. Nice guy. He could do it all. If he wanted to add a relationship with me to his resume, it would likely be a bigger challenge than landing at the Avalon airport.

When I planted my feet on terra firma, I began to breathe normally. The wind had cleared away the clouds. The air was crisp and the sun warmed my face. We walked to the terminal building and boarded a van that took us along a winding road through the arid hills. We passed a herd of mangy buffalo, which, according to the driver, was brought to the island in the twenties to work as extras in a movie. When the film wrapped, the actors and crew went back to the mainland. The buffalo stayed on the island. I hoped they were still getting residuals, because it could be a long time until their next acting gig.

Twenty-five minutes later we arrived in Avalon, the larger of two small towns on Santa Catalina Island. We strolled along Casino Way, a narrow walking street lined with palm trees and small shops. Beyond the small, pebbly beach was a harbor filled with dozens of boats tethered to white mooring balls.

We found the golf cart–rental stand where Aidan Malloy had once worked, but he wasn't there. His former boss told us he had taken a job as a busboy at the Catalina Country Club, so we hiked a short distance up the hill, past a row of Hansel and Gretel cottages, where we found Aidan Malloy filling saltshakers at a busing station on the patio outside the restaurant.

Malloy was a lanky, good-looking kid in his late teens. He told us he'd moved to L.A. to find work as an actor. He'd been living with an aunt in Rancho Park and supporting himself by working at Rossi's restaurant while he waited for Hollywood to come calling. He'd grown up on the island, where the main mode of transportation was golf cart, so he wasn't an experienced driver. Denting the Bentley had dampened his hunger for life in the big city. Getting fired was the tipping point. He decided to come home to rethink his future. I showed him the photo of Eugene and asked if he was the person he spoke to on Saturday night.

"That's the guy," he said. "He told me he was a reporter, investigating the murder of that cleaning woman. He wanted to know if I was working the night she died."

"And were you?"

Aidan unscrewed the caps of all of the saltshakers and began wiping them with a towel. "Yeah. From six till eleven. He was interested in a car I saw parked behind the chocolate shop."

"A black Mercedes with a dealer plate from Garvey Motors in Alhambra?"

He eyes opened wide in surprise. "Yeah. How'd you know?"

"Just a wild guess."

"Wow. That's awesome."

"Not really. I saw it, too, around eight fifteen."

Aidan began filling each shaker with salt from a carton. "I drove through that alley about a million times a night, checking for parking spaces. I saw everybody who parked there. The Mercedes came at about seven thirty."

"Did you see anybody going in or out of the store?" I said.

"I saw the cleaning woman come out earlier in the evening. I can't remember what time it was. She was throwing a plastic sack into the Dumpster."

Jordan was leaning against a nearby wall, watching me operate. He listened intently but didn't interfere. The guy was perfect.

"Did you recognize the driver of the Mercedes?" I said.

"He was all dressed up, so I figured he was one of the owners."

"Dressed up how?"

"Suit. Tie. You know, geezer wear."

"Was he tall, short, young, old?"

Aidan topped off the shakers and replaced the caps. "I'm eighteen. Everybody looks old to me. It was dark outside, but he seemed like average height."

"What else did Eugene ask you?"

"A bunch of questions, mostly about Mr. Rossi. I told him what I knew, which wasn't much. He almost blew a gasket when I told him about the cell phone I found by the Dumpster Thursday night."

My gaskets were ready to blow, too. "What did it look like?"

"It was a girl's phone, real dorky. And purple. It had all these sparkly things pasted all over it. The battery was dead, so there was no way to find the owner. I kept it for a few days in case somebody came back asking for it, but nobody ever did. I finally tossed it out when I got to work on Saturday."

Helen Taggart had described Lupe Ortiz's cell phone as purple and gaudy. It had been missing since the night of the murder, at least according to Detective O'Brien. The phone had to be Lupe's. She must have dropped it when she went out to empty the trash.

"Where did you toss it?"

"In a trash can on Bedford."

"So what happened next?"

"Your friend wanted to leave his old Volvo by the curb for a few minutes. He couldn't find a place to park, and he wanted to see if the phone was still there."

"Nectar was closed. Why didn't he use those spaces?"

Aidan held his palms up in a gesture of apology. "There were already cars parked there."

"So you let him stay?"

"I felt sorry for him, but I told him he had to be back in ten minutes—max. He said okay, but he didn't come back for half an hour. Man, I was sweating bullets. It was only a matter of time before Rossi noticed the guy wasn't in the restaurant. He gets totally freaked out about parking because it's hard to find space for the customers."

"Did Eugene find the phone?"

"Yeah, but I guess it took him a while to fish it out. Boy, was it ever grody. I told him the battery was dead, but he kept trying to find a signal, anyway. When he couldn't get it to work, he asked me where the nearest Radio Shack was so he could buy a charger. I told him not to bother. It was cheaper to buy a new phone."

I was proud of Eugene. It took an enormous amount

of courage for a world-class germophobe like him to scavenge through a garbage can looking for clues. He obviously bought the charger, because I'd found the Radio Shack receipt in his desk drawer.

"What else did he say?"

"Not much. I saw Rossi watching us. I told him to move his car, and he did."

"Did he say where he was going next?"

Aidan finished with the salt and began the same ritual with the pepper shakers, starting with the caps. "He said something about the CIA. I thought he was full of it, but he paid the valet fee and tipped me ten bucks, so what did I care?"

I didn't understand why Eugene wanted to talk to the CIA, but I was pretty sure they wouldn't want to talk to a fake reporter. I imagined him being held in an undisclosed prison in a country that ended in *stan*.

"Did he say who at the CIA he planned to contact?"

"The guy's not with the agency anymore. He's some kind of teacher at Santa Monica College."

Dale Ewing taught there, too. It was a big place, but maybe he'd heard of a colleague who once worked for the CIA. As soon as I got back to the mainland, I planned to ask him about it.

A middle-aged woman wearing a white chef's apron came out of the bar. She put her hands on her hips and glared at Aidan.

"Look," he said, "you have to go, or I'll get fired from my second job in a week. That would be a record, even for me."

I gave him my business card and asked him to call

if he thought of anything more. Jordan and I returned to the main drag and bought a couple of burgers from Eric's on the Pier. After that, we walked to Descanso Beach, where we sat on a retaining wall overlooking the bay and had an impromptu picnic.

Jordan told me he was from Chicago, an only child. His father was a judge. His mother raised money for various charities. He'd attended Yale as an undergrad, and Harvard University Medical School. Although he didn't say, I gathered the family money went back more than just a couple of generations. Regardless of whether his money was ancient or merely old, Jordan Rich had lived a life of privilege. Maybe his name had been a self-fulfilling prophecy.

My story wasn't as straightforward. I told him my mother was a working actor who wasn't always working, until she married an aging hippie yoga teacher with memory lapses and a trust fund. He listened to my story. Said it sounded like an interesting life. *Maybe*, I thought, *but not when you're living it*.

"Have you ever been married?" he said.

"Once. You?"

"I was engaged, but we never set the date."

"Don't tell me she cheated on you and you found out."

He was quiet for a moment. "Nothing so dramatic. The truth is we had different priorities. We just grew apart. I'm glad we found out before things got complicated."

We retraced our path along Casino Way, stopping at Big Olaf's for a homemade waffle cone before heading to the van station. It had been a pleasant day, but Eugene was still missing and I had to find him. For some reason, he wasn't checking in with me. Either he didn't want to or he couldn't. I just hoped it was the former.

I pondered what I'd learned about Eugene's movements so far. On Saturday, he found Herbert Osteen on the Internet and called his wife. He stopped by Nectar that night to search the alley behind the store where he found Lupe's cell phone. Later, he drove to Radio Shack to buy a charger.

On Sunday morning, he packed a bag and told his mother he was going away on business. Maybe he planned to drive to Montecito. If so, he never made it. He may have collected enough information from Osteen on the telephone to make the trip unnecessary. Osteen told him about quetzal feathers and chocolate pots, and referred him to Marianne Rogers at the Natural History Museum.

Eugene left a message on my machine on Monday, telling me he was okay but he'd gone deep undercover. He also visited Marianne Rogers and learned about the stolen chocolate pot. If Eugene suspected the pot was an authentic relic of an ancient culture, he would have tried to find out where Helen got it. Maybe he already knew. He'd been talking to her on the telephone every day and had learned her whole life story.

On Tuesday, Eugene called Lupe's cousin to learn the name of the customer who'd given her the pot. Connie didn't know, but during that call he found out about Lupe's difficult life in Guatemala.

Roberto Ortiz had told me the chocolate pot's former

owner had called Lupe so many times she no longer answered her telephone. If Eugene had been able to read her call history, the numbers he found might have led him straight to her killer.

Charley was on the trail of Lupe's customers, so I decided to contact Dale Ewing and ask him if he knew a former CIA agent who now taught at Santa Monica College. Finding the guy was a long shot, but Ewing was a friendly informant; at least that's what I thought.

Chapter 29

Despite Friday-afternoon traffic, by three o'clock I made it from the Long Beach airport to my office, where I tried but failed to reach Dale Ewing. When I searched the Santa Monica College Web site looking for information on his classes, I discovered he taught a three-unit political science class called International Politics, which explored the "issues of war and peace among states in the international system." It was a topic that needed more attention than a three-day-a-week course at a community college, but at least it was a start. The class was held every Monday, Wednesday, and Friday from 2:45 to 4:05 p.m. I didn't want to compete for Ewing's attention with hoards of students, so I called the school and learned he held office hours immediately following his classes. I decided to arrive early so I'd be first in line.

Ewing's office was a small cubbyhole in a building on the main campus. I tried the door, but it was locked. I looked up and down the hallway. Nobody was around. I paced for a few minutes, reading notes on the bulletin board—students looking for a ride home for Thanksgiving break and notices for herbal weight-loss remedies.

My watch read 4:10. Ewing's class had been over for five minutes. I hadn't booked an appointment. I gambled he'd come back to his office before leaving campus, even if he had no formal appointments. If he didn't show, I'd try calling again, but I preferred talking to him in person. Charley claimed it was easier to read people when you sat face-to-face. I didn't know how far away the room was from his office, so I decided to wait a little longer.

Ewing's schedule wasn't posted outside the door. Maybe it was inside, taped to the wall. The lock looked flimsy. I could probably defeat it with the lock-picking set Charley had given me. I reasoned that it was only illegal if you got caught. I was still warring with the idea when I heard footsteps coming toward me.

I turned to see a young woman wearing skinny jeans and a black hooded sweatshirt. She was carrying a stack of books. Her eyes were wide with wonder and her body was ripe for trouble. She shifted the books to her left arm, took a set of keys from the pocket of her hoodie, and unlocked the office door.

"Excuse me," I said. "I'm waiting for Dale Ewing. Do you know where he is?"

With the keys still in the lock, she pulled a tissue

from her pocket and wiped her nose. "He'll be here in a few minutes. I'm just dropping off some books. Do you want to wait in the office? At least there's a place to sit."

"That would be great. Thanks."

She sneezed and blew into the soggy tissue.

"You have a cold?" I said.

"Allergies. Every November when the Santa Ana winds blow."

"I have a friend with the same problem. He uses an air purifier."

"Yeah? Maybe I'll try one. Nothing else seems to help."

She opened the door and waved me in. Ewing's office was the size of a large closet, with room enough for a desk and a couple of file cabinets. Several cardboard boxes were stacked in a corner. On the desk were copies of journals and what looked like student exam papers. I sat on a chair and waited.

The student's nasal passages vibrated as she tried to breathe. "I'm Pooh, by the way, Dale's research assistant."

Pooh? It was all I could do to keep from asking her if she'd found Eeyore's missing tail, or if Piglet had really seen a Heffalump in the Hundred Acre Wood.

"Tucker Sinclair. How long have you worked for Dale?"

She set the books and her backpack on the desk. "About six months. I take every class he teaches. He's sort of a mentor of mine."

"So," I said, "what does your mentor do for you?"

She had a dreamy look in her eyes. "Dale's just there for me all the time. He lets me use his office to study. He gives me suggestions for class papers and edits my work. Right now he's trying to get me an internship for next semester."

Based on the gaga expression on her face when she mentioned Ewing's name, I gathered Pooh was infatuated. I wondered how Ewing felt about her and if Helen had been barred from his house because of paint fumes or editing complications. I was beginning to suspect everybody had a secret agenda.

"What kind of internship?" I said.

"He thinks I should be an analyst for the CIA when I get out of school. My dad is a software engineer, so he's taught me a lot about computers. Dale says the government is looking for people like me."

I cocked my head and frowned. "How do you get a job with a spy agency?"

"They recruit on campus for permanent jobs, but not for internships. Dale has juice with some big mucky-muck with the agency in Washington, D.C., so he wrote a letter of recommendation for me. I'm still waiting to hear back."

"How does Dale Ewing know this guy?"

"He used to work for the CIA. He doesn't tell a lot of people, so please don't spread it around."

I remembered Ewing's use of *collateral damage* that day in Helen's condo. At the time, I'd thought he'd been in the military. I would never have guessed the CIA. He didn't seem the type. Despite Ewing's confidence in Pooh, she was going to make a lousy spy.

Somebody needed to tell her that loose lips sink ships. If she told *me* about Ewing's secret past, she'd likely told others.

"What did he do for the CIA?"

"I shouldn't say."

"Come on, Pooh. You've already told me he worked for the agency. I promise not to tell anyone else. I'm just curious. That's all."

Behind me I heard a man's voice answer. "I was a political analyst, a desk jockey."

I glanced toward the door and saw Dale Ewing walking into the room, wearing his signature tweed jacket and carrying a stack of notebooks.

"Among other things," he went on, "I researched political decision-making processes of various European Union members and attended a lot of embassy cocktail parties."

I took a deep breath, searching for an appropriate response. "Does Helen know?"

He set the notebooks on his desk. "Of course she does."

"Would she have told anybody else?"

"She may have. Pooh's correct. I don't broadcast my resume, but it's hardly a secret."

"Did my assistant call you in the past few days?"

Ewing wrinkled his forehead as if that would help him remember. "Eugene? No, but if he called my house, I may have missed it. I've been moving furniture, getting ready for the painters. I accidentally pulled out the telephone cord and broke the plastic clip. I had to drive to the hardware store to get a new one."

Pooh's cheeks were turning scarlet.

"What's wrong?" I said to her.

She swallowed hard and looked at Ewing. "He called last night when I was here working on a class assignment. He said Helen Taggart told him you used to work for the CIA in Guatemala, and he had some questions to ask you about the civil war."

My gaze darted to Ewing. "You were stationed in Guatemala?"

He crossed his arms over his chest in a defensive posture. "Yes, and please don't give me grief about the CIA's role in the civil war. It was wrong. Okay?"

Pooh collapsed in the chair behind Ewing's desk. "I told Eugene I'd written a paper about the war."

Ewing shot her a benevolent smile. "I suggested Pooh write about the conflict because it has some thought-provoking historical issues and a legacy that's still alive today in L.A."

"How so?" I said.

"Many Guatemalans came here during the war and applied for asylum. It's taken years or even decades for those cases to reach the courts. Now that they have, the government is ruling against them. Thousands of people have already been deported."

"I told Eugene all that," Pooh said, "but it wasn't what he wanted to know. He asked where he could find old police records about a theft from some museum in Guatemala City. I told him I didn't know. He'd have to call back and talk to you."

Eugene had talked to Aidan Malloy on Saturday and told him he was planning to contact the CIA. That was almost a week ago. I wondered why he'd waited so long to call Ewing. Maybe he hadn't yet put all the puzzle pieces together.

Ewing checked his watch. "He hasn't called yet. Sorry we couldn't be of more help. Pooh and I are going for coffee. Would you care to join us?"

"No, thanks," I said. "I have work to do."

It was comforting to learn Eugene was still alive and well, but I had a creepy feeling he was getting too close to the truth for his own good. The clock was ticking. I just hoped Charley could find the former owner of the Mayan spouted chocolate pot—and soon.

I still thought it was possible Lupe's killer was the same person who broke into Helen's condo. Charley hadn't had much success interviewing her neighbors, but that had been on a Friday. Tomorrow was Saturday. People would be home from work. I planned to make another sweep of the condo complex to see what I could find.

Chapter 30

As soon as I arrived at the cottage, I brought Muldoon home from Mrs. D's place. He looked hungry, so I scrounged around in the refrigerator, looking for something for us to eat. I'd already served the panini, which limited my choices to a tub of sour cream that had expired two months before and a sack of petrified baby carrots. There was still a can of politically correct, environmentally aware dog food and a handful of kibble, which was good news for Muldoon and bad news for me. The market wasn't far away, but the thought of pushing a cart down the aisle and waiting in the checkout line sounded like too much effort. Muldoon ate the dog food, and I dipped a couple of sweet pickles in a glob of peanut butter and called it dinner.

After that, Muldoon and I retired to the couch and listened to Bill Withers sing, "Lean on me when you're not strong." It made me think of Jordan Rich and all the reasons there were to fall for him. He was intelligent, kind, compassionate, and financially secure. I swept that last word from the list as an invalid reason to fall in love. Security was for quitters.

Somewhere in the middle of "Grandma's Hands," Muldoon started barking. A moment later, I heard a knock on the side door. I crept to the window and peeked outside. A petite blonde wearing a puffy ski jacket that made her look like a plus-sized Teddy bear stood on the deck. It was my mother, looking droopy and tired. When I opened the door, Muldoon stopped for a quick hello before racing toward a flock of gulls on the beach.

"Are you sure you were at a retreat, Pookie? You don't look very relaxed."

She leaned over and picked up a suitcase, triggering multiple alarms in my head. My mother used to live with me. Then she met Bruce and he'd moved in for a while, too. I loved my mother, but I wasn't ready to have either of them as roommates again.

"What's going on?" I said.

She walked passed me into the house. "I thought I'd stay with you for a couple of days."

"Pookie—"

"I need a quiet place to think."

"Do you hear all that barking out on the beach? That doesn't sound very quiet. Besides, how can rooming with me be more peaceful than the Happy Baby pose on one of Kismet's cushy yoga mats?"

Pookie continued down the hall toward the spare bedroom. "I can't think with Bruce around."

I left the door open a crack so Muldoon could get back inside. Then I followed my mother, wondering if the same cosmic vacuum that had sucked out Bruce's brain had attacked hers, too.

"Bruce is an annoying distraction," I said, "but he's your annoying distraction. Why mess with a good thing?"

Pookie set her suitcase on the bed. "Things change."

Her comment surprised me. My mother knew I didn't approve of Bruce. I thought she could have done better, but she wasn't defending him as she normally did. That was a bad sign. She opened the suitcase and began sorting clothes. Clean ones on hangers. Dirty ones in a pile on the floor. She must have come to my house without stopping by her apartment to repack. Another bad sign.

"Okay," I said, "what's going on?"

She stopped sorting and met my gaze. "My agent called while we were up north. I've been cast as the lead in an independent film directed by Raj Territo."

The name sounded familiar. It took me a moment to remember why. Territo had won a Best Director Oscar a few years back for an indie film that took the world by storm.

"Is he still big in Hollywood?"

"The biggest."

"Do you want the part?"

"Are you kidding? It's like a dream come true. The

script is brilliant. Most actors wait their whole careers to find a part like this."

"That's great news. Congratulations."

She picked up a denim jacket with the word JACKIE embroidered on the back. It was the name of the character she'd played ten years before in *The Hot L Baltimore*. The jacket had been part of a costume she'd been allowed to keep when the play closed.

"Filming starts next week in Toronto," she said.

I sat on the bed next to the suitcase. "Uh-oh."

"Right. Uh-oh. Bruce doesn't want me to go."

"I'm sure he doesn't, but he's got to understand what a great opportunity this is for you."

"He doesn't understand. He wants me to say no. We've been arguing about it for days. This film role may be *my* dream, but Kismet is *his*. He thinks I'm trying to destroy it."

Dueling dreams seemed to be the penultimate problem couples faced. What came next was usually the division of community property in the divorce.

"Bruce can manage the studio for a couple of weeks," I said. "Petal can help him."

"Petal is going back to school next quarter. She can only work on weekends. Besides, Bruce says he can't run the studio by himself, even with Petal."

"Then you'll just have to hire somebody. A temp."

The suitcase was empty now. Pookie snapped the latch shut just as Muldoon rejoined us after his run with the gulls. His tongue was hanging out and his paws were covered with sand. He glanced at the pile of clothes on the floor, and moved over to claim them as his bed. Pookie set the suitcase in the closet and closed the door.

"Bruce doesn't want strangers working at Kismet," she said.

"He can't have it all his way. He has to compromise."

"He says Kismet was built with his money, and I agreed to help him run it. He thinks I should honor my commitment."

"Why is he pulling that 'my money' crapola on you now? This is a community-property state. You're married. What's his is yours and vice versa. Besides, you put as much of your blood, sweat, and tears into that place as he did. The studio is up and running. He followed his dream. Now he should let you follow yours."

Pookie moved Muldoon off the pile of dirty clothes and headed for the laundry area. "He doesn't see it that way."

I trailed behind her. "Look, Pookie. You're pushing fifty-two. Opportunities like this don't come along that often anymore. This could be your last chance."

"I know, Tucker. I just have to think it through."

The solution was clear to me, but it wasn't my marriage or my future at stake. My mother would have to wrestle with the issues and make her own decisions.

She'd just poured soap under the running water of the washing machine when I remembered the spouted chocolate pot was still in the dryer. I pulled it out, wondering why Marianne Rogers hadn't called me back. That must be some kind of family emergency she was dealing with. I could identify. I'd had a few of those myself.

"What's that?" Pookie said, pointing to the box.

That's when I realized she didn't know Eugene was deep undercover. She didn't know anything.

"I'll tell you, but it's a long story."

She closed the lid of the washing machine. "Will I need a glass of wine?"

"Yup. Maybe more than one."

While Pookie wrestled the cork out of a bottle of Sauvignon Blanc, I looked around the house for a hiding spot for the chocolate pot. The garage wasn't secure. Every place else seemed too obvious. I thought about leaving the box at Mrs. D's house, but she got woozy after a couple of martinis and had a history of breaking vases. I finally hid the box in a ratty cooler in a cupboard above the washing machine. I just hoped it would be safe there until I could drop it by the museum.

Pookie nestled into the cushions of the living room couch next to Muldoon and his yellow cashmere sweater. I sat in an adjacent chair and told her about Lupe's death and Eugene's undercover search to find her killer. I laid out all of the contacts he'd made in the past several days, just to keep them straight in my own mind.

She curled her body into a tiny ball. "I just hope you don't get sucked into another situation where you could get hurt."

"Charley's in charge of the investigation. I'm just helping out."

"How is he, anyway?"

I told her about Lorna Tate pushing Charley to have a baby, which I realized was yet another example of a dream conflict. Lorna wanted a baby. Charley wanted Lorna. Maybe there wasn't much of a conflict after all.

"I think it's sweet she wants his baby," Pookie said.

I raised my eyebrows in surprise. "Charley will be close to eighty when the kid starts college."

"So? By that time they'll have had a good eighteen years together. I think men enjoy children more when they come later in life. He might love being a father again."

I wanted to say, *Yeah, when pigs fly*, but I realized Pookie might be right. Charley could be cranky sometimes, but he was a stand-up guy. He'd make a good father. His resistance might soften if Lorna stopped forcing the issue and let him get used to the idea.

"I feel petty complaining about my acting career when your life is falling apart," she said. "I mean, seriously. What else could happen?"

That's when I told her about Joe Deegan's engagement. She hit all the right notes in her response—his marriage to the evil Carly McKendrick wouldn't last, he'd regret letting me go, and that tired old saw about how there was somebody wonderful waiting for me just around the corner.

I didn't buy any of it, but after a while I realized how satisfying it was to be sharing a glass of wine with my mother and airing my dirty laundry while she washed hers in my machine down the hallway. I didn't know how I'd feel about my new roommate in a day or two, but for tonight she was just what the doctor ordered.

Taking about Eugene reminded me that I had an obligation to call Detective O'Brien and tell him Lupe Ortiz's cell phone wasn't missing anymore. He wasn't going to be happy. The phone was a vital piece of evidence in a homicide investigation. Deep undercover or not, Eugene should have come in from the cold and turned it over to the authorities. He hadn't, and that could cause problems.

It was late. I didn't expect O'Brien to be at work, but I called and left a message, anyway. At least he couldn't say I didn't try.

Chapter 31

I arrived in Brentwood early Saturday morning. I knocked on Helen's door, but she didn't answer. She must have already left for Nectar. As I turned around, I heard somebody blowing his nose. I peeked through the trees that screened Helen's sidewalk from the one next door. A man in his thirties was walking down the path toward the street. He looked pale and wilted like a celery stick that had been left too long in the refrigerator. I could see the impressions of a pair of knobby knees under his sweatpants as he struggled with a black plastic garbage sack.

I parted the tree branches and said, "Excuse me."

He dropped the sack and whipped his body into a karate stance.

"Stay back! These hands are registered weapons."

I almost laughed. He was skinnier than Eugene and

his feet were so large they looked as if they could anchor him to the ground in a hurricane. He seemed weird enough to be the man Charley had interviewed through a closed door on Friday.

I stepped onto the sidewalk in front of him. "I didn't mean to startle you. I'm looking for Helen Taggart, but she's not home. Have you seen her today?"

His brows were heavy and low over his eyes, which made him seem feral. "No. I haven't been out much. I'm just getting over a cold." He picked up the bag. "Excuse me. I have to take this to the garbage before I get chilled."

"If you're sick, I'll take it."

He hesitated and then he handed me the bag.

"My name is Tucker Sinclair. I think you spoke to my colleague a few days ago. Charley Tate. He wanted to know about the burglary at Helen's place last Thursday night. You told him you hadn't seen anything."

"What I told him was I hadn't seen anything out of the ordinary."

His response seemed evasive. I wondered what he was hiding.

"If you saw anything at all, I'm sure Helen would like to know about it. Some cash was stolen from her place that night."

"Oh, please. You'd think somebody broke into Fort Knox, the way people are acting. I actually had a reporter from the *New York Times* come to my door yesterday to interview me."

A weight pressed against my chest, making it difficult to breathe. "Did this reporter give his name?"

"It was one of those pretentious nicknames, Buff or Biff, something like that."

"Bix Waverly?"

"Yes, that's it. Good old Bix."

"What did you tell him?"

"Just what I told your so-called colleague. I didn't see any strangers around the area that night."

"Did you see *anybody*?"

His eyes narrowed. "Are you a private eye, too?"

"No. I'm a business associate of Helen's."

"I don't want to get involved in her problems. I make a point to distance myself from the neighbors. It's safer that way."

"Look, you have nothing to fear from me. I'm just curious to know what you saw."

"You won't tell anybody?"

"What's said on the sidewalk stays on the sidewalk."

He scowled. "Are you making fun of me?"

"Not at all."

He looked around to make sure nobody was close by. "I drank a lot of cough medicine on Thursday. I slept off and on all day. Just before midnight, I heard a loud noise. It woke me up. It seemed to be coming from the condo next door, so I got out of bed and went for my binoculars."

I felt my eyes open wide. "Binoculars?"

He grabbed the garbage bag out of my hand and held it protectively against his chest. "I know what you're thinking, but I'm not a pervert. I'm a bird watcher. I'd been monitoring the progress of a *Carpodacus mexican-*

nus that's been building a nest in the eaves outside my kitchen window. There's nothing wrong with that."

"I agree. So what did you see?"

He set the bag on the sidewalk. "The kitchen door was open and the light was on. Then it went out and another light came on in the upstairs bedroom. I know it was the bedroom because my condo is the mirror image of the one next door. I looked at both units before I chose this one. I liked mine better because streets border the other unit on two sides. I'm a light sleeper and I didn't want traffic noise keeping me awake."

"So, the light in the bedroom went on. . . ." I prompted.

"Yes. The mini blinds were down but the slats weren't closed. I could see a man. I just assumed it was Helen's boyfriend. I've never met him before, but I can hear them sometimes through the bedroom window . . . you know . . . making noise."

"Was he alone?"

"As far as I know."

"What was he doing?"

"Pulling out dresser drawers and scattering clothes everywhere, and I know why. You hear about it all the time. People pretend to burglarize their own apartments so they can collect money from insurance companies."

"You think this was insurance fraud?"

He put his hands on his hips. "Please don't make me state the obvious."

I tried to make sense of what he'd just told me. It was

mind-boggling that Helen was so desperate for money she'd recruit Dale Ewing, a former CIA analyst, to defraud an insurance company for chump change. If she were going to take that kind of risk, she would have claimed more was missing.

"Did you tell the police what you saw?" I said.

"They knocked on the door, but I didn't open it. I told you before. I don't want to get involved."

"What did this guy look like?"

"Short, stout, black hair. And he was wearing a suit."

The neighbor was more than a little strange. He admitted to overdosing on cough medicine, which may have distorted his recollection, but the man inside Helen's apartment didn't match the description of Helen's boyfriend. Dale Ewing was tall and his hair was white. It sounded more like the man Aidan Malloy had seen getting into the Mercedes parked outside Nectar the night Lupe was murdered.

"If I showed you a picture of Helen's boyfriend, do you think you could tell me if he was the man you saw that night?"

The neighbor seemed less sure of himself. "I have to go inside now. I'm getting cold, and I don't want to have a relapse."

He grabbed the garbage bag and hurried inside his condo. A moment later, I heard three sets of dead bolts click into place.

I was just walking back to my car when Charley called. He asked me to meet him at the office. He had some important news.

Chapter 32

"There's a research foundation up in Thousand Oaks that collects birds from all over the world," Charley said. "They test DNA to find out why birds are dying or why their eggs are getting so thin. And guess what? They have a drawer full of quetzals."

Charley was sitting at his desk, trying with little success to pry something out of his stapler with his lock-picking tools.

"That's not all," he went on. "The place gives tours to the public. A couple of days before Lupe Ortiz was killed, one member of the group seemed overly interested in the quetzals. The purpose of the foundation is to educate the public about birds, so the guy was allowed to get up close and personal with the display. When the tour was over, one of the scientists noticed a quetzal was missing."

"Did they confront the guy?" I said.

Charley banged the stapler on the desk. "Nah. They can't prove he took it. They considered it an unfortunate loss and moved on."

"Do they know who the guy is?"

"He gave John Jones when he made the reservation, but I'm sure that's not his real name. He left a telephone number. I talked the docent into giving it to me. I called, but there's no answer and no voice mail."

"Is there another way to find out who the number belongs to?"

Charley gave up on the stapler and used a paper clip to attach several sheets of paper that looked like one of his case progress reports. "I tried. It isn't listed. The police would have to issue a warrant to get the records."

"So you think this guy stole a quetzal and left its feather by Lupe's body. Why?"

"He may have known her son was a gangbanger and wanted to set him up for the murder. If so, it was a good call. It worked."

"That means the guy planned to kill Lupe when he came to Nectar that night."

"Maybe he got tired of playing games with her. He wanted the chocolate pot back and he wanted Lupe dead for making his life difficult."

"So what do we do now?" I said.

"I've been following up on the list of customers you gave me. I've contacted everybody on the Westside and in the Valley. None of them recognized Eugene's picture. Only three of the owners knew Lupe Ortiz by name. None of them knew about the spouted chocolate pot. I still have a few places to check in the east. If those don't pan out, we'll have to get more names from Jay-Cee. I have to meet with a client this morning, but I'll try to get through the list by tonight."

"Nerine Barstok asked me to pick up a bag of sugar. I'll already be in Silver Lake. Give me the names and I'll check them out."

He hesitated. "Okay, but make up a pretext. I don't want anybody knowing what you're up to. If you sense trouble, get out. Fast. Call me if you have any questions, and don't do anything stupid."

"Thanks for the vote of confidence, Charley."

"Sorry. You know what I mean."

Charley gave me the address and contact name for a suntan salon in Arcadia and a dry cleaner in Montebello. I added the suspected quetzal thief's number to my cell phone address book. It was improbable, but maybe I'd be able to connect it to one of the businesses I was going to visit.

Pookie was still ensconced in my spare room, weighing her future, so Muldoon would be safe with her until I got home. After I left the office, I stopped at the market for a five-pound sack of sugar before heading to Eugene's apartment.

Nerine opened the door, releasing the aroma of baking peanut butter into the November afternoon. She was wearing an apron and what looked like one of Eugene's cats on her head. On closer inspection, I realized she had the same uncontrollable cowlick in the same spot as his. Her hair must have been plastered down with spray the first time I saw her, because I hadn't noticed it before. Somehow it made her seem more human.

Nerine took the bag of sugar and gestured for me to come in. When I stepped over the threshold, I stared in disbelief. She had rearranged Eugene's furniture. His knitted afghan was missing from the couch. Magazines that he would never read were lined up with military precision on the coffee table—*Southern Living*, *Redbook*, and *Golf Digest*. Big Ben was now hanging on the wall in the kitchen, overlooking trays of cookies covered with waxed paper. She must have found more sugar somewhere, because she looked as if she was going into competition with the Girl Scouts.

She studied my dumbstruck expression. "It helps me cope."

"Have you heard from him?"

"No. I finally had to tell the colonel our son was missing. He wanted to fly out here and lead the charge, but I told him to wait."

"I'm surprised he'd do that for Oops."

Her cheeks turned scarlet. "That was a nickname. The colonel's little joke. He didn't mean anything by it."

"Excuse me, Nerine, but you can't really believe that. Every time he said it, he was reinforcing the fact his son was a mistake, and even more hurtful, he was unwanted."

She took off her apron "Eugene *was* a mistake. I can't change that. Marilyn was already ten when he came along. The colonel and I thought we were done with diapers and colic and sleepless nights. It was a shock to both of us."

"Then why didn't you give him up for adoption?"

She scowled. "Don't be ridiculous. That sort of thing isn't done by people like us."

"If you'd given him up, he might have had a happier life."

She looked stunned by my comment and averted her gaze. "I've often wondered which came first, the chicken or the egg. Did my son turn out the way he is because of us, or would he have been that way regardless of how we'd raised him?"

"Eugene is a great person. Maybe he turned out that way in spite of you."

She took the remark with deep-seated stoicism. "It's not easy being a parent. You never set out to make mistakes, but somehow you always do. Maybe the colonel and I made more than our share, but regardless of what you think, I love my son, and if anything ever happened to him, I don't know what I'd do."

I felt guilty for giving her a hard time. Besides, who was I to criticize? I had no idea what it was like to be a parent. I barely knew how to raise Muldoon.

"Charley and I are doing everything we can to find him," I said.

Nerine nodded. "Eugene's credit card bill hasn't come yet. I've been opening all the mail except for personal letters. I hope he won't mind."

I smiled to show support for her shift in attitude. "I think he'll understand."

A plastic bag full of peanut butter cookies was sitting on my passenger's seat and Eugene's apartment was already in my rearview mirror when my cell phone rang. It was Riley Deegan.

"Joe called," she said. "I don't know what you said to him, but he apologized to me. Said he was sorry he hadn't been more supportive. That's the best news. Do you want to hear the second-best news?"

"Shoot," I said.

Riley squealed with excitement. "Emma called me from Las Vegas. She and Noah eloped. They called to thank me for introducing them. She said she found her soul mate and apologized for taking that roll of toilet paper the night of the singles' party. She and Noah were in Claudia's bathroom, putting their clothes back on, and she didn't realize she'd slipped it into her tote bag. I did it, Tucker. I made my first match. Luv Bugs is going to work, isn't it?"

I smiled. "Yeah, Riley. It's going to work. Congratulations. You did a great job."

"So when can we get together and talk?" she said.

"How about next week? Call me on Monday and we'll set something up."

The smile spread to my entire face as I closed the phone and prepared to interview Lupe's clients.

Chapter 33

Best-Way Cleaners was located in Montebello, an Italian word that means "beautiful mountain." It's a medium-sized residential and industrial city located in the San Gabriel Valley, about eight miles east of downtown Los Angeles. The place has oil wells, the Barnyard Zoo at Grant Rea Park, and an annual murder rate that generally stays in the single digits.

I parked in one of the three available spots behind the dry cleaning store and went inside. Hanging on one of the walls was a flag that featured a broad white stripe sandwiched between two turquoise stripes of equal width. Centered in the white was a laurel wreath, two crossed rifles, and a quetzal perched on an unrolled piece of parchment that read LIBERTAD 15 DE SEPTIEMBRE DE 1821. On the other wall was a plaque that read PROUD TO BE A GUATEMALAN AMERICAN. I didn't make too much of that. Montebello's population was predominantly Hispanic.

A stout woman in her fifties stood behind the counter. Her hair was too evenly black not to be dyed. She was chatting amiably with a male customer. According to the information I'd found in Lupe's personnel file, the owner's name was Isela Navarro. I watched as the woman counted a pile of crumpled dress shirts. There were fifteen of them, a three-week supply.

She acknowledged me with a nod. "Be right with you."

Neither she nor the customer seemed to care that I was waiting. Both were more interested in exchanging a series of whiny complaints that went back and forth like a tennis volley. He railed about the high parking fees at the Staples Center. She griped about European shoes being too narrow for her feet. The machine at the counter spit out two pieces of paper. Mrs. Navarro handed one copy to the customer and put the other on top of his shirts. As soon as he left, she turned to me.

"Now," she said. "You."

Charley told me to invent a pretext, so I used the first one that popped into my head.

"I'd like to pick up some dry cleaning for my brother. I'm sorry. I forgot to bring the ticket with me. Maybe you can check his name. Bix Waverly."

"We don't use names. What's his phone number?"

I paused for a moment to think. It didn't matter what number I gave her. The pretext was just an excuse to start a conversation. I rattled off my office number and watched as she typed it into the computer. I expected her to say she couldn't find it in the database, but her response sent me reeling.

"He picked it up already. This morning. One hand-knit sweater. Right?"

I jammed my hands into the pockets of my jacket to keep them from trembling. "I guess I made the trip for nothing. Thanks for checking." I paused and pointed toward the wall. "That's a beautiful flag. I've never seen one up close before."

She nodded. "Sometimes it makes me sad to look at it and remember. I had a good life in Guatemala. I went to parties with important people. Now look. My hands are rough from too much work." She held them out so I could inspect her ragged cuticles.

"Did you leave because of the war?"

"The war was the war. It did not affect us much. I didn't want to leave. My husband made me."

I remembered Dale Ewing talking about the asylum seekers who'd moved to L.A. from Guatemala during the war and the problems they were having now. Members of the disbanded national police had come here, as well. I wondered if Mrs. Navarro's husband fell into either of those categories.

"Was your husband in the military?" I said.

Her laugh sounded like a bark from a humorless dog. "Manuel? In the military? He was an accountant at a museum in Guatemala City."

My face began to tingle. A moment later, I heard a door close in the back of the store. A man dressed in a suit and tie appeared from behind a rack of hanging clothes. My heart felt as if it had just dropped into my stomach. He was the customer I'd met at Nectar who had given up his place in line to accommodate the rude woman with the Fendi handbag.

"Well," she called to him. "Look what the cat dragged in. Where have you been, Manuel? My feet ache from standing too long, and my head hurts from the cleaning fumes. I need a break."

Manuel Navarro stared at me with a puzzled frown. My pulse was racing. My thoughts were in overdrive. Isela Navarro was his wife, the one who had warned him that his guilty pleasures would kill him one day. She said something to him in Spanish in an abrasive tone. He responded with a dismissive hand gesture as if he had heard the criticism before and had ceased to give it much weight. It was no wonder that the relationship had soured. She'd given away his price-less Mayan spouted chocolate pot to the cleaning woman.

Isela crossed her arms over her chest and looked at Navarro with a defiant stare. He ignored her, and a moment later she disappeared into the back room, leaving the pile of dirty shirts on the counter.

He walked toward me. "I did not know business doctors made house calls."

I didn't dare mention Eugene's name, so I made up another story, hoping it would allay any suspicions he had.

"What a coincidence. I didn't know this was your place. I got your name from Jay-Cee Janitorial Services. I'm looking for somebody to clean my office, and they gave me a list of clients to call for references. Your wife's name was on the list. So, how would you rate the service?"

If he noticed the strain in my voice, he didn't let on. He pulled a cloth drawstring sack from underneath the counter and began stuffing the dirty shirts inside. "I do not know. Isela manages the cleaning people."

"Then maybe I should talk to her."

"You are not likely to get a warm reception at the moment. Something I've done, I'm sure."

"How did you find out about Nectar?" I said.

Navarro put the receipt in the sack and tied it closed with the drawstrings. "Lovers of cacao have networks of spies. I cannot tell you which one told me of this particular shop."

"Since you're such a chocolate aficionado, I wonder if you ever noticed the Mayan spouted chocolate pot Helen had on display in her retail store."

It was a risky move to mention the pot, but I felt safe enough. Mrs. Navarro was in the back room, and I wanted to judge her husband's reaction. Navarro was so quiet I thought he'd stopped breathing.

"I do not remember such a thing. Is there some problem with this chocolate pot that you should make the long journey to my dry cleaning store to ask me about it? I hope it has not been stolen."

"No. It's in a safe place. No one can get to it."

"And what is so special about it?"

"It may be valuable."

"So you are looking to return it to its rightful owner?"

"Perhaps."

A bell tinkled above the door. I turned and saw a woman enter the store, carrying several items of clothing draped over her arm. Navarro greeted her with a nod.

"I would like to help you," he said to me, "but now is not a good time. Perhaps we can meet tomorrow. There is a place near the chocolate shop called the Brighton Café. I will be there at eleven."

He turned away from me, making it clear he considered our conversation over. Behind him, a rack of hanging laundry parted, exposing the face of Isela Navarro. Her eyes were dark with suspicion.

I left the store and rounded the corner, staying out of Navarro's line of vision. I pulled out my cell phone and dialed the number for John Jones, the man who had toured the quetzal display. I watched as Navarro patted his breast pocket. He pulled out a phone and squinted as if he was reading the caller ID. He studied it a moment, frowned, and closed the phone.

It was time to call in the cavalry.

Chapter 34

Charley told me to go home and sit tight. He'd contact Detective O'Brien at the Beverly Hills police department to let him know what I've found out about Navarro. I planned to take his advice, but first I decided to stop by the office to see if I could find more information on the man that might help the police make a case against him.

It was Saturday and traffic was light, so I got to the office at around three thirty and logged on to my computer. Manuel Navarro was a common name. My Internet search produced thousands of links. Many were in Spanish. I scrolled through page after page of listings before I finally moved on to sites dealing with stolen antiquities, Mayan spouted chocolate pots, and the Guatemalan civil war. I stared at gruesome photographs of bodies in mass graves, just as Jordan Rich had described the night we'd gone to the theater. I found nothing connecting Manuel Navarro to any of it. Even so, I could still piece together a theory based on what I knew. Some of the details may have been wrong, but the story held together.

Lupe and her mother had come to Los Angeles to seek asylum from death squads in the Guatemalan civil war. Navarro came to Los Angeles because he was running from the law. He'd stolen a priceless antiquity from the museum where he worked as an accountant.

Navarro opened the dry cleaner's in his wife's name to cover his tracks, and she hired Lupe to clean the store. According to Roberto, Isela Navarro had been clearing out a storage room. She found the chocolate pot, thought it was junk, and threw it out. Lupe found it in the trash and got permission to keep it. Isela Navarro told me she didn't know why her husband had made her leave Guatemala, so she probably didn't know he was a thief.

It was difficult to say when or why Navarro discovered the pot was missing. Maybe he routinely checked it. In any event, he discovered his wife had given the pot to Lupe. He began hounding her to get it back, only to find it was in Helen Taggart's chocolate store, where Lupe meant it to stay. Navarro must have been frantic. Not only was the pot valuable, it also tied him to a crime that could have landed him in a Guatemalan prison.

Under the guise of buying chocolates, Navarro traveled to Helen's store. On one hand, he must have been relieved to see the chocolate pot displayed on the shelf out front. On the other, he had to be worried someone would break it or even steal it before he could get it back. Maybe he thought the customers would provide enough cover for him to take the pot without being discovered. That didn't work, so he had to try another approach.

Navarro must have driven to Nectar on Thursday, knowing Lupe would be there, intending to take back the pot using whatever means necessary. He arrived at seven thirty. Bob Rossi had already delivered the garlic shrimp, but the door was still unlocked. Navarro killed Lupe and planted the quetzal feather by her body to implicate Roberto. It wasn't until afterward he discovered the pot wasn't in the store anymore.

Helen's neighbor saw somebody matching Navarro's description in her bedroom at around midnight. He could have found Helen's home address on a packing slip in her office or on some other correspondence. Later than evening, he broke into her condo, only to find that the pot wasn't there, either. He didn't know at the time, but it was in the trunk of Helen's car. I wasn't sure why Navarro had come back to the store on the Friday after the murder when I was there helping Kathy. Maybe he'd become addicted to Nectar's chocolates or maybe he was just a murderer returning to the scene of the crime.

Lupe's cell phone led Eugene to the dry cleaning store. I wondered where he would go next. To Navarro's house? I opened Charley's property-records data-base. Navarro's primary home was in Alhambra, but my heart started to race when I saw he owned a second home—in North Hollywood. Eugene had called Mr. Winn's message machine yesterday morning to say North Hollywood was the new capital of California. It *had* been a clue. I jotted down the address and shut off the computer.

I thought about the man I'd seen lurking in the shad-ows near my car at work. It must have been Navarro. He'd seen me at Nectar Thursday evening. He must have waited around until the police arrived. Maybe he'd even seen me load Helen's collectibles into the trunk of my car. At the time, he couldn't have known what was in those boxes, but in his search for the choc-olate pot, he'd eliminated both Nectar and Helen's condo. If he connected all the dots, he must assume that I had the pot or at least knew who did. So where would he look next? The only place he hadn't tried yet—my house. He had my home telephone number. It was on the business card I'd given him the first time we met at Nectar. I included it because I often worked at the beach. I wanted my clients to be able to reach me there. With my number and a little ingenuity, Navarro could locate my address.

Pookie and Muldoon were at the cottage. I had to warn them.

I called both the house and Pookie's cell phone. She didn't answer. I hoped she and Muldoon had gone home to Bruce. In some dark corner of my mind I knew that wasn't true. I looked up the number for the Malibu sheriff's department and dialed. Then I ran for my car.

It was already dark by the time I got to my beach cottage. There was no dark Mercedes or patrol car parked on the street near my cottage, only Pookie's lime-green VW Beetle sitting in the driveway. I pulled into the garage and cut the engine, scanning the area for something I could use as a weapon. The old broom I found propped up in the corner wasn't going to do much good. The pepper spray was my only defense.

My heart hammered as I tiptoed up the steps to the deck and peeked through a side window. The house was dark, but the door was locked. I used my key and stepped over the threshold, inhaling the odor of cigarette smoke. Nobody in my life smoked, except Manuel Navarro. I remembered his nicotine-stained fingers and the burning cigarette arcing out of the Mercedes window the night Lupe was murdered.

It was cold inside my house—too cold. The pilot light in the furnace must have gone out. My hand fumbled along the wall for the switch. Light flooded the room. I gulped in some air and surveyed the damage.

All of the kitchen cupboards were open. Pots and pans were scattered everywhere. Items that had been in my grandmother's steamer trunk now littered the floor—family photographs, some seashells my father had collected on the beach when he was a child, his camera equipment. I felt violated and angry. Mostly I felt scared about my mother and Muldoon. My gaze continued around the room until it had made a full circle, stopping at the French door. One of the glass panes near the handle was shattered. Cold November air seeped into the room.

My chest felt as if it was about to explode. Even if my mother had been in the bedroom with the door closed when Navarro broke the glass, Muldoon would have heard. He would have been barking his head off, raising hell. I called Pookie's name. No response. I tiptoed past the kitchen toward the bedrooms in the back of the house, until I reached the utility room. Lying on the floor was the cooler in which I'd hidden the chocolate pot. It was empty.

I was heading toward the telephone to call for help when I heard the side door creaking opening. It wasn't the deputy. He would announce himself before entering the house. Shoes clicked against the entryway tile. Someone was in the house.

"Tucker? Why is it so cold in here? Did you turn off the heat? Oh, my God! What happened?"

It was Pookie's voice. A moment later, Muldoon ran down the hall toward me, barking and sniffing like crazy. Relief flooded through me. I collapsed on my knees next to him, burying my face in his thick coat.

"Where were you?" I said to Pookie.

"You don't have to shout, Tucker. I was at Mrs. D's place, trying to think of a stage name for her singing act. She wants something easy to remember, like Cher."

I grabbed my purse. "Somebody from the sheriff's

department is on the way. I'll explain later. Take Muldoon and go back to Mrs. D's until the cops get here."

"Maybe I'll call Bruce and ask him to come over. He can board up the window. Where are you going?"

I flew out the door and down the steps to the sand. "To find Eugene."

Chapter 35

It was close to nine when I arrived in North Hollywood, a neighborhood dotted with ordinary houses, neat lawns, and stone planters filled with annuals that tolerated the Southern California fall weather. The area was quiet. It felt safe.

As I drove down the street looking for Navarro's address, I saw Eugene's Volvo parked on the street about a block away from the house. I got out of the Boxster and put my hand on the Volvo's hood, an old trick Charley had taught me. It was still warm from engine heat. The car hadn't been there long. I pulled in behind the Volvo and stuffed my pockets with the flashlight, my cell phone, the pepper spray, and the lock-picking set. Then I secured my purse in the trunk and headed for Navarro's house.

It was a one-story place. The curtains on the front

windows were closed, which made it look dark and foreboding. I made my way to the two-car detached garage, but couldn't see anything because the windows were blacked out with some sort of covering. I tried the side door, but it wouldn't open. I spent several precious moments working a tension wrench and diamond pick until the lock popped open. Inside the garage, I found a black Mercedes with an advertisement where the license plate should have been. It read GARVEY MOTORS—ALHAMBRA. Navarro must be inside the house. What I didn't know was if Eugene was with him.

I kept to the shadows, walking down a sloping driveway to the right of the garage until I reached a metal gate. The latch wasn't visible from the street, so I reached over the top and released it from the back side. When the gate swung open, I guided the pin back into its notch to avoid making noise.

There were no lights in the side yard, so I ran my left hand along the rough stucco wall. A short distance down the path I stepped into a pile of dried leaves. The crunching sound was deafening. I froze, listening for any hint that I'd been discovered—footsteps, doors opening, a "Who's out there?" I waited through a minute of silence before moving on.

As my right hand wrestled with overgrown foliage from an untrimmed hedge, my left hand bumped into a metal downspout. More noise. A spiderweb brushed across my face. I controlled the urge to cry out. My hand left the house and followed the curve of a retaining wall that grew taller as the path turned left and descended into the backyard, which was hidden from the neighbors by thick trees and shrubs. As I stepped closer, I could see light spilling from a sliding glass door. I peeked around the corner of the wall and saw what looked like the edge of a bed.

A wide stairway with six steps led to the glass door. To see the whole bedroom, I had to get to the other side of the steps without being seen. I crawled on my belly along the path until I reached a chest-high wall on the far side of the steps. Above was a brick patio. I stepped on a raised drain cover and used all of my strength to pull myself onto the cap of the wall, teetering for a moment at the top before recovering my balance. Falling would make noise, and I'd be discovered.

I rolled into a squatting position, keeping low. If anybody glanced out the window, they'd be looking at eye level, not toward the ground. At least I hoped so. I crept to the corner of the house to have a look.

The chocolate pot was sitting on the bed next to a gray handgun. I scanned the room and spotted a small plastic rectangle lying on the carpet. It looked like Eugene's air purifier. I craned my neck until I saw a foot sticking out of the closet. I recognized the shoe. It was Eugene's. The shoe moved. Relief washed over me, then white-hot anger. I wanted to smash the glass and charge in to rescue him, but I knew that would be a deadly mistake.

I needed to get help. As I stood to leave, I saw a flash of dark blue in the hallway outside the bedroom. I pressed my body against the side of the house and saw Manuel Navarro walk into the room. He looked placid.

He said something to Eugene and paused as if he was listening for a response. The window was open, but not wide enough for me to hear the conversation.

Eugene was still alive, but I couldn't guarantee he was going to stay that way much longer. Navarro had killed Lupe Ortiz over the chocolate pot and he wouldn't hesitate to kill Eugene. I considered my options. If I called 911, I'd have to leave my hiding place and waste precious minutes explaining what was going on. If Navarro heard me talking, I'd put Eugene in jeopardy.

Charley would send the police, but I didn't have time to use a middleman. I had to go directly to the authorities. To Joe Deegan. I dialed his cell phone number and left a text message with Navarro's address followed by the words *send help* and the number *187*, the California penal code for homicide.

Deegan would recognize my telephone number and know the call was from me. He also knew Eugene was missing. Even if he couldn't guess precisely what the trouble was, he would call his LAPD buddies at the North Hollywood station and ask them to check out Navarro's house.

I turned off my cell phone. If Deegan called back, I didn't want it to ring or even vibrate. Any sound might reveal my hiding place. I kept my eye on Eugene's foot, hoping he wouldn't say anything to get him in more trouble. A moment later, Navarro left the bedroom and didn't return for what seemed like an eternity. Not knowing where he was or even if he was still in the house filled me with panic. If the cops didn't arrive soon, I'd have to break my vigil and go for help.

At least fifteen minutes passed as my limbs grew stiff from the cold. Just as I stood to stretch, Navarro walked back into the bedroom with the wooden box Marianne Rogers had given me for the chocolate pot. Navarro swaddled the pot in the packing material and laid it in its container. He looked as if he might be preparing to leave.

Eugene's foot was still visible, but it was no longer moving. Navarro picked up the gun and turned toward the closet, toward Eugene. I had to distract him. I turned my phone back on, desperate to get a signal. It seemed to take forever.

A moment later, Navarro whipped around toward the hall as if something had startled him. With the gun still in his hand, he ran from the room. It had to be the police at the front door. I didn't care about being discovered now. I had to warn them about the gun.

I ran down the stairs and retraced my steps around the curved path to the gate. That's when I saw a black Ford Explorer parked at an odd angle to the curb. It was Joe Deegan's. I exited through the gate and let it slam shut. I didn't care if it made noise now. My lungs burned. My legs were stiff and painful. I heard a loud explosion and then another and another. My heart pounded as if *it* would explode.

I jogged up the driveway toward the street. Stepped over a stone planter. Ran to the door. It was ajar. The center panel was staved in, as if somebody had kicked it. I smelled gunpowder. My throat felt hoarse and raw as I yelled Deegan's name. No response.

Lights flicked on in the neighbor's house. A dog barked. I pushed on the door, but it wouldn't open. Something was in the way. Even without looking, I knew what it was. I squeezed through the opening and saw Manuel Navarro slumped on the floor a few feet away. A gun lay near his feet. Blood pooled around his body. I turned and saw Joe Deegan splayed out with his back against the door. A vivid circle of red was spreading from a wound to his chest. Math calculations kept me from panicking. A cup? A pint? Less? More? Then I heard sirens. Why were the cops taking so damn long?

Eugene was alive and safe where he was, at least for the moment. Deegan was the only thing on my mind now. I fell to my hands and knees next to him. My fingers went to his neck, feeling for a pulse. Found it. He was still alive. I tore off my jacket to cover his wound, hoping it would stanch the flow of warm, sticky blood that was seeping from his chest. I bent to his ear, shouting for him to hold on. Help was on the way. No response. I was stunned by fear, and then outraged enough to kill Manuel Navarro myself if he wasn't already dead.

Chapter 36

Venus had been right. Eugene was tougher than we thought. He refused a ride in the ambulance, so I loaded him into the Boxster and followed the paramedics to the hospital, an upscale place where the eighteen-dollar valet parking fees and the prenups of its A-list neighbors were not negotiable. When I pulled into the circular driveway, a swarm of uniformed valets lined up to take my car.

Eugene was dehydrated and emotionally shaken but mostly intact, more concerned about abandoning his beloved Volvo than hearing the results of his EKG. I told him there was too much chaos at the scene to rescue the car, although I promised to help him pick it up in the morning.

For four hours I sat in a chair next to his bed in the ER, waiting for Nerine to arrive by taxi to pick him up. My clothes were soaked in Deegan's blood, so the nurse gave me a hospital gown and bathrobe to wear, and disposed of my garments in a biohazard bag.

Every few minutes, I pestered her about Deegan—how he was, where he was. She was pleasant enough, but she couldn't tell me anything. In desperation, I called Jordan Rich and asked him to use his connections to find out what was happening. He had privileges at the hospital and knew the thoracic surgeons who would likely be working on Deegan. He pledged that they were all top-notch doctors, and the trauma center's equipment was state-of-the-art.

Eugene pleaded with me to go to Deegan. He said he'd be fine by himself, but I wouldn't leave him alone. There was nothing I could do until I heard from Jordan Rich. Still, it was torture waiting for the call.

"We were all sick with worry," I said to Eugene. "Why didn't you tell us where you were?"

He leaned back into the pillows and crossed his legs. The hospital-issued brown ankle socks with white gripper patches on the soles made him look like a bear cub.

"You would have only tried to stop me. I had to do this on my own."

"Because of your mother?"

"Because of me. I have to learn to face life without crutches."

"Knitting isn't a crutch. It's more like a hobby."

"You know what I mean, Tucker. You baby me too much. Charley, too. I know you care about me, but the nest is getting crowded. You have to let me fly. If I crash and burn, I'll get up and try again."

It's difficult to see your shortcomings laid bare, but Eugene was right. I did baby him too much, but not because I lacked confidence in him. He was capable, creative, and loyal to the core. Maybe I just wanted to protect him because his mother never had.

"I promise to do better in the future," I said. "So, how did you find out it was Navarro who killed Lupe Ortiz?"

"I saw the number for Best-Way Cleaners on Lupe's cell phone call history. When I drove to Montebello to check it out, I found a Mercedes parked in the back lot. It had a Garvey Motors sign on the license plate, just like the one you saw the night of Lupe's murder. I staked out Navarro's place for several days, and last night I followed him to the North Hollywood house. Tonight I decided to go back when he wasn't there to see what I could find. He surprised me while I was taking pictures of the house with my cell phone. The next thing I knew, he was pointing a gun at me. The rest, as they say, is history."

"You must have been scared."

"Totally! Especially when I saw the chocolate pot. I knew he'd gotten it from you, and I knew you wouldn't give it up without a fight. That's when I realized I was in big trouble."

"Do you have any idea what Navarro planned to do with the pot?" I said.

"Sell it. I heard him on his cell phone, haggling

over the payment. He insisted on all sorts of complicated wire transfers, and the buyer wasn't going for it."

"I can't believe you're still alive," I said.

"Maybe the quetzal feather was my *nahual*, protecting me from Navarro. I'm just sorry I couldn't find out where he got it."

I told Eugene about the research foundation in Ventura and the missing bird from the quetzal display. Just then a nurse came by and pulled the privacy curtain around us. I heard the wheels of a gurney rolling up to the next bed. Eugene and I exchanged worried glances. We had experienced too much trauma in the past few days. We didn't want to see any more of it.

"Nerine was really worried about you," I said, "and the colonel was ready to fly to L.A. to lead the search party."

"I think you have my father confused with somebody who cares. I don't look forward to hearing the lecture about how I screwed up again."

"You didn't screw up, Eugene. You found Lupe Ortiz's killer."

He smiled. "Yeah, I guess I did. Does Charley know?"

"Not yet. I'll call him as soon as your mother springs you out of here."

It was painful to watch the reunion between Eugene and his mother. Nerine stood ramrod stiff. Didn't know what to do. I was afraid she would offer him a cookie and spoil the moment, but seconds later he threw his arms around her in an awkward embrace. She cried.

Told him Liza and Fergie were at the apartment meow-
ing and missing him like crazy. I wondered if Nerine
would ever tell him they'd spent the past few days at
a kennel.

After Eugene and his mother left, I sat in the lobby.
While I waited for Jordan to contact me, I called Char-
ley to let him know what had happened. He said,
"Shit," and then he repeated the word five more times.
He wanted to come to the hospital to get me. I told him
no.

"Why don't you quit doing all that business crap and
come to work for me? At least I could keep an eye on
you. Three years on the job and you'd be a full-fledged
PI."

"Oh, sure. As if that would ever happen."

Charley was mothering me just as I'd done to Eugene,
but I wondered if that's what all good friends did for
each other. Maybe it was better than the alternative—
having nobody who cared about you at all.

"How's Lorna?" I said.

There was a long pause before he answered.
"Pregnant."

I was stunned. "I thought the test turned out
negative."

"It was wrong. She went to a doctor. She's eight
weeks along."

"Are you okay with that?"

He didn't answer right away. I couldn't see him
through the telephone line, but I knew he was running
his freckled hand over his crew cut, as he always did
when he had weighty issues to consider.

"Ask me in seven months."

As soon as I ended the call with Charley, I dialed Jordan Rich's number. He apologized for not contacting me sooner, said he'd only just learned the latest news about Deegan's condition. His tone seemed matter-of-fact, as if he was dictating a doctor's report.

"Detective Deegan was unconscious and in shock when they brought him into the ER," he told me. "The wound was just to the left of midline, at the midchest level, and his breathing had telltale sucking sounds. They inserted an endotrachial tube and began breathing for the patient. Next, they performed an emergency thoracotomy to address the low blood pressure. At that time, they evacuated copious blood from the chest and incised the pericardium, evacuated the blood from around the heart, and repaired a bullet hole in the left ventricle of the heart. After that, his blood pressure came up with transfusion, and they sent him to the operating room. The upper aspect of the liver was lacerated by the bullet, which finally lodged against a rib. The left lower lobe of the lung was also penetrated. All this resulted in the hemopneumothorax."

"Jordan, no offense intended. Just tell me in English. Is he going to be okay?"

He hesitated before answering. "They repaired his liver laceration and sent him to the surgical intensive care unit. That was about two hours ago. He's breathing on his own, and they've removed the respirator. All his vital signs are stable. At the moment, he's semiconscious. I've pulled some strings and cleared you to visit, but he may not be able to communicate."

All I could manage was a halting "thank you." I closed my cell phone and asked the nurse for directions to Deegan's room.

Chapter 37

On the way to Deegan's room, a burly guard in uniform stopped me at the elevator. "You gotta sign in. What's your name?"

"Tucker."

That was apparently good enough for him. He wrote *Tucker* on a sticky name tag and handed it to me. So much for security. I could have been at a chamber of commerce mixer.

As I entered the elevator, my throat felt as if it had developed an inoperable tumor. I checked in at the nurse's station and explained that Jordan Rich had cleared me to visit. The charge nurse checked Deegan's chart and directed me to the recovery room, where several uniformed LAPD officers stood guard near the automatic double doors that admitted gurneys, doctors, and nurses.

I assumed Deegan's mother and his sisters were on their way. Carly, too. I thought of Riley and the feelings of loathing she had toward Deegan's fiancée. Soon she would feel that way about me, too. There would be no strategizing about Luv Bugs the next week. By then, she wouldn't even be speaking to me. I didn't want to be around when she arrived. I couldn't face her, knowing she would probably never forgive me for what happened to her brother.

I walked past carts and equipment until I saw Deegan lying in a bed, hooked up to tubes and machines. He looked pale and vulnerable. I remembered our conversation earlier in the week when he asked me if he looked like he needed protecting. He did now. I slid a nearby chair to the bed. Deegan's eyes were shut. I reached over the rail and touched his arm, fighting to maintain control of my emotions.

"Hey, Deegan. It's Tucker."

He didn't respond. I'd never seen him so still before. Even when we were together and I would watch him sleep, there were always signs of life. I laid my hand on his forehead. It was cool. I held his hand. I felt prickles on my nose. My eyes began to swell. I let the tears flow.

"Damn you, Deegan. If you die, I swear I'll come after you in eternity and kick your ass."

I laid my head on the sheet and allowed mascara to smear the pristine white cotton. Sometime later, I heard a voice say, "Knock, knock." I looked up and saw Jordan Rich. He had on green scrubs under his white doctor's coat and a stethoscope visible in his coat pocket. I must have looked like a wreck, with makeup running down my cheeks. My nose was red from crying and I still had on those dorky hospital PJs.

"Sorry," he said. "I didn't mean to interrupt."

I let go of Deegan's hand and dabbed at the tears with the sleeve of the robe. "It's okay. He's asleep."

"He's on a lot a drugs. They want to keep him quiet."

"I guess I'm not helping."

Jordan's expression looked pained, as if somebody had just punched him in the stomach. "I didn't realize you and Detective Deegan were so close."

I felt sad for him, for all of us. Riley Deegan's mission for Luv Bugs was to put people together who should be together, and stop everybody else from making bad decisions. I didn't know in which category I belonged. Jordan Rich was a kind and genuine man, a great catch for some woman, maybe even me.

"Detective Deegan is engaged," I said. "We're just friends."

His smile seemed tentative. "He'll be okay, Tucker. I'll make sure of that. I'm going to watch over him myself."

My vision grew blurry with tears. All I could do was muster a nod of my head.

"There are people here to see him," Jordan said. "Visitors are only allowed in one at a time."

I stood. "Okay. I'll go."

He held up his hand to stop me. "Why don't you stay a few minutes more? I'll tell them to wait."

Jordan left the area, closing the privacy curtain behind him. I sat in the chair and picked up Deegan's hand again, lacing my fingers through his. His skin was cold and dry.

"There's so much we never said to each other. I don't know why. Maybe we were too proud or too independent or too stubborn. I know you can't hear me, but I'm going to tell you how I feel. I love you. I've probably loved you from the moment we met. I think you loved me, too, so I'm trying to figure out why we never told each other and why our lives were never in sync. I know it doesn't matter anymore, but I just wanted you to know."

I wasn't sure what I expected him to say—*I know we can never be together, but I'll love you till the day I die*? That sounded too close to reality to be of comfort. I kissed his hand and tucked it under the sheet. I put the chair back where I'd found it and walked toward the exit. I didn't expect to see Joe Deegan again, so I turned to get one last look. His eyes fluttered and then opened. I wasn't sure how long he'd been conscious or if he'd heard anything I'd just said to him.

"Hey, big guy. It's Tucker. I was just leaving. You have lots of people waiting to see you."

He said something, but the words were barely audible. I walked back to the bed and leaned over him.

"I couldn't hear what you said."

His voice was a raspy whisper. All I could make out was a single word—*Stretch*.

Also Available

from

Patricia Smiley

Short Change
A Tucker Sinclair Mystery

Los Angeles-based Tucker Sinclair has her
hands full trying to get her consulting
business off the ground. But it won't be
easy: with her clients' businesses
threatened—as well as their lives—
the stakes are deadly high.

"Tucker Sinclair is smart, unflappable, and
wickedly funny." —Denise Hamilton

**Available wherever books are sold
or at penguin.com**

Amazing
Attributes
of Aging

Silly &
Sacred Stories
of Blue Garter
Friends

Judy Appel & Mary Huntley

For more information, contact:
Minnesota Heritage Publishing
205 Ledlie Lane, Suite 125
Mankato, MN 56001
www.mnheritage.com

ISBN: 978-0-9794940-7-9

Library of Congress Catalog Number: 2009920881

Published by Minnesota Heritage Publishing

Printed in the United States of America
By Corporate Graphics, North Mankato, MN

First Printing: April 2009

Edited by Betsy Sherman

Original watercolor of Blue Garter
By Carolyn A. Petersen

Cover design by Sara Joyal

To order visit www.amazingaging.com
Or call: 1-651-439-0399 or 1-507-388-3690.
Reseller discounts available.

For You, Diane, my
favorite "sis" of a lifetime!
Love You, forever — —
Weeny

Dedicated to

Mature Women Friends

whose power
will soon shatter
the American glass ceiling

The A's on the medallion symbolize the A's in the title,
Amazing Attributes of Aging.

The S's intertwining the A's symbolize the subtitle,
Silly and Sacred Stories.

Acknowledgments

*A*s lead authors of this project, we have been delightfully inspired by our longtime friendship to share the phenomenal story of our Blue Garter Gang, which originated in 1958. As we shared the idea and potential outcomes of the project with our Blue Garter Gang of friends, we gained energy and inspiration to keep going. During our birthday gatherings, we enjoyed the discussions among these amazing women. After several conversations about ideas and many e-mails during the last six years, we have brought together over 50 years of reflections from 21 friends of the Blue Garter Gang.

We are grateful to those who hosted gatherings where book conversations took place on a shaded patio, porch, in a living room in front of a blazing fireplace, or around huge dining room tables:

Judy Strand Appel in Sun City, AZ

Mary Hesla Huntley in Mankato, MN

Virginia (Ginge) Klenk in Moorhead, MN

Ann Warren Schmidt in Shelburne, VT

Elizabeth (Liz) Nelson Shriver
in Cleveland Heights, OH

Marlys Case Sloup in Door County, WI

We are thankful to those who shared their writings for the manuscript:

Karen Marie Anderson	Louise Nelson Anderson
Judy Strand Appel	Mary Kolling Brion
Ruetta Beck Dykstra	Georgia Koberoski Hanson
Mary Hesla Huntley	Sharon Carlson Kalahar
Janna Polzin Morgan	Judy Pyles Newhouse
Carolyn Meyer Petersen	Ann Warren Schmidt
Liz Nelson Shriver	Marlys Case Sloup
Peggy Vihstadt Warren	

We are appreciative to our Blue Garter friends who gave faithful listening ears and supportive voices to the unfolding story of who we were, who we are, and who we have become:

Jean Bond Comfort	Ginge Klenk
Sandra Donaldson Lowery	Mary Johns Miller
Lois Christensen Schoeneman	Jane Williams Thom

We are delighted with the artistic talent of Carolyn Meyer Petersen, who created an original watercolor painting of the blue garter. Her artwork is the featured illustration on the cover and in the book.

We acknowledge the reality that this particular gang of friends had many other friends during the growing-up years and through high school. No one really remembers exactly how this group of friends became the Blue Garter Gang. We believe it had to do with whoever was together at a certain point in time and who was going on to college. Some may perceive the group as elitist. However, it was never our intention. We regarded ourselves as open and inclusive.

We enthusiastically thank everyone who listened, talked, laughed, cheered, questioned, shared real perspectives, and created printable words and photos. We express our gratitude to Brian Bibbs, Mary's son-in-law, for his website design and technical support. We also thank our spouses, Ray and Ken, who shared in the evolution of the manuscript in a variety of ways: they drove us to meeting sites in Prior Lake and Apple Valley, engaged in serendipitous conversations with us when writers' block occurred, and most of all, were supportive, loving, and encouraging.

Table of Contents

Foreword

> If you are lucky and have wonderful friends who stay with you and were with you all of your life, there are marvelous things about getting older.
>
> *Inge Morath*

*I*nge Morath, who was born in Austria in 1924, produced that wonderful quote which captures the spirit of *Amazing Attributes of Aging*. Marvelous things can happen as young girls grow up together in friendship. *Silly & Sacred Stories of Blue Garter Friends* collects the memories of the authors' 50 year friendship among Minnesota women of the generation that followed Inge.

Inge was a well-educated woman who learned many languages beyond her native German, including French, English, Romanian, Spanish, Italian, and Chinese. In 1951 she declared herself a portrait photographer; later she became established as a well-known artist and a remarkable, multitalented writer. During her travels with people in the movie-making industry, she met playwright Arthur Miller, whom she married after his divorce from Marilyn Monroe. They lived together happily in Connecticut. Inge died of cancer at age 78 in 2002.

Morath, Inge. "A Certain Kind of Energy." In Cathleen Rountree, *On Women Turning 70: Honoring the Voices of Wisdom,* p. 58. San Francisco, CA: Jossey-Bass. 1999.

A Carefree Toast
from left to right: Mary Huntley, Ginge Klenk, and Judy Appel

Toasting a Passage

Three longtime friends gathered to celebrate their 62nd birthdays in 2002. Each had chosen early retirement from her career. They were eager to experience their newly found carefree spirit and to soak up the warmth of a southwestern winter. Little did they know it was about to become the beginning of a six-year project of reflecting, reminiscing, sharing, and laughing through the years of their lives in knowing each other. Their early years were special, for they were part of a generation of women who were among the first to experience retirement from a career. A joy-filled project began with what women often love to do: go out for lunch.

Here's their story.

As we settled into our chairs in a charming Tex-Mex restaurant in Carefree, Arizona, the three of us— Judy, Ginge, and Mary—were relaxed, warmed by the April sunshine. We were at the end of our weeklong girls' get-away. It was lunchtime of our last day together.

Our waitress for the afternoon was a woman about our age. She was wearing a yellow ribbon in honor of her grandson, who had just gone off to Afghanistan to fight the Taliban as a part of President George W. Bush's "war on terror" following the devastating "September 11, 2001, terrorist attacks." We sincerely shared her concern for life and for all of our futures. We told her that with our special Blue Garter Gang connections, we had stayed friends since high school graduation. Having bonded with us in thoughtful chat as she served our delicious meal, our server presented us with a complimentary triple-fried ice cream sundae smothered with fresh strawberries and whipped cream and gave us a hug!

"You should write a book," she commented. "It seems like you have a special story to tell."

Our bellies full, we took on the challenge. Who had we become? How had our adolescent friendships shaped our adult personalities? We had led parallel but vastly different lives after school graduations. Why were we having so much fun together again now that we were growing older?

Our lives had begun in a medium-size town at "the bend of the Minnesota River," or Deep Valley, as Maud Hart Lovelace called it in the Betsy-Tacy book series. Mankato is a town of hills and valleys and streams, a college town where "getting a good education" was expected and was provided at a reasonable cost. We were products of parents who experienced the Great Depression. Many of our fathers gave the beginning of their adult lives to serve in World War II. Our mothers grew strong and independent in their absence. Much was expected of us as we grew up in the 1940s and 1950s. We were to respect our elders, work hard, not get into trouble, go to college, and make something of ourselves.

We three had navigated years of our youth—the excitement and the adventures of marriage, family, college degrees, and professional careers. We were about to begin the journey into the next phase of our lives. Our parents were in poor health or had passed away. As retirees, we were no longer defined by spouses or by our professions. Some of us were grandparents. Health problems were raising challenges for us. Change was present in nearly every area of our lives. Our comfort zone was being challenged. We wondered where we were going next in our lives. The book about blue garter friendships began to take shape.

The three of us brainstormed over several months, selecting words to best describe our generation as aging women. In our reflections, we found that carefully chosen words described us—first as individuals, then as longtime friends, and finally as members of the larger community of the world to which we had become contributors.

This revelation led us to create the "Amazing Attributes of Aging Women." The text for this section of our book is like a dictionary because it uses English words with their meanings arranged alphabetically. However, all of our entry words are specific descriptions of the mature women we have become. The first entry is always a "Self" word. The second is a "Friend" word. The third is a "Community" word. This dictionary is the specific and logical tool we have developed. The Blue Garter women reflect on the attributes of their unique adult personas in the "Silly and Sacred Stories" section of our book.

After a year of writing, sharing, and more reflecting, we gathered again in sunny Arizona. This time the three of us were joined by two other women from our Blue Garter Gang. We donned 1950s aprons and became the Five Kitchen Divas as we put together a luncheon for women more experienced than we, three charming octogenarians.

After lunch, we read our first writings to our guests and asked for their feedback. They said, "Give us more; tell us more about the Blue Garter friends."

This conversation revealed that our developing book needed to include the voices of the Blue Garter group of friends. When many of us gathered to celebrate our 65th

The Octogenarian Luncheon
Top L to r: Carolyn Petersen, octogenarian Mary Cox, Retta Dykstra,
Mary Huntley, Ginge Klenk.

Botton L to r: Judy Appel, octogenarians Helen Marsh and Audrey Strand.

birthdays, we shared the manuscript. This was the perfect
time for us to meld our ideas and invite more participation.
Discussion followed, including feedback from people not
associated with our own high school class who wanted to
know more about us as individuals. Time and again readers

said that we were so fortunate to have had such rich and lasting connections held together by our Blue Garter Gang. These repeated comments have inspired some of us to share our personal stories.

We also reviewed biographies of famous women for additional words of wisdom and validation. Their voices gave our text color and depth. They are quoted throughout our descriptions of aging women.

Nesting Dolls

Nesting Dolls of Aging

Maturing women perceive themselves and their issues as changing from decade to decade. Victor Hugo describes certain stages of life this way: "The forties are the old age of youth, while the fifties are the youth of old age."

Madeleine L'Engle metaphorically adds, "The nice thing about aging is that you don't lose all the other ages you have been. You are like a nesting doll."

Blue Garter women are now past their second youth. Along with other women of substance, beginning with our own mothers, we have the freedom and the ability to bring forth some of our passions that have been quietly nesting as forgotten dolls of the past. We are ready to recognize the inherited genes of our birth that have been nurtured by our friends and our environment as we have grown up and become strong women.

It is very difficult for a woman to admit to anything that sounds like bragging in public. Minnesota women born in the 1940s were brought up to be kind, inclusive, and humble. With the wisdom of age, Blue Garter women defined themselves using "The AAA's Dictionary." We modestly reveal our passions in the "Sharing Silly and Sacred Stories" section of our book. All active mature women are harboring these sacred strengths.

We encourage you to use the following chapter of our book to help you find your strengths. Three descriptive attributes have been carefully selected for each letter of the alphabet in this dictionary. The definitions are taken from the Webster's *New Collegiate Dictionary*. Some words are accented with hyperbole. We have also liberally quoted memorable statements from famous mature women to give practical examples of each attribute.

Aging women are special characters with special strengths. Each has acquired a unique patina through the years. A well-developed woman's personality can never be duplicated. Her design is worth displaying so that it can be passed on to succeeding generations. Celebrate your well-earned, beautifully unique nesting doll of aging. Nurture it among lifetime friends and your community.

Amazing Attributes of Aging Women

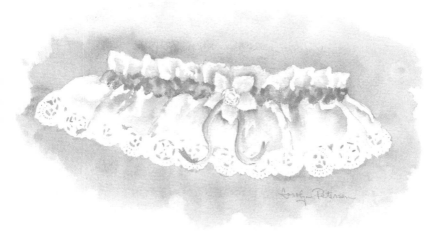

The AAA's Dictionary

The first word for each
alphabetical letter is an attribute of

Oneself

The second word is an attribute of
one's relationship with others

Our Friends

The third word is an attribute
of a member of the

Larger World Community

A

Aging Women Are:

Allied: *united by kinship*

Affirmed: *said positively, declared firmly, asserted to be true*

Adapting: *adjusting oneself to new or changed circumstances*

"At 65 we are beyond the stereotypical 'blue garter' stage; we can be ourselves…find people who validate you…you are doing something that is important…have great passion."

Riane Eisler, eminent author, attorney, and social activist

B

Aging Women Are:

Brave: *willing to face danger, pain, or trouble; not afraid; having courage*

Buoyed: *cheerful, held by lightness*

Bountiful: *giving freely and graciously; generous*

"A woman is like a teabag—only in hot water do you realize how strong she is."

Nancy Reagan, U.S. First Lady 1981-1989

C
Aging Women Are:

Compassionate: *feeling or showing the urge to help others, sympathizing deeply*

Connected: *linked; united together*

Cheerful: *happy and optimistic*

"Women in their seventh decade have woven themselves into the tapestry of life. Among the roles of the grownup Blue Garter women are animal genealogist, artist, athlete, author, board chair, care partner, day care provider, friend, musician, grandmother, historian, international volunteer, librarian, photographer, tax preparer, teacher, and wife."

Judy Appel and Mary Huntley,
authors

D
Aging Women Are:

Direct: *honest and to the point; straight forward; frank*

Distinguished: *celebrated; eminent*

Discerning: *having or showing good judgment or understanding; astute*

"I feel totally prepared to do my strongest work yet."

Mary Ellen Mark,
distinguished photographer

E
Aging Women Are:

Experienced: *made wise, competent*

Evolved: *developed by gradual changes; unfolded*

Empowering: *giving ability; enabling, permitting*

"The wisdom of 60 year old women consists of many rich experiences which have been reflected upon until they can be communicated emphatically with others."

Joan Cleveland,
author

F
Aging Women Are:

Free: *not constrained or stilted; easy and graceful*

Focused: *centered on an activity; attentive*

Founded: *established, organized*

"Perhaps physical and emotional stamina is a matter of habit."

Said late in her life by Golda Meir,
Prime Minister of Israel 1969-1974

G

Aging Women Are:

Gentle: *kindly, serene; patient*

Gleaned: *collected gradually*

Generous: *giving*

> "Running in a circle, someone is in front and someone is behind. Therefore, try to stand in the center. Let the circle revolve around you. Try to be a marvelous pivot. Send out your rays. All your rays will not touch the circumference at the same time. There will be some light and some shadow. But a bit of each is needed by all."
>
> *Pearl Bailey,*
> *American singer and actress*

H

Aging Women Are:

Hopeful: *having expectations of good*

Hailed: *greeted with cheers*

Harmonious: *having similar or conforming feelings, ideas, interests; in accord*

Carpe diem, "Seize the day."
C'est la vie, "That's life."

I

Aging Women Are:

Independent: *not controlled by another*

Interdependent: *mutually relying on others for support*

Inspiring: *arousing positive thoughts or feelings*

"The older you become, the more likely you are to be an exception."

Carolyn Bird, author

J

Aging Women Are:

Joyful: *welcome, happy*

Joined: *participating with others*

Judicious: *wise and careful*

"Innate female spirituality underlies an often unspoken commitment to protect our world from the ravages of greed and violence."

Joan Borysenko,
author of A Woman's Book of Life

K

Aging Women Are:

Knowing: *skillful, well informed, astute, intuitive view*

Kindred: *of like nature, similar*

Kin Keepers: *historians, connectors*

"She is more precious than rubies, and all things thou canst desire are not to be compared unto her."
Proverbs 3:15

L

Aging Women Are:

Liberated: *released*

Loving: *devoted*

Laughing: *making explosive sounds of the voice and the characteristic movement of features of the body (in response to an unexpected altered perception)*

"Positive laughter matters, it releases tension, and is the celebration of a loving heart for living well."
Mary Huntley and Edna Thayer, authors

"...the greater part of our happiness or misery depends on our dispositions and not on our circumstances."
*Martha Washington,
U.S. First Lady 1789-1797*

M
Aging Women Are:

Mindful: *aware, heedful, careful*

Mirthful: *joyful, inner pleasantness,*
sense of merriment

Magnetic: *powerfully attractive,*
bringing people together

"The Plains Indians held the family circle sacred: Girls were taught spiritual and moral responsibilities of life. Grandmothers passed wisdom and respect to grandchildren."

C. J. Bradford and Laine Thom, authors

N
Aging Women Are:

Natural: *not artificial or manufactured*

Nurturing: *affectionate or kindly feeling*

Networked: *having contacts or exchanging*
information with others

"Loss of fertility does not mean loss of desire and fulfillment. But it does entail a change… The woman who is willing to make that change must become pregnant with herself, at last."

Ursula K. Le Guin, prize-winning author

O

Aging Women Are:

Organized: *having an orderly state of mind*

Optimistic: *taking the most hopeful or cheerful view of matters or expecting the best outcomes*

Outspoken: *bold or candid*

Elizabeth Cady Stanton, social activist and founder of the women's movement, once said to Susan B. Anthony, "It is better to be a thorn in the side of your friend than his [her] echo."

P

Aging Women Are:

Peaceful: *not quarrelsome; peaceable*

Perceptive: *able to perceive quickly and easily; having keen insight or intuition; penetrating*

Productive: *marked by abundant production or effective results*

"Handling even a single success...the use of talent, the sharing, the holding on, the giving out and pulling in, requires special preparation. At this stage you should be hoping that if God favors you, you will maintain your sense of values... your sense of gratitude."

Pearl Bailey, American singer and actress

Q

Aging Women Are:

Quiet: *not ostentatious or pretentious*

Qualified: *having the necessary or desired characteristics; competent*

Quotable: *worthwhile reciting or suitable for repeating*

"Classical values are truth, beauty and decency."

Susan Sontag, American literary theorist, novelist, and filmmaker

R

Aging Women Are:

Rational: *showing reason; not foolish; sensible*

Respectful: *full of or characterized by showing courtesy; showing deference or dutiful regard*

Resilient: *recovering strength, spirits, good humor quickly; buoyant*

"Keep your eyes on the road, your hand on the plow, your finger in the dike, your shoulder to the wheel and push like hell."

Vivian Baxter, mother of poet and author, Maya Angelou

S

Aging Women Are:

Spiritual: *characterized by the ascendancy of the spirit; showing much refinement of thought and feeling*

Sharing: *receiving, using, experiencing, in common with another or others*

Socially intelligent: *able to navigate human society, its needs, organization, and development*

"I know that tears rolled down my cheeks and that I held my head in my hands when the voting was over, but all that I recall about my feelings is that I was dazed; I had never planned to be prime minister. I only knew that now I would have to make decisions every day that would affect the lives of millions of people, and I think perhaps that is why I cried."

Golda Meir

T
Aging Women Are:

Tranquil: *free from disturbance or agitation; calm, serene, peaceful, placid*

Tactful: *having a delicate perception of the right thing to say or do without offending; skill in dealing with people*

Tenacious: *persistent; stubborn*

"Her love of life and of all living things was her outstanding quality, of which everyone speaks. More than anyone else I know, she embodied Albert Schweitzer's 'reverence of life.' And while gentle and compassionate, she could fight fiercely against anything she believed wrong."

Rachel Carson, marine biologist, author of Silent Spring, speaking about her mother

U

Aging Women Are:

Unique: *having special qualities*

Uplifting: *raising to a higher moral,*
        social or cultural level

Understanding: *having a sympathetic rapport with*

"The only real security is not in owning or possessing, not in demanding or expecting, not in hoping, even. Security in a relationship lies neither in looking back to what it was in nostalgia nor forward to what it might be in dread or anticipation, but living in the present relationship and accepting it as it is now"

Anne Morrow Lindbergh, pioneering aviator, author, wife of Charles Lindbergh

V

Aging Women Are:

Vivacious: *full of life and animation; lively*

Valiant: *resolute; determined*

Vital: *essential to the existence or*
      continuance of something;
      indispensable

"On the feminine psyche: Women can give everything with a smile, and with a tear take it all back."

Coco Chanel, French fashion designer

Aging Women Are:

Whole: *integrating all aspects of one's being, including the physical, mental, social, and spiritual*

Welcoming: *greeting with pleasure and hospitality*

Wise: *having or showing good judgment*

"Behind every successful woman is herself."

Dolores Huerta, founder with Cesar Chavez of the United Farm Workers of America Union

X

Aging Women Are:

eXacting: *demanding great care, patience, effort*

eXquisite: *of highest quality; consummate*

Xenophilial: *having an attraction to or admiration of strangers*

"Women's values are gradually beginning to shift the zeitgeist in this country, though, not just through political action, but in doing what women do naturally, relating to other women."

Lois Banner, feminist author who introduced women's studies into college curricula

Y

Aging Women Are:

Yea-sayers: *having an affirmative or positive attitude*

Yielding: *bending easily, flexible, productive*

Young-at-Heart: *representing or embodying a new tendency, social movement, progressivism*

"Sister, change everything you don't like about your life. But when you come to a thing you can't change, then change the way you think about it. You'll see it new, and maybe a new way to change it."

Maya Angelou, quoting her grandmother

Z

Aging Women Are:

Zaftig: *having a full shapely figure*

Zesty: *having keen enjoyment, gusto*

Zeitgeistful: *having the spirit of the age; trend of thought and feeling of the period*

"…in order to give birth [you] have to let go of everything inside you."

Mattilda Coumo, First Lady of New York State 1983-1995 and founder of Mentoring USA

From A to Z and with 78 amazing attributes of aging women, the Blue Garter friends continue to grow, admire one another's passions, share new challenges, and live in friendship.

"The Garden of Eden is behind us, and there is no road back to innocence; we can only go forward. The journey we started must be continued. With our blazing candle of curiosity, we must, like Psyche, make the full circle back to wholeness, if we are ever to find it."

Anne Morrow Lindbergh

Revealing
The Blue Garter Story

Through the Eyes of the Principal's Daughter

Unique, the most unique class I have ever seen. The whole class—so close, so together. Remarkable!

Milton Vihstadt

These thoughts were expressed on numerous occasions by my father, Milton Vihstadt, our principal. I listened; I heard; I had a sense of pride. I was part of this very special bond. I felt it, for I lived it—our unique class, the Mankato High School graduating class of 1958. What made our class of nearly 300 students so unique, so close-knit? Could it be that "our gang" played a part in developing and strengthening the school's atmosphere? We were no small gang, no small clique hanging out with just best friends. There were 36 of us who enjoyed each other's friendships. We were together; we were close; we were unique. Every weekend would find us together at athletic events, potlucking before and slumber-partying after. If no athletic event was scheduled, there were dances to attend, picnics planned, or gatherings at each other's homes. Thirty-six of us? Not always—but we all knew we were welcome to join in with whatever was happening. We were accepting, congenial, compatible. We loved being together!

High School Reunion Gathering 1998
Top L to r: Judy Appel, Carolyn Petersen, Mary Huntley, Jane Thom,
Marlys Sloup, Sharon Watson, Liz Shriver, Judy Newhouse.
Botton L to r: SACK Kalahar, Ann Schmidt, Peggy Warren, Retta Dykstra,
Janna Morgan, Ginge Klenk at Maggie's Restaurant, Mankato

High School Reunion Gathering 2003
Top L to r: Mary H., Judy N., Hermine Hirshberg, Peggy, Carolyn, Liz, Ann,
Jean Comfort, SACK.
Botton L to r: Mary Brion, Marlys, Mary Miller, Karen Anderson, Judy A.
at Maggies Restaurant.

Those in our gang had originally come from six neighborhood schools channeling into four junior high schools: Lincoln, Franklin, North Mankato, and College Lab School. As 10th graders, we all joined together at Mankato High School. Each of us came with our early elementary and junior high connections and friendships. Now, through extracurricular activities and personal interests, our range of friends and acquaintances broadened. Could it be that our curiosity and individuality, combined with our congeniality and our acceptance of each other, affected the relationship of other class members? Did our demeanor influence the overall class? Did this play a part in making the class of 1958 unique—so close, so together?

These friendships that developed during the 40s and 50s have continued. Today we cherish the opportunities we have to be together. Being with each other is always special. Time and distance do not seem to matter, for when we're together it's "kind of magic." It takes no time for us to feel as though we are back 50/60 years—same voices, same personalities, same real friends sharing hopes, dreams, and memories.

Gang member Peggy Vihstadt Warren

Yes, as Peggy said, it had become our custom to spend Friday nights before football and basketball games potlucking at the home of a friend. Oftentimes a Friday night dance or a picnic or a slumber party would follow the athletic event. On our graduation day, we realized that our times together were ending.

Following our parents forewarning that the only people who had jobs during the Depression were college graduates, we all were enrolled as freshmen for the fall 1958 college term. Most of us, limited by finances or family obligations, enrolled at Mankato State College in our own town. The University of Minnesota and the colleges of Gustavus Adolphus, St. Olaf, Carlton, Colorado Woman's, North Park, Antioch, and Wooster; Iowa State University; and Swedish Hospital were some of the choices made by more adventuresome friends. Dancing with our boyfriends to the strains of "Moments to Remember" on graduation night, we exchanged tearful goodbyes to our youthful high school innocence on June 5, 1958. We made plans to gather again in August after our summer jobs were over to exchange addresses as well as to buoy ourselves for the unknown adventures ahead. But now we would dress up for lunch at the Holiday House, a nice restaurant with notable cuisine and ambiance, near St. Peter, Minnesota.

We had such a great time at our luncheon that before leaving the Holiday House, we agreed to meet again in December during our first college Christmas break. Elizabeth (Liz) Nelson would host the gathering in her parents' home. We were each to come wearing a sweatshirt from our college. The Blue Garter Gang was formed officially at the holiday reunion.

At first we referred to ourselves as a gang, a commonly used term at that time that meant a group of people with like interests who hung out together. Blue Garter friends could tell their parents that they were getting together with the "gang," and they knew just who we would be with and that we would meet their standards for propriety.

As high school graduates in 1958, many of us were expected to have a college diploma and a wedding band by the time we were 22 years old. The tradition of the bride wearing something old, something new, something borrowed, something blue, and a penny in her shoe was also prescribed. The best friend of our soon-to-be bride sponsored a bridal shower to which all of the Blue Garter Gang were invited. A pretty, lacy blue garter then became a memento and the gang's gift to the prospective bride at that event. It became a tradition for the bride to be photographed at her wedding with her bridegroom holding up her wedding dress exposing a seductively garter-attired leg (see Appendix for Blue Garter Traditions).

Something Blue
Carolyn's legs with blue garters, 1961.

Each bride provided copies of her engagement announcement, shower and wedding invitations, napkins, and the formal bridal photo complete with newspaper article to our Blue Garter historians after the wedding. Mary Hesla and Peggy Vihstadt were chosen as the original Blue Garter Gang co-chairs. They were both very dependable and were staying in town to attend college, so no immediate changes in addresses or phone numbers were necessary. Mary and Peggy were to maintain our scrapbook as well as keep an accurate record of our addresses. A 15-by-12-inch white Webway scrapbook with "The Blue Garter Gang" embossed in gold on the cover holds our treasured engagement and wedding archives.

Through the years, our Blue Garter Gang members have settled in 13 states. Two members have passed away, a result of cancer at a young age. Over time the showers and weddings have ceased, but other excuses to reunite have replaced them.

Blue Garter Lunch 1989
L to r: Jane Todd, Judy Newhouse, Ginge Klenk, Judy Appel,
Mary Huntley, Lois Schoeneman at Country Pub

Blue Garter Lunch 1990
Top row l to r: Jane Thom, Retta, Mary H., Judy A., Marlys, Judy N., Liz.
Bottom row l to r: Weez Anderson, Mary B., Mary M., Caroyln
at Schumacher's in New Prague, MN.

Early on, we had luncheons in the summers when many of us returned to Mankato to visit our parents. On June 30, 1989, Louise Nelson Anderson organized a luncheon at the Country Pub, another elegant restaurant near St. Peter. Ginge Klenk was visiting from West Virginia. Seven friends met that afternoon, coming from at least four Minnesota communities. A flowered journal was initiated that day by Louise—better known to us as Weez—to record the names of the attendees and to describe the setting and the event. More than 20 such gatherings at cafes or homes have occurred since that time. In 1990, it was suggested that we consider celebrating our 50th birthdays with a roving birthday card. There were 27 names from the original group on our Blue Garter list at that time. The plan was for each of us to write a bit of news about ourself and about our family on the birthday card when it arrived. Then we were to mail the card to the next birthday person listed. That card and the letters never made it all the way around to everyone.

When 14 of us gathered for our 60th birthday celebration, 10 years later in 2000, we finally retrieved the Blue Garter birthday card and all of the letters attached to it! Mary Hesla Huntley was our hostess for that special weekend slumber party. We reconnected with each other, our town, and our old Mankato West High School, and we visited with three parents of our gang members still living in town. We brought potluck dishes to share. Mary Huntley baked our special Waldorf Astoria $300 Red Velvet birthday cake using Mary Kolling Brion's recipe. Marlys Case Sloup began a gift exchange.

In 2005 we met again. this time as the guests of Liz Nelson Shriver. Cleveland Heights, Ohio, was the destination for this grand-style birthday celebration. This photo documents our adventure as we were all seated in the "Rocket Car,"

Rocket Car

which with honking horn and blaring siren whisked us throughout Cleveland waving and shouting, "We are celebrating our 65th birthday!" As we passed the Browns' football stadium, crowds entering clapped, whistled, and cheered us on! In a more spiritual setting that day, an urban-historian friend gathered us in Wade Chapel, with the Tiffany stained glass apostles above. We lit candles and sang "Will the Circle be Unbroken?" Delicious food made by our Blue Garter gals, the baking of our traditional birthday cake, a gift exchange, and conversation with our friends invigorated us again.

Ann Warren Schmidt invited us to her home in Shelburne, Vermont, in September 2006, for our 66th birthday celebration.

We were refreshed by the lovely garden setting, neighborhood walks, viewing Lake Champlain, brunch at the Shelburne Inn, and a fair at the historic Shelburne Farm.

Vermont Gathering 2006
Top row l to r: Peggy, Judy N., Ann, Karen, Retta.
Second row l to r: Mary B., Mary H., Jane, SACK, Liz.
Bottom row l to r: Janna, Mary M., Marlys, Judy A.

Door County 2007
Top row l to r: Jane, Karen, Judy A., Mary B., Carolyn,
Sandi Lowery, Liz, Peggy, Ann.
Bottom row l to r: Janna, Marlys, Retta, Mary H.
along the Lake Michigan Shoreline.

The long weekend together created even more enthusiasm for our next gathering.

Marlys Case Sloup, a Wisconsinite, invited us to The Lodge in Door County, Wisconsin, as the place for our 67th birthday celebration in 2007. She and her husband, Joe, chose to rent this huge house for the special gathering. The weather was cool, the autumn scenery spectacular. We toured the Lake Michigan shoreline, hiked, attended a play, shopped, and enjoyed the locals' acclaimed ice cream cones in Egg Harbor. Using The Lodge's full kitchen, we took turns preparing favorite potluck foods for our Blue Garter family. Inspired by our scrapbook archives and sharing photos, we told stories. Playing Mary's newly invented "Blue Garter Bingo," and vying to win Marlys' specially wrapped prizes, created silly, congenial fun.

After 60 years of friendship, Mary Hesla Huntley is still our historian and the keeper of our Blue Garter archives.

We are affectionately grateful for her faithful stewardship of our history, which is now contained in five volumes of photos, wedding announcements, birth announcements, letters, Christmas cards, luncheon journals, honors, retirement celebrations, sympathy expressions, reunion programs, and even adult slumber party memorabilia.

The kin-keeper role is now shared with Mary Kolling Brion. Her gifts of photography and scrap-booking have generated new albums for us. Our 60th, 65th, 66th, and 67th birthday party mementos are beautifully displayed along with those of our 50th high school reunion gathering in October 2008.

Being there for each other and sustaining the common bond of friendship gives us hope. Through knowing, through our kindred hearts, and through our responses to kin keepers we grow more deeply connected.

Blue Garter Gang
50th High School Reunion
Top row l to r: Jane, SACK, Marlys, Mary H., Georgia Hanson,
Janna, Peggy, Liz, Lois.
Middle row l to r: Judy A., Judy N., Carole Hamre, Jean, Ann, Mary B.
Bottom row l to r: Retta, Carolyn, Ginge
at Ann's mother's home in Mankato.

Sharing Silly and Sacred Stories

Blue Garter Friends

From our past came the Mankato High School cheer: "Everywhere we go, people want to know, who we are, so we tell them, we are the Scarlets…." Now, when we gather for our birthday reunions, people want to know who we are, so we tell them we are the Blue Garter friends. Our story goes wherever we go: Mankato, Cleveland, Shelburne, Door County, and wherever we travel from Washington, California, Colorado, Minnesota, Wisconsin, Illinois, Ohio, Vermont, Massachusetts, Arizona, North Carolina, Arkansas, and Georgia.

Each of us has a unique response to "who we are" as a Scarlet, as a Blue Garter friend, as an aging woman. Our reflections and perspectives are shared in this chapter of stories. Some stories reflect specific AAA's, some are inclusive of many attributes, some are messages of gratitude, and some are adventuresome passions. All speak to the varied aspects of what makes this group of nearly lifelong friends stay connected. Our relationships had varied beginnings. All of us were connected in high school and have stayed friends such that when we gather, we begin where we left off the last time. Everyone is openly embraced, and the joy of friendship and aging together is felt over and over again.

Blue Garter friends grew up believing we had many best friends. Our friends have been there for us through many of the needs described in the following excerpt. Blue Garter friends represent the "Wonderful Women in Our Circle."

To The Wonderful Women in My Circle

When I was little, I used to believe in the concept of one best friend, and then I started to become a woman. And then I found out that if you allow your heart to open up, God would show you the best in many friends.

One friend is needed when you're going through things with your man. Another friend is needed when you're going through things with your mom. Another when you want to shop, share, heal, hurt, joke or just be. One friend will say let's pray together, another let's cry together, another let's fight together, another let's walk away together.

One friend will meet your spiritual need, another, your shoe fetish, another, your love for movies, another will be with you in your season of confusion, another will be your clarifier, another the wind beneath your wings.

But whatever their assignment in your life, on whatever the occasion, on whatever the day, or wherever you need them to meet you with their gym shoes on and hair pulled back, or to hold you back from making a complete fool of yourself.

Those are your best friends.

It may all be wrapped up in one woman, but for many it's wrapped up in several; one from seventh grade, one from high school, several from college years, a couple from old jobs, several from church, on some days your mother, on other your sisters, and on some days your daughters.

So whether they've been there 20 minutes or 20 years, praise God for the women that have been placed in your life to make a difference.

Author Unknown

Gloria Steinem reminds us that as women in our 60s, we all have a full circle of human friendship qualities, but we have them in a unique combination that could never happen again. The Blue Garter women, who have searched to find the origins as well as the evolution of these personal stories, know that wonderful memories have emerged. We joyfully share them with you on the pages that follow as essays, poetry, and photos.

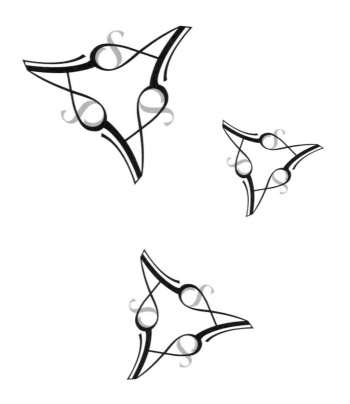

An Evolving Athlete

Judy Strand Appel

*I*n the context of "The AAA's Dictionary," the letter E best describes me as I have searched for my unique mature identity. I am experienced, I have evolved, and I now can be empowering. I have become an athlete!

My home at the far end of the road in West Mankato was the source of a stream of walking friendships. That also meant that I walked a little further than many of my friends. Little did I know at the time that all of this extra athletic activity was manufacturing endorphins within my brain that I would continue to crave for a lifetime. I was well aware of the gift of special time that I spent with many friends daily. I became a kind of Labrador-dog personality. I didn't drool over each person, but I came to love each as a unique individual.

Beginning in kindergarten at Roosevelt School, I met a voracious reader of horse stories at the first intersection; then we continued walking on down to the capable scientist's home, then to the gentle, quiet, beautiful daughter of our Blue Bird leader, and finally to a jolly friend who lived nearly adjacent to the school.

When we got older and took the route to Lincoln Junior High School, the progression added more amazing friends: the exacting seamstress and mathematician; the giggler; the usually late, but always accurate and joyful, and the brilliant. On the reverse walk, we could split at the top of the slough, bringing along the ubiquitously vivacious, the more brilliant, as well as Miss Creativity.

I still was the last one home every day.

For Mankato women attending junior and senior high school, there were very limited opportunities to participate in organized athletics. Cheerleading and Girls' Athletic Association (GAA) were about all. Our eighth grade science teacher, Merv Nelson, was the Mankato High School men's golf coach. Mr. Nelson was a precise and decisive man who held his red pencil the same way every day as he corrected our snappy check tests. We all worked very hard for him and took pride in meeting his high standards. He had only one flaw: He did not allow girls in his golf practice area, located underneath Mankato High School. Here between the immense concrete pilings that supported our beautiful new school, Mr. Nelson had creatively suspended a couple of army surplus tarps from the rafters. The natural dirt floor provided a state-of-the-art golf teeing area kept at a naturally air cooled temperature in all four seasons.

Over time we ladies, led by classmate Liz Nelson, approached Mr. Nelson en masse about the possibility of him teaching us the golf fundamentals. He reluctantly agreed. (I think that he really enjoyed working with us over time.) For Liz and me golf was wonderful. My left-handed friend Carolyn, found it a real challenge, however; our "loner" golf clubs were cast off from right-handed men! Mr. Nelson was such a perfectionist as he taught the grip, the arm positions in the backswing, and the weight shifts, that even with his back to me as I worked out, he would hear the sound of my swing and shout, "Judy, keep your left arm straight!"

Years passed, and MHS women never competed in golf events. But Liz did break one barrier for women by becoming Mankato High School's first female Student Council president.

I continued to be fascinated with the challenge as well as with the satisfaction of using my body to successfully complete golf shots. Although the ambition and the drive to compete were innate, I did not have much stamina. My parents always said that it was because of my light case of polio that left my muscles weakened and aching after the summer of 1951.

It was my husband, a fine competitive golfer and coach, who kept golf alive as we raised our four children. We had great fun on occasional weekend golf blitzes. Leaving as soon as he got home from teaching Friday afternoon, we drove to Dodge Center to play our first nine holes, finishing just as the sun set. The next morning, getting up early, we got in 18 holes at Eastwood in Rochester. Ray always walked and carried. I could handle the walking part. I had to use a pull cart to tote my clubs. Our day would end by playing 18 more holes (riding in a power cart) in Prescott, Wisconsin. Although I'd be exhausted by the last hole, my swing became more consistent. Ray and I would go home on the top of the world!

I joined a golf league and competed in my first tournament after age 40. It all began as Ray convinced me to play in the Women's Club Championship at Oak Glen Golf Club in Stillwater. Wonder of wonders, I became one of the first Women's Net Club Champions at that new course in the early 1980s. Carolyn also got back into golf as her children became more independent. She scored a hole in one using her three-wood at Inverwood Golf Course in 1994. Carolyn and I connected again with our golf soon after. Eventually we went on to play together in Minnesota Women's Golf Association (MWGA) events. Reflecting Merv Nelson's excellent fundamentals instruction, Carolyn and I were on the winning team in the 2005 MWGA Mid-Handicap Tournament. We also won the MWGA Four Ball, First Flight Master's Division championship medal in 2007 and the outright Master's Championship in 2008.

The year before Ray and I retired, we joined a private golf club for the first time. Now I am a part of a whole new group of wonderful women. At Stillwater Country Club, female role models of all ages struggle daily to stay healthy and to improve their golf game in a friendly yet competitive setting.

My golfing goal still is to achieve a single-digit handicap. My tee ball has always been the best part of my golf game. Unfortunately, my short game has always been inconsistent. In 2001 I settled into a practice routine of hitting about 300 balls a day in our yard to cure that deficit. I'd start with a 30-yard hit, and next go to an 80, then on to 100- to 125-yard irons, with all shots aimed for a five-gallon bucket. It got to be a lot of fun listening for the balls to hit the target. Within a few weeks my effort was rewarded. I scored two holes in one nine weeks apart! This amazing feat gave me the opportunity to speak up and promote women's golf at our club, with at least a few men listening intently. Stillwater Country Club was an old boys' club until the mid 1990s, when the club became one of the last in Minnesota to stop paying a tax penalty for discrimination against tee times for women golfers. As President of Women's Golf at Stillwater in 2005, I saw men begin to take pride in the physical accomplishments of their women golfers. Today the club is being ably served, and with pride, by its first female board president.

While I have yet to achieve my handicap goal, in 2007 I won the 18-hole SCC Valley Cup league championship. I have great faith that as long as I can stay healthy, along with the aid of my friends and family, my athletic ability will continue to evolve.

Remembering Yesterday's Passions Today

Janna Polzin Morgan

ecalling memories, I have been thinking back a long ways. I was born and grew up in our small town in southern Minnesota, Mankato. I can remember walking home in grade school looking at the colored leaves in the fall and enjoying all the multiple bright colors that our maples and oaks produced. It was pretty much the same group of us that would walk together going to school: Judy Strand, Sharon Watson, and me. We all went to the same grade school. Those friendships would last for all of these years.

In winter, the crunch of our boots as we trudged along on those crisp days seemed quite noisy. We usually had some kind of scarf over our lower face to keep our nose and mouth warm. In springtime we looked for spring flowers to be emerging, remembering that "April showers bring May flowers." Summertime was supreme. We lay on our backs on the plush green grass and looked up at the clouds floating by. If you had a good imagination, you could picture all kinds of shapes that the cloud formations created.

My first passion was reading. From junior high all the way through high school, I literally read hundreds of animal or horse books to feed my thirst for animals. I can remember that one day alone, I read seven books. With two brothers and two sisters, all younger than me, I learned at an early age how to tune out extraneous noises. I'm sure my mother bemoaned the fact that she had to call me several times to do things, because I didn't hear her. I was in my own dreamland. I wondered if being a veterinarian was my calling.

My second passion, as it were, was animals. I had a tendency to bring home stray dogs. I know Mom had to find several homes for critters that I brought home. I'm sure they were happier, but I wasn't. However, like many other young girls, I reached an age when I wanted a horse. That desire didn't go away. Finally my parents gave in and bought me a horse. Those were some of the happiest days of my life. I rode with a number of other young people who enjoyed riding as much as I did: Judi Krost, Sis Carney, Darlene Denzel, Judy Strand, Nan Blethen, Chuck Burke, Howard True, and Jim Miller. We must have ridden every back trail within miles. We met new people that way, too. We all participated in events at our local saddle club, even sometimes trailering our horses to nearby towns for competitions there. That must have given me my competitive spark because all through my life, I have competed with my animals.

When I went away to college, my horse was sold. I shed many tears over that. In college, since I didn't have a regular form of exercise, I started walking. I walked many a mile, burning off energy, that school didn't take care of. I signed up for horseback riding classes every semester so that I had some outlet. I didn't get credit for some of the last ones, but I didn't care because at least I was getting some small enjoyment out of going riding. Twice I rode in the National Western Stock Show, representing the college in English Pleasure classes.

After college, marriage, and children, my husband and I had an opportunity to get a mixed-breed puppy. She looked like a diminutive Irish setter, long-coat and red. Her name was Tuffy, and she lived to be 14 years old. She broke in several of our succeeding dogs and was good with our children, and I enjoyed her.

As the years passed, I had a stronger desire to get a dog that I could show in the American Kennel Club venue and "real" shows. I worked my way through a number of dogs, each one better than its predecessors. I bred several litters and kept one puppy out of each litter, or at least co-owned several of them. Co-owning means to share the dog and expenses with one of the owners physically caring for the animal.

The American Kennel Club looks at statistics at the end of each year and tallies how many dogs of a breed have been defeated by other dogs in the same breed. For dogs that win Best of Breed and go on to compete at the end of the day in group competition, there is another tally done. Each breed is assigned a group e.g., herding dogs, working dogs, sporting dogs. I had the No. 8 working dog in 1997 for competition in groups, a Rottweiler named Duke. He was the basis for my ongoing breeding program. He was the sire of the No. 4 Rottweiler, Eddie, in the working group in 2004. Eddie competed in herding events the following year and placed No. 2 for all herding dogs in the United States. The herding events use ducks, sheep, and cattle in competition. Duke was the grandfather of the No.1 Rottweiler dog, Nemo, in group competition in 2007.

I am delighted that this boy was genetically strong enough to carry through for several generations.

Using my knowledge of and experience with Rottweilers, I searched for and found a small breed of dog that pleased me, the toy Manchester terrier. Within two years, I co-owned a bitch named Ruby, who climbed the charts rapidly. She was No. 2, in the toy competition, at group level for both 2007 and 2008.

Showing the dogs led me off on another tangent. As I thought about breeding them, I realized I had to research their background or pedigree. I had already made several trips to Germany to see shows there; my dogs are a German breed. While in Germany, I picked up several stud books on the ancestry of my dogs. When people realized that I could do a pedigree for my dogs, they soon asked if I could do one for theirs too. I did, and then enlarged my scope to all AKC breeds. This involves a great deal of detail work and always teaches me something new about different lines in each breed. It gave rise to my business, Evrmor Pedigrees.

Having moved away from southern Minnesota, I have enjoyed the reunions that our class has had. Instead of feeling isolated because I was in a different geographical area, I feel like I have never moved away. The camaraderie that we Blue Garter women built has never left us.

I think that, having moved away from the group, I learned independence. I learned to be resilient and resourceful in my problem-solving. I am convinced that our strong friendships fostered all of this.

I found that most of us have stayed married all these years. Was it our similar upbringings? Few of our parents divorced, and neither have we. My dad died about nine years ago, but Mom didn't stop going places. At 87, she is still out exploring new places. In 2008, I met her in Arizona where she rented a condo for the winter. The year before she was in Florida. Our parents have been active, and so are we. Maybe it is our hardy pioneer stock, but our parents have lived long lives, and I expect to see our group do the same. Our attitudes are upbeat and positive. That doesn't mean that we don't have negative moments, but our response is generally positive and we solve our problems, rather than give up on them.

I'm always anxious to learn new things, and I suspect many of my classmates are the same. Again, did our parents and teachers instill this into us? "The world is our oyster" might be our theme.

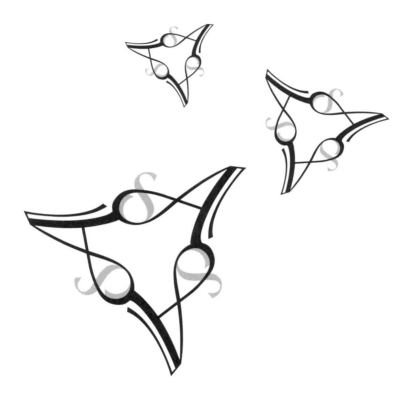

Passing on Wisdom and Respect

Ruetta "Retta" Beck Dykstra

I claim the letters I for Independent, C for Connected, and O for Optimistic as I consider The AAA's Dictionary. My parents brought me up to be independent. I have been connected to my Blue Garter friends for decades. My husband and I have raised our sons to be optimistic people.

The Blue Garter girls came into my life at Roosevelt School when I was in kindergarten. Our school was approximately a five-block walk from my house. It was a neighborhood school. Unless the weather was really fierce, students walked from the four cardinal directions, all converging on the school's playground until the bell rang every morning, interrupting our play. We had an excellent academic beginning. During first grade, a new social element pulled some of us together when the mother of our classmate Lynnette LaGow agreed to become our

Blue Bird leader. Such good memories remain of those days. Although we met regularly in the LaGows' basement to complete projects, it was together as Blue Birds that we all had our first away-from-home camping experience at Camp Patterson. Some of us were only seven years old at the time, so Mrs. LaGow was required to stay with us for the whole week and to act as our counselor. Lynnette's younger brother Dewey, a preschooler, came along and became the mascot of our cabin. Dewey now has fun telling people that he slept with Judy or Jane or Carolyn! Leading our group was a family affair for the LaGows. At our Halloween party with peeled-grape eyeballs and spaghetti blood vessels, Lynette's grandmother claimed that my warts would disappear under the pressure of her fingers on them. Unfortunately, all these decades later, the wart on my left hand, Tall Man, remains in need of further treatment. During those Bluebird and Campfire years, we started the amazing Friday evening potluck supper tradition that served to solidify our bonding in later years. As we moved on to junior high and high school, the core Blue Bird group from Roosevelt School expanded to include girls from other schools who shared our adventurous spirit.

Mankato was a safe town. Young children were free to grow and to discover. My friend, Sharon, and I often walked home Friday nights from the YMCA to my home in West Mankato without fear. After babysitting down the street on Westwood Drive, I thought nothing about walking home alone at 1 a.m..

My husband, Jim, and I came from stable backgrounds with caring parents who had high expectations for their children. According to my father, there was only one way to do things: the right way. I am not sure if my mother was of quite the same temperament, but she either agreed with my father or went along with his standard. Maybe that is why my Wear Ever pots and pans, wedding gift from my father, are still shiny and bright after 50 years of service. Perhaps it is because of my genes that I am more comfortable following a recipe than winging it.

We encouraged independence in our children, just as my mother encouraged that trait in me. Both Jim and I are Iowa State University graduates with degrees in engineering and math. The program was rigorous, but we persevered, upholding the high expectations of our parents in completing the work. Our sons, Hans and Jonathan, born early in our marriage have followed in our academic footsteps. Jon received an anthropology degree from the University of California, Berkeley, and then went on to Wayne State Medical School in Detroit. Today he is a family physician living near Portland, Oregon, with his wife and twin children. Hans graduated from the University of Texas with a PhD in theoretical physics. He followed that with a postdoctoral position at Fermi Lab near Chicago and now has a career in computer programming. Hans and his wife also are proud parents of twin sons.

Both of our sons were Merit Scholars. Although Jim disagrees, I think our sons were easy to raise. There was no hyperactivity or cupboard-climbing. They could entertain themselves and play well together. Their toys were shared. Perhaps that led us to follow the adage "Don't sweat the small stuff." When the boys were arguing or fighting, Jim would ask each about his version of the situation. That seemed to easily resolve the problem, as each had to fess up to his part. The boys were able to care for themselves as we traveled for extended periods of time while they were in high school. While attending a business conference, we left them alone for more than a week. I left notes for their teachers in case there was some unusual behavior. Hans's English teacher seemed impressed that we had entrusted him with this responsibility. I later read in an entry in a journal Hans kept for his English course that he was most pleased to be left on his own.

Jim and I never paid for car insurance for either of our sons. In Canada, high school kids with cars were rare. Kids biked or walked on the trails to school. When we moved to California, we told Jon, then 16, that our income would require his contribution to our insurance payment if he chose to drive. Considering all the options, he chose to ride his bike. Of course, the winters near San Jose were mild. Hans won a free-ride scholarship to Michigan State University and spent several years there as a teaching assistant. We were amazed that upon graduation, he had saved enough money to pay cash for his first car.

As parents, we often refer to the glass half-full versus the glass half-empty. I am the half-full person, thinking that any pursuit is likely to be successful, even though there are obstacles. I can deal with the pursuit *not* working out. If Hans or Jon was unhappy about a test score, I asked, "What is the worst that can happen? If you can deal with that, you can approach a teacher." I used the same approach with a Boston Scientific colleague who often seemed nervous about decisions. It seemed to be an approach that served her well.

An optimistic attitude has served me well all my life. Today in my retirement, I substitute teach. I really enjoy working with bright and challenged math students. Weaving the wisdom of independence, connectedness with others, and optimism, I continue to teach and live my life respecting students, family, and friends.

Embracing the Artistic Gene

Carolyn Meyer Petersen

I was a firstborn child. In fact, when I think of my Blue Garter friends, I realize that most of us were firstborns. That may say something about why we all went to college and were driven to be successful. Because I was older than my siblings, my parents were firmer with me. They expected that I would be honest, trustworthy, and home on time (especially when I went out at night). Because they trusted me, they were willing to give me freedom and independence—with limitations, of course! That sense of freedom and independence I felt growing up in Mankato has stayed with me throughout my life.

When my friends and I graduated from high school, it was expected that we'd go to college, become teachers or nurses and get married, in that order. I never quite fit that mold. I knew before graduation that neither of those professions was appealing to me. A degree in journalism was a possibility, since in high school I had thoroughly enjoyed the imaginative aspects of working as second-page co-editor of *The High News*. However, by my sophomore year at the University of Minnesota, design caught my eye. I settled on a degree in Related Art from the School of Home Economics. This degree supposedly prepared one to go into the creative fields of fashion merchandising or interior design. I stayed in the program through my junior year at the university.

The fall after my junior year, I was married. It was Vietnam War time, and my husband, George, was about to enter law school. Back then first-year law students were not permitted to work. Since George could not afford to go to law school on his own, we decided I would leave college to seek employment and put him through. For years when asked what I'd gotten my degree in, I'd say, "I have my PhT, my Putting Hubby Through degree."

By my 40th birthday, George was a distinguished district court judge, our kids were in junior high, and I had an opportunity to return to the U of M and complete my Related Art degree. Soon after becoming a full-time student, I decided I needed a degree in something that had a more practical application. That's when I applied to the School of Journalism and was accepted. Three years later I finished my degree with an emphasis in public relations. In the spring of 1983, with my entire family looking on, I proudly donned cap and gown to walk Northrup Memorial Mall as a graduate. After graduation I worked in public relations and eventually in the field of hospital volunteer management.

Even though I was working, I continued to walk along an artistic pathway. While at the U of M the first time, I had made myself a promise: At different steps in my life, I would become successful at a number of art media. Those were batik (a wax and dye art process), weaving, potting, photography, and watercolor painting.

Initially I immersed myself in weaving. When I joined the Weavers' Guild in the mid-1960s, George built me a floor stand to hold my table loom. I designed and wove placemats, ponchos, and wall hangings, using natural dyes and homespun sheep's wool. By the early 1970s I had an itch to expand my creativity by trying my hand at throwing pots—making pottery, that is! George again came to the rescue when he built me a kick wheel. Weekly I learned to pot under the tutelage of Richard Abnet, a well-known and accomplished potter. My family could see it coming: They received bowls, cups, ashtrays, vases, teapots, plates, and jars that I'd thrown, glazed, and fired. I was gleefully up to my elbows in wet clay, water, and glazes.

From the late 1970s through the mid-1980s, I created batik wall art. At the Uptown Art Fair in 1983, I made my most successful sale to Augsburg Publishing House in Minneapolis for its permanent collection. They purchased a piece I entitled "Nativity." Augsburg reproduced it as the wraparound cover of their 53rd book edition of *Christmas: The Annual of Christmas Literature and Art.*

Throughout the years, I've taken photographs and am known as the family photographer. It's a form of artistic expression I have always enjoyed. I particularly like using Adobe Photoshop Elements to enhance my photos. I've been known to eliminate saddlebags and double chins from those of us a little older. I even added a touch of a smile to an otherwise beautiful photo of one of my granddaughters. It really brings a smile to my lips when I think of the creative ways I've manipulated photos.

I believe I inherited my creative talents from my mother. She was an artisan all of her life. When Mom was a young girl in Dayton, Ohio, she won a citywide drawing contest. As she grew up, she used her artistic talents to design and sew clothes, probably out of necessity. At 19 she made her wedding dress and trousseau. All her life she was a passionate seamstress. My sisters and I always believed

Mom would rather sew than eat. I remember like it was yesterday all the clothing she sewed for us, including reversible pleated Pendleton wool skirts and jackets. She also sewed one outfit for Mary Kolling Brion. In turn, Mary's mom knit collars and cuffs for the Eisenhower-style jackets that were part of our ensembles. Mom never taught my two sisters and me how to sew. She always said she was too busy with her own sewing—most special to me was my peau de soie, ivory-colored wedding dress which she designed and sewed in 1961!

True to my self-promise, I have explored all of the creative mediums I set out to learn, the last being watercolor. In recent years I have been stretching myself by strengthening my skills as a watercolor artist. While listening to a good Hayden symphony, I can paint for hours, losing all sense of time and space. I feel a sense of freedom, and my creative spirit takes over. Pleasure is my reward for my painting. I also am passing along my love of painting to two of my grandchildren who often ask to come over and paint with me. I imagine in the years ahead I'll spend a lot of time at my artist's table absorbed in new painting discoveries. Though I don't know what my future holds, I do know it looks colorful and bright!

A Twin, Joyfully Joined

Louise "Weez" Nelson Anderson

The mid-20th century in the upper Midwest of America brought a new challenge to the C.D. and Betty Nelson family of North Mankato, Minnesota. The entire family of seven—two parents and five children—was struck with the dreaded disease of poliomyelitis (polio). Not realizing the seriousness of it at the time, having just low fever, mild aches, and slightly painful breathing, the dad didn't even miss work. The children were kept home from school for two to three days, and life went on as usual. Then three weeks later, the second-eldest son, Tom, became very ill with a high fever and severe debilitating weakness. He was taken to the University of Minnesota Hospital and immediately placed in an iron lung for a month. After he was weaned from the lung to breathe on his own, he was transferred to the Sister Elizabeth Kenny Institute in Minneapolis for the following 10 months. He returned home with his parents in the spring of 1949 in a wheelchair. His life was resumed within his family of loving and caring parents and siblings.

I, as his twin sister, assumed a number of roles: therapist, with a morning regimen of leg exercises; transporter, by pushing him to school in his wheelchair, where he was piggybacked up the stairs to the fifth-and-sixth grade classroom on the second floor; and chief facilitator of his paper route, as I pulled him in a wagon and he rolled up the papers and threw them onto front steps. Thus was our life as a family coping with the fact of polio and its devastating aftereffects on one of our own. I will recount some of the struggles, successes, and strengths of this very brave, dear twin of mine, who faced a lifetime of experiences to come.

There were no handicap accesses or assists available for those with special needs in the 1940s, 1950s, or even 1960s, making polio a life-changing challenge for Tom. We kept things as normal as possible for a 10-year-old boy who had a brace on one leg and was not yet able to walk on his own. As one of our childhood friends recalled, "Tom was never left behind; we always found a way to bring him with us in all of our childhood activities." Another friend remembers, "Tom was the same before and after polio," citing his calm acceptance of what was. His droll sense of humor kept all of us on an even keel of dealing with life. I remember only one episode of anger in our growing-up. Tom had just started walking with his "Kenny Sticks" before our junior high years, and he was knocked down flat on his face in the hallway by our lockers. My locker was next to his. I helped him up, gathered his books together, and walked him to his next class. He was beet-red and totally frustrated, but didn't say a word. We never spoke of it again.

Senior high was a different story. Tom was manager of the wrestling team, which was the chosen sport of his older brother, Hans. He was also a sportswriter in our weekly school paper and was elected senior class president by nearly 300 of his peers. Those experiences of total acceptance, support, and encouragement served him well. He went on to a prestigious college and then law school on an academic scholarship and entered the workforce as an attorney for the Federal Power Commission. Even though he got his driver's license in high school like everyone else did, to insure his safety, his Washington, D.C., friends made sure he never drove anywhere in the city alone.

Living his adult life with the effects of polio was the biggest challenge of all. He returned to Mankato to pursue the rest of his career in private law practice. He was a champion of the poor; he defended his clients much of the time pro bono, accepting only what the person could afford. Tom's greatest success was achieving full compensation for a person whose family was killed in a car crash. It was difficult for Tom to do courtroom work; standing with only his sticks for balance was hard.

Tom's health declined during his middle years. He cut his practice to half-time, then one-third. By age 50, Tom was noticeably more fatigued and weaker. He retained his usual calm demeanor and quiet steadfastness, offering us advice only when asked, and was always up for watching an athletic competition with any or all of us. Tom spent his last two years surviving a divorce and visiting Florida for a short respite from Minnesota's harsh winters.

On the last day of March in 1993, Tom quietly slept away. His family had never experienced deeper grief; I felt a huge hole in my heart, which will never be filled in this lifetime. My husband, Joel, expressed it by confiding to me several months later that Tom had always been his favorite. I will conclude by restating my mom's last paragraph in Tom's bio written by her on the sheet distributed at his memorial service: "Tom's clear thinking, unique personality and sturdy independence made him always at our family's center and in our hearts. For 45 of his 50 years, his life was hard; be grateful with us that his death was easy."

Now, 16 years later, I am only beginning to realize that my life was meant to be lived as a twin—Tom was meant to be that twin with me. Later, three more beautiful children were born into the Nelson family; fortunately, they were able to be vaccinated against the scourge of polio.

The introduction of our Blue Garter friends came at a perfect juncture in my life. Our family had moved to West Mankato. I had to find new friends, in a new neighborhood, and attend a new school. My first friendship was with Ginge Klenk. Our parents played bridge together and suggested we might enjoy each other's company. We found we had much in common and became lifelong friends. As a result of walking to school with classmates, we both became actively involved in the activities of our high school. My mother reminded me that I could not be in the "YCDE" (You Can't Do Everything) Club; however, I was the violin concert mistress in the orchestra, a varsity cheerleader, a Dolphin, and a Spanish club member, and was active in other extracurricular activities. Ginge and I both were in a larger group of wonderful friends. This group of like-minded young women later referred to themselves as the Blue Garter Gang. We have enjoyed this base of support and camaraderie and shared delightful experiences throughout our lives!

My own nuclear family of a wonderful husband and two amazing adult daughters has completed my life's circle of family and friends. I sincerely believe my experience with these great groups prepared me for a successful and heartwarming career with people as an aerobics instructor and swimming teacher. Hopefully, I have given as much as I have received.

Nurturing Locally and Globally

Judy Pyles Newhouse

Carhopping was a common form of employment in the 1950s but isn't as well known in this century. In our town, carhopping seemed to be the job for teenagers during the summer months.

The Oasis root beer stand was just two blocks down the hill from our house and where I worked for many summers. I learned a lot from that job; unlike at the other root beer stands in town, we didn't write down the orders. The owner found this to be a good marketing tool, and it certainly helped me in many areas of my life.

One area was teaching Spanish to 400 elementary students. I was able to memorize all their names. Throughout my life, I've had an interest in people's lives. They always appreciate my remembering details about them.

My husband and I raised four children, two biological and two adopted. When our two birth sons were almost four and one, our nephew, who was five, came to live with us, and we adopted him. We both longed to add a girl to our family, and when our Costa Rican neighbors told us that we could adopt from their country, I knew adopting a girl was a possibility. The boys were almost nine, eight, and five when my husband and I flew to Costa Rica to meet our daughter, who was only two months old. The people there called her "Chiquita Linda," which means beautiful little girl.

The only information we had about our daughter's birth family was that there were older siblings. When Karen graduated from high school, we took her to Costa Rica so she could experience where she was born and possibly to find her other family. In their language, they would call our experience a "milagro" or miracle. We discovered she had six brothers and sisters. We met all but one sister and her birth mother and father. Karen said a hole in her heart was filled because of this experience. The story generated local interest, and a three-page article titled "Karen's Roots" was published in the Sunday edition of the local newspaper.

Because of my love for people, our family hosted four exchange students. My horizons really expanded from being raised in a medium-size town and carhopping to connecting with young people from another part of the world.

It would be difficult to choose only one letter in "The AAA's Dictionary" to define myself. I learned to be joyful waiting on all different personalities at the root beer stand. When I reflect on raising our four children and hosting our Guatemalan students, I would have to say that I was nurturing. My friends think of me as full of life and active;

therefore, I see myself as vivacious. And finally, I love to be welcoming, since I love to entertain and be hospitable in our church family, our immediate family, and others outside the circle.

I am very thankful for the life I've had so far and hope to be a blessing to everyone with whom I come into contact.

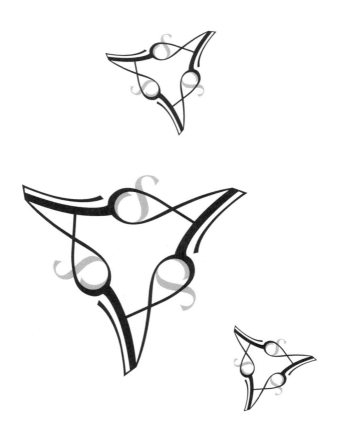

Laughing All the Way

Mary Hesla Huntley

*B*lue Garter friends always have fun together, even before they knew about being named the Blue Garter Gang. I remember living in the Betsy-Tacy-Tib neighborhood of Mankato. This was a neighborhood described in the books written by Maud Hart Lovelace, who was born in Mankato in 1898 and lived on Center Street. I lived in Tib's house on Byron Street during a period when it had been converted into a duplex. My lifelong friendships with Liz and Janet, who lived a block away, began at that time. Our kindergarten days at Lincoln School with Miss Radcliff as the teacher were exceptional. She was about our height, wore a perpetual smile, and loved all of the children. She provided the beginning of an education that many of us remember as enjoyable and positive.

After World War II was over, I moved to a house close to the Mankato State Teachers' College campus. For me, neighborhood friends changed, school friends changed, and all of it was fun. I acquired "Lab School" friends during those four years of elementary school. Even now our images of teachers, classroom activities, and students in the classes continue to be vivid.

When the instrumental music program began in the public schools beginning in fifth grade, more changes occurred. Going to Union School during fifth and sixth grades meant playing the cello and making new friends. Being the jacks champion was as good as it got for me in the domain of athletics. However, it was the beginning of a life revealed some 40 to 50 years later. I still have the joke book I wrote in the sixth grade. Friends shared riddles and rhymes, and I wrote them down or copied them from *The Weekly Reader*. Funny art doodling was included. I had more new friends.

We roamed purposefully all over town. Sometimes we walked places; sometimes we biked. Families typically had only one car, so we were on our own for getting places. According to today's standards, we were a liberated group; our freedom was vast. Mankato was a safe place to be. There was trust from loving parents. Whatever worries parents had were not shared with children. Children were allowed to be, to have fun, and to enjoy growing up. Our play was truly our work. Neighborhood games included Hide and Seek, Kick the Can, and Annie, Annie Over. We played until it was dark. Our mothers called us to come inside at bedtime. There was no television to watch.

Because there were connections made before going to high school, forming a new community of friends was much easier. Friends welcomed friends. The warmth of friendship translated to a sense of devotion to friendship and being open to new friends, rather than forming cliques among a few people.

Even though I chose to stay at home and attend Mankato State College, I felt liberated, with a sense of being on my own. Nursing was my major in college. I enjoyed caring about and for people. Behavioral health became my specialty area in graduate school. I was interested in how to help people rediscover their quality of life and happiness. Getting a graduate degree posed a new set of challenges. I was the one who said I would never go back to school after four years of college. Now, I felt really liberated as I began to explore more career opportunities. Even though I also said I would never be a teacher, nursing education was calling to me. I was soon hooked on working with students and being involved in the other side of academic life.

However, life in academe has its own set of expectations. One expectation was to earn a doctoral degree. I had found my comfort zone, and going back to school again was not part of it. I was treading carefully—I checked out various universities, and even took some summer courses just to see if it seemed like a good choice. Again, I was hooked. The next summer I packed my bags, loaded the van with some furnishings for an apartment, learned to operate a computer, and off I went 16 hours south on Interstate Highway 35 to Denton, Texas. It had been 18 years since I was in a degree program. I was scared beyond scared.

Talk about being liberated—it was the most liberating experience of my whole life. I left behind a loving and supportive family of a husband, two teenage children, a cat, and a dog. Tears streamed down my face as I drove south on 35 to attend Texas Woman's University. I had never lived alone before. I had never had my own apartment. At first it was awkward, then it was delicately delightful, then it was absolutely wonderful. I could not admit it to many, but I was free, I was on my own and loving it. I was healthy, studious, judicious, and totally directed toward my goals. My loving family was ever present and supportive. We were only a phone call away. I asked my aging parents, who lived in Florida, to please do their best to stay healthy during this time—it would be the best gift ever for me so

I could stay focused. They did it. My dad died two years after I graduated.

I knew from the beginning of that educational experience that I would study the relationship between laughter and wellness. I knew in my heart of hearts that those variables influenced each other—now, to find out how. I was able to use nearly every course to study the twists and turns of this relationship, finally culminated in a completed dissertation, PhD graduation, and then back home to teach the course, Laughter and Wellness for Nursing Practice. A strong emphasis was to develop ways to laugh with oneself and others not laugh at others. Twenty-some years later, and after five years of retirement, a book about laughter and wellness was published by me and a nurse colleague. It is finding its way across the country. Who would ever guess a person could connect with being liberated because of love from a devoted family, and could fully experience the wonders of laughter all the way from a sixth grade joke book to authoring a book, *A Mirthful Spirit: Embracing Laughter for Wellness.*

Laughter is one of the strongest attributes shared by this Blue Garter group of friends. For me, it was first the laughter over playful times, sharing jokes, and just seeing the joy of life unfolding before us every day. We did not realize at the time what was happening. However, we did have the wisdom to chow down Chuckles candies as a symbol of our silly times together. In retrospect, we realize our great fortune. Now I share these memories, Chuckles candy, and lots of laughter with my grandchildren.

Balancing Faith, Family, and Friends

Elizabeth "Liz" Nelson Shriver

$\mathcal{L}$ooking back is refreshing. Just as visiting hometown Mankato gives me a renewed connection with my roots, recalling so many events of the early years puts me back in touch with the people and places that remain treasured memories. Throughout all stages of my life, there seem to be common threads: faith, family, and friends. Balancing all of those has always been a challenge.

In my family, I happened to be the youngest, the queen of all positions. Most things went my way. My older sister and brother were role models and very good to me while they were at home. And when they left, I especially enjoyed the friendships of neighbors and friends my own age. My parents were always dedicated church members and offered that to me as a source of inspiration and service. It has continued to be meaningful to my spiritual growth.

Friends from childhood to this day have been solid sources of loyalty, knowledge, and fun. I remember the formation of the Blue Garter Gang in our family living room. We all gathered in December 1958, wearing our college emblem sweatshirts and having completed one quarter or semester of college. My parents were always happy to have my friends share our home. They knew all the girls and were as interested in their lives as if they were family. I hope that my home is as welcoming as I remember my Mankato home.

Leaving home to attend the College of Wooster in Ohio determined the direction the rest of my life would take. Wooster was a perfect match for me. The rich liberal arts focus combined with a Christian foundation challenged me in every way. The small campus was a comfortable atmosphere for making new friends. The best event was at a dorm dinner on Valentine's Day my freshman year when I met a boy, now my husband of 46 years. Dave and I married and ventured to Cleveland, Ohio, ready to take on the world.

We immediately embarked on new experiences. I taught in an urban school. Dave attended graduate school at a large university. We made new friends from backgrounds so different from our own and were introduced to so many rich experiences and challenges, from urban problems to race relations. Since we were so far from our homes, many of our friends became extended family and continue to remain close to us.

Our family grew to include four children and nine grandchildren. The family roles keep changing. Now we are supporting our own children in their roles as spouses and parents. Always, the family has been my greatest joy, challenge, and support.

It was a thrill to host a gathering of the Blue Garter Gang in our home to celebrate our 65th birthdays. One of the highlights was to have a close Cleveland friend, Sandra Vodanoff, lead a tour of my Mankato friends through the Wade Chapel in Cleveland, where we were in awe of the beautiful stained glass designed by Louis Tiffany. It became a special spiritual moment for all of us to share as Sandra sang "Shall We Gather at the River?" and we lit candles in memory of our loved ones.

We have all been searching for an answer to why we continue to enjoy our early childhood friends so much after all these years. One of our group, Mary Hesla Huntley, has kept us together through her amazing collection of memorabilia related to all of our lives from childhood to the present. She has remained in Mankato and been the anchor.

She, too, has been challenged by the balancing of events in her life that keep faith, family, and friends a focus. We are grateful for the way she has included us as her lifelong friends. She has taught us that along with all that life deals us, we need to keep in touch, lighten up, and laugh a lot. It works!

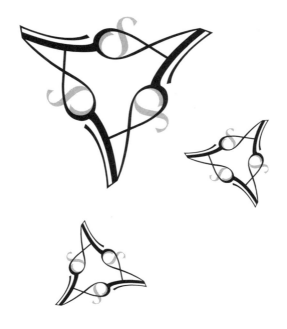

Overflowing with Music

Georgia Koberoski Hanson

I have always loved my memories of growing up in Mankato. Our home was in the middle of a nursery in a beautiful valley. We were surrounded by the many varieties of the prettiest trees, flowers, and shrubs that a nursery would have. Going for walks or bike rides was always special, because we were in the midst of all that beauty. The hills around were wooded and perfect for hiking to find the first wildflowers of the season or just plain relaxing away a Sunday afternoon. However the 1950s was a unique time. Many things we don't even think about anymore were major problems to us then. The fear of an attack by the Russians caused us to practice blackouts in our community. It was very scary to a child. The threat of illnesses we no longer have to deal with, especially polio, were major issues because vaccines had not yet been discovered. Antibiotics were still relatively new.

The heavy snows of the winter of 1951 brought about devastating flooding the following spring in Mankato. The extreme dampness of that summer seemed to harbor bacteria and germs, causing major illnesses to run rampant in our community. A major polio epidemic took the lives of several young people, including our 14-year-old neighbor boy and my brothers' best friend, also 14. It crippled many more. Two of my brothers became extremely ill at this time. Their symptoms were paralysis, extreme pain in the limbs, and dangerously high temperatures. We assumed it to be polio. However, when tests came back negative we had to look further for answers. Eventually rheumatic fever was diagnosed. One of my brothers proved to be deathly allergic to penicillin. Complications with Saint Vitus' dance were ravaging my other brother. Doctors seemed to be puzzled for answers. Therefore, my parents in desperation to help their very ill children, moved the family to another state seeking alternative help for their sons.

Our family spent six weeks from the middle of September to the first part of November living in a small apartment, seeking care for my brothers. They got better, but were by no means well when we returned to Mankato to continue treatment with the specialists there. We had two hospital beds brought into our kitchen/dining room so that my brothers would be part of family activities. We spent many more months caring for them at home. It was a very difficult time for all of us. The positive ending to this story is that my brothers recovered and went on to live happy, productive lives.

That was the beginning of seventh grade for me. It was also when students from other schools joined us for junior high at Lincoln School. What an exciting time! However, when we were out of state, my other brother and I did not go to school. I had missed all those weeks of classes, and we were all still very busy caring for two sick boys at home. It was a very hard time for me. Fortunately, we had kind, caring teachers who recognized my dilemma and allowed the make up work to "go away." The social situation was different. My best friend had moved away at the end of sixth grade, and now all these new students had taken over "my" friends so I felt completely lost. It would be a whole year before I began to feel like one of the bunch again.

Mankato High was a great place to be. We had amazing teachers! I feel so lucky to have been there at that time. Perhaps the teachers at Mankato High have always been of such quality, but we surely felt lucky to be there then. We knew our teachers were the best! We were also told by Mr. Vihstadt, our principal, that we were the "best class Mankato High has ever had!" What a reputation to live up to! I am certain that each of us worked just that little bit harder to live up to the idea of being the best.

Perhaps my fondest high school memories would have to be those connected to the debate team. Mr. Fitterer was an awesome debate coach. He was dynamic, funny, inspiring, and just plain nice. He pushed us to be the best we could be, encouraging us to set goals for ourselves and work our hardest to attain them. Traveling to out-of-town meets at colleges and universities, eating out, staying in hotels—all of this was unusual to everyday life back in the 1950s. It surely was a big part of the educational package of being a debater. Of course, traveling together and working hard together also was preparing us for our adult lives ahead. I am so grateful for this high school experience.

The friendships being created at this time in our lives, whether they were new or old, were also shaping who we were as individuals. We were evolving into the group we came to call the Blue Garter Gang. Our pregame potlucks, the slumber parties, and Sunday afternoon birthday tea parties were all contributing to our becoming the women we are now. As a piano teacher, I can't imagine how I would have survived and enjoyed so much the many recitals we have had in our home and in public without the experience of those Sunday tea parties! We Blue Garter girls were and still are a diverse group of women who were growing up in a special time. Life was more simple then. I watch the world of my grandchildren today and think how scary it will be to have to find one's way in the very complicated world of tomorrow.

College years were not a realization of my fondest dreams. Living in Mankato and going to college in my hometown was never in my plans; however, it was my parents' plan, and they made that decision for me. I had always been a serious piano student and had taught piano with the guidance of the wonderful Mrs. Silber in high school, so being a music major was right for me. I noticed a cute guy playing tuba in the band—Lowell Hanson by name. To make a long story short, we became a couple and married upon his graduation. Together we moved to Montana.

Our years in Montana were very rewarding. Lowell was a high school band director, and I was the piano teacher. It has been a great working combination! Our three daughters were born in Montana, and we spent 12 years working hard to create fine music programs for young people. We have always been lucky to live in communities that were eager for the kinds of services we had to offer. Life was wonderful.

Eventually I began to wish that we were closer to our parents and families. They were missing out on their grandchildren growing up, and our children were missing out on having a relationship with their grandparents. We decided to leave Montana—it was very hard—and return to a Minnesota place nearer to our families.

Montevideo was the community looking for us. It is a lovely town much like Mankato with the two river valleys, only much smaller. We have had 35 wonderful years here. Lowell has retired from teaching high school band, but does substitute work in music at area schools, still has the community band he started 25 years ago, and works hard at a local nursery. He worked on my parents' nursery back in our college days; little did we know that it would come to be something of a second career for him.

I have said I will probably teach piano until I can't—either physically or mentally—because I love it. It is simply a part of who I am. I recently discovered that there are compositions hiding away in my head: Some of them are four-part piano quartets, some are duets, and some are solos. My composing began because we had difficulty finding piano quartet music for my more advanced students. I jokingly said I would have to write one, having no idea that one was floating around in my head. I am looking forward to the possibility of attempting to have some of this music published and continuing to enjoy this kind of work in the years ahead. It is terribly exciting, kind of like the excitement of reading a very good book!

We are a lucky couple. Our children have all chosen to return to the Montevideo area. Our grandchildren are an extremely important part of our lives. Everyone loves to come to our lake place in the summer. Our life is very full.

I regret having been a delinquent Blue Garter member for many years. I hope to be far more faithful in the years ahead. Finding that my friend Ginge had returned to the Mankato area finally gave me the impetus I needed to look up my long-ago friend. The years sort of fell away. She encouraged me to attend our 50th class reunion and also to reunite with the Blue Garter group. I found to my delight that they were still all of what they once had been, with the added bonus of the wisdom formed by the many years that have gone by. I am so glad for this rediscovery.

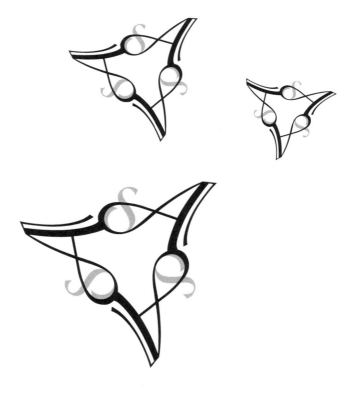

Ties That Bind - Faith, Family, Friends, and Fun Travel

Sharon Ann "SACK" Carlson Kalahar

A special group of girls was born in 1940, girls who remained friends forever! I remember critical events in Mankato that left vivid imprints on my brain. I remember hot summer days when Tourtellotte Pool was closed because of the polio outbreak; having my tonsils out in a doctor's office; my dad walking the block at night to make certain all shades were pulled and no house lights could be seen during the nighttime civil defense blackouts during World War II; buying sugar with ration stamps while shopping with my mother at Popular Foods grocery store; squeezing the dot of red food coloring into the white shortening that came in a plastic bag. My brother and I fought over who would get to squeeze the food coloring, which changed the white

Oleo margarine package to a buttery yellow. We had limited understanding of the impact all this had on our lives.

Little did I know that my Lab School days, high school education, summer camps, travel, and church every Sunday morning and evening would influence my life so strongly. In 1945 I started kindergarten. With the encouragement of Effie Conklin, a neighbor and art professor at the then Mankato State Teachers College, I was enrolled at the College Lab School. As a lab school, several student teachers were always on-site observing and perfecting their skills. I can remember the kindergarten room with its cloakroom; the playroom with large blocks, planks, and screws; and a piano room. My favorite third grade memory is petting two cute and cuddly baby lions that visited our school from the Mankato Zoo. In fourth grade our teacher held "health checks" every morning. Hands, nails, and teeth were inspected for cleanliness. Throughout the year she continued to stay on top of the health issues of each student. When I had chickenpox, books couldn't even be sent home because I was contagious! The science fair that year brought project expectations. My dad, an optometrist, helped dissect a pig's eye; it was displayed in a tall test tube so each layer of the eye could be seen.

Did I mention that girls could wear only dresses or skirts, and no slacks? This practice was not appreciated by someone like me who did not like "dressing up." By the sixth grade, we could wear slacks on Friday—TGIF! Spelling has never been one of my strong points. Once I was told that if I received 100% on a Friday test, I would be allowed to attend a Youth for Christ rally. I did not cheat, but I saw a student teacher correct one of my words so that I could get that 100%. He knew how badly I wanted to go to that special event.

For grades seven through nine, there were many advantages to being on a college campus and having access to various science, art, and athletic facilities. One memory with junior high friends focused on nicknames. Mine was SAC, representing my initials. It stuck and prevailed through high school and college. My mother did not like it very much. She always called me Sharon around my friends. When I married and took the name Kalahar, my nickname just expanded to be SACK. Among my Blue Garter and college friends, my name is still SACK.

I remember the flood of 1951. The Blue Earth and Minnesota Rivers flooded both North Mankato and lower Mankato. The homes of many people were nearly destroyed by the high water. We housed our pastor, his wife, and three children for several days. Later another family came to stay with us. It was a bit cozy with four adults, three boys, and two girls in a small four-bedroom, one-and-one-half bath home. My parents generously welcomed everyone.

My paternal grandparents were always available and only a bike ride away. Grandma always had cookies ready and an overnight room for my brother and me when our parents went out of town. Grandpa Andrew Carlson had been the custodian at Mankato State Teachers College where I attended grades K-9. My Carlson grandparents were even caretakers at Stony Point Bible Camp on Loon Lake in Lake Crystal, Minnesota. I attended camp there at least one week every summer. Having family conveniently nearby was coincidental—or was it?

A great time was had by all the kids from our Covenant Church district for both summer camps and winter retreats. We all became friends. It was important that I be at church on Sunday mornings and Sunday nights. This was expected by my parents even if I wanted to go out on summer Sunday nights with my friends.

In addition to the kids attending Bible Camp and Camp Fire Camp at Lake Washington, we made many summer trips as a family, both by car and train. My parents were very involved in the National Optometric Association and attended many annual conventions. This gave my brother and me the opportunity to visit historical spots and national parks even as our country was painfully stressed by war. Imagine the gift of experiencing the beauty of Mt. Rushmore, Old Faithful, and the tall, majestic redwoods, and the horse stable in Kentucky where Man o' War was raised. One time during the intense heat of June, we drove in a car with no air conditioning. The gift that day was a refreshing swim in the Atlantic Ocean off the coast of Miami. History and the social study of the United States came alive for me. I learned to love traveling and living history.

After ninth grade, my classmates and I from the Lab School began attending Mankato High School. I knew some of the students there from my church and through my parents. Peggy Vihstadt, daughter of the high school principal, became one of my best friends. We had known each other from Kiwanis children's activities. Both of our families had moved to West Mankato where we walked to school together. Later I drove us and our younger brothers to school—lucky me.

When I was old enough to work, Carolyn Meyer and I detasseled corn for the Green Giant Company during the summer. This was an extremely itchy job, but we thought the money was great! During those important school years, there were 15 or so girls who became very close. We attended Friday night football and basketball games and dances. We pulled taffy, held potluck dinners, and enjoyed teas with our mothers. For homecoming, each homeroom decorated a float, and there was a parade down Front Street. After these activities, we and our dates went to someone's house for a party or to a local park for a cookout. Morning summer school was a must to earn more credits toward graduation; afternoons we swam at Lake Washington Club.

After my high school graduation my parents and I were delighted to receive my acceptance to our church-affiliated college, North Park, which is now a university. It was the only school I had applied to! I was reunited with my friends from Bible Camp the day I moved in. I also met Bill Kalahar, my future husband, during the four years before I received my degree. College was a great time for me. High school friends came to visit. Going to college in the big city of Chicago, riding the El to Marshall Fields in the Loop to shop, and taking the train from Evanston to Mankato were all adventures. The North Park experience prepared me for my first teaching job in Glenview, Illinois, where I taught students from the Naval Air Base.

Bill joined the Air Force and became a military officer. We were married with a military-style wedding in Mankato. Our first assignment was to Bellevue, Nebraska. However, Bill was soon sent to the Panama Canal Zone, and I went home to Mankato where I delivered our beautiful daughter, Lisa. Baby and I lived with my parents until suitable housing was available in the Panama Canal Zone. After leaving the military, we moved to Park Ridge, Illinois. Lori was born. Bill was transferred to Atlanta in 1972. Kristen was born. While living in Atlanta, we realized our marriage was not working. It was time to make a change. The pain of divorce was deep for me, the girls, and for my extended family. Through my faith in God and my close friends, I feel that I have grown spiritually from facing the tough choices that had to be made. New self-confidence led me to new independence and to my dream job as a first-grade teacher at the Galloway School in Atlanta. Travels associated with the school took me to Ecuador, Galapagos Islands, Costa Rico, Mexico, and China.

My three daughters are a blessing to me. Lisa and I share the love of teaching first graders. Her family and I have enjoyed summers at the beach on St. Simon's Island, Georgia. Lori's interest in traveling in and out of the U.S. has provided us with several memorable trips. Travel, photography, and spending time with family have given Kristen and me special times together. Four grandchildren who call me Nana have brought the joys of watching them grow and play soccer. Now my family's tradition of traveling together has begun with big-city family adventures to Boston, Chicago, Washington, New York, and Philadelphia.

While life has taken me and my Blue Garter friends in different directions, now many years after kindergarten or high school together, we remain in close contact. Wherever or whenever we gather, we celebrate our friendships held together by lifelong ties that continue to bind us.

Declaring and Believing It Will Happen

Karen Marie Anderson

A is for Adventure, and U is for the Unknown, and both are exciting to me and have been motivating me most of my life. Compared to my classmates, my situation was quite different. There was no one to walk to and from school with, no talking and playing along the way, picking pretty weeds in the spring, and sliding on the ice on a cold winter day. No friend's mother invited me in for hot cocoa and cookies to warm me up. No, my first adventure with young town girls was in the ninth grade. I rode 13 miles into town every day in a yellow school bus with a bunch of farm kids. Surrounded mostly by boys, some of whom still had on their "barn boots," to put it politely, I wanted to distance myself from some of them.

Going to school in town was a new and unknown adventure. I had gone to a country school of only four classrooms, with two grades in each room, from first through eighth grade. In my grade during those eight years, sometimes I was the only girl with about five or six boys. In my own family, I was the only girl, with three brothers.

Therefore, it was so exciting to go to the big city school in Mankato. Compared to the little town of Judson, Minnesota, with a population of only 100, I would be meeting lots of girls. I loved it! I would have girls to talk about boys with, girls to study with; we could discuss life's problems together. We could potluck together, have slumber parties and birthday parties. I was so happy! This was my first experience with a whole gang of girls who weren't cousins. They were friends. I was also very lucky. Mrs. Stanley Jones, a well-known piano teacher in town, who I took piano lessons from, introduced me to a couple of her talented students who were my age. She wanted me to know someone when I stepped off the yellow bus at my new town school. I also had a really nice big brother who drove me into town to pick me up on Saturday mornings after I had stayed overnight with some of my new girlfriends.

Girl power and Woman power—we certainly didn't call it that 50 plus years ago, but we knew there was a special strength and consciousness when we were together. We could talk about and do almost anything. This was the beginning of the Blue Garter Gang, our special friendship. Of course, there were still some problems, like dating, or not dating; our complexions (I don't even want to write the p----- word); worrying about being too fat or too thin or too flat-chested; hairstyles; and, oh dear, wearing glasses. You couldn't even be an airline stewardess if you wore glasses in the 1950s. I wore glasses.

Strange as it might seem now, we arrived at the name Blue Garter Gang because we gave a blue decorative garter at the bridal shower of whomever was getting married. There were some girls in the group who got married during college or upon college graduation. I always admired the ambition and focus of these girlfriends. This was the end of the 1950s and the early 1960s. They wanted it all: a husband, a good college education, a career, and babies.

At that time in my life, marriage was not of interest to me. I just had a desire to travel and see the world. I wanted to explore the unknown in person and not just through the National Geographic, which my extraordinary Swedish grandfather sometimes read to me. He would tell me his stories too, including how he left Sweden by himself when he was 13 years old. I had already decided by fourth or fifth grade that I would have to see the Seven Wonders of the World. I didn't know how I was going to accomplish it, just that—it was what I wanted to do.

Growing up on a turkey farm with plenty of land surrounding us was a wonderful experience. We had an abundance of things to do all the time depending on the season. My dad was the King of Invention and had fun with his family. He built a huge swimming pool for us out by our woods that tapped into a freshwater stream before it went down into the valley. There was a spillway with a water wheel and a diving board. There was also a small changing house and a fireplace for outdoor cooking. We called it Anderson Park. Mom and Dad were always there for my three brothers and me, no matter what was going on. We were each "Number One!" in their eyes.

I decided to go to Gustavus Adolphus College, located about an hour from where I grew up. College life was exciting. I had a hard time deciding what I wanted to do. I switched majors from interior design to social work, and then to painting and art. My career path was not clear. Then one day at the beginning of my junior year, the Air Force, Army, and Navy came calling. They were looking for teachers. I knew this was it! I would be a teacher in the

Air Force and see the world. I immediately went to the registration office. I switched all my classes to education so that I could teach the children whom I already adored working with.

After teaching for two years in the Twin Cities area, I landed a job with the Air Force in Japan. It was with the Department of Defense, and we, the teachers, were first lieutenant officers with all privileges. It was very exciting. We could take space-available trips as long as we were back at school in time to teach our classes.

When I returned home from Japan, I thought I could easily settle back into my old life teaching and living in Minneapolis, but it wasn't the same. It was wonderful to see my family and friends and to be part of one another's lives again, just like it was yesterday. There were family reunions, Blue Garter reunions, showers and weddings, and luncheons. It was great fun to be home again, but I still had the urge for more unknown adventures.

Once again, that great "aha" moment came when I least expected it. It was minus 20 degrees, with snow up to the windowsills, and I was reading the *Star Tribune*, the Minneapolis daily paper, and looking at the employment opportunities, and there it was: "International Schools from New York hiring for jobs abroad. Interviews tomorrow at the Lemington Hotel, downtown." I returned from that initial job interview with a strong-enough feeling that I told my roommates maybe I should give them notice, since I thought I would be heading to West Africa soon. That did come true. I spent the next three years in Ghana, helping to establish an international school for Kaiser Aluminum. We oversaw the building of a $1 million school. As the first teacher hired, I taught every grade in the first couple of months. I developed amazing insight into the cultural and political transitions of West Africa as they evolved before my curious eyes over the years 1965-1968.

After completing Phase 1 of my long-range plan—visiting 57 countries—I was ready to return to the United States for Phase II, moving to San Francisco. That would be where I would get married and settle down at age 30. I was 32 on my wedding day, two years off my schedule.

It was a crazy time to move to San Francisco, a year after the Summer of Love in the Haight Ashbury. I thought America had gone off her rocker. I had been away for four years, and America had flown the coop. So much had changed, but I was very happy to be back in the USA!

In 1976 the most magnificent event of my life occurred when I gave birth to my son, Nathaniel. During the nine months of this production, I was aware of the miracle I was creating. I worked every day until the weekend he was born and had amazing energy. He is the joy of my life.

You Can't Take the Country Out of the Girl

Karen Anderson on John Deere Tractor in Vermont.

After spending nearly 40 years in California, I still say I'm going "home" to Minnesota—to my mom, brothers, their families, and our family farm. When I'm there, I try to connect with as many of my Blue Garter friends as possible. As we have started to retire and have more time, we have spent some long weekends together in interesting places sharing our wisdom and humor. It is truly a blessing.

In closing, I was trying to think about my life and if there were any lessons for all of us. I think the main theme is to "Declare What You Want and Believe It Will Happen."

Now I'm about to start my singing career with some lessons. It will happen.

Heartfelt Interracial Pioneer

Mary Kolling Brion

I am Mary Kolling Brion, part of the "North Mankato" group. I went to school from kindergarten through ninth grade there. It was a big move to go across the river to Mankato High School. There were so many more students, all strangers! Peggy and Sharon had moved to Mankato earlier, leaving Marlys, Ann, and me to break into the Mankato group. I feel very blessed to have been accepted and included. I have many fond memories of potlucks, sports events, slumber parties, picnics, and just hanging out with new friends. After graduation, we all went our different paths, but our Blue Garter Gang kept us connected. It was so meaningful to be a part of each of our weddings and to celebrate together. The Blue Garter shower was very special. Over the years, the importance of these friends in my life has become clearer. No matter if we have seen each other frequently or once in 40 years, that deep feeling is loud and clear. I have many other friends whom I have met in the passing years, and they can't understand how we have all stayed in close touch for over 50 years.

The Blue Garter Gang has a very special place in my heart. After graduation, I left Mankato to pursue my nursing education at Swedish Hospital in Minneapolis. I met my future husband soon after. He was an intern from the Philippine Islands. I will try to make you understand the significance of that. First, I was leaving safe Mankato to go to the big city. I was very naïve. Besides, in 1958 interracial relationships were very rare and not often accepted. I must say, we never encountered any major problems, but there were a few times of uneasiness. My family was very accepting. My next hurdle was my Blue Garter friends. I should have known they would be great, but I wasn't sure. They made Nanoy feel very welcome. They treated him like one of the gang. I can't tell you how much that influenced my life.

Through the years we have gotten together, sometimes with spouses and sometimes just us girls. Each and every encounter has been special. We have all had our own burdens to bear and have valued the Blue Garter support. As we celebrated our 50th high school reunion in 2008, we looked backward and, more importantly, forward to continuing this special connection of the Blue Garter Gang.

Friendships Crossing the River

Peggy Vihstadt Warren

What a gift God gave to me: the opportunity to experience growing up at "the bend of the Minnesota River"! Remembering early North Mankato years with neighborhood friends, church friends, and school friends brings back treasured memories—off to the old North Mankato school, gathering friends along the way, and trudging through Wheeler Park. Of course, we trudged back home for lunch each day, for you didn't eat at school unless you lived in the country or your mother worked. A mother working outside the home was rare! In the winter we walked tall snowdrifts, playing King of the Mountain, and ice skated at every possible opportunity.

Come spring, we hiked the foothills to pick wildflowers. Summer found us spending many hours riding bikes and proudly wearing our "Knothole Gang" buttons, as we watched the North Mankato Merchants baseball team at Tanley Field. Mary Kolling, Louise Nelson, and I started together, and through the years enjoyed North Mankato events with many remembered grade school friends. Marlys Case and Sharon Anderson both joined us in North Mankato for fifth grade. They arrived just in time to experience the flood of 1951. We were all out of our homes for at least a month, living with friends across the river in Mankato. Memories of attending school at the Centenary Methodist Church, standing in line outside the Knights of Columbus Hall for typhoid shots, and living through the cleanup and needed repairs are all vivid in my mind. Louise moved across the river to Mankato in the sixth grade, and in seventh grade Sharon did the same. Moving from Butterfield, Ann Warren joined us in the seventh grade.

Ann, Marlys, Mary K., and I developed a close friendship spending many hours together and today share fun North Mankato memories. We had great times gathering in Marlys' kitchen to make Chef Boyardee pizza while listening to her record collection. There are memories of sitting around Mary's dining room table for Camp Fire activities and for her birthday parties. We loved sleepovers at Ann's. Ann's bedroom, the entire upstairs of their house, seemed huge, like her own little apartment. We bunked there often, and it was there that we held our annual Christmas gift exchanges. Everywhere we went, we walked. Coming up Range Street, we'd meet Ann at the corner of Belgrade and Range and then head over the bridge to downtown Mankato for a movie or to shop. Perching on a stool at the Candy Kitchen, we loved to sip a cherry Coke before heading back over the bridge.

My family moved to West Mankato before I entered high school in 10th grade. It took no time at all to renew and make new high school acquaintances. Through Camp Fire, church, and family friends, I already knew many people. Of course, Louise and Sharon had at one time been in

North Mankato. Mary Hesla, Sharon Carlson, Liz Nelson, Ginge Klenk, Judy Pyles, and Jane Williams were among those I already knew. Our gang began to grow. In no time at all, Ann, Marlys, Mary K., and I, who had come from North Mankato, were gathering with many new friends. Sleepovers in Ann's upstairs were now becoming slumber parties in basement rec rooms and living rooms. Trips to the movies and to downtown now involved more than just the four of us. We loved it—new friends, new experiences, and adventures.

Birthday parties often found us dressing up for an afternoon birthday tea with fancy sandwiches, cookies, mints, nuts, and punch. Learning to drive meant picnics were planned and frequent trips were taken to Lake Washington to swim and bake in the sun. Summer jobs found many of us working with friends carhopping, flipping burgers, or dipping cones.

Y-Teens, class plays, choir, band, orchestra, decorating for dances and working on homecoming floats, a journalism trip to Chicago, going to Minneapolis to the state basketball tournament—so many memories keep flashing into my mind. How fortunate to have had the wonderful experiences that built our strong foundation. Our high school graduation on June 5, 1958, was not the end, but was the beginning of lifelong friendships that are now so precious to each of us— so close, so together, so unique!

From illustrator Flavia Weedn's greeting card collection:
> Sweet memories are woven from the good times we've had with friends. Some of us keep things...pieces of times cherished and memories we can't throw away. If I could sit across the porch from God—I'd thank Him for lending me all of you.

Thank you, Blue Garter friends, for being you!

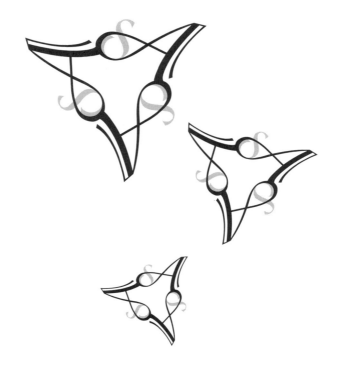

Earthwatch Connects Turtles and Friends

Marlys Case Sloup

I've been keenly interested in sea turtles for many years, and being able to work directly with the turtles and the research scientists was a dream come true. Volunteering with Earthwatch became a way to travel to exotic places, meet interesting people from all over the world, and create new friendships. In 1991 my great desire to travel took on new meaning! The story of my first Earthwatch expedition and creation of a special travel companionship with Anna Lea began.

Earthwatch Expedition—Saving the Leatherback Turtles

Earthwatch had been suggested to me as an alternative way to travel solo and to work with scientists studying the natural world. So on June 12 I flew to Frederiksted, St. Croix, U.S. Virgin Islands. Cottages by the Sea was the rendezvous site and home for 10 volunteers and the principal investigators, Peter Dutton and Donna McDonald. I flew in a day early so I had time to enjoy the beach and the night sky before others arrived for the 11-day project.

Every night after our evening meal, the research team drove out to Sandy Point Beach. There we were assigned partners and a stretch of the 10-mile sandy beach to patrol. Most nights we were on the beach from 8 p.m. until 5 a.m., although some mornings we saw the sunrise if a turtle came in to lay her eggs at that time. Imagine walking the soft sand or in the surf, listening to the sea, and observing the night sky for nine hours at a time. Of course there were the rest periods at the point where we had cookies and water and time to solve three-minute mysteries. As we walked, our night eyes scanned the beach ahead for moving turtles and tracks in the sand. Sometimes we were fortunate to observe a giant leatherback, a creature changed very little since dinosaur times, as she emerged from the sea and started to drag her heavy body along the beach. Being very quiet and using no lights, we observed as she chose a nesting site, body pitted, and with her hind flippers dug her pear-shaped egg cavity to a depth of 70 cm (28 inches) in the warm sand.

Once the egg cavity was dug, we could do our work: measuring her carapace, looking for unique body markings and injuries, checking for the number on a flipper tag. If there was no flipper tag, one was attached to the back edge of a front flipper. With one person holding a back flipper away from the egg cavity opening, a volunteer counted the eggs, usually 80 to 100, as they were being laid. All data were carefully recorded on the daily log sheets. We also had to do a triangulation, measuring from the nest to two stakes along the upper beach. These measurements were recorded so the nest could be located 60 days later after the eggs had hatched. When the female completed her egg laying, she diligently camouflaged the nest. We were sure to be out of reach of her powerful three-foot front flippers and the flying sand. It was so awesome to watch her return to the sea, leaving giant tractor-like tracks in the sand before she disappeared into the dark surf. Some nights we dug up nests that had hatched, freeing baby turtles still in the sandy nests. Then we would guard the babies as they crawled over the sand on their perilous journey to the sea. There were always yellow-crowned night herons and ghost crabs ready for a snack!

Scientists know that leatherback turtles return to the beach for their egg-laying rituals 3 to 10 times a season, each time laying 80 to 100 ping-pong-ball-sized eggs. Scientists also believe that a nesting female returns to the same beach where she hatched and that she lays eggs every two to three years. The rest of her life is spent swimming and feeding in the ocean. Leatherback turtles are also known to swim out of the tropical waters to find jellyfish, their favorite food.

A Special Friendship Begins

While on this first Earthwatch expedition on St. Croix, I met Anna Lea. Among the volunteers, we were the only two travelers to bring binoculars. So on our free afternoons we went bird watching. Conversations revealed we were the same age, both public school teachers of early reading, of the same political persuasion, and had a passion for travel.

While in St. Croix on this first Earthwatch expedition, I received a phone call from the director of language arts and reading in the Madison, Wisconsin, schools. She offered me a position as the second Reading Recovery teacher leader to help support the expanding Reading Recovery program for struggling first-grade readers. That meant I would be leaving my classroom teaching position at a school where I'd taught for 21 years and had many special professional colleagues. It also meant I would need to live in Ohio, as I would be studying for nine months at Ohio State University in Columbus. At age 51, I would be going back to school as a full-time student to train as a Reading Recovery teacher leader. I would be living alone for the first time in my whole life. I would also be a beginning Reading Recovery teacher in an Ohio school working as a student teacher.

After conferring with my husband, Joe, by phone, I decided to accept the new position. Since Anna Lea was living in Columbus, she offered to help me find a place to live for the nine months I'd be going to the university. I often marvel at how serendipitous it was that we should meet in St. Croix at that particular time. In July, Joe and I drove to Columbus and spent two days locating an apartment and arranging for furniture rental. The rest of the summer was a whirlwind of activity as I cleaned out my classroom, said goodbye to friends, packed for my year away, and moved myself (two loads in our Honda Accord) into my furnished apartment in Lancaster, 25 miles south of Columbus.

It was during this intense year of study as a Reading Recovery teacher leader-in-training and interning as a Reading Recovery teacher in the Lancaster Public Schools that Anna Lea helped to add balance and support in my life. I ate dinner with her after classes one day a week, and we often went bird watching on Sunday. We always talked about my classes, how hard I was studying, and all I was learning about how we learn, and in particular about how young children learn to read and write. As a Title I teacher, Anna Lea was interested in my studies and new insights and asked many questions. Although she thought I was crazy to be studying so hard "at my age of 51," three years later she accepted the challenge of studying to become a

Reading Recovery teacher at her school. She served in that position for the last five years of her school career.

Even though Anna Lea lived in Ohio and I lived in Wisconsin, we became special friends and for 12 years were travel partners, exploring the natural world. We traveled to the Falkland Islands, South Georgia and the Antarctic Peninsula, to Ecuador and the Galapagos Islands, on safari in Kenya and Tanzania, and went snorkeling off the coast of Belize and bird watching in Trinidad and Tobago. We volunteered for other sea turtle projects in Costa Rica, Belize, Surinam, and Topsail Island, North Carolina. We helped an Earthwatch scientist study sea grasses along the coastline of San Salvador in the Bahamas. In August of 2002 we were again Earthwatch volunteers for Hawksbill Turtles of Barbados. Just before we were to leave, Anna Lea was diagnosed with stage four lung cancer. I went alone to Barbados. Anna Lea started treatments. Thinking positively, we signed up to travel with World Wildlife Fund to China to see the pandas and important natural attractions in May 2003. This would complete our goal of observing wildlife on all seven continents.

When May of 2003 arrived, all travel costs were paid, and we had our plane tickets and visas, but Anna Lea was too weak to travel. Instead of going to China, I flew to Columbus to spend a week with Anna Lea in her home. She lived for three weeks after I left, and she died on June 12, 2003. That was the same day I returned home from my second "Saving the Leatherback Turtles" Earthwatch project in St. Croix. I had just introduced my nephew and his wife to the excitement of being Earthwatch volunteers and seeing the nesting leatherback turtles up close on the tropical night beach. Anna Lea would have been so proud to know that over the 12 years since our first project, the efforts of Earthwatch volunteers had made a big difference in the number of nesting females returning to lay eggs at Sandy Point.

This special friend, Anna Lea, taught me so much about friendship, the excitement of adventure travel, and the dignity of life. Through my professional studies in Reading Recovery and my travel adventures, I have also learned more about the potential within myself. Now in my retirement, I feel ready for more new adventures. Friends often tell me that my adventuresome spirit and independence are an inspiration to them.

Braving the World for Peace

Ann Warren Schmidt

*M*adeleine L'Engle's analogy of old age being like a Russian nesting doll, or the analogy of the skin being peeled away from an onion, is very appropriate when, at 68, one looks back over the years and at who one was and who one has become. The solid core of the doll within the center, formed in one's early years, is still there, deep inside the layers of the experiences that have followed.

I spent only six years in Mankato, from grade seven in junior high through high school graduation from Mankato High School in 1958. That is a short amount of time compared to the many years and experiences that have followed. It is also probably the fewest number of years of any of the Blue Garter members. It may also explain why I do not remember the many streets, houses, neighborhoods, events, and people the Blue Garter girls reminisce about. Yet it was developmentally a critical period and very influential in forming that small, solid core of my nesting doll. The Blue Garter group members all know how fortunate we are to still be here, having just celebrated our 50th anniversary of graduation from high school. We are also fortunate to have united to support one another and provide continuity to our lives.

What was so influential and significant about those high school years for me? It was a brief time. As we read and reread the school newspaper, *The High News*, and the yearbook, the *Otaknam* (Mankato spelled backwards, weren't we clever), at our slumber party gatherings now, and continue discussions, the impact of those years becomes clearer and clearer.

We were innocent children of the 1950s. It was a time when there was no war and little unrest. Many issues such as divorce, battering, homosexuality, cancer, and special needs were swept under the rug or put into the far recesses of the closet so that we were protected from any disturbing unpleasantries. Most articles and features in our school publications were about our many service sororities, academic clubs, music groups, theater, debate groups, parties, and dances. We could join and join and join, very inclusively—there were more than enough organizations for everyone. We could also be presidents, treasurers, queens and princesses, actors, editors, and musicians. We could organize dances, variety shows, carnivals, meetings, fundraisers, and class trips. As we read about some of these high school organizations today, they seem to have had little purpose except for opportunities to belong and be recognized and feel responsible and important.

We preceded women's liberation, and there were few opportunities for athletic participation. Nonetheless, we found our strengths in other areas. It was the best of times.

I loved all of the activity, the participation, the recognition, friendships, and "responsibilities."

But I also felt that there was a bigger world to see and more to be done. I wanted to go away to college and to see the world. The support that I had been given during those few high school years gave me the strength and confidence to do so. In fact, I had an unrealistic sense of confidence. I could succeed at anything I wanted. There was no question in my mind that I could get into any college I chose, even though I had no knowledge of what my SAT scores were and was not really a scholar. My mother had suggested Antioch College in Ohio, which had an innovative cooperative education system. It required that students apply academic knowledge in the practical world of work, and through doing so, winnow down career choices or strengthen career skills. This had great appeal in that I didn't need to spend all of my time in the classroom and I could see the world, my primary interest.

Thus was developed the next nesting doll, the next layer of the onion. I applied to only one school, Antioch. I was, of course, accepted, and went "east to college." I could do it. Hadn't I been the editor of *The High News*, the president of Chi Epsilon, the treasurer of some other organization? I joke that Ohio was about as far east as one could acceptably go from the Midwest, or one would reach New York and the climate of decadence and snobbery and the lack of Jell-O salads and tuna hot dishes (with crushed potato chip topping).

Besides being a fine college with a wonderful cooperative education program, Antioch was also a bastion of radical ideas: Men were allowed into women's dormitories, protests were held to integrate the local barber shop, guest lecturers came to town to talk about the House Un-American Activities Committee. "We Shall Overcome" was practically the school song. This was quite a distance from Phi Delta Rho and *The High News*. But it reinforced and strengthened the value of inclusiveness that I had learned in Mankato. Another nesting doll, another layer of onion skin.

Antioch was a five-year program because more than an additional year was spent in cooperative job experiences. Nesting doll after nesting doll was added with each job. I worked as a secretary for the Experiment in International Living in Putney, Vermont. I had learned to type with Miss Weese at Mankato High, which was the ticket to seeing the mending walls of Robert Frost. And although I didn't travel internationally, I planned trips for people who did— and I loved it.

Next I had the opportunity to move to Chicago and work as an assistant kindergarten teacher in Winnetka. What I didn't know how to do in the classroom I finessed, with the confidence instilled from my Mankato High days. I navigated the big city. I loved it! The next job was at The *Washington Post* as a copy boy. No such thing as girl journalists in 1960. I thought I may want to bring my interest in journalism from Mabel Lou Ahrens and *The High News* to the big time. I was in heaven. Washington, D.C.! It was pre-Woodward-and-Bernstein days, but I went to the Senate and the White House and the National Press Club with reporters. I attended parties with other copy boys in Georgetown. What a great way to learn and see the world.

A job at the Southside Jewish Community Center in Chicago and another in the Peace Corps offices in Washington D.C. completed my co-op experiences—more nesting dolls and layers.

When my husband and I were married on our college graduation day, we really went off to see the world, about as far from Mankato as one could travel. This, for me, was the ultimate in adventure. We were Peace Corps volunteers in a remote jungle village in northern Malaysia. With the layers from Antioch, the core from Mankato in my doll, and the support of my husband, I was able to do it: two years in a house on stilts in a Muslim village with no water, electricity, or English spoken.

After we returned to the States and settled for graduate study and a more traditional life, our family began. Our first child, Kate, was born. As we considered a second child, it seemed a good thing to adopt a child for whom it might be difficult to find a family—at that time a child of African-American heritage. Through our daughter, Amy, we have had the privilege of being included in the black American culture, something we might not have otherwise experienced.

Our next adventure was the adoption of David at age six, our son who has struggled with special needs and the effects of abuse. I have been taken to another place with David, that of increased sensitivity to those who have extraordinary challenges.

And then at 65 I had the opportunity to rejoin the Blue Garter girls. I felt like something of an imposter, as I had attended none of the showers and weddings that were the foundation of the group. Nevertheless, I was welcomed with open arms and the feeling that only a few days had passed since 1958. We have been able to reflect together on the experiences in Mankato and at Mankato High School that influenced the creation of all our core nesting dolls. Layers and layers of other dolls have been added for all of us, influenced by that Mankato High School beginning. We have been blessed to come together each year. And it has been more fun than anyone should be allowed after all these years!

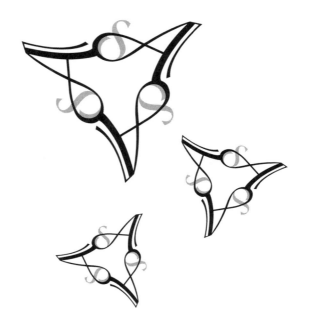

Mentoring the Community Teeny-Boppers

Why has this group continued to need or to want the companionship of each other? These women have many connections: husbands, children, colleagues, and family. Perhaps the answer can be found in the strong, nurturing network of Mankato community mentors who patiently brought together spirited 1950s teenagers.

> Don't slouch...Stand up straight...Wash your hands...Brush your teeth...Do the dishes... Make the beds...Take care of your clothes... Watch your brother...Stay away from him... Practice your music lesson...Be home at 10 p.m....Don't let me catch you....Be careful... Put on your play clothes...Change your shoes...Clean up your plate...Drink your milk...Watch out for your reputation...Come when you are called...Remember your family name.

Our parents were categorized as very strict, moderately strict, or minimally strict. These attitudes were surely formed by family struggles during the 1920s Depression years of their growing up. For us, family ties were cemented by the frightening memories of World War II blackouts; joyful reunions as fathers jumped off the braking, steam-shrouded troop train alongside the Mankato Depot in the dark of the night; the tears shed as daddies' furloughs ended; the house deadened with his departure on another deployment. The "clean plate" club was organized during our era. Basic staples of sugar, meat, rubber, and gasoline were rationed. Many of our mothers were forced into the workplace by financial need. Wastefulness was not acceptable. Respect for our parents' sacrifices occasionally gave us the face-saving comeback of "My parents won't let me go or won't let me do it." Our parents demanded that we be respectful and honorable consumers of the community's resources. That devotion and careful guidance gave us the skills to become independent. As a result, our presence and participation were welcomed within the community's institutions as we grew up.

We were blind to socioeconomic differences. Basically, our community functioned without division. Many of us never knew the background of a friend's father or where he worked. Home sizes varied based on family size. Our lawns connected within a larger neighborhood. The vacant lot served as our park and playground. Mothers waved as friends passed and said, "Have a good day." We did have a lot of fun as we were allowed to roam the town under their watchful eyes.

As Blue Birds and Camp Fire girls, we spent several summers at Camp Patterson on Lake Washington. Here new friends were made as we walked around a tub of wax, held onto wicks, and learned to make candles. Today we laugh at the image that presents. Red Cross swimming instruction, horseback riding, rituals such as revelry, taps, campfires, and singing were indelibly stamped into our memories. Chaperoned by college-age women, we were counseled and sheltered during vicious nighttime thunderstorms. Soaking wet, we shuttered the continuous screening around our cabin. Shivering, we wrapped ourselves in rough wool army blankets and huddled together telling ghost stories, until exhausted we fell asleep in our bunks.

Mankato was a college town. Parents could choose between public and parochial schools as well as campus schools for their child's education. We had excellent teachers. Our teachers coped cheerfully with huge classes. Mary Huntley says of her kindergarten teacher, Miss Radcliff: "She was exceptional; about our height, and she carried a perpetual smile. She loved all of the children."

Isn't he cute...Did you hear about her...I read about it in "True Confessions"...They call it rape...Did you say "rake"...Don't you know about intercourse...They were drinking...Kicked off the football team...I got my period...Have you tried Tampax... Come over...I'll ride my bike over this afternoon... Tell me all about it...See you later.

Holding hands with our first school boyfriend, dimes jingling in our sagging pockets, we tiptoed gingerly down the distant hall together to buy war bonds. Toothless, square, 45-pound, 45-inch tall kindergarteners found comfort in coeducational settings. Our school district moved some of us on to one of two different junior high schools in seventh grade, however. That fall it seemed that suddenly the girls were taller than the boys.

Our school nurse and boys' physical education teacher segregated our class one day unannounced. The subject for the girls was menstruation. We were given a booklet graphically showing the female reproductive system. The nurse thoughtfully answered most of our questions but left the big one—how do you get pregnant—for us to discuss with our mothers. A Kotex coupon was also included. What the boys learned from the coach we never will know. However, from that day on, the same kindergarten boy who had been our best friend began to whisper with his buddies and to laugh behind our backs as our breasts budded and hair growth made us itch.

That new school setting opened our eyes to other firsts as well. Boys carrying books for girlfriends, school dances, basketball games, cheerleading tryouts. One by one we finally got our first periods. We called it by the code word "Gretchen." No one knew anyone named Gretchen. The nickname, Gretch, was a way to keep the feminine "curse" more friendly. Eventually more facts of life were gleaned secondhand, the original source being an older sister or cousin or whispers between best friends. We became giggling girls as we gathered in each other's homes for potlucks and slumber parties and hashed over our questions and new discoveries, all with the blessings of our parents.

The community took over to give us a safe environment for boy-girl mingling as teeny-boppers. There was the public library, located at the time on Broad Street. To do homework or to work on a project together required a time-consuming physical jaunt, and we settled down for productive study after all of that required exercise. Generally our families did not have a second car, so walking, biking, or taking the city bus was the rule to get us to our destination on time.

There was also the Alpine Attic. a community-sponsored facility on the second floor of the YMCA building located at the corner of Second and Cherry streets. Here junior high kids could congregate on Friday nights for socializing. There was dancing to jukebox records and low-cost refreshments. An older lady, Mrs. Adams, became a friend to all. She played the records and supervised the concession area. She probably knew everyone, and all the parents as well.

Outdoor ice skating rinks brought many teens together on cold winter nights. Handsome young men employed by the city recreation department supervised and looked out for our safety. They played music, kept the wood stove steaming hot, and gave us the thrill of a game of Crack the Whip as well as a boy-girl waltz to close each skating session.

Extracurricular activities supervised by teachers and community volunteers became part of the scenario in high school. There was choir, drama club, band and orchestra. Private piano lessons and recitals formed new alliances for some. Sports for girls were extracurricular activities, but cheerleading was popular. Tryouts for coveted cheerleading spots happened for football, basketball, and wrestling. The school plays, student council, debate team, journalistic activities, service clubs, and Y-Teens were among the array of choices for all. This eclectic approach to involvement in the broader community of school activities strengthened Mankato High School's climate with the talents of a variety of individual thinkers. In practice, it also gave young women more respect for the capabilities of less-known friends as well as acquaintances. We learned that it was our attitude, our confidence level, and our self-esteem that were the keys to personal happiness.

> Have you memorized your Bible verses...I have confirmation every Saturday morning... It will be my first Communion...We are going on a Luther League retreat...I accepted Christ as my personal savior at Green Lake Bible Camp.

Our gang was also mentored by our faiths. The phrase "under God" was added to the Pledge of Allegiance in our era. Ecumenical religious instruction was offered to public school students weekly for a half day in nearby churches during the school day. There we were instructed in basic scripture, including the Book of Proverbs. Interestingly, as we researched for this book, we found that although most of the proverbs were traced to King Solomon, the proverbs themselves are female instructions in moral virtue—While God is masculine, wisdom is female.

The Bible New Revised Standard Version, Proverbs 3:13-18 states:

> Happy are those who find wisdom and those who get understanding, for her income is better than silver, and her revenue better than gold. She is more precious than jewels, and nothing you desire can compare with her. Long life is in her right hand; in her left hand are riches and honor. Her ways are ways of pleasantness and all her paths are peace. She is a tree of life to those who lay hold of her; those who hold her fast are called happy.

Mary Hesla Huntley's father praised our laughter. "Giggling girls are having fun growing up." Sharon Anderson had the best chuckling laugh and began our gang's Chuckles candy routine. Whenever we were at a movie or an athletic event, we brought our Chuckles candy packages and enjoyed more chuckles. Ann Warren Schmidt even named her car the Chuckle Wagon. Mary still has the joke book that she wrote in the sixth grade. Today she is coauthor of the book *A Mirthful Spirit*, promoting the healthful properties of smiling and laughter.

We thank our faithful network of generous Mankato mentors. They successfully launched an entire gang of 1950s teeny-boppers. We are richly blessed women celebrating our 50th year of nurturing friendships.

Cherishing Fond Memories

Celebrating a well-lived life will be the final chapter in all of our great friendships. As this passage creeps up on us, we are being prepared by our parents' decline. We now wear a thick coat that has been tanned either by the devastating loss of their presence and counsel or by our core stature that has been strengthened by their dignity. Some of us have been allowed the supreme gift of holding a hand in passage. A confidently completed life is a great joy.

Saying goodbye to a special friend must be faced in an even more intimate context. Marlys Case Sloup best described this in saying goodbye to her friend Anna Lea:

> I learned about pain and end-of-life care, and about the importance of a network of caring friends. So many had been calling, coming to visit, bringing food, taking her to the doctor, picking up and organizing her medicines, talking care of the business of running her home. While I was there 24 hours a day for seven days, we came to realize just how sick Anna Lea was. With the help of hospice care, Anna Lea died at home surrounded with the support and love of her many friends. She taught me so much about friendship...and the dignity of life.

As Blue Garter friends, we have grown up knowing one another's primary families. In sharing annual birthday and holiday greetings, we have become very close to one another's extended Blue Garter families. None of us has been spared the pain of tragic loss. We have felt the pain of death, divorce, and career challenges. Fifteen of us had lost both parents by the time we were 66 years old. Three lost a spouse as a result of illness; four have experienced the shocking death of children or siblings. Cancer and other diseases of decline are a part of our lives now as we age. With these changes, we are even more aware of the preciousness of our time together.

Sharing these stories of death and loss is difficult; listening is becoming easier. As we come to know death more, we come to realize that the last stage of life is as important as the first stage, when we shared birthing or adoption stories. Our kindred minds and hearts make new connections. We will truly become each other's keeper of fondly cherished memories. While saying goodbye to those we love, we celebrate life knowing each has made a difference.

Celebrating Lifelong Friendships

A landmark UCLA study suggested that women respond to stress with a cascade of brain chemicals that cause them to make and maintain friendships with other women. It seems that when the hormone oxytocin is released as part of the stress response in a woman, it encourages her to tend children and to gather with other women. Studies suggest that when she engages in this tending or befriending, more oxytocin is released, which further counters stress and produces a calming effect.

Whether the Blue Garter Gang members have been oxytocin junkies since their birth in 1940, we may never know. What we do know is that "it takes a village to raise a child," as notably stated by Hillary Clinton when she was U.S. First Lady in 1996-2000. The truth of this memorable quote was already in evidence with this group of girls growing up in Mankato and attending high school together.

Now a much smaller core of about 21 Blue Garter women communicate regularly and make a concerted effort to maintain a close connectedness. Others choose to remain on the outer perimeter by confiding with one or two friends. Some connect only through e-mails. Not everyone chooses to meet with our group when we have reunions. We live in the present, accepting our friends within their limits. Whether there is active communication or just a sense of silent companionship, we all continue our concern for each other in heart and in spirit, and we look forward to gatherings of our complete circle of friends.

Carolyn captured that spirit with this poem:

Sunny Delight in Arizona

In the fall of '03 Mary's e-mail did come
To visit Judy in Sun City for a week in the sun.
Five of us accepted and made plans to spend time
With forever friends, strengthening ties that bind.

We flew in on a Sunday with Mary's casserole in hand
A full week lay ahead with many plans quite grand.
Who was awaiting our arrival in the Valley of the Sun?
Why, Sun City Express, and we were off to Quail Run.

We made lunch for three ladies on Monday at one
Audrey, Helen, and Mary Cox, they were really quite fun.
Mary regaled us with poems for an hour, then two,
And entertained one and all, there was much ado!

Off to Triology at Vistansia on Tuesday for a tour
Of 12 model homes, most certainly the allure.
Then on to Dillon's Grand for onion rings and Burnt Ends
We sipped margaritas on the deck, just six lifelong girlfriends.

Our evenings were spent sitting out under the stars
Reminiscing about our lives for hours and hours.
Weez's call from Arkansas was absolutely delightful,
But we're guessing her phone bill was really quite frightful!

We talked of our lives o'er the past 50 years' time
While nibbling and drinking infamous Two-Buck Chuck wine.
We drove to the Heard to see artifacts from the Southwest
A guide showed us throughout, she was absolutely the best.
We were genuinely in awe of pottery, baskets, and art
We heard of Indian travails and left part of our hearts.

Our trip to Sedona was filled with laughter and glee
Five women on a trip, feeling light-hearted and free.
We used a cane and a code to secure parking at the top
When visiting Holy Cross Chapel perched high on red rock.
"Killdeer" was the code, flippantly shouted during the day
Its use made us laugh through the setting sun's last ray.

An all day rain occurred Friday, a rare sprinkling for sure
Spoiling plans for White Tanks hiking,
but making shopping the lure.
We lunched at the Elephant Bar, an Asian fusion delight
And returned home to play bridge
into the early hours of the night.

We left for home on Saturday,
our time together too soon ended
We couldn't have had a better time or
found a better way to spend it!

Carolyn Meyer Petersen

Today the elastic in our faded old blue garters is dried up and limp. This book chronicles the memories of who we have joyfully become as our friendships have grown more meaningful with age.

As seventh-decade women, we can both question and doubt ourselves without panicking today. We know that the core doll of our birth is continually growing enriching layers. As individuals, we really haven't changed much. We still need our lasting friends to validate and to encourage us to be our independent selves. Although statistically, 1 in 5 women over 60 live in some type of poverty—whether it is emotional, economical, or physical poverty—our individual spirits continually surprise us.

Dr Borysenko shared her wisdom of relationships in these words:

> By keeping active and involved in the world, by using our voices, we can truly become grandmothers of vision. And with nature's simple elegance, the more we use our wisdom, the more the neural circuitry that supports it will continue to develop. Perhaps the next generation will look back on the elders of the late 20th century as the foremothers of a new millennium in which the spirit of relationality restored balance to a troubled world.
>
> *Joan Borysenko, PhD*
> *Psychologist, author distinquished*
> *pioneer in integrative medicine*

Many of us have released what was inside us to make room for a new birth. Older years have given us the gift of contentment, hope, and personal dignity. We lift up our glasses in a celebratory toast to evolving, maturing, aging women. We invite you to continue to seek and to experience the joys of your lifelong friendships.

Appendices

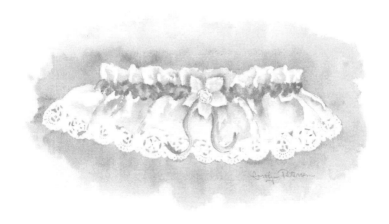

Savoring Our Old and New Recipes

Vegetables & Side Dishes

Breads & Muffins

Desserts

Tastefully Simple

60th Birthday Gathering

Mankato, Minnesota ~ 2000
Friday, August 4, 2000

Chicken Linguine Salad	Cuke Mostaccioli Salad
Frog's Eye Salad	Onion Dill Bread
Almond Bars	Red Velvet Cake

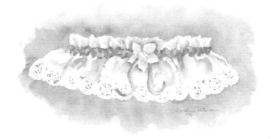

Chicken Linguine Salad *(makes 6 very generous servings) Carolyn Petersen*

Ingredients:	Dressing:
1 1/4 pounds chicken breast	1/2 cup red wine vinegar
1 jar capers, drained	2 tablespoons lemon juice
8 ounces fresh mushrooms	1/2 cup oil
1 jar pitted kalamata olives	4-6 garlic cloves, crushed
1 can artichoke hearts, drained	1 tablespoon dried basil leaves
1 box penne pasta	2 teaspoons salt
1/2 cup parsley	2 teaspoons oregano
	1 1/2 teaspoons pepper

Directions:
1. Boil pasta according to directions. Rinse in cold water; drain.
2. Cut artichoke hearts into bite-size pieces; slice olives lengthwise; wash and slice mushrooms.
3. Toss all ingredients with dressing.
4. Chill several hours or overnight.

Cuke Mostaccioli Salad

Judy Newhouse

Ingredients:

1 pound mostaccioli	1 large jar pimiento
2 teaspoons prepared mustard	1 medium cucumber, unpeeled and sliced thin
1 1/2 cups cider vinegar	1 tablespoon parsley flakes
1 medium onion, chopped	1 teaspoon salt
1 1/2 cups sugar	1 teaspoon garlic powder

Directions:

1. Cook noodles, drain; coat with one to two tablespoons of oil and drain.
2. Mix all additional ingredients and add to noodles.
3. Mix and let stand overnight.
4. Keeps in refrigerator one week.

Onion Dill Bread

Lois Schoeneman

Ingredients:

1 package yeast	3/4 cup sour cream
3 1/3 cups bread flour	3 tablespoons sugar
1/4 teaspoon salt	3 tablespoons minced dried onion
1 unbeaten egg (room temp.)	2 tablespoons whole dill seed
1/4 cup water	1 1/2 tablespoons butter
3/4 cup cottage cheese	

Directions:

1. Mix together yeast, flour, salt, and egg.
2. Put dry ingredients into bread maker.
3. Heat other ingredients and add to bread maker.
4. Push button.

Frog's Eye Salad

Sharon Kalahar

Ingredients:

1 cup sugar
2 tablespoons flour
2½ teaspoons salt
1¾ cups pineapple juice
   (from 2 20-ounce cans)
2 eggs, beaten
1 tablespoon lemon juice
3 quarts water
1 tablespoon oil

1-pound package of acini di pepe
3 11-ounce cans mandarin oranges
2 20-ounces cans pineapple chunks, drained
1 8-ounce container cool whip
1 cup miniature marshmallows (or more if desired)

Directions:

1. Combine sugar, flour, and ½ teaspoon salt.
2. Gradually stir in juice and eggs over medium heat. Stir until thick. Add lemon juice and cool to room temperature.
3. Bring water, 2 teaspoons salt, and oil to boil. Add acini di pepe and boil until done. Drain and rinse; drain again and cool to room temperature.
4. Combine pepe with egg mixture and stir lightly but thoroughly. Cool overnight in refrigerator. I put it all in a large zip-lock bag.
5. Add remaining ingredients; mix thoroughly. Return to refrigerator to cool. Lasts a week.

Almond Bars

Judy Newhouse

Ingredients:

Crust:
- 1 cup butter
- 2 cups flour
- 1/2 cup powdered sugar

Filling:
- 8 ounces cream cheese, softened
- 2 cups sugar
- 2 eggs
- 1 teaspoon almond extract

Frosting:
- 1 1/2 cups powdered sugar
- 1/4 cup butter
- 1 teaspoon almond extract
- 1 1/2 teaspoon milk (may need more)
- Sliced almonds on top (best to toast them)

Directions:

1. Mix crust ingredients together and pat into 9 x 13 inch pan (or use a jelly roll pan so they aren't so thick).
2. Bake for 20 minutes or less at 350 degrees.
3. Beat together the filling ingredients and pour over crust.
4. Bake 15-20 minutes at 350 degrees.
5. Cool, frost, and top with almonds.

Waldorf Astoria $300 Red Velvet Cake   *Mary Brion*

Ingredients:
2 1/2 cups flour
1/2 cup cold butter
1 1/2 cups sugar
2 eggs
1 ounce red food coloring
2 teaspoons cocoa
1 tablespoon vanilla
1 teaspoon salt
1 cup buttermilk
1 tablespoon white vinegar
1 tablespoon baking soda

Frosting:
3 tablespoons flour
1 cup milk
1 cup sugar
1 tablespoon vanilla
1 cup cold butter

Directions:
1. Cream butter, sugar, and eggs.
2. Make paste of red food coloring and cocoa.
3. Add to creamed mixture.
4. Add buttermilk, salt, and vanilla alternately with flour.
5. Mix soda and vinegar (mix and add at last minute).
6. Add and beat mixture.
7. Grease and flour four 9-inch round pans, and pour into pans evenly. (Or use two 9-inch pans and cut in half after baking.)
8. Bake at 350 degrees for 20-30 minutes. Watch after 20 minutes to avoid overbaking.
9. For frosting, cook flour and milk until thick and cool.
10. Cream sugar, butter, and vanilla until very fluffy.
11. Add cooled milk and flour mixture.
12. Beat until creamy.
13. Makes enough to spread on top of each layer and around sides. Will just cover with nothing to spare.
14. Refrigerate, as the frosting is very soft. Keeps well in the freezer.

60th Birthday Gathering
Mankato, Minnesota ~ 2000
Saturday, August 5, 2000

Blueberry Health Muffins   Fresh Fruit

Egg Casserole   Breakfast Bake

Coffee and Juice

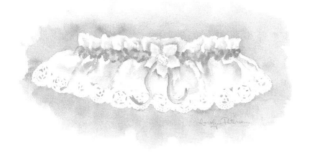

Blueberry Health Muffins *Makes 16 muffins*   Judy Appel

Ingredients:

1/4 cup safflower oil	1 cup unbleached flour
3/4 cup brown sugar	1 teaspoon baking soda
1 egg	2 teaspoons baking powder
1 cup 1% buttermilk	1/3 cup oatmeal
1/4 teaspoon salt	1/3 cup wheat germ
	1/3 cup blueberries

Directions:

1. Mix in order given: column 1 and then column 2.
2. Mix lightly after adding blueberries.
3. Pour into muffin pan.
4. Bake at 400 degrees until done, about 20 minutes.

Breakfast Bake
Mary Huntley, from Taylor Corporation Cookbook, 1998

Ingredients:

1 6-ounce package Pepperidge Farm onion and garlic croutons
1 package Jimmy Dean sausage, regular flavor, browned and drained
1 32-ounce bag frozen shredded hash browns
4 eggs
2¼ cups milk
¾ teaspoon dry mustard
2 cups shredded cheddar cheese

Topping:
½ cup milk
1 can cream mushroom soup
½ cup shredded cheese

Directions:

1. Layer croutons in greased 13 x 9 inch pan.
2. Add 1½ cups cheese and sausage.
3. Mix together eggs, 2¼ cups milk, and dry mustard; pour over mixture. Cover and refrigerate overnight.
4. When ready to bake, mix cream of mushroom soup with ½ cup milk and pour over all.
5. Top with frozen hash browns and sprinkle with remaining ½ cup cheese.
6. Bake at 325 degrees for 1½ hours. Cover last 15 minutes.

Egg Casserole

Serves 12

Mary Huntley

Ingredients:

8 eggs
4 cups scalded milk
1/8 teaspoon pepper
8 slices bread, buttered, and cubed
1/4 teaspoon dry mustard

3/4 pound American cheese, cubed
10-12 slices bacon cooked or ham, cubed (optional)

Directions:

1. Place cubed bread in greased 9 × 12 inch pan.
2. Sprinkle ham/bacon on top, then cheese.
3. Beat eggs, add seasonings, stir in milk. Pour over bread.
4. Refrigerate overnight.
5. Bake at 325 degrees for 1 hour.

If preferred, may add 1 tablespoon minced onion and 1 package frozen chopped broccoli. Also good with diced onion and green pepper.

Sunny Delight

Sun City, Arizona ~ 2004
March 28 - April 3, 2004

Spinach Lasagna	Broasted Potatoes and
Swiss Chard Tart	Vegetables
Lemon Pie	Rhubarb-Pineapple Jam
Bean Salad	Sand Beef
Baked/Poached Chicken	White Sugar Cookies

Spinach Lasagna
Mary Huntley

Ingredients:

12 uncooked lasagna pasta	1 10-ounce package frozen
1 64-ounce jar spaghetti	chopped spinach, defrosted
sauce	and drained
1 16-ounce ricotta cheese	3 cups mozzarella cheese
1 pound ground sausage	1 4-ounce package of
(turkey or beef)	shredded parmesan cheese
1 1/2 cups onions, chopped fine	

Directions:

1. Layer sauce, pasta, sauce, half of meat, and onion.
2. Add half of ricotta cheese mixture, half of spinach, and 1 1/2 cups of mozzarella cheese.
3. Repeat layers and top with Parmesan cheese.
4. Refrigerate 24 hours before baking or freeze, defrost, and bake.
5. Bake 45-60 minutes at 350 degrees. I bake covered for 30 minutes and uncovered for 30 minutes.
6. Let set a few minutes before cutting into pieces.
   Also good warmed over.

Swiss Chard Tart
Judy Appel

Ingredients:

1 package of puff pastry	3 tablespoons of ground flax
1 large sweet onion, thinly sliced	seed
12-15 Swiss chard leaves or other greens, ribboned	1 egg
1 handful of golden raisins	Salt
	Nutmeg

Directions:

1. Sauté onion and chard until wilted yet crisp. Cook down but keep crisp.
2. Add raisins and flax seed.
3. Continue cooking until warm throughout. Cool slightly.
4. Add an egg, well mixed.
5. Add salt and nutmeg.
6. Brush 2-3 individual sheets of pastry with olive oil or spray.
7. Place in pie dish. Arrange vegetable mixture in pie dish.
8. Top with 2-3 upper layers of pastry (brushed with oil).
9. Rip a sheet into ribbons and crimp on the top.
10. Roll up and crimp the top edges to resemble pie crust.
11. Sprinkle with more flax seed.
12. Bake at 375 degrees until golden brown (about 45 minutes). Watch to make sure it doesn't burn.

Lemon Pie

Recipe from Judy Appel's stepmother, Audrey Strand

Ingredients:

1 medium lemon
4 eggs

1 1/2 cups sugar
2/3 stick butter

Directions:

1. Cut lemon into chunks, remove seeds, and place in blender.
2. Add rest of ingredients and blend until smooth.
3. Bake at 350 degrees in unbaked pie crust for 40 minutes.

White Sugar Cookies

3 dozen   Recipe from Judy Appel's grandmother

Ingredients:

1 cup butter, or use half butter,
   half margarine
1 cup sugar
1 egg, beaten
1 teaspoon vanilla

2 cups flour
1/2 teaspoon baking soda
1/2 teaspoon cream of tartar
Pinch of salt

Directions:

1. Cream butter and sugar.
2. Beat in egg and vanilla.
3. Mix in other ingredients.
4. Roll into small balls, dip in sugar, and press onto cookie sheet with watered fork (I use my design stones).
5. Bake at 370 degrees for 11 minutes.

Bean Salad

Recipe from Ginge Klenk's sister, Nancy

Ingredients:

$3/4$ cup sugar
$2/3$ cup Heinz cider vinegar
$1/3$ cup oil (Canola)
1 teaspoon salt
1 teaspoon ground pepper
1 can dark red kidney beans

1 can garbanzo beans
1 can cut wax beans
1-2 cans green cut beans
   (4 cans of beans total is
   good)
1 medium onion, sliced thin

Directions:

1. Heat sugar, vinegar, oil, salt, and pepper together slowly to dissolve sugar. Do not boil.
2. In separate bowl, mix beans together.
3. Pour liquid over beans, mix, and stir periodically.
4. Marinate 24 hours and serve cold.

Broasted Potatoes and Vegetables

Judy Appel

Directions:

1. Wash and cut up potatoes, carrots, onions, and any other veggies into a large bowl.
2. Pour about 2 tablespoons to $1/3$ cup olive oil over potatoes and veggies.
3. Sprinkle with thyme and rosemary.
4. Roast 425 degrees for 20 minutes. Turn with spatula.
5. Reduce heat to 300 degrees.
6. Total broasting time 45-60 minutes.

Sand Beef

Retta Dykstra, from *The Chinese Cookbook* by Craig Claiborne

Ingredients:

1 pound flank steak, well trimmed	1 tablespoon dry sherry or shao hsing wine
1 tablespoon cornstarch	1/4 cup onion, finely chopped
1 tablespoon dark soy sauce	1 teaspoon sugar
2 small jalapeno peppers, seeded and chopped	1/4 teaspoon MSG—optional
Salt to taste	Cayenne—optional to taste
2 tablespoons curry powder, or more, to taste, see note	1 bunch scallions, greens only, cut in 1 1/2-inch lengths or garlic chives
2 tablespoons chicken broth, peanut, vegetable, or corn oil	

Directions:

1. Place the meat on a flat surface and slice across the grain into the thinnest possible slices. This is easier to do if the meat is partially frozen. Place it in a mixing bowl and add 1 tablespoon of oil, the cornstarch, wine, and soy sauce.

2. Work well so that the meat is thoroughly blended with the other ingredients.

3. Combine the onion, scallions, and red or green hot peppers and set aside.

4. In a wok or skillet, heat 1 or 2 tablespoons of oil, and when it is hot but not smoking, add the beef. Cook, stirring, just until the meat changes color. Transfer the beef to a bowl.

5. Add a little more oil to the pan and then the onion mixture. Add the sugar, salt, and MSG and cook about 30 seconds, then add the curry powder and cayenne. Return the meat to the pan and add the chicken broth. Cook, stirring, until the sauce starts to boil.

6. Add the scallion greens or garlic chives. Cook, stirring, until blended and thoroughly hot. Do not overcook.

7. Serve over rice.

Notes: The amount of oil is reduced dramatically from the original. I much prefer Sun Brand Madras curry powder for this dish, available in many supermarkets. It is very flavorful and not very hot. You may want to add a little cayenne to increase the heat level. Chopped scallions are replaced with scallion greens only; use garlic chives if available. Garlic chives make a great addition if you can find them or grow them in the garden. One of the springtime treats I vividly recall from trips to China are garlic greens, simply stir fried with a little sesame oil and soy sauce. I make this dish frequently and have adjusted it to suit our tastes. It freezes tolerably well and can make a quick weekday supper. A solidly frozen triple batch has made it on a coast-to-coast flight to serve at a family gathering. It's now even a favorite at each Blue Garter gathering.

Baked/Poached Chicken

Judy Appel

Directions:
1. Place chicken breasts or pieces in baking dish.
2. Add juice of 4 lemons or use wine.
3. Add lots of fresh garlic cloves
   (at least one per chicken breast).
4. Sprinkle chicken with sage, thyme, and salt.
5. Cover and bake at 350 for one hour.
   Use higher temperature when oven is full.

Rhubarb-Pineapple Jam Recipe from Audrey Strand's sister, Helen Marsh

Ingredients:
7 cups diced rhubarb
4 cups sugar or less
1 14-20 ounce can crushed pineapple—do not drain
1 6-ounce package. strawberry Jell-O

Directions:
1. Put rhubarb, sugar, and pineapple in large pan for 2 hours;
   stir occasionally.
2. Bring to a boil and cook for 5-10 minutes.
3. Take off the burner and add Jell-O. Stir well.
4. Pour into jars and refrigerate.

65th Birthday Gathering

Cleveland Heights, Ohio ~ 2005
October 7-10, 2005

Craisin Salad

Sand Beef

Seasoned Pretzels

Waldorf Astoria $300 Red Velvet Cake

Seasoned Pretzels

Mary Huntley

Ingredients:

2-3 pounds round pretzels
1 bottle Orville Redenbacher popcorn oil
1 package dry Hidden Valley Ranch dressing

1 tablespoon garlic powder
1 tablespoon dill weed

Directions:

1. Mix liquid in bowl with seasoning
2. Dump pretzels and liquid into a large zip-lock plastic bag for one hour.
3. Keep turning back and forth in rolling action every 10-15 minutes.
4. Leave in the bag to absorb seasonings and oil.

Craisin Salad

Ingredients:

1 bunch red leaf lettuce	**Dressing:**
1 bunch green leaf lettuce	$^1/_2$ cup chopped red onion
1 head iceberg lettuce	1 cup sugar
8 ounces shredded mozzarella	2 teaspoons dry mustard
cheese	1 $^1/_2$ teaspoon salt
4 ounces shredded parmesan	$^1/_2$ cup red wine vinegar
cheese	Blend above, then add 1 cup
1 pound crumbled bacon,	of oil
optional	
4 ounces slivered and roasted	
almonds	
1 large package Craisins	
(cranberry raisins)	

Directions:
1. Toss greens, cheese, bacon, almonds, and Craisins.
2. Blend dressing ingredients and add 1 cup oil.
3. Mix well.
4. Toss half of dressing with salad ingredients and add more as desired.

Red Velvet Cake

66th Birthday Gathering

Shelburne, Vermont ~ 2006
September 15 - 18, 2006

Moussaka
Chicken Caesar Salad
Banana Bread
Out-of-This-World Chocolate Cake
Ben and Jerry's Ice Cream

"Gathering in the Kitchen--Appetizer Time"

Moussaka (Greek Lasagna)
Ann Schmidt

Ingredients:

3 medium-size eggplants
8 tablespoons butter
3 large onions, finely chopped
3 pounds ground lamb
1 small can tomato paste
1/2 cup or more red wine
1/4 teaspoon cinnamon
1/2 freshly chopped parsley

Salt to taste
Black pepper to taste
6 tablespoons flour
1 quart milk
4 eggs, beaten until frothy
Freshly ground nutmeg (lots)
2 cups ricotta cheese
1 cup fine bread crumbs
1 cup parmesan cheese

Directions:

1. Preheat the oven to 375 degrees.
2. Peel the eggplants and cut them into slices about 1/2-inch thick. Put on cookie sheet, brush with olive oil, and bake at 350 degrees until soft (about 20 minutes).
3. Sauté onions in olive oil until brown. Add ground meat and cook until brown (remove fat drippings, as there will be a lot).
4. Combine the tomato paste with the wine, parsley, cinnamon, salt, and pepper. Stir this into the meat and simmer over low heat, stirring frequently until all the liquid has been absorbed.
5. Make a white sauce by melting butter and stirring in flour with a whisk. Meanwhile, bring the milk to a boil and add it gradually to the butter-flour mixture, stirring constantly. When the mixture is thickened and smooth, remove it from the heat. Cool slightly and stir in the beaten eggs, nutmeg, and ricotta cheese.
6. Grease the 11 x 16 inch pan and sprinkle the bottom lightly with bread crumbs.
7. Arrange alternate layers of eggplant and meat sauce in the pan, sprinkling each layer with parmesan cheese and bread crumbs.
8. Pour the ricotta cheese sauce over the top and bake one hour, or until the top is golden brown.
9. Remove from the oven and cool 20 to 30 minutes before serving. Cut into squares a la lasagna. Great warmed over.

Ann has adapted this recipe over the years, originally from *The New Times Cookbook*.

Banana Bread

Ingredients:

1/2 cup shortening (margarine)	2 cups flour
1 1/2 cups sugar	1 teaspoon baking soda
2 beaten egg yolks	1 teaspoon baking powder
2 well-mashed ripe bananas	1 teaspoon vanilla
2/3 cup whole milk (add 1 teaspoon vinegar to milk)	1 cup chopped walnuts
	2 egg whites

Directions:

1. Cream shortening well.
2. Add beaten egg yolks, mashed bananas, and vanilla.
3. Blend together flour, baking soda, and baking powder.
4. Alternate adding flour mixture and the sour milk, ending with flour.
5. Fold in chopped nuts.
6. Beat egg whites until mounds form, and gently add to mixture.
7. Place in well-greased 8 x 5 inch loaf pan.
8. Bake at 350 degrees for one hour or until toothpick comes out clean.
9. Cool for 5-7 minutes and remove from pan.

Out-of-This-World Chocolate Cake
Mary Huntley, similar to Betty Crocker's Better-Than-Most-Anything Cake

Ingredients:
- 1 German chocolate cake mix
- 1 can sweetened, condensed milk
- 1 14-ounce jar butterscotch caramel topping
- 12-ounce container Cool Whip
- 1 cup crushed Heath bars

Directions:
1. In 9 x 13 inch pan, prepare cake mix as directed on the box. Cool.
2. With fork handle or straw, poke 24 holes in the cooled cake.
3. Pour one can sweetened condensed milk over cooled cake.
4. Pour butterscotch caramel topping over milk.
5. Top with 12-ounce container of Cool Whip.
6. Sprinkle Heath Bars on top.
7. Chill.

O the Lord is Good to Us—Friends Singing Thanks in Door County

67th Birthday Gathering

Door County, Wisconsin ~ 2007
September 27 - October 1, 2007

Jack and Red Pepper Quesadillas
Orange and Green Olive Salad
White Chicken Chili
Toffee Bar Torte
Lasagna
Cowboy Caviar
Oatmeal Muffins

L to R: Karen Anderson, Janna Morgan, Carolyn Petersen, Sandi Lowery,
Mary Huntley, Retta Dykstra, Judy Appel is serving the muffins, Liz Shriver.

Jack and Red Pepper Quesadillas

Serves 4

Carolyn Petersen, from *Cooking Light* magazine

Ingredients:

4 whole wheat 6-inch tortillas
8 tablespoons Monterey jack
    cheese, shredded
8 tablespoons bottled roasted
    red bell peppers, chopped

4 tablespoons fresh cilantro,
    chopped
8 teaspoons green onions,
    sliced

Directions:

1. Coat one side of each tortilla with cooking spray.
2. Place tortillas, coated side down, on a large baking sheet.
3. Sprinkle each tortilla with 2 tablespoons chopped red pepper, 1 tablespoon chopped cilantro, 2 teaspoons sliced green onion, and 2 tablespoons cheese.
4. Fold each tortilla in half.
5. Bake at 400 degrees for 5 minutes until cheese melts.
6. Cut into wedges and serve.

Orange and Green Olive Salad

Serves 4

Carolyn Petersen, from *Cooking Light* magazine

Ingredients:

2 tablespoons honey
1 1/2 tablespoons fresh lemon
    juice
1 tablespoon extra virgin olive
    oil
1/4 teaspoon ground cumin

Dash salt
4 cups fresh baby spinach
4 peeled navel oranges, cut
    into 1/4 -inch slices
4 tablespoons green olives,
    chopped

Directions:

1. Combine honey, lemon juice, olive oil, cumin, and salt. Mix well.
2. Arrange spinach on four plates, top with sliced oranges, and drizzle with honey mixture.
3. Top with 2 tablespoons chopped green olives.

White Chicken Chili for the Crock Pot or Stove

Recipe from Carolyn Petersen's husband, George

Ingredients:

2 cans (14 ounces) navy or
  Great Northern beans,
  drained and rinsed
1 large onion, chopped
1 stick butter (or less)
$^1/_4$ cup flour
2 cups nonfat half-and-half
4 cups chicken broth (or more)
1 teaspoon tabasco
1$^1/_2$ teaspoon chili powder
1 teaspoon ground cumin

$^1/_2$ teaspoon salt
$^1/_4$ teaspoon white pepper
1 rotisserie chicken, skinned,
  boned, and pulled
4 ounces pepper jack cheese,
  cubed 1/2 inch
1 11-ounce can Mexican corn,
  drained
2 cans (4 ounces) mild green
chilies, chopped

Caveats:

1. Six tablespoons butter in the roux is very rich and fatty; may want to start with less.
2. Three cups chicken broth at start of cooking may leave the chili thicker than desired.

Directions:

1. Coat crock pot with vegetable spray and add the pulled, shredded-into-bite-size pieces of chicken.
2. Add beans, corn, green chilies, and cheese.
3. Heat 2 tablespoons butter in a skillet over medium heat, and cook onion until softened. Set aside.
4. Warm 1 cup chicken broth and 2 cups half-and-half before adding to the roux (below).
5. In a 6-to-8 quart kettle, melt remaining 6 tablespoons butter (or less) over low heat, and whisk in the flour. Cook roux 3 minutes, whisking constantly.
6. Stir onion into roux, and gradually add chicken broth and half-and-half, whisking constantly. Bring mixture to a boil and simmer, stirring occasionally for 5 minutes, or until thickened. Stir in tobasco, chili powder, cumin, salt, and pepper.
7. Add mixture to crock pot and stir. Add 2 cups chicken broth and stir.
8. Cook on low 2 to 2$^1/_2$ hours and then turn to warm until serving.
9. During cooking time, stir and add 1 or more cups chicken broth to thin as desired.

Toffee Bar Torte

Ingredients:

6 egg whites	1 pint heavy cream
$1/2$ teaspoon cream of tartar	Dash of salt
$1/4$ teaspoon salt	6 $3/4$-ounce toffee bars
2 teaspoons vanilla	crushed or 3 1.4-ounce
2 cups sugar	bars, or 1 8-ounce bag
	chocolate and toffee
	bar bits

Directions:

1. Beat egg whites until frothy. Add cream of tartar, $1/4$ teaspoon salt, and vanilla. Beat until soft peaks form. Gradually add sugar, beating until stiff peaks form.

2. Cover 2 cookie sheets with brown paper. Draw 9-inch circle on each—trace using a 9-inch round cake pan. Spread meringue evenly within the circle.

3. Bake 275 degrees for 1 hour (if your oven is particularly hot, bake at 250 degrees for 50 minutes).

4. Meringue should be lightly brown on top.

5. Do not open the oven. Turn off the oven temperature and allow meringue to dry in the closed oven for at least two hours.

6. To prepare layer cake: Whip cream, add dash of salt. Reserve $1/4$ cup of crushed toffee bar bits. Fold remaining toffee bar bits into whipped cream.

7. Spread $1/3$ mixture between layers and frost top and sides with remainder. Sprinkle reserved toffee bar bits over the top.

8. Chill 8 hours or overnight.

Tip: If using toffee bars, freeze first, and then pound to more easily crush into bits.

Lasagna

Mary Brion

Ingredients:

2 pounds ground beef
  or chicken
Chopped onion
2-3 cloves chopped garlic
12-ounce can tomato paste
2 14-1/2 ounce cans diced
  tomatos
1 teaspoon salt

3/4 teaspoon pepper
1/2 teaspoon oregano
1 box lasagna pasta
3-4 cups shredded mozzarella
24 ounces cottage cheese
Parmesan cheese

Directions:

1. Brown ground beef or chicken.
2. Add chopped onion, garlic, tomato paste, diced tomatoes, salt, pepper, and oregano.
3. Cover and simmer 30 minutes.
4. Cook 1 box lasagna pasta.
5. Layer pasta in two pans, one 9 x 13 and one 8 x 8.
6. Then layer 4 ounces mozzarella (I use 3-4 cup bag divided between 2 pans), 1/2 pint cottage cheese(I use most of a 24-ounce container), 1/2 meat sauce. Then repeat layers.
7. Sprinkle parmesan cheese over top.
8. Bake at 350 degrees 45-60 minutes. (I cover with foil for 3/4 of cooking time.) Let stand 10 minutes before cutting.
9. Can cover pan with foil and freeze before cooking. Then thaw and cook covered until15 minutes left. Foil and cook until center is hot.

Cowboy Caviar

Mary Brion

Ingredients:

1 cup canola oil	1 orange pepper
$^1/_2$ cup cider vinegar	1 medium onion
$^1/_2$ cup sugar	Drain and wash:
4 stalks celery	1 can pinto beans
1 green pepper	1 can black beans
1 red pepper	1 can shoepeg corn
1 yellow pepper	

Directions:

1. Combine oil, vinegar, and sugar in saucepan. Heat until sugar dissolves. Cool.
2. Dice vegetables; combine in bowl with beans and corn.
3. Add oil, vinegar, and sugar mixture (when cool).
4. Mix and marinate overnight.

Oatmeal Muffins

Makes 12 muffins   Judy Appel

Ingredients:

1 cup cooked oatmeal	1 teaspoon baking powder
1 cup flour	$^1/_2$ teaspoon baking soda
$^1/_2$ cup orange juice	Pinch of salt
(add this last to moisten	1 teaspoon cinnamon
to the proper consistency)	$^1/_2$ to 1 teaspoon ground
$^1/_4$ cup liquid shortening	cloves
1 egg	Raisins, if desired
$^1/_2$ cup brown sugar	

Directions:

1. Mix and divide between 12 medium-size muffin cups.
2. Bake at 400 degrees for 20 to 25 minutes.

Tastefully Simple® Products

Bountiful Beer Bread Mix®
Spinach & Herb Dip Mix®
Corn Black Bean Salsa over cream cheese, topped with shredded
   cheese, and served with vegetable flavored chips
Absolutely Almond Pound Cake Mix™

At each of our Blue Garter Gatherings Tastefully Simple products have been a real hit. Mary Kolling Brion introduced us to the Bountiful Beer Bread Mix and the Spinach & Herb Dip Mix at our 60th Birthday Gathering. Then we learned that our Blue Garter Friend, Liz Nelson Shriver's oldest son, Andrew, and Joani Nielson are life partners.

Joani is the Founding Partner & COO along with Founder & CEO, Jill Blashack Strahan of Tastefully Simple. The original national home taste-testing company is based in Alexandria, Minnesota. Recipe and serving suggestions for the items listed above plus more can be found at the tastefullysimple.com web site.

Blue Garter Friends have enjoyed new delicacies at each gathering as well as following the wonderful success story of the Tastefully Simple business. Even though Blue Garter gals enjoy cooking, they are part of the new generation that gravitates toward convenient gourmet cuisine.

Blue Garter Tradition

Most Blue Garter friends referenced in this book had church weddings, chose not to see the groom until escorted down the aisle, and had photos taken following the wedding service. A reception was held in the church's fellowship hall with punch, pretty sandwiches, fancy cookies, and a tiered wedding cake served with egg coffee. The top tier of the cake was saved for the couple's first anniversary. There were no spirits served; wedding dances were rare. Many of the weddings were recorded on black and white photos. Many wedding customs prevalent today were also prevalent when these Blue Garter friends married. One such custom was the blue garter.

The significance of wearing a blue garter dates back to ancient history. The garter represented the virginal girdle. Removal of the garter by the groom signified the bride giving up her virginity. A bride's garter also symbolized luck and good fortune for the couple. In the 14th century, European guests thought that having a piece of the bride's clothing would bring them good luck. Pieces of fabric were literally ripped from the gown. Brides did not like this, and the custom of throwing something to the guests began. The garter became one of those items; it was tossed to a group of male guests. At times men became impatient for this to happen, got drunk, and would try to remove the garter from the bride. Brides did not like this rowdiness, so the custom changed again. The groom removed the garter from the bride's leg so it could be tossed among male guests. The custom included the bride first tossing her bouquet to the women guests in hopes it would be caught by an unwed woman. In a perfect world, the garter would be caught by an unwed man, and the two recipients of the tosses might then become the next couple to wed.

The color blue was associated with "something blue" being part of wedding traditions. Blue symbolized purity, faithfulness, and fidelity. Christians associated the blue color with the purity of the Virgin Mary. Thus, the blue garter became the "something blue" that brides could wear as part of their wedding attire.

Bridal garters are still in style. There is now the opportunity to purchase two matching garters—one the bride keeps and one that is tossed. Some wedding planners, however, say that half of the bridal couples today include bouquet- and garter-tossing as part of their activities. This group of Blue Garter friends recommends a couple chat about the tradition, its potential nostalgia and wholesome fun for guests, and then decide.

References:

Becker, Hollee A. *Wedding Customs: Tracking Tradition.* http://www. theknot.com (accessed January 18, 2009).

Staff, Mike. *Bouquet and Garter Toss: Should We or Should...* http:// www.wedalert.com (accessed January 18, 2009).

The Traditions of the Wedding Garter. http://www.orangecountywedding plan.com/weddinggarter.htm (accessed January 18, 2009).

Bibliography

Aburdene, Patricia and John Naisbitt. *Megatrends for Women.* New York, NY: Villard Books. 1992.

Angelou, Maya. *A Song Flung Up to Heaven.* New York, NY: Random House. 2002.

Bailey, Pearl. *Talking to Myself.* New York, NY: Harcourt Brace Jovanovich, Inc. 1971.

Banner, Lois W. *In Full Flower: Aging Women, Power, and Sexuality, A History.* New York, NY: Alfred A. Knopf. 1992.

Barry, Kathleen. *Susan B. Anthony: A Biography.* New York, NY: University Press. 1988.

Bennett, Joyce and Wendy Byle. *ABCs of Your Success.* www.abcsofLiving.com. 2008

Berkowitz, Gale. *UCLA Study on Friendship Among Women.* Study done by S.E. Taylor, L.C. Klein, and B. P. Lewis. *In Natural Health California Newsletter,* June 2003. http://www.naturalhealthcalifornia.com (accessed July 2008).

Bird, Carolyn. *Lives of Our Own: Secrets of Salty Old Women.* New York, NY: Houghton Mifflin. 1995.

Borysenko, Joan. *A Woman's Book of Life: The Biology, Psychology and Spirituality of the Feminine Life Cycle.* New York, NY: Riverhead Books. 1996.

Brafford, C. J. and Laine Thom. *Dancing Colors: Paths of Native American Women.* San Francisco, CA: Chronicle Books. 1992.

Cleveland, Joan. *Simplifying Life as a Senior Citizen.* Griffin, NY: St. Martin's. 1998.

Edwards, Susan. *Erma Bombeck: A Life in Humor.* New York, NY: Avon Books. 1997.

Hertog, Susan and Nan A. Talese. *Anne Morrow Lindbergh: Her Life.* New York, NY: Doubleday. 1999.

Hogrefe, Jeffrey. *O'Keeffe: The Life of an American Legend.* New York, NY: Bantam Books. 1992.

Hugo, Victor. In Cathleen Rountree. *On Women Turning 50: Celebrating Mid-Life Discoveries.* p. 5. New York, NY: Harper Collins. 1993.

Huntley, Mary and Edna Thayer. *A Mirthful Spirit: Embracing Laughter for Wellness.* Edina, MN: Beaver's Pond Press. 2007.

Kidder, Tracy. *Old Friends.* New York, NY: Houghton Mifflin. 1993.

Lear, Linda. *Rachel Carson: The Life of the Author of Silent Spring.* New York, NY: Henry Holt and Co. 1997.

Lee, Carol W. and Renee Hermanson, (eds.). *Blue Garter Club: Ties That Bind Fourteen Christian Women for 40 Years.* San Antonio, TX: Langmarc Publishing. 1992.

L'Engle, Madeleine. In Cathleen Rountree. *On Women Turning 70: Honoring the Voices of Wisdom.* p. 9. San Francisco, CA: Jossey-Bass. 1999.

Madsen, Axel. *Chanel: A Woman of Her Own.* New York, NY: Henry Holt and Co. 1990.

Meir, Golda. *My Life.* New York, NY: G.P. Putnam's Sons. 1975.

Morath, Inge. Wikipedia. http://en.wikipedia.org/wiki/Inge- Morath (accessed August 2008).

Rountree, Cathleen. *On Women Turning 70: Honoring the Voices of Wisdom.* San Francisco, CA: Jossey-Bass Publishers. 1999.

Rountree, Cathleen. *On Women Turning 60: Embracing the Age of Fulfillment.* New York, NY: Three Rivers Press. 1997.

Rountree, Cathleen. *On Women Turning 50: Celebrating Mid-Life Discoveries.* San Francisco, CA: Harper San Francisco. 1993.

Russell, Jan Jarboe. *Lady Bird: A Biography of Mrs. Johnson.* New York, NY: Scribner. 1999.

To The Wonderful Women in My Circle. Author Unknown. http://www.flobaribeau.spaces.live.com (accessed July 2008).

Snowdon, David. *Aging With Grace: What the Nun Study Teaches Us About Leading Longer, Healthier, and More Meaningful Lives.* New York, NY: Bantam Books. 2001.

Vaillant, George. *Aging Well.* Boston, MA: Little, Brown, and Co. 2002.

Webster's New World Large Print Dictionary. New York, NY: Macmillan General Reference. 1989.

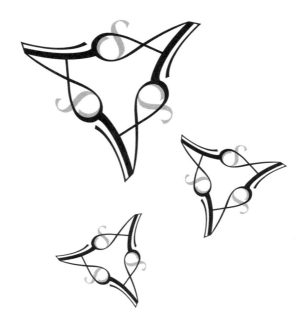

About the Authors

Judy Appel

*J*udy retired from the joy-filled rigors of teaching elementary school-age children in 1997. Her plan was to develop a new career as a writer. Along the way, she authored a newspaper column, *A Teacher's Insight*, as well as collaborating with her father in a four-year-long project of memoir writing. The touching experience of carefree interaction during the "farewell" period of a dear father's life became an inspiration for Judy. She began serious investigation into the topic of aging. February 2006, her husband, Ray, was diagnosed with Parkinson's disease; a month later her father passed away. These life-changing realities intensified Judy's quest for better understanding of the enigmas of aging. Serendipitously, lifetime friends, Mary Huntley and Ginge Klenk, came to visit in celebration of their retirement in 2002. *The Amazing Attributes of Aging: Silly & Sacred Stories of Blue Garter Friends* project began during that visit. Now, seven years later, Judy looks back with pride upon the personal odyssey that she partnered with Mary Huntley. Searching Mary's lovingly-cataloged archives of friendship, attending reunions, engaging in intimate conversations with childhood friends as their life stories were recalled—all have been deeply felt joys. Only with devoted friends could a project like this come to completion. Nancy Tsuchiya's "Writing Your Life Stories" class, and its strong community of Hoover Room memoir-writing pals, brought a wealth of inspiration and validation, as Judy wove her life experiences and research into this manuscript.

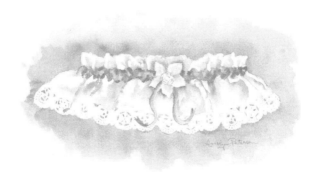

Mary Huntley

Several years before retiring, there was only a small hint of interest in writing one book, not three. Beginning January 2002, retirement offered some new twists and turns for a person who enjoys being busy. To Mary's surprise, she launched her first book in 2003 with two colleagues, recording the history of the School of Nursing where Mary earned her undergraduate degree in nursing and later taught for 30 years. In 2007, the second book entered the market. Along with her coauthor, the belief is shared that laughter makes a difference for a healthful, productive, and happy life. Underlying her passions for nursing and a mirthful spirit are the friendship connections that emerged through living in Mankato, Minnesota, attending nursery school through college. Judy and Mary made their first connections in Sunday School, were confirmed together, and later lived in the same neighborhood. They rode to high school each day with Judy driving her beloved old Hudson convertible. They traveled west across the country together by train between their sophomore and junior years in college. Those were the days. While in college, Judy introduced Mary to her husband of 46 years; and yes, Judy was a bridesmaid in their wedding two years later. Mary's and Judy's friendship, along with all the Blue Garter friends, is a treasured phenomenon. Every opportunity to be together gladdens their hearts. Sharing her passions by writing about them and doing so with cherished friends brings great joy.

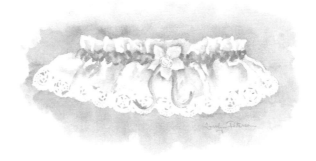

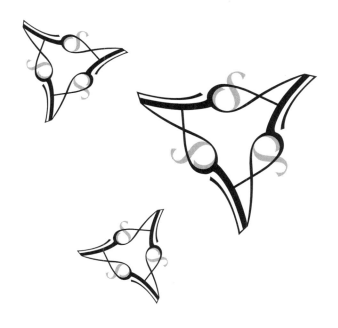

To Order Books

Name _____

Address _____

City _____

State _____ Zip Code _____

Phone _____ Email _____

I would like to order:

_____ Book(s) at $15 (U.S. $) each including
sales tax

__$3.00__ Shipping and handling for one book
with one-to-two week delivery.

_____ For multiple books and/or faster
delivery, contact the authors
for discounts and fees.

_____ Total

Please send a check payable to AHA Aging to:

AHA Aging
11277 Neal Avenue North
Stillwater, MN 55082
USA

For presentations, book signings, and multiple book orders,
Contact us through our website: www.amazingaging.com